PENGUIN BOOKS

BEYOND THE BOTTOM LINE

Tad Tuleja is the author or coauthor of fifteen other books, including books on selling techniques, precious metals investment, competition in American society, and other social issues of concern to government and business leaders.

BEYOND THE BOTTOM LINE

How Business Leaders Are Turning Principles into Profits

Tad Tuleja

A Stonesong Press Book

Penguin Books

For Paul Fargis, one of the good guys

PENGUIN BOOKS
Viking Penguin Inc., 40 West 23rd Street,
New York, New York 10010, U.S.A.
Penguin Books Ltd, Harmondsworth,
Middlesex, England
Penguin Books Australia Ltd, Ringwood,
Victoria, Australia
Penguin Books Canada Limited, 2801 John Street,
Markham, Ontario, Canada L3R 1B4
Penguin Books (N.Z.) Ltd, 182–190 Wairau Road,
Auckland 10, New Zealand

First published in the United States of America by
Facts on File Publications 1985
Published in Penguin Books 1987

LIBRARY OF CONGRESS CATALOGING IN PUBLICATION DATA
Tuleja, Tad.
Beyond the bottom line.
Reprint. Originally published: New York: Facts on
File, c1985.
Includes index.
1. Business ethics. 2. Executives—United States—
Conduct of life. 3. Industry—Social aspects—
United States. I. Title.
HF5387.T84 1987 174′.4 86-17078
ISBN 0 14 00.9365 6

Printed in the United States of America by
R. R. Donnelley & Sons Company, Harrisonburg, Virginia
Set in Melior

CONTENTS

Consider any great organization—one that has lasted over the years—and I think you will find that it owes its resiliency, not to its form of organization or administrative skills, but to the power of what we call beliefs and the appeal these beliefs have for its people.

This, then, is my thesis: I firmly believe that any organization, in order to survive and achieve success, must have a sound set of beliefs on which it premises all its policies and actions.

Next, I believe that the most important single factor in corporate success is faithful adherence to those beliefs.

And finally, I believe that if an organzation is to meet the challenges of a changing world, it must be prepared to change everything about itself except those beliefs as it moves through corporate life.

—Thomas J. Watson, Jr.
Former chairman, IBM

We know that a business cannot operate in a vacuum, concerned only with profits and markets and oblivious to the impact it has upon the rest of society....Now, perhaps for the first time, we are part of a real attempt to integrate two different value systems: those that are oriented toward making a living with those that are oriented toward making a life.

—Robert A. Beck
Chairman, Prudential Insurance

A great society is a society in which its men of business think greatly of their functions.

—Alfred North Whitehead

ACKNOWLEDGMENTS

In researching the progressive policies of American business, I used two basic sources: printed matter and personal interviews. The books, articles, and other printed material to which I refer in the text are cited in "Notes." My first debt of gratitude is to the many corporate public relations departments who sent, or steered me to, this material.

Any quotations and attributions that are not cited in the "Notes" come from my interviews, both in person and by telephone, with the following corporate managers:

Aetna Life and Casualty Company: John H. Filer, chairman (ret. 1984); Geraldine E. Morrissey, senior communications specialist; and Robert H. Roggeveen, national programs manager for the Aetna Life and Casualty Foundation.

Control Data Corporation: William C. Norris, chairman and chief executive officer.

Dayton Hudson Corporation: Peter C. Hutchinson, corporate vice-president and chairman of the Dayton Hudson Foundation.

Hewlett-Packard: Mary Anne Easley, manager, public relations services; and John C. Young, president and chief executive officer.

IBM: Richard T. Liebhaber, director of business development and practices, now senior vice-president with IBM-owned Satellite Business Systems.

Johnson & Johnson: James E. Burke, chairman and chief executive officer; and Lawrence G. Foster, corporate vice-president, public relations.

Johnson Wax: Samuel C. Johnson, chairman.

J. C. Penney Company: Robert B. Gill, vice-chairman of the board.

The Pillsbury Company: Terry T. Saario, vice-president, community relations, now president of the Northwest Area Foundation.

Prudential Insurance Company: William E. Brooks, secretary of the Prudential Foundation; and Richard A. Mathisen, senior public relations consultant.

Xerox Corporation: Robert Gudger, manager, corporate

responsibility; and Marion Whipple, community and employee programs manager.

My interviews with these individuals took place between July 1984 and January 1985. I am grateful to them and to their companies for their hospitality and cooperation.

In addition, I owe thanks to Michael Rion, president of Hartford Seminary, for an illuminating interview about ethical thinking at Cummins Engine Company and in American business at large; and to James May and Albert Eisele for arranging my interviews with, respectively, Samuel Johnson and William Norris.

My appreciation to Professors Dwayne Willard and David Paas of the University of Nebraska at Omaha for allowing me to participate in their stimulating course on business ethics in the spring of 1984, and to Professor Kenneth Bond of Creighton University for supplying me with a bibliography that considerably cut my research time. Thanks also to David Sheaves of the Institute for Research in Social Science at the University of North Carolina at Chapel Hill for sending me a helpful packet of Harris and Gallup poll results.

Both *The New York Times Book Review* and *Party Line*, a weekly newsletter for public relations specialists, ran requests for information for me free of charge; my thanks especially to Betty Yarmon, managing editor, for arranging the query in *Party Line*.

Of the numerous authors to whose cited works I am indebted I should mention particularly the team of Milton Moskowitz, Michael Katz, and Robert Levering. Their justly popular reference works, *Everybody's Almanac* and *The 100 Best Companies to Work for in America*, saved me incalculable hours in the library. The "Corporate Performance Roundup" columns in *Business and Society Review* (of which Mr. Moskowitz is senior editor) were also an invaluable resource.

To Robert B. Miller and Stephen E. Heiman of Miller Heiman Inc. I am grateful not only for an insightful interview but for a satisfying "Win-Win" association that exemplifies the ideals proposed in this book.

To my wife Andrée my appreciation, as always, for her warmth and wit and, in this project particularly, for keeping me on my toes.

INTRODUCTION
What This Book Is Not

One legacy of the Watergate fiasco, and of the attendant flap over illegal campaign contributions, was the creation of a cottage industry in the study of "business ethics." Responding to an outraged public's suspicion that free enterprise was inextricable from corruption, writers in and out of academia set themselves to investigating the commercial impulse to see whether it was inevitably or only accidentally linked to profiteering, social irresponsibility, and general turpitude. Business executives, pictured as larcenous agents of a decadent economic system, were challenged to defend not only their personal probity but the morality of capitalism itself.

In the ten years that have passed since the Lockheed, Northrup, and Gulf Oil scandals, this inquiry into the ethical standards of business has shown little sign of abating. Under the Reagan presidency, the tone of the examiners may have softened, but the volume of their work is still high. A recent bibliography of business-ethics articles lists over 2,000 items published between 1976 and 1980 alone—and that's not counting dozens of books. Whether you read *Business Week* or the *Journal of Purchasing and Materials Management*, it is hard to escape the impression that business ethics has become for the 1980s what Theory Z was for the 1970s: a cutting edge of B-school chic.

Any writer adding to this literature has an obligation to his readers to say how his contribution will be different, so that they may identify what room of the cottage he is in. In my case the obligation has pragmatic force since, unlike many writers on the subject, I am trying to reach not so much students of the corporate drama as its actors. Few corporate executives have the leisure (not to mention the patience) for a scholarly review of the literature; readers will want to know, now, "What will this book do for me?"

In addressing the professional business person and those interested in that person's problems, I hope to provide a useful, provocative overview of the major ethical dilemmas facing management today. My intent is to demonstrate that, while there may be no single "right" answer to a manager's moral dilemma, there are still ethically sound (and ethically unsound) ways of approaching solutions; and to demonstrate, by reviewing the experiences of successful companies that take their ethics seriously, that "good works" are quite compatible with a healthy bottom line.

I can focus this description of intent a little better if I state what the book is not.

First, it is not a book about ethics with a capital "E"—that is, about the nature of justice or about "how we know" what is right and what is wrong. Since the book's readers will almost certainly be legatees of the Hellenic and Judeo-Christian traditions, I assume that we share approximately the same moral ideals. For example, I take it as generally agreed that truthfulness is a virtue and that murder and theft are wrong. To the philosophically minded who find this assumption unwarranted, I recommend Chapter 2, which lays out its underlying logic.

Second, the book does not present "business" ethics as being in some mysterious way distinct from ethics in general. I reject the notion that business has, or should have, its own moral rules, just as I reject the notion that a moral atrocity in one culture can be, or should be, "justified" by custom in another. I embrace the absolutist bias that says if torture is wrong in Sandusky, it is also wrong in Teheran; that if the teenage car thief goes to jail, so should the embezzling CEO. The corporate executives I have spoken with virtually all agree with this bias. In order for business to prosper, they say, it must play by the same rules as everybody else.

Third, the book does not address the significant but somewhat esoteric issue of corporate personality, or the related issue of personal liability in cases where ethical and legal principles are violated by the management of a firm. Some observers, critical of the very notions of "conscience" and "moral duty" as applied to large organizations, contend that since a corporation is not a person, it should not be held accountable for the actions of its members, nor should it reasonably be held to have "sinned" when one of its executives goes wrong. The common practice of fining a corporation for the errors of its management, they say, is itself morally questionable, since it punishes the stockholders for the supposed crimes of their agents.

Compelling as it is, this argument cannot really be properly addressed within the scope of this book. I admit that corporate agents, like any agents, occupy an ambiguous moral position vis-a-vis those who employ them. And it may be true that when a corporate officer is personally responsible for his company's tax evasion or oil spill, simple justice would suggest that he, and not the stockholders, pay the piper.

Custom, however, dictates otherwise—and not entirely through caprice. It is not frivolous to say that because stockholders profit from managerial virtue they should also suffer for managerial vice. For the purposes of this study, with some reservation, I accept this judicial fudge and take the corporation as a person—with all the risks that such personhood implies. When I use the term "corporate responsibility," therefore, the fastidious may safely read "responsibility of the corporate managers."

Finally, I have reluctantly but rigorously avoided the nettlesome issue of systemic ethical dilemmas—what Marxist analysts are fond of calling the "internal contradictions of capitalism." The moral objections raised by critics of the free enterprise option—concerning the profit motive, competition, worker alienation, "wage slavery," and so on—are of abiding concern to anyone interested in social questions, but they too are beyond the scope of this book. Here I take corporate capitalism as a given, and ask two related questions:

1. Within the "System" as currently organized, can people who work for and manage our great corporations behave in a morally responsible manner?
2. If they can—that is, if it is possible to work for a corporation and still be ethical—then do they?

I believe that both questions may be answered, and answered strongly, in the affirmative. The larceny of some people aside, vast numbers of American business professionals can and do behave in a perfectly respectable fashion. And they do so even though their ethical decisions are frequently confusing, costly, and misrepresented by the press.

But of course there are businesses and there are businesses. Obviously, American corporate life has not been without its share of abuses. Indeed, when I began my research months ago, I anticipated finding the worst, and envisioned the book as a stick to make the Bad Guys shudder. I found what I was looking for, but I also found that many of my investigative colleagues had already beaten up on Firestone and Pinto and Nestlé for me. One more trip through the corporate chamber of horrors, I was forced to acknowledge, might generate more old heat than new light.

Luckily, there was another route. It was to tell the story of a remarkable, and substantial, group of corporate citizens who not only took ethical imperatives seriously but made a good deal of money by doing so. That story had not been adequately told, and I hoped that telling it might have a couple of beneficial effects that an anti-business polemic would not. For those business people who were already taking ethics seriously, it would provide encouragement. For those who were convinced that morality was an impediment to success, who argued that it was irrelevant or who just didn't want to think about it, such a "carrot" approach might do what the "stick" approaches had not: convince them there was gain in being good.

So I sent off inquiries to the Good Guys, starting with about fifty firms which cropped up consistently in *Business and Society Review* as exemplars of responsible social behavior. After sorting through the responses—pounds of annual reports, codes of corporate behavior, news clippings, speeches, and correspondence—I selected about a dozen companies for interviews. The people I spoke to there, whose comments illuminate the book, convinced me again and again that their firms not only are ethical but succeed in making it pay.

Most of the firms discussed here are large multinational corporations. I concentrated on the big guys for two reasons, the first sociological. Since I was interested in the links between corporate and social behavior, it seemed imperative to start with businesses that had the widest possible impact on our society. This also enabled me to test the sociological commonplace that bigness leads to insensitivity and corruption.

Second, the big firms were simply more accessible. It's easier to obtain information on ethical codes and conduct from a company with a twenty-member public relations department than it is to get it from a small family business; that is a paradox of expansion. I apologize for resorting to expediency to the thousands of American companies that cannot afford such departments. I am aware that people in these smaller companies do justice, love mercy, and walk humbly with their God. They were just too difficult to get to.

My focus on the firms profiled here, finally, should not be taken to mean that I find them morally infallible. The text will show that, in many instances, I disagree with their moral choices. But business virtue does not consist of choosing the "right" answer 100 percent of the time. It consists of establishing a corporate culture that encourages asking the right questions. And all these firms do that.

It should go without saying that they are not the only American corporations to do so. No doubt there will be more than one corporate employee who, after reading this book, will wonder angrily why his or her company is not mentioned. To those persons I plead economics: I have profiled as many "good" firms as I could, given finite resources and competing ends. The resulting list of these companies is certainly not comprehensive; it is merely representative—and exemplary.

Part I

Principles and Premises

1 BUSINESS ETHICS Contradiction in Terms?

"Do other men, for they would do you." That's the true business precept.

—Charles Dickens

In former periods business was identified as secular, and service as sacred. In proportion as we have discerned that between secular and sacred no arbitrary line exists, public awareness has grown that the golden rule was meant for business as much as for other human relationships.

—James Cash Penney
Founder, J.C. Penney Company

A recent *Wall Street Journal* article asked whether the term "business ethics" should be considered, like "jumbo shrimp," an oxymoron. After reviewing the current furor over ethics in American business circles, the article concluded that the term was not in fact self-contradictory: In many firms, moral questions were being taken as seriously as questions about productivity and the tax laws. A fundamental goal of today's business leader, the paper acknowledged, was to ensure that corporate success be achieved without compromising standards of personal integrity and fair play.

To many people this goal is invisible. When they are asked to rate the ethical standards of U.S. business professionals, they agree that those standards have always been low, and that in today's often troubled economy, things are only getting worse. To most of the general population Dickens's observation hits the mark; Penney's is hypocrisy or wishful thinking.

Public opinion polls are unambiguous on this point. In the summer of 1983, for example, the Gallup Organization investigated popular beliefs regarding the honesty of various professional groups. Only 18 percent of those polled put the standards of business executives at "high" or "very high." That placed them far behind physicians, teachers, bankers, policemen, and funeral directors, and only slightly ahead of those traditional lodestones of public opprobrium, members of Congress.

Another Gallup poll, conducted for the *Wall Street Journal* in October 1983, found that about half the people interviewed believed that business values have declined in the past decade. Nearly three-quarters were convinced that business people routinely pad their expense accounts.

A Harris survey conducted in the same month corroborated the public's dissatisfaction with the way American businesses are being run. Only 18 percent of those surveyed expressed "great confidence" in the leaders of major companies—down from 27 percent in the early 1970s and 55 percent in 1966. It should be noted that public confidence in *all* institutions declined in this period—but no institution, including Congress, underwent such a precipitous drop in faith as did business.

The businessman's poor reputation is evident not only in these official pulse-takers' results, but in the many unofficial indices of public affection that appear in our mass literature and culture. Benjamin Franklin, in producing the best-sellers of his time, endorsed the Puritan virtues of industry, thrift, and fair dealing as essential to worldly success; a modern Poor Richard who suggested such a linkage between probity and profit would be ridiculed as a cat's-paw or a fool. The postwar expansion of the American economy may have seemed a miracle to Wall Street, but in the movies and pulp novels and TV the "typical" executive behind that miracle is depicted as a knavish go-getter willing—indeed, eager—to ruin associates for the sake of a three-car garage.

Literary historian Emily Stipes, in a recent study, identifies cynicism as an abiding element in the American people's perception of the businessman. "Most businessmen depicted in post-1945 serious literature," she writes, "are still characterized as greedy, unethical, and immoral (or amoral)." With few exceptions, this comment applies to the productions—serious and frivolous—of the theater and electronic media as well.

I recall vividly, for example, the two fictional businessmen that seemed to me the most "realistic" portrayals of the type as I was growing up in the 1950s. They were Budd Schulberg's Sammy Glick, a pathologically competitive climber willing to subvert any allegiance for personal gain; and Sloan Wilson's Tom Rath, the Man in the Gray Flannel Suit, whose claim to moral distinction was that he saw through the vapidity of corporate culture. Schulberg (negatively) and Wilson (positively) hinted at the same conclusion: The true home of the man without scruples was the American business firm.

Almost thirty years later, children are still getting the same message. In the recent television series "Nine to Five," the boss, Mr. Hart, is a grasping buffoon, ready to sacrifice his employees on the altar of his own success. In the 1984 pilot series "Empire," executives in a strife-torn corporation are seen as pitiful and pitiless boardroom sharks, using soft soap, backstabbing, and guile not so much as means to personal advancement but as ends in themselves. And in the extremely successful prime-time soap opera "Dallas," oil baron J.R. Ewing is a philandering, avaricious sneak whose supreme pleasure in life is watching rivals go bankrupt.

The image of the corrupt business person is not ephemeral or merely "entertaining." It informs the entire society; it shows how business is understood, by people both within it and outside. The image is accepted so unquestioningly that it becomes a cliché—and once it becomes a cliché, it is questioned even less. The unprincipled businessman becomes, like the bungling bureaucrat or the deceitful communist, a cultural given. And smugness sets in. The single most common response I heard when I told people I was researching a book on business ethics was this: "That shouldn't take very long."

Sniping at the businessman is not a new sport in our culture. Before Ben Franklin left his teens, Puritan father Cotton Mather had already sounded the monitory strain. "There is one thing in the condition of many Rich Men," he wrote in the 1727 tract *Agricola*, "which cannot with sufficient Horror be thought upon. Great Estates, like unto great Rivers, often are swelled by Muddy Streams running into them. Some of the Wealth is Ill-gotten Wealth. Dishonest Gain has increased it."

And Mather was no *vox in deserto*. As the nation expanded, geographically and commercially, so too did the stridency of commercophobes who feared private enterprise as a betrayal of the national promise. Our vaunted national respect for getting ahead has been meliorated, throughout our history, with a deep suspicion of success. This suspicion has fallen with particular severity on success achieved in the marketplace.

The high-water mark in anti-business sentiment was the turn of the twentieth century, when muckrakers excoriated the trusts for engaging in practices that, admittedly, deserved the full measure of their scorn. Stock-watering, price-fixing, graft, kickbacks, product adulteration, desecration of the environment, and a widespread contempt for the public—all were in ample supply in the "robber baron" era. Today, remembering railroad king William Vanderbilt's famous quip "The public be damned," it is hard to deny that the protests of writers like Upton Sinclair and Ida Tarbell were needed correctives to the excesses of the Gilded Age.

No business executive today would have the temerity to echo Vanderbilt's gaffe. On the contrary, all major companies employ communications experts to draw up corporate codes of conduct, demonstrate social concern, and in general justify the ways of Mammon to man. Today's organization men are heavily involved both in doing good works in the company's name and in telling us about them. We are far from the day when a tycoon like John D. Rockefeller could dismiss his critics with this fillip: "Great prejudice exists against all successful business enterprise—the more successful, the greater the prejudice." Or when he could justify his own accumulative urge with the modest observation "God gave me my money."

Yet in spite of the rapprochement that now exists between business and some of the press, muckraking has not expired. In many instances, the communications experts labor in vain to upgrade the image of their firms because, as in the days of yellow journalism, it is scandal rather than virtue that sells papers; no matter how long and diligently an oil company may have worked to safeguard the environment, it is still the oil spill that makes page one.

Not that American businesses have been blameless. To suggest that corporate profligacy is an invention of a commerce-hating press would display the same tendentious illogic that saw the Watergate debacle as a creature of the *Washington Post*. A 1980 *Fortune* report on the "lawlessness" of U.S. firms, for example, released a sobering statistic. Of the 1,043 companies that had at some point in the 1970s been among the top 800 domestic concerns, a total of 117 had been implicated in at least one violation of the law. The culprits ranged from aerospace giants like Northrup, caught giving illegal campaign contributions, to chemical companies like Allied, nailed for price-fixing and tax fraud, to smaller suppliers like Heublein, found bribing a state official.

This survey, moreover, was extremely limited in scope. It concentrated on only "five offenses about whose impropriety there is little argument": bribery, fraud, illegal political contributions, tax evasion, and antitrust violations. It said nothing about such "lesser" offenses as discriminatory hiring practices or false advertising. Nor did it mention such legal but arguably unethical practices as the willful pollution of rivers or the peremptory closing of plants. Allied Chemical was scored for collusion, not for dumping kepone into Virginia's James River. Firestone was identified as a tax cheat, not as the maker of the ill-famed Firestone 500 radial tire. If muckraking has been enjoying a new heyday recently, it is largely because corporate managers have been providing plenty of new muck to rake.

Given the morally questionable practices in which our large businesses are still being implicated, no one should be surprised that most people do not trust corporations. Without intending to minimize the gravity of the situation, however, I believe there are some consolations—perhaps even some encouragement—to be drawn from the public outcry over corporate sins.

First, the outcry indicates ironically that morality *does* matter in business—that, to answer the question posed by the title of this chapter, "business ethics" is not a contradiction in terms. Cynics quote the proverb "You've got to have a little thief in you to get ahead," and say that success is impossible in business unless you are willing to lie, cheat, and steal. University of Kansas ethics professor Richard De George calls this opinion part of the "Myth of Amoral Business," and he notes succinctly how the public outcry over commercial immorality gives this myth the lie:

> If it were true that business is viewed as amoral, that it is not expected to behave according to moral rules, and that it is appropriate for it to do whatever is necessary in order to increase its profit, then there would be no surprise, shock, or uproar when a business acted immorally. The uncovering of bribes and kickbacks would not be news.

The fact that such revelations are news indicates to De George that, in spite of what the Myth suggests, business is expected to be moral. The disruption of standards gives offense only because those standards are generally accepted as valid.

One corollary to this observation: In an economy where the consumer is sovereign, it may be expected that sooner or later public outrage will tend to raise the overall level of business conduct. It took a generation of protest, the work of numerous investigative committees, and tomes of reformist reportage, but eventually the mining industry pulled ten-year-old children out of the mines. Keeping them there was no longer seen as compatible with common standards of decency; in a democratic community, where those standards had become law, the mineowners had to comply or go under. Is it unrealistic to suppose that the current round of protestation will eventually have a similar restraining effect on business crime?

Indeed, it may already have had that effect. Journalists tend not to emphasize blemish-free firms because the average newspaper reader would rather hear about scandals than about the day-to-day progress of a decent company. But statistically it seems clear that most American businesses, large and small, are managed effectively year after year without ever running afoul of the regulatory agencies that are meant to keep "wicked" business in check. The 117 firms cited in the *Fortune* study, for example, represent 11 percent of the total. That means nine out of ten American firms got through the freewheeling 1970s without stepping on the toes of either the Justice Department or the SEC. Not a bad record for "bad" guys.

A second reason for encouragement is that it is corporate leaders themselves who are most upset by moral lapses—at least with regard to certain abuses. Consider the Gallup survey done in 1983 for the *Wall Street Journal*. When asked if it would be wrong to conceal $2,500 in income from the government, 95 percent of the executives polled said it was; only 75 of the general public agreed. Charging the company for a cab ride not taken was wrong to 76 percent of the executives but only 52 percent of the public. Asked whether or not they would hire an applicant who had overstated his previous salary, 63 percent of the public said they would, compared to only 47 percent of the executives.

The pragmatism of the company steward is clearly a factor here, since in the abuses cited the ostensibly more ethical executives preferred choices that would also work toward the long-term good of the firm. Does their concern for frank accounting and disclosure procedures reflect a higher ethical awareness in general? And does that awareness enable them to make better moral judgments with regard to people outside the company—customers, for example, or society at large? These questions will be addressed frequently in this book.

A final reason for encouragement is that the public suspicion of business suggests we are in the process of a fundamental, and fundamentally healthy, change in the way we view the role of business, particularly corporate business, in our national life. The outcry over abuses may be only the cutting edge of a major reassessment. Americans today are asking the private sector to go beyond the traditional bottom line of cost-benefit analysis, dividends, and profit; they are asking the nation's business leaders to adopt strategies for a new bottom line—one that takes not just shareholders but the entire population as its constituency.

Public expectation about business's role in society has already undergone one significant shift, from the nineteenth-century view of the corporation as a producer of goods, services, and profit to the modern view of the corporation as a manufacturer of jobs as well as widgets. That shift, which began a century ago and is still going on, produced Big Labor, the federal regulatory apparatus, and whispered hints of a coming industrial policy. The second shift, which began only after the Second World War, is already having far wider implications than the first; it is a shift toward seeing the corporation, in uneasy cooperation with the government, as a major force for social change.

Of course the corporation has always had tremendous social impact, even when that impact, engineered by robber barons, was thought to bring more woe than weal. Today the common weal—or, to use the constitutional term, the "general welfare"—is seen more and more as being the corporation's proving ground—and its responsibility. Private-sector giants are now expected to pick up where government leaves off in managing the problems of the inner cities, the dispossessed, and the environment that the corporations themselves have damaged.

Recent budget cuts may have made this supposed obligation more obvious and urgent, but well before Reaganomics corporate concern for social problems was already being seen by many not as a matter of charity but as a morally obligatory surcharge on the private sector's "obscene" profits. Led by environmentalist and consumer groups, the American people began in the 1960s to demand a revival of stewardship. Henceforth the role of the large firm in society would not be that of the economic privateer whose actions, nudged by Adam Smith's invisible hand, *indirectly* benefited others; it would be that of the "partner in progress" whose enormous wealth and resources must be *directly* applied to common ills.

Loyola University professor Thomas Donaldson, who has written widely on the moral responsibility of corporate officers, acknowledges this second shift in expectations:

> Corporations today are meeting their social responsibilities considerably better than they were fifteen years ago. But at the same time public estimation of the ethical character of business has slipped. To me, that is proof of a changing mandate from the public. Society has raised its standards; it expects more from a corporation.

Donald MacNaughton, the former chairman of the Prudential Insurance Company, goes even further. "Business is not simply an economic institution," he said recently, "but a socioeconomic institution with a primary responsibility to society as a whole, and a secondary responsibility to stockholders and employees."

That is a remarkable admission to be made by a major business leader. To the traditional laissez-faire capitalist—whether he is a tycoon like Vanderbilt and Rockefeller or a more benign analyst like Milton Friedman—such a view is heresy. Maybe. But it is hard to deny that it is also the wave of the future. The fact that the head of a multibillion-dollar organization can now utter (and be praised for) such a sentiment shows how our view of corporate responsibility has changed.

A few examples will indicate how far-reaching that change can be, and how some American corporations, seeing the handwriting on the wall, are already expanding their traditional commitment to morality by making it not only personal but social. If you doubt that "business ethics" can be a driving force in a corporation's culture, consider the following cases.

Levi Strauss & Company. The original blue jeans manufacturer is well known in corporate circles for its high-intensity but low-profile commitment to community relations and minority hiring. Its commitment to fair treatment for its employees is less celebrated but just as impressive. Workers have owned large portions of Levi Strauss stock since 1912, and San Francisco's Haas family, which has run the firm since the 1920s, takes the needs of these employee-owners seriously.

In 1979, when the company broke the $2-billion sales mark, management voted 42,000 employees cash awards ranging from fifty dollars for a newly hired worker up to $350 for those with greatest seniority. Cynics might see this merely as a way of avoiding potential trouble on the line; that would not explain why the company also sent its *retirees* checks of $100 each.

Levi Strauss shows the same attention to "people needs" when business is not so good. In 1978, although the company overall had a record year, declining jeans sales forced workweek reductions in some plants. To help soften the impact on the affected workers, the firm sent "distress payments" ranging from $75 to $175 to workers in twenty-eight plants; the total compensation, sent to union and nonunion employees, was $1.4 million. Further cuts in 1984 were accompanied by what *Business Week* called "generous severance and retraining benefits."

International Business Machines. IBM now employs over 335,000 people worldwide, yet it manages to sustain the feeling of being a small, family-owned business, because the simple ethical beliefs of its founder, Thomas J. Watson, are still very much a part of daily affairs.

Twenty years ago Watson said that the first and most important of those beliefs was "respect for the individual." Adherence to this belief has earned IBM a reputation as a great company to work for, the almost fanatical loyalty of its people, an unrivalled customer service record, and a growing recognition as a responsible corporate citizen. Although it is better known in the business community for its many satisfied customers, its service to society at large is nearly as impressive. For example:

- The IBM Fund for Community Service supports civic, cultural, and scientific organizations.
- The company's Social Service Leave Program enables employees to take paid leaves of absence to lend their talents to public improvement projects.
- Through its Faculty Loan Program, IBM staffs colleges and universities with large minority and handicapped student bodies.
- Through its Job Program for the Disadvantaged, the company lends equipment and supplies to local job-training organizations.

Johnson & Johnson. The people who gave you the Band-Aid and tearless shampoo made two management decisions recently that reinforced their image as an ethically managed firm. One was to help revitalize its corporate base, New Brunswick, New Jersey, rather than move to an area less stung by urban blight. The other was to withdraw 31 million bottles of Extra Strength Tylenol from the market in the fall of 1982, after several people were killed by poisoned capsules.

The decision to make New Brunswick a model "company town" has met with some opposition from community groups who feel that the "new New Brunswick" typifies racist gentrification. More on this issue in Chapter 7; for the present it is enough to say that the majority of New Brunswick's people have welcomed the corporate aid.

The corporation's handling of the Tylenol scare was described by one business writer as "the case example of the decade on how to do it right." Few disagree with that assessment. Not only did J&J mount the massive $100-million recall effort without being asked to do so by the FDA; it also tested millions of capsules in conjunction with federal inspectors, offered to replace free of charge the containers that frightened consumers had discarded, and initiated a tamper-proof packaging system that became a standard in the industry.

This "people matter" approach to a problem that was not J&J's fault, and over which it had no control, quickly reaped rewards. By December—only a month after the recall—Tylenol had already regained 80 percent of its pre-crisis sales position. CEO James Burke enjoyed the extremely rare privilege (for a business executive) of being publicly congratulated by Phil Donahue and his audience. And the *Washington Post* recognized that J&J had successfully portrayed itself as "a company willing to do what's right regardless of cost."

Dayton Hudson Corporation. This Minneapolis-based retailer, which owns the Target, Hudson, and B. Dalton chains, does not issue an official "code of social responsibility." It doesn't have to. For over a generation the company has been demonstrating that responsibility by sharing its profits with the multitude. Most corporations donate less than 1 percent of their pretax profits to charity; since 1946—long before "social responsibility" or "business ethics" became catchphrases—Dayton Hudson has been giving away the full 5 percent allowed as tax-deductible under law.

The Dayton Hudson "Five Percent Policy" is a model against which much corporate philanthropy is now measured, and following Minneapolis's lead, many communities now have Five Percent clubs to encourage local businesses to adopt similar policies. A remarkable symbiosis has developed between Dayton Hudson and its host city, with the company funding numerous civic projects and also backing the new downtown shopping center, Nicollet Mall, which the *New York Times* called "a landmark in urban planning as well as a keystone in the revival of downtown Minneapolis."

Of course that's good business. "A healthy community leads to healthy business in the long run," Dayton Hudson CEO William Andres said in 1982. But the firm's involvement also extends to projects from which it is difficult to imagine a conventionally acceptable return on investment. The company's 1982 report on community funding, for example, listed these grants:

- $5,000 to a day-care center of the Native American Coalition of Tulsa, Oklahoma
- $5,000 for general support of the Rape and Abuse Crisis center in Fargo, North Dakota
- $5,000 to replace a broken furnace at Goodwill Industries of Greater Wichita, Kansas
- $15,000 to the United Negro College Fund
- $35,000 to the Mexican-American Legal Defense and Education Fund.

Members and clients of these organizations may of course become Dayton Hudson customers, and the company's largesse may be repaid. But you would have to be uncommonly cynical to interpret grants to native American children, battered women, black collegians, Hispanic defendants, and the indigent as *simply* a pandering for sales. There's more going on here than public relations. There's clearly a commitment to decency, or fairness, or ethics.

These examples may be criticized on a number of counts. Let me address three of them.

First, it may be charged that, far from illustrating a fulfillment of social responsibility, such endeavors as funding day-care centers and loaning faculty to minority colleges are actually blatant denials of the corporation's primary social responsibility, which is to increase its profits. Milton Friedman defended this proposition fifteen years ago in a now classic essay, and has continued to do so eloquently ever since. I have already said in passing that I believe the "wave of the future" in this respect will run counter to Friedman's desires. Since it is perilous to dismiss a Nobel laureate in an aside, I will confront his thesis at greater length in chapters 7 and 8. Suffice it to say here that, whatever the economic wisdom of increased corporate responsibility for social concerns, the trend toward greater involvement is unlikely to abate in the near future. The question then becomes: What kind of involvement is ethical? The above mentioned companies seem to me to represent, in principle and in practice, the right kind of involvement.

A second objection to the examples may be that my rosy description fails to take into account the "ulterior motive" of profit. The managerial decisions cited, it may be claimed, were not purely motivated. On the contrary, Dayton Hudson scores a public relations coup every time it funds a ghetto self-help project, and J&J withdrew Tylenol only because it risked market disaster if it failed to do so. In other words, what looks like altruism on the surface is really a sophisticated brand of selfishness.

The logic of this argument is as impeccable as the argument itself is irrelevant. A psychologist may find it valuable to determine the "real" reason behind James Burke's appearance on the Donahue show, and a market specialist will certainly want to assess the effect on sales of the recall decision. In the context of this book, however, those are tangential issues. I am interested in knowing how much "good" and how much "ill" the new bottom line brings into our society—regardless of the motives of its practitioners.

It can be argued, moreover, that all human activity is a "sophisticated brand of selfishness." I will look at this idea in the following chapter, and try to show that the presence on a corporate or a personal level of ulterior motives does not necessarily vitiate the goodness (or the badness) of an action. To someone who is primarily interested in the social effects of certain corporate cultures, it makes no more sense to chide a CEO for currying public favor with a grant than it does to denounce the country vicar for giving alms as a way of winning favor with the Almighty.

A final objection: The cases given are false examples; that is, they are not representative of the behavior of the firms involved, or of the System itself, as a whole. The real day-to-day operation of business, those who make this objection say, is core-rotten; the good deeds cited here are simply window dressing. A second version of this objection is that big guys like J&J and IBM behave in an ostensibly ethical manner because they have enough money to cover their tracks: that is, they can afford to be moral—on the surface.

In both versions, the window-dressing argument comes down to this complaint: Big corporations have virtually unlimited resources, and we have no obligation to be grateful if they give a minuscule portion of those resources to non-profitmaking concerns. They should be giving much more. And no matter how much they give, nothing can make up for the fact that their "business as usual" is dirty pool.

To someone who believes this firmly, no amount of evidence to the contrary is going to matter. To those who suspect that, in spite of its excessive tone, the basic thrust of this characterization is on target, I can offer these tentative observations—all of which will be discussed in later chapters:

First, I am well aware that American corporations in general are not in the habit of emptying their coffers for social purposes. Even the highly acclaimed Dayton Hudson gives only 5 percent. Its spokesmen explain that, while they would like to give more, this would make them uncompetitive in a market in which the other firms give so much less.

But noting that a given firm is niggardly in its largesse does not necessarily imply that it treats its own employees badly, that it cheats on its taxes, or that it routinely poisons the air. Social service projects may fairly be characterized as window dressing; before you denounce a firm for putting up curtains, though, you have to find out what's going on behind them.

Second, in any consideration of corporate ethics, you need to weigh the various responsibilities that a company may have (or may be thought to have) to all of its constituencies—the constituencies whom J&J chairman Burke called, during the Tylenol crisis, "partners dealing with the same problem." The issue of conflicting responsibilities will be raised in Chapter 3. For now, it is important to remember that what looks like a good deed to one person may look like betrayal to another. Corporate executives don't have it any easier than the rest of us when it comes to balancing moral claims. Sometimes, since they are human, they blow it.

Finally, *because* they blow it, I am not out to prove in this book that any of the companies I profile are either blameless or infallible in their judgments. I believe that there is a demonstrable difference between a moral corporate manager and an immoral one, but I do not suppose that the difference resides in the one possessing moral infallibility and the other not—that is, in the moral manager always coming up with the "right" answer to a corporate dilemma. Human judgment is notoriously unstable, but moral attitude—what some ethicists call "moral character"—is not. Ethical judgment consists not in getting the right answer all the time, but in consistently asking the right questions. The companies profiled here, I am convinced, do that with some consistency.

"Asking the right questions," of course, is neither a comprehensive nor a precise definition of ethical behavior. Plato asked what he thought was one very central "right question" over two millennia ago, when he had Socrates proclaim throughout the *Republic*, "What is justice?" Philosophers ever since have been, in Alfred North Whitehead's famous phrase, "writing footnotes to Plato," and not a few of the footnotes have involved ruminations over that question. The best of today's corporate managers, whether or not they know their Plato, are carrying on that rumination.

To see how they are able to do this, we need to spend one chapter on theory. Looking briefly at some "professional" philosophers will help us to define a moral context. Such a context is important because corporate ethical decisions do not exist in a vacuum; they are the outcome of a long tradition. Understanding that tradition will clarify what I mean by "right questions." It may even give some clues as to where the right answers lie.

2 ETHICAL MODELS
An Overview

What is the highest of all realizable goods? As to its name there is pretty general agreement: The majority of men, as well as the cultured few, speak of it as happiness; and they would maintain that to live well and to do well are the same thing as to be happy. They differ, however, as to what happiness is, and the mass of mankind give a different account of it from philosophers.

—Aristotle

The golden rule is that there are no golden rules.

—George Bernard Shaw

The *New Yorker* magazine, never notoriously affectionate to business, once ran a cartoon in which several executives are gathered in a corner office, visibly puzzled. One of them presses an intercom button and pleads with his secretary, "Miss Dugan, will you please send someone in here who can distinguish right from wrong?"

In implying that top managers may lack the fundamental ethical knowledge that we expect of a seven-year-old, the cartoon reflected the public cynicism of the Scandalous Seventies. The commercophobic jibe was that crime in the executive suites derived not so much from venality as from an atavistic innocence. The boys in pinstripes, was the message, are too stupid to know that they're bad.

As comforting as it may be to embrace this smug view, honesty compels us to admit that it is not only business executives who suffer from moral retardation. Not knowing right from wrong, far from being an idiosyncrasy of the merchant class, is part of the human condition. We are all of us, to one degree or another, too ignorant to know right from wrong, or too weak to act on the knowledge. If this were not the case, Jesus's comment to the people of Jerusalem—"Let him without sin cast the first stone"—would not have its peculiar pungency. Nor would elaborate legal codes have had to be devised as crutches for the confused.

Plato made the case in a famous parable over two millennia ago. He imagined the condition of human beings as that of bound prisoners in a cave, sitting with their backs to a fire between which and the prisoners move objects whose shadows are cast on the far wall. The prisoners see the shadows alone, and what we see and know—the objects of thought, the impressions of our senses, and our opinions about them—are (Plato said) like those shadows on the cave wall, indistinct and ephemeral copies of a formal, ideal reality we can never know. We behave as if we understood what was real, and true, and good. But even the most enlightened among us—those whom Plato called "philosopher kings"—are in the end only guessing. "In the world of knowledge," Plato says, "the last thing to be perceived and only with great difficulty is the essential Form of Goodness."

Twenty-four centuries of footnotes have not substantially undermined that perception. In the boardrooms and barrooms, the day-care centers and think tanks, we are still guessing. "Most of the interesting moral questions in the practice of business," the Committee for Education in Business Ethics (CEBE) concluded recently, "are not obvious but rather constitute genuine moral dilemmas." That is true outside of business, too. Which is why the debate goes on.

It would be presumptuous of me to suggest that I can better Plato, or even the CEBE, and this is not a philosophy text. So I will not review the epistemological queries that lie behind Plato's conclusion, nor touch on modern surveys of the wall. My aim in this chapter is modest. I want to show, by looking at some common approaches to ethics, how the ethical framework most of us share—that of the Hellenic and Judeo-Christian traditions—can be justified by logic, not just temperament. Granted that both logic and my own cultural biases are provisional, I still believe that this shared framework can be shown to make at least as much sense as any other.

To decipher the shadows on the cave wall, human beings have come up with a huge range of investigative procedures. In Western moral theory, four such procedures have been perenially popular. Two of them—the utilitarian theory of Jeremy Bentham and the formalist theory of Immanuel Kant—will be introduced in a moment and will reappear throughout the book. But I want to begin with the other two, since they are both more widely endorsed and more easily dismissed as reliable guides for social thinking.

First, ethical *absolutism* or, as it is commonly known today, ethical *fundamentalism*. If you are an ethical fundamentalist, you decipher the shadows in a relatively straightforward manner. You look up the meaning in a book. Or you get the word from someone else who has read (or written) the book.

This conventional, literalist approach to morality, which relies on revealed rather than constructed wisdom, has been the mainstay of ethical systems for most of our species' history. In traditional societies, where religion advances social cohesion, God's word and the rule of law are often perceived as identical. But even in "freethinking" societies like ours, the courts often take their cues from long-forgotten moral codes that were written down originally as approximations of divine injunctions. To a lawyer, the "chapter and verse" approach to moral questions is congenial, and indeed the secular equivalent to religious fundamentalism is an appeal to the majesty of the law.

The principal limitation to taking "the Book" as your moral authority is that there are so many books to choose from. Consider only the Bible and the Koran. What is obvious to reader Falwell is anything but obvious to reader Khomeini. The difficulties of reconciling even these two holy writs lie behind such escapades of illogic as the Iranian hostage crisis and the Crusades. Think of the aggravations that arise when you add in the Analects of Confucius, the works of Darwin or Freud, or the statutes of the state of Wyoming.

Furthermore, as liberal theologians have long recognized, holy writs are notoriously interpretable, at least on matters of import. If you need advice on oblations, you can find more than you really want to know in Numbers and Leviticus and Deuteronomy. If you need counsel on something that matters today—capital punishment, say, or adultery—you will encounter lacunae, parables, and inconsistency. You will be even more at sea if you seek advice on employee compensation, leveraged buyouts, or the ethics of closing a plant. The fervor with which television fundamentalists proclaim the unity of scripture while disagreeing on political options underscores the point that, for the business person seeking moral guidance, the Bible is no more helpful than the law.

But the most serious objection to fundamentalist morality is that it permits a True Believer to avoid responsibility for actions, by allowing either the Book or one of the Book's authorized readers (minister, mullah, or judge) to dictate his or her moral choices. Such a surrender of personal accountability segues tragically into the Good German defense: I was only following orders; I did as the law commanded. Playing the shadow game "by the book," therefore, leads to a false sense of security that can be ethically very perilous.

Ironically, the same peril awaits those people who are generally considered fundamentalism's greatest antagonists: the ethical relativists. If the fundamentalist claims that all moral questions can be decided by referring to an external authority, the relativist denies the existence of that authority, and concludes that therefore they cannot be decided at all. The shadows are only shadows. Moral opinions are only opinions.

This second popular approach to ethics, which derives from anthropological liberalism, has grown in favor as the world has become more cosmopolitan and as our own cultural prejudices have been revealed. It's harder to chide the heathen than it used to be. A hundred years ago the British army, quite rightly, outlawed the traditional Indian practice of suttee, or widow-burning, on the grounds of immorality. Today it is possible for rite-tipsy anthropologists to call this "cultural imperialism."

At its extreme the relativist view leads the True Unbeliever into quicksands of illogic. Richard De George maps these clearly. He points out that if you believe that every opinion is as defensible as every other one, you must also accept the following:

- First, your judgment about an action is not really a judgment at all, but merely an expression of your personal feeling about it. The implication is that nothing external really exists, only your view (of the nonexistent).
- Second, you are not allowed to disagree with anyone about the morality of an action. If you do disagree, you must admit that you are expressing only a baseless conjecture, unconnected to reality.
- Third, neither you nor anyone else can ever be mistaken in a judgment, since you're making no claim on the facts, only on your "view" of them. Therefore, you can say one thing today, the opposite tomorrow, and be right both times.
- Finally, you are empowered to alter the morality of an action by expressing a different opinion on it. "If a moral judgment is only the report of an emotion or the expressing of an emotion, then by changing his emotion a person changes the morality of the action."

The inanity of these propositions should be evident to the most generous of relativistic spirits. And all of them derive logically from the conviction that because you can't prove it in print, it's no use making a claim.

While it is clear that moral opinions are culturally determined and that reasonable people can disagree on many specifics, it does not follow that all opinions are equally laudable, or that lack of a single standard means we should forget about standards altogether. Ultimately, it is just that leap of faithlessness that makes ethical relativism barren.

Like other forms of cynicism, relativism provides a refuge for the frustrated purist, who reacts to the news that the rules have changed (that "God is dead," for example) by saying the game is no longer worth playing. In this century, especially among business people, ethical relativism has also become an excuse for not looking too closely into the morality of other cultures. If everybody's opinion is equally defensible, you are spared the uncomfortable task of questioning the morality of bribes or of doing business with repressive regimes.

And this points to the root of the problem. It is not so much its inconsistency as its denial of accountability—a characteristic it shares with fundamentalism—that makes relativism ultimately arid. Precisely because they allow this kind of denial, both ethical relativism and ethical fundamentalism have considerable appeal among people who are frightened by the complexities of moral choice. To the reflective business person, aware that moral decision-making is likely to involve a little work, they provide no real assistance.

Fortunately, there are alternatives.

The premise of *utilitarianism*, the third moral theory, is that no action is good or bad in itself, but only with regard to its consequences: It's the ends, not the means, that count. Because of its focus on ends, utilitarianism is known as a teleological philosophy (from the Greek *telos*, end); since its inception it has been the most widely endorsed of teleological ethical systems.

The father of utilitarianism, the eighteenth-century British reformer Jeremy Bentham, popularized the adage with which the utilitarian sensibility is generally identified. A good, or moral, action is one that promotes "the greatest happiness of the greatest number." An immoral action is one whose consequences limit that happiness.

To those critics who charged that "happiness" was an indistinct end, Bentham responded with another famous rule of thumb. As common sense shows, he said, happiness can be equated with pleasure, and unhappiness with pain. That which brings us pleasure is therefore identified as good, that which brings pain as bad. The original premise is thus modified: whatever brings a net outcome of pleasure is classified as moral; whatever brings net pain is immoral.

The pleasure/pain dichotomy was marginally more precise than the happiness/unhappiness formulation, but it did not get the utilitarians out of the woods. The remaining problem was how to *quantify* pleasure and pain, so that the total "amounts" of goodness or badness in alternative choices of action might be compared. Suppose, for example, that one division of a multidivision company is so unprofitable that it is threatening the survival of the firm as a whole. Consider these choices:

1. You can lay off employees in the unprofitable division, thus bringing them pain but maintaining the pleasure of the rest of your work force; or

2. You can keep the division running, thus maintaining the pleasure of its workers but risking eventual pain for everybody if the division's losses necessitate future payroll cuts.

In choosing between these options, you encounter two difficulties. First, it is impossible to predict with any accuracy exactly what the consequences would be either of closing the plant or of keeping it open; all such managerial decisions are based on informed speculation. Second, in order to compare the expected consequences in terms of happiness and unhappiness, you have to measure the two. What units do you use? How many board feet of pleasure are equal to a half quart of pain?

Bentham addressed this problem by proposing a "hedonistic calculus" in which the goodness or badness of an action would be calculated based on a sophisticated analysis of each potential pleasure's (and pain's) "intensity, duration, certainty or uncertainty, propinquity or remoteness, fecundity, and the purity of the value in question." When these variables were figured in, Bentham said, reasonable people would with some accuracy be able to distinguish between low-yield and high-yield pleasures, to assess the relative (if not absolute) preferability of actions based on the "units" of pleasure and pain. If you could count, you could tell right from wrong.

As a straightforward, materialistic approach to moral questions, utilitarianism has proved remarkably durable, largely because—as Bentham and his followers pointed out—the hedonistic calculus, with all its imprecision, is a fairly accurate metaphor for the way the nonphilosopher compares choices anyway, all the time. "Utilitarianism," De George says, "is simply the result of making explicit the ways we ordinarily argue about policies, laws, and actions."

To the business professional this should be obvious. When you use any type of cost-benefit analysis, you are employing utilitarian thinking. And this is appropriate. If you want to know whether a given decision is ethical or not, it makes sense to ask how much good (pleasure) and how much bad (pain) it will bring, and then compare the two. It's done all the time, and it works.

But there are problems with this ledger approach to ethics. Let me address the two most serious ones: the likelihood that subjective bias will distort the calculation, and the utilitarian's incomplete explanation of how a balance sheet on morals serves justice.

Subjective bias. Critics of utilitarianism say that in calculating the net sum of good and bad in a potential action, I am not likely to be dispassionate and impartial, but to weight my own happiness more heavily than that of others. The injunction to promote the general good may be ignored, consequently, if it conflicts with what I see as my own pleasure. Moreover, I am likely to make my own case special, to make myself an exception to every utilitarian rule.

That this is no idle apprehension we see in business every day. It's doubtful that Lockheed's management would have defended bribery as a *generally* moral action, or that the distributors of defective merchandise see the greatest good for the greatest number in the crapshoot they play with their products. To every manager faced with the choice of honoring the general good or of honoring his own good by increasing profits, the temptation is strong to weight the scales.

To Bentham and his chief apologist, the philosopher John Stuart Mill, this was a manageable problem. Yes, they admitted, the hedonistic calculus could be perverted. But so could every other system. "Is utility the only creed," Mill asked in his 1863 tract *Utilitarianism*, "which is able to furnish us with excuses for evil doing, and means of cheating our own conscience?" With the proper education, the early utilitarians were convinced, rational individuals would understand the ultimate conjunction between their personal happiness and that of the greatest number. With the proper education, they would see things impartially and act well.

Maybe. But we're far from providing that type of education today, and until we attain such a pedagogical paradise caution is in order. Bentham's contemporary, the Anglican bishop Joseph Butler, acknowledged the subjectivist limitation of the theory with a famous quip. God, he said, is almost certainly a utilitarian, but human beings had better not be, until their judgment improves.

The justice problem. The second objection to utilitarianism is that in their zeal to honor the "greatest good" principle, utilitarians are apt to thwart justice: to deny certain persons their rights because those rights run counter to the widest possible happiness. Conversely, they are likely to overlook evils, if by doing so more people turn out to be happy.

The first possibility is poignantly dramatized in Swiss playwright Friedrich Dürrenmatt's *The Visit*, popularized on Broadway several seasons ago by Ingrid Bergman. In this play the residents of a tiny, poverty-stricken town are offered a proposition by an old woman who grew up in the town, moved away, and is now enormously wealthy. She will donate enough money to the town to solve all its material problems if the residents, collectively, will execute her former lover, an old man named Albert who, fifty years earlier, had seduced and abandoned her.

In terms of sheer numbers, the calculation is easy. We are asked to weigh the death of one man, who will probably die shortly anyway, against the potential happiness of an entire town. True, death is a stiff price to pay for one youthful indiscretion. But in terms of the hedonistic calculus, isn't execution what's called for?

The converse example is that of the corporate officer who is discovered embezzling company funds, but who is also an able manager, a devoted husband and father, a responsible civic leader. How severely should he be punished?

This is no hypothetical example. The chairman of a major American firm was recently indicted for exactly this infraction, and the judge who sentenced him, obviously a utilitarian, gave him three months' probation. Evidently he felt that anything longer would have created, not only for the defendant but also for his family and community, too great a net amount of pain. So the wrist slap was "moral."

But there's something wrong here. As rational in mathematical terms as Albert's execution and the executive's light sentence might be, they still don't "feel right" to most people. Nor should they. There is something basically unjust about such decisions, in spite of their coherence to the calculus. To discover what that something is, we need to go beyond utility and examine a fourth theory, that of the deontologists.

Deontology is the study of moral obligations (from the Greek deon, obligation). To the deontologist, the utilitarian emphasis on consequences is a heresy, and a dangerous one at that, because it allows people to justify all sorts of immorality with the excuse that the end is worth the means.

To the deontologist, morality means conforming to certain unyielding principles, which are *in themselves* worthy of respect, whether or not adherence to them leads to the greatest good for the greatest number. One such principle is that of justice, often defined as giving each person his or her due. The deontologist would be less likely than the utilitarian to fudge this principle by executing Albert or letting the embezzler off easy.

Deontology is a *formalist* theory, because it demands that an action, to be considered moral, pass certain formal tests—that is, conform, whatever the consequences, to a universally recognizable, and universally valid, logical structure. The most distinguished proponent of formalism was the German philosopher Immanuel Kant; nearly two centuries after his death, it is still Kant's description of formal moral tests that command the most attention among ethicists.

The basis of all such tests was his celebrated doctrine of the Categorical Imperative. This imperative, he claimed, was the only test of moral action that was universally consistent with human reason. To Kant, all truly moral actions conformed to a moral law that had to be obeyed by all rational people (that is, was imperative) because it was unconditioned by time and place (that is, was categorical).

Kant devised three versions of the Categorical Imperative, each one stressing one of three interrelated characteristics by which a moral action could be recognized. The clearly moral action would:

1. Be universalizable. That is, it would make sense, consistently, for everybody in a similar situation to take the same action.
2. Demonstrate respect for individual human beings. It would treat others not as means, but as ends in themselves.
3. Be acceptable to all rational beings. If the action were made the basis of a universal law, receivers as well as initiators of the action would agree that it was just.

As these formulations of the Categorical Imperative make clear, one quality that mattered a great deal to Kant was that of consistency of action. That quality has been held in high regard since Plato's time, and as the discussion of personal bias under utilitarianism indicated, it is a quality that has a distinct bearing on ethical questions today. It is by no means an archaic or purely formal argument to insist that individual (and corporate) actions be internally consistent, or that they should remain consistent even when applied on a broad scale. The public or corporate official who claims that "grease" money is all right in his case, but that nobody should make a practice of offering it, is committing the logician's one mortal sin, that of self-contradiction.

Although formalist ethics may seem less immediately applicable to business than utilitarianism, the Categorical Imperative is quite as relevant to the world of affairs as it is to the realm of abstract ideas. Philosopher Norman Bowie uses the Kantian formulations to demonstrate not only the relevance of the moral law to business but the impossibility of doing business without it. He considers whether the deceptive practices often attributed to businessmen can be condoned, and concludes, echoing Kant, that they cannot because they fail the test of consistency. If every business person routinely cheated on tax forms, used misleading advertising, or broke contractual agreements, then no party to a business transaction could be confident of the outcome, and business would self-destruct. Like De George, Bowie recognizes that commerce presupposes morality—the morality of universal norms. The business community recognizes it too. Bowie identifies why:

> To universalize cheating would be self-defeating. Kant's point is implicitly recognized by the business community when corporate officials despair of the immoral practices of corporations and denounce executives engaging in shady practices as undermining the business enterprise itself.

So too with such guardians of probity as the Better Business Bureau. The Bureau monitors its members' behavior not to restrict their options but to enhance them. Like all pro-business watchdogs, it understands that free enterprise depends on fair play.

This suggests that honesty might be the best policy for a quite selfish reason. The ethical choice, says Kant, is the choice that you would find acceptable even if it were done *to* you rather than *by* you. In other words, the ethical person really takes not "the moral law" but himself or herself as the norm for judging actions. Only if you don't mind being lied to yourself can you engage in lying to others; if you want your business associates to honor your contracts, you must honor theirs.

It will be obvious that the Categorical Imperative, which endorses consistency of action and invokes the actor's own desires as a test of that consistency, is an elaboration of a much better known injunction: "Do unto others as you would have them do unto you." "Kant's moral philosophy," writes Bowie, "can be viewed as an extensive reworking of the Golden Rule." It may not be so obvious that the Golden Rule, commonly thought of as the benchmark of "altruism," actually enshrines selfishness. Like the Categorical Imperative, it takes one's own feelings and desires as standards against which behavior toward others should be measured. The implication of the Golden Rule is that you should ask not "How do *you* feel?" but rather "How would *I* feel if I were you?"

It is precisely this self-centeredness of the Golden Rule that makes it so valuable, and so widely acknowledged, as a guide. To inquire of yourself, "How would I feel in the other fellow's place?" is an elegantly simple and reliable method of focusing in on the "right" thing to do. The Golden Rule works not in spite of selfishness, but because of it. Jesus, that supreme psychologist, was also a supreme egoist. That is why he understood love.

To the "altruistically" inclined, this comment might sound cynical. But it is nothing of the kind. It simply acknowledges a central psychological fact; that whether you call yourself moral or Machiavellian, in the end you are on your own side. The altruism that Jesus is supposed to have encouraged is really that sophisticated brand of selfishness that is often called "enlightened self-interest."

One irony of social history is that those people who live by this principle of self-interest generally do well in business. It's a logical irony. Treating others as you would want to be treated usually means treating them well, and people who are treated well tend to come back for more. While someone who feels he's been wronged reacts by taking his business somewhere else.

Many of the successful companies I will be talking about in this book are believers in Kantian ethics, subscribing either consciously or unconsciously to the categorical injunctions that moral actions must be universalizable, must treat individuals with respect, and must be acceptable to receivers as well as to givers of the action.

They feel strongly enough about it to make it part of official statements. I have already mentioned IBM in this regard: Thomas

Watson's identification of "respect for the individual" as the company's guiding belief is a classic example of formalist thinking. Johnson Wax promises to "respect the dignity of each person as an individual human being." And former J.C. Penney chairman Donald Seibert, recalling that James Cash Penney's first store was called The Golden Rule, calls the deontological principle of enlightened self-interest "the foundation of morality."

My own attachment to enlightened self-interest is evident. Yet I appreciate the common-sense value of utilitarianism, especially to business people, and in this book I will be using an ethical model that combines elements of the Benthamite and Kantian systems. By combining the two approaches, I hope to avoid the measurement tangles common to utilitarians on the one hand, and the potential impracticality of formalists on the other.

The utilitarian's premise is that moral actions maximize happiness. The Kantian starts with two related premises. First, moral actions are consistent with a universal moral law. Second, they show the respect for individuals that each of us would want to be shown if we were on the receiving end of the action. The premise of my synthetic model can be stated very informally: Businesses must treat individuals fairly, just as they would want to be treated if they were themselves individuals.

Another way of stating the premise would be to say that businesses must fulfill certain *obligations* to individuals: that managers should try to determine what it is they *owe* others. A working axiom of this book is that an ethical company tries seriously to meet its obligations to everybody with whom it interacts.

But who is "everybody?" And what, precisely, are those obligations?

3 THE BROADENING BASE

A corporation is best pictured...as having a full gamut of stakeholders with each of whom a constructive relationship must be established or negotiated.

—Henry B. Schacht, chief executive officer
Charles W. Powers, former vice-president
for public policy, Cummins Engine Company

We think our giving program should be accountable to the same stakeholders as the rest of our company—our customers, employees, communities, and stockowners....Serving society is not optional to our business. It is the foundation upon which our business rests.

—Peter Hutchinson
Chairman, Dayton Hudson Foundation

Not many years ago, the idea that businesses had obligations beyond that of making money for their owners struck most business people—and most of the general public—as an eccentric proposition. There was no need for a Milton Friedman to defend a limited social role for corporations or to excoriate those who would expand it; such a defense, up to a generation ago, would have been aimed at straw men.

In the 1950s attitudes began to change, as people began, in Thomas Donaldson's phrase, "to expect more of a corporation," not only ethically but socially. Keith Davis and Robert Blomstrom, authors of *Business and Society*, a standard text on business's widening role, credit Howard R. Bowen's 1953 book *Social Responsibilities of the Businessman* with focusing a turnaround, while acknowledging that the book didn't so much create as reflect an attitudinal shift following the Second World War:

> Society had solved most of its economic problems arising from the Depression of the 1930s, so it was ready to move on to new ground. With economic problems minimally out of the way, social problems became more visible. In essence the abounding success of the economic machine had created an affluence which released society from economic bondage and allowed it to turn to other challenges.

There is a world of qualification in that tiny word "minimally," and the recession-torn 1970s have reminded us that the economic system is far from purely rationalized yet. But the basic observation is sound. The demand to increase profit was appropriate to a developing and unstable corporate economy; current demands on business, implying obligations beyond profit-making, have arisen in a mature economy whose players have learned to soften, if not eliminate, the uncertainties of the free market.

As Davis and Blomstrom point out, it's not only attitudes that have changed; the system itself has evolved. Like every institution, the corporation "may change its way of working with people, its manner of relating to other organizations, the activities it performs, and other characteristics. All these changes relate to its attempt to meet human needs and remain viable in the system." Corporations have always attempted to do both these things. Today, however, the two aims are less separable than they used to be. Remaining viable in our mixed economy means meeting human needs. As the Business Roundtable put it in a 1981 statement, "The long-term viability of the business sector is linked to its responsibility to the society of which it is a part."

Human needs are now widely identified, moreover, as comprising more than a paycheck and good products. Few business leaders would be as blunt as former Prudential chairman Donald MacNaughton was in acknowledging that the corporation as a "socioeconomic institution" owes a *primary* responsibility to society and a *secondary* one to employees and stockholders. But even conventional profit maximizers must now recognize that the nature of corporate obligation has changed. The base of customer support and social involvement has broadened, so that the corporation has assumed obligations (not always willingly) to groups that may have no direct connection with the operation or ownership of firms.

At Cummins Engine and Dayton Hudson, as the epigraphs opening this chapter suggest, these groups are described as "stakeholders." Other firms use different terminology to acknowledge the same broadening corporate base. Some examples:

- Armstrong World Industries, the Pennsylvania flooring specialist, lists among its "principles" the obligation to "serve fairly and in proper balance the interests of all groups associated with the business—customers, stockholders, employees, suppliers, community neighbors, government, and the general public."

- Johnson Wax, in its policy statement "This We Believe," specifies five "groups of people to whom we are responsible, and whose trust we have to earn." These are employees, consumers, the general public, neighbors and hosts, and the world community.
- At several companies, including John Deere, J.C. Penney, and Reynolds Aluminum, corporate constituencies are spoken of as "publics," deserving of the same respect as the public at large.
- Since the 1940s, Johnson & Johnson has attempted to fulfill responsibilities to four groups identified by name in its corporate Credo: all those "who use our products and services," "our employees," "the communities in which we live and work and...the world community as well," and stockholders.
- In a recent statement on "Philosophy and Direction," Aetna management insists that corporations consider "what their multiple constituencies—employees, agents, shareholders, customers, and the public generally—demand of them."

The examples are representative, not exhaustive. I mention these companies because they recognize explicitly the broadened constituency. The concept of multiple publics, though, is also recognized by firms that do not articulate it in print, and even by firms that resist the idea. In today's corporate arena, the broad-base model is impossible to avoid.

The term I use in this book to describe corporate publics is the one in place at Dayton Hudson and Cummins: stakeholders. One reason for this choice is personal. I originally heard the term about ten years ago, when I was writing "social issue profiles" for the Philadelphia research firm Human Resources Network. These profiles, which were addressed to business leaders, government officials, academics, and others with a professional "stake" in the economy, came out under the rubric "Stakeholder Outlook."

Second, I like the term "stakeholder" because it both evokes and enhances the more familiar term "stockholder." The original stakeholders of any public company were its shareholders and investors, and it is appropriate, when speaking of a broadening base for the corporation, to see the new members of that base as having interests roughly analogous to those who put up the first stakes.

Finally, I find the term attractive because it suggests the dynamic interplay that goes on between a corporation and the people it serves, or who serve it. In a country whose business is business, all of us are stakeholders to some degree in the operation of major firms. Whatever our personal feelings about Big Business, we all have a stake in how it performs its social roles. The term "stakeholder" reminds us of that reality.

At Cummins, dealing with "the full gamut of stakeholders" has been recognized as a necessity for twenty years. As we shall see, this willingness of a company to negotiate with a broadening base, far from vitiating its effectiveness, can actually enhance its performance, in the economic as well as social sphere. Cummins is evidence of that, as are many of the other firms in this book.

These firms don't all recognize the same groups as being stakeholders, and that is true in the general corporate population as well. A heavily regulated industry would probably identify government, however grudgingly, as one of its constituencies; a nonregulated industry might not. A mutual insurance company might recognize its policyholders as both consumers and, in a modified sense, "stockholders" too; at a nonmutualized company the two groups would be more distinct.

In this book I concentrate on five stakeholder groups that are recognized as important by most firms, across industry lines and in spite of business location or size. Although the general corporate obligation to each of these groups is the same (that is, to treat each with respect, and to do so consistently), there are also specific obligations that arise because of the nature of the groups—and specific resulting issues. As a prefiguring of these issues, which will be addressed in detail in Part II, I'll briefly describe the five groups. They are shareholders, employees, customers, local communities, and society at large.

Shareholders. Owners still come first. Although the justice of this is debated, the reality is unavoidable under capitalism. The reason is simple. Unless management serves its shareholders well—so that they receive a fair return on their investment—the firm will not survive. The obligation to manage investors' money efficiently and honestly underlies all other obligations, because an unprofitable firm can meet no obligations.

But in "efficiently" and "honestly," there's a rub. Because the two are not always identical, we need to ask which profitable money-management practices are acceptable and which are not. In Chapter 4, therefore, we will look at the moral questions raised by the use of expense accounts and executive perks supposedly to advance shareholder interests.

Employees. The responsibilities that an employer owes to the stakeholders he or she employs begin with, but do not necessarily end with, the obligation to pay each worker a fair, contracted salary or wage for services rendered. Recompense may also include such benefits as health care insurance, pension security, and (in the more progressive companies) unconventional perks like free day care, free lunches, and the option of flexible working hours.

Beyond this, there are ethical considerations in the issues of labor-management relations, affirmative action, and job security. In Chapter 5 we will see how several "model" companies try to provide an open, secure, and productive environment for their people.

Customers. Some years ago the president of a major computer firm described his firm's attitudes toward customers: "Our support and service policy is to leave our customers surly but not rebellious." The ultimate fallout from that attitude, in terms of lost credibility, was severe, as any student of the Golden Rule could have predicted. Fortunately, such antediluvian attitudes are becoming increasingly rare. In many companies today, far from being thought of as a mark or an inconvenience, the customer is considered the market's sovereign.

In Chapter 6 we will see how companies that practice a "close to the customer" philosophy (to use the Peters/Waterman phrase) manage their obligations to avoid misrepresentation, to sell safe and reliable products, and to refrain from price-fixing and other anti-consumer trade practices. By measuring the philosophies of these "creative marketing" companies against their profitability, we will determine in what respects a disavowal of caveat emptor is a factor in bottom-line success.

Local Communities. Not even Milton Friedman would be likely to object to a corporation honoring the first three stakeholder groups: that's just good business. But he would stop there, denying that business responsibility extends beyond the groups with whom business directly engages in commerce. He would deny that companies have obligations to their local (or national) communities beyond the minimal and negative obligation not to dump toxic wastes into the water supply or otherwise endanger the common weal.

Many companies today reject this minimalist view of community obligation, and do involve themselves socially (this usually, though not always, means "financially") in the communities where they do business. In Chapter 7, after reviewing the Friedman thesis, we will investigate the ethical issues that confront the manager who takes the local community as a fourth stakeholder. As many firms attest, this approach can have market advantages. But what moral dilemmas are faced by the corporate manager acting as "good citizen"?

Society at Large. Finally, what responsibility, if any, does a corporate manager have to the wider social community—to the state, the nation, even the planet? Many companies today address this question forcefully in terms of both space and time: space in the sense that they see themselves as impacting on a wide social and ecological constituency; time in the sense that they take account of the effects of corporate decisions on unborn generations.

In their attention to the possibly harmful social effects of corporate actions, and in their awareness that businesses can also tremendously enrich the social environment, these managers are reviving the nineteeeth century concept of stewardship, necessarily modified today by the presence of Big Government, consumer and environmentalist pressure groups, and the mixed economy itself. In Chapter 8 we will see how firms that embrace a national role try to draft alliances with government and other social actors.

Identifying the obligations of corporations to their various stakeholders leaves unanswered some ticklish but fundamental questions. The most basic one involves the potential for a collision between, rather than a coincidence of, the interests of different groups.

Marketing executive Harold Johnson in a thoughtful essay on "Ethics and the Executive" identifies this as a basic moral problem in business. "Often what would appear to be the moral act from the standpoint of one corporate constituency may result in hardship to others." Johnson rightly, if a bit sanguinely, recognizes the difficulties here as inevitable under democratic capitalism: In a society that encourages "counterpulling individuals and groups," managerial dilemmas of this sort "in part reflect the independence of free persons." Yet he acknowledges, less blithely, that this doesn't solve the problem. What should the ethical manager do when he must serve one stakeholder well, but at another's expense?

A Johnson & Johnson senior manager, at a meeting designed to test the efficacy of the company's traditional Credo, expressed the problem of balancing interests in a provocative metaphor. The interests of the constituencies identified in the Credo he likened to juggler's balls, three white ones representing the needs of customers, employees, and communities, and one red one for the stockholders' needs. In juggling conflicting claims, he said, the only thing a manager really knows for sure is that he cannot drop the red ball, because that would mean the end of the business. But what about the other three? Ideally, you don't want to drop any of the balls—to slight any constituency. And that, as the manager recognized, is a lot more complicated than keeping your eye *only* on the red.

One common example of this dilemma I alluded to in the discussion of the utilitarian calculus: that of the manager who can increase overall corporate profits by closing an unprofitable plant. A traditional managerial solution here is to close the plant immediately because that will make more quick money for the stockholders, whatever the social cost. Labor's traditional solution is to keep the plant going, whatever the cost to the firm. The modern manager, aware of multiple corporate commitments, does not have the luxury of adopting either of these simple solutions. Commonly, he or she must balance the interests of all concerned parties, which often leads to a compromise that leaves nobody feeling well served.

William Brooks, who as secretary of the Prudential Foundation confronts this kind of dilemma daily, speaks of the "inevitable conflict" that arises, most pointedly in progressive firms, between the requirements of line production and broader social goals. "It's relatively easy for the line manager to decide what's most important," he says. "But senior management has to look at everything. We have to temper the line charges even though we recognize that we all depend on the line for our survival. Sometimes you feel like a chameleon."

The dilemma is no less complicated, and the alternate solutions no less unsatisfying, when the issues at hand are "minor" and the social effects internal. Indeed, the conflict of allegiances that is most likely to give a manager nightmares is also the one most likely to arise in day-to-day operations: that involving people with whom he or she works every day. A John Deere manufacturing executive, C.C. Peterson, recently applauded his company's "compilation of beliefs, of concepts, of attitudes, of ways-of-proceeding that represent, in a modest way, an ethical philosophy of conduct." Yet this philosophy, he admitted, could be of only limited help in the case of many "ethical anomalies"—cases where the venal and the venial, the principle and the personal, seem to fuse. He gave the following examples:

> You believe you have a moral and legal duty to convey knowledge of...illicit activities to the proper authorities in your company. But what would you do if the illicit activity is minor or transient, and is committed by a lifelong friend?
>
> What would you do if you learned that an executive earning $50,000 a year had been padding his or her expense account by about $2,000 a year? Suppose the amount was greater or lesser: what would you do then?
>
> Is a machine shop supervisor right or wrong in discharging an older worker who drinks too much, who has become a danger to... coworkers but for whom the supervisor has no other job?

In such areas, Peterson says, there are no clearly "right" answers. "Some of us would go one way in answering them, and others would go precisely 180 degrees in the opposite direction." And both ways might be considered "moral." Is there a way beyond this impasse?

As I've already mentioned, it is not my intention to suggest that you are a Good Guy if you check Box A and a Bad Guy if you choose Box B. The challenge to today's management is not to score high in morality-testing, but to provide a context in which, even though the choices remain difficult and even though there is no clear moral distinction between them, the *process* of decision-making remains ethically well grounded because it derives from an understanding of competing claims, and the need to seek a fair balance among them.

Michael Rion, now president of Hartford Seminary, was in the 1970s director of corporate social responsibility at Cummins Engine. While there he set up a series of workshops designed to give company managers on-the-job training in ethical thinking, by asking them to question "who gets hurt and who doesn't" in cases involving such issues as hiring and firing practices, pricing mechanisms, and plant safety. The goal of the workshops, Rion told me, was not to tell people what was "right" and "wrong" in individual cases; in business, he admitted, "the answers are typically not clear-cut, because reasonable people can disagree on what is ethical and what is not." The goals, rather, were to "draw out people's concerns, to ask what fairness really means in individual cases, most of all to reinforce a framework for thinking through the issues and the questions."

In this book I hope to supply some of that same opportunity for "thinking through the issues and questions" that the experiment at Cummins Engine helped to give that company's managers, and that Cummins and many other firms are still supplying today in somewhat less formal ways. As Rion would certainly agree, it is not so much getting the right answer as it is learning to ask the right questions that creates an ethical context, in or out of the business environment.

Such a context can be nourished best, I believe, if we keep a rudimentary moral philosophy in mind. One that is both logically reliable and applicable to business is that of "checked utilitarianism"—a utilitarianism whose essential focus on the greatest good for the greatest number is continually tested, in individual cases, against the requirements of a formal moral law.

Those requirements, you will remember, are that actions be consistent, that they demonstrate respect for persons, and that they be acceptable to rational beings whether they are initiating or receiving them. Naturally, not all of these requirements can be met in every case. In some cases none of them will be met. In many cases, pressed for time and/or uncertain about the potential outcomes of a decision, a manager may find that these complicated formulas seem irrelevant.

In such cases a "short form" check might be in order. The short-form check I would suggest combines the utilitarian injunction to avoid pain with the formalist requirement that every moral action be acceptable to the receiver. Simply stated, it is that the corporate manager, in considering decisions, should check them against a bedrock injunction, the injunction to *do no harm*. That injunction is frequently attributed to Hippocrates, and thought of as an underlying principle of his famous physician's oath. Yet it is clearly no less applicable to the market than it is to the clinic or emergency room. As any health professional can tell you, "doing no harm" may well be an ill-defined and unattainable ideal. But it is still worth aiming for.

Many critics of the business community, of course, will say that this ideal is far from enough. It is not sufficient, they will claim, for a chemical company not to dump its freakish compounds into our water supply; any company with a capacity to harm in this manner obviously also has the capacity to help—and morality demands that that capacity be immediately and widely employed. The chemical company's obligations, for example, may begin with an ethical injunction against dumping; they may end only when the ecosystem of Love Canal is restored.

The question of whether or not corporations have affirmative obligations to do good as well as negative obligations not to harm extends into an organizational context some of the oldest and most personal of moral questions. Clarence Francis, former chairman of General Foods, recognized almost forty years ago that the distinction between affirmative and negative injunctions, then being discussed in business circles, really grew out of the ancient ethical transformation from the "Thou shalt not" tenor of the Old Testament to the "Love thy neighbor" approach of the New. In a remarkable expression of utilitarian faith, Francis predicted that the future of business enterprise rested with those who took the more expansive view of responsibility:

> The Decalogue, after all, did no more than impose certain necessary restrictions on human conduct. A new era began when the Sermon on the Mount opened mankind's eyes to the possibilities of affirmative good will. I am not ashamed to predict ... that the next age of business leadership will belong to those who count their success in terms of the greatest possible service to the greatest number of people.

This "service first" approach to corporate responsibility, somewhat anomalous in the 1940s, has become less so today, but of course there are still plenty of business leaders who find Francis's type of optimism misplaced. Many still feel today that, for a corporation at least, avoiding harm is quite enough, and that to expect a large business to behave like the Good Samaritan is to shackle it with unnatural intentions.

"Avoiding harm," however, is more accessible as a general principle than as a benchmark in individual cases—as the more sophisticated business analysts understand. For example, John Simon, Charles Powers, and Jon Gunnemann, authors of the excellent study of corporate responsibility *The Ethical Investor*, "affirm the prima facie obligation of all citizens, both individual and institutional, to avoid and correct self-caused social injury," yet they understand that this basic negative injunction can cloud the ethical issue in a business context, particularly when the harm generated by a managerial decision is indirect and/or unintended. Chiding those who see "ethics," social outreach, and fiscal irresponsibility as an indissoluble triad, they observe:

> Most of the debate on corporate responsibility, by rather carelessly focusing on what we have termed *affirmative duties* rather than the *negative injunctions* and by raising efficiency to the level of the highest virtue, has obscured what seems to be the fundamental point: that economic activity, like any human activity, can have unwanted and injurious side-effects, and that the correction of these indirect consequences requires self-regulation. This is the meaning for the business corporation of what we have called the 'moral minimum'—the negative injunction to avoid social injury—which cannot be set aside where there are reasonable ways to obey it.

I will not solve the issues raised by this observation here, although, as I have hinted in mentioning the Friedman thesis, they will arise in some of the later chapters. I mention negative injunctions versus affirmative duties now to prepare the reader for future complexities and to demonstrate that as a baseline for moral decision-making the Greek physician's rule of thumb—what the authors of *The Ethical Investor* call the "moral minimum"—is a relatively simple one to agree on.

At Cummins Engine it is part of the creed. Michael Rion defines a fundamental management task as the dual one of "learning how to avoid harm and respect stakeholders." Cummins CEO Henry Schacht and the company's former public policy vice-president, the same Charles Powers who coauthored *The Ethical Investor*, also refer to this rock-bottom test of ethical decisions:

> Stakeholders should have avenues of access to set forth their claims and to say that they are being hurt. In turn, the corporation has a responsibility to respond appropriately and to ensure that at the very least its activities do noo diminish the health and welfare of those it affects.

At the very least, indeed. Phrased in this manner, the Cummins philosophy is one that even the opponents of "social responsibility" should recognize as common sense. For a company that is unresponsive to someone's claim that he or she is being *hurt* is unlikely to be responsive to other claims. In an "informative economy" inhabited by increasingly sophisticated and demanding consumers, an attitude so disrespectful of basic human needs will not carry you far. Eventually the failure to observe this elementary check on behavior leads to what Schacht and Powers call "a social dynamic in which everyone loses."

Including the company that has failed. Again we see that, at least in theory, business success relies on basic ethical concerns.

Let's see now how well this theory translates into practice.

Part II

The Five Stakeholder Constituencies

4 THE INITIAL STAKEHOLDER
What Is Owed the Owner?

It is generally conceded that management is obligated to preserve and protect the interests of stockholders—to operate the company in such a way that does not waste corporate resources and thus endanger or threaten stockholder investment.
—Keith Davis and Robert Blomstrom

If there is no bottom line, then there is no opportunity to go beyond it. The creation of wealth is the foundation on which all else rests.
—Thornton Bradshaw
Chairman, RCA

In spite of the broadening of the corporate base, and in spite of the growing recognition that business has obligations to multiple constituencies, it is still generally agreed that the first duty of a company's managers is to serve as honest and efficient fiduciary agents—that is, to earn profits and dividends for shareholders. Few managers today would be so blunt as to echo former General Motors chairman Thomas Murphy, announcing that his company's purpose was to make not cars, but money. But even the most avowedly progressive executive must seek a profit, and must acknowledge that, in most boardrooms, shareholder needs often take precedence over the needs of other stakeholder groups. American business may be moving beyond the old bottom line of maximizing profit at all cost, but at this point, and for the foreseeable future, owners still come first.

There are a number of reasons why this managerial bias toward one stakeholder group is not as "unethical" or "servile" as defenders of corporate democracy might suggest.

First, there is Bradshaw's point. No matter how righteously it acts, a company that slights its owners' concern for profit will, in the long run, not be able to act at all. Bradshaw rightly implies that fulfilling even the most elementary obligations to nonowners—the provision of goods, services, and jobs—depends on serving the owners first. That is the most practical reason for letting shareholder needs take precedence.

Second, modern managers, in a way quite different from their nineteenth-century predecessors, hold positions of corporate stewardship and not just proprietary interest. Senior executives do tend to hold large blocks of stock; but in most cases those blocks are pebbles compared to what was owned by the Commodore Vanderbilts and J.P. Morgans of the past. The "robber barons" were themselves the principal owners of their firms, and if they used those firms as bulldozers against the public weal, they had recourse to the fallacious but plausible-sounding laissez-faire argument, "It's my money and I can do what I want with it." Today's managers cannot use that argument. Since their firms are publicly owned, they must answer to a plethora of individual shareholders for the way they preserve and protect their assets. That they themselves are also part owners in no way diminishes the moral demands of their stewardship.

The argument is sometimes made that, since most shareholders own very little and are uninvolved in the real functioning of corporations, they do not really have owners' rights. The comment, which has greater pragmatic than moral force, was lucidly rejected by Eells and Walton almost twenty-five years ago: "It is one thing to say that the risk-bearing stockholder has little function; it is quite another to say that he deserves little respect." The Kantian notion of respect for persons is the key. Mrs. Smith may own only one share in my corporation, but following the Categorical Imperative, I am obliged to manage her investment as soundly as if it were ten thousand shares. If the concept of private property means anything, it means that in cases of joint ownership, the dime is as sacred as the dollar.

This means that the basic obligation to stockholders suggested by the Davis/Blomstrom epigraph is not simply a practical but a moral imperative. And from it all other obligations derive. Davis and Blomstrom, for example, itemize such shareholder legal rights as the right to dividends if they are declared, the right to inspect the company books, and the right to vote on mergers. All of these rights grow out of the more fundamental right to good stewardship. A good steward "preserves and protects"; in doing so, he refrains from such clearly irresponsible practices as lying, stealing, and wasting the assets entrusted to him. In mundane terms this means that the good manager does not tell Mrs. Smith that her dime is worth twelve cents when in fact it is worth nine; does not invest it frivolously; and does not pocket it and fly to Brazil.

A third and more negative reason for managers to think of owners first is that in many cases of unethical business behavior, it is the owners who are harmed. I've suggested that the injunction "Do no harm" could serve as a check against unethical behavior. Apply this test to the most commonly cited corporate abuses—book-cooking, the abuse of the perquisite system, the padding of expense accounts—and who comes out the victim? The immediate victim is the company. Indirectly, that means shareholders.

This fact is easy to ignore, and it is ignored, all the time. Anyone who has worked in a large corporation can attest to the ubiquity of expense-account padding—and to the nonchalant attitude that usually greets its discovery. In 1976, at the height of post-Watergate soul-searching, the *Harvard Business Review* published the results of a survey on executive ethics. In one test question, readers—the majority of them middle to upper management—were asked to judge the propriety of an executive earning $30,000 a year padding his expense account by about $1,500 a year. Only 9 percent of those surveyed felt that such behavior was "unacceptable, regardless of the circumstances." Nearly 90 percent believed such fiddling to be fine "as long as the executive's superior knows about it and says nothing." Translation: It's all right to burglarize Mrs. Smith as long as your boss holds the ladder.

Many, I know, will find this analogy suspect, precisely because such offenses are so common in corporate life. Most managers would have no difficulty in condemning flagrant abuses such as falsification of stockholder reports or embezzling of company funds. The confusion arises in the gray areas between the clearly illegal and the merely "improper" practices. I want to spend most of this chapter on these problem areas, because it's there that management's obligation to "protect and preserve" owners' assets is brought into sharpest focus, and most frequently tested.

George Craig, a middle manager in ABC Industries, which did half a billion dollars in sales last year, is a decent, hardworking American with a salary in the mid-forties. He's recognized as an able manager, and his pattern of business behavior is typical of others at his level. Last Friday, for example, ABC sent him to an industry conference in Bay City. His schedule that day included the following:

- At 11 a.m., just before leaving the office to catch his flight, George used his section's copy machine for reports he would need at the conference. At the same time he copied several pages of personal material unrelated to company business.
- At noon, on his way out the door, he stopped by a supply cabinet to withdraw a pocket calculator which, he knew, would be as useful to him at home as it would be at the conference. The supply room was empty, and he signed no requisition slip.

- It was a short walk to the limousine service that made regular airport runs, so George used the service, at an out-of-pocket expense of eight dollars. In his expenses book he recorded a twenty-dollar cash outlay for a taxi.
- Arriving in Bay City, George ate dinner at The Pines, the city's most exclusive restaurant, with Preston Brock, a business associate. Sparing no expense, he and Brock put eighty dollars worth of lobster thermidor and Montrachet on the ABC credit card.
- After dinner, George returned to his hotel room, where he called a friend he had not seen in many years. The extended personal chat went on the ABC hotel bill.
- Before retiring, George turned the cable television set to the Playboy channel; the X-rated movie also went on the company bill.

Admittedly, the above schedule of account-padding is fairly heavy, but it is hardly fanciful. George's irregular billings are certainly not isolated examples, and if he seems less temperate than most conference participants, his is an excess of degree rather than kind.

What, if anything, has he done wrong? Reasonable and well-meaning people will disagree on that, as surveys indicate. The 1983 *Wall Street Journal* survey of attitudes toward business standards showed a considerable range of opinion with regard to just such cases. And it showed marked divergences between the general public's view and the executive subculture's view of such common practices as pushing the bar bill to the limit and the appropriation of office supplies. Some specifics:

- There was disagreement over photocopier use, but few condemned the practice out of hand. A typical response was "Big deal. It costs the company a penny a copy."
- Although only 40 percent of the public admitted having taken home office supplies, 74 percent of the executives did. Few of them would have been outraged at George's home use of the calculator.
- Only 15 percent of the public said they had used company phones for personal long-distance calls, as compared to 78 percent of the executives. That's four out of five top managers who wouldn't see George's chat as cheating.
- Charging an employer five dollars for a cab ride not taken struck 76 percent of the executives as wrong; only 52 percent of the general public agreed.
- Eating at the best restaurant in town on a business trip was rejected by 39 percent of the executives polled. But in an illuminating breakdown of these managers, it appeared that two-thirds of those stating ethical reservations were not permitted this perquisite themselves.

This last finding is unsettling. And it was true across the board. In every perquisite investigated except one (flying first class), there was "a clear connection between questioning a perquisite and not getting it oneself." This runs us right into the old bugbear of self-deception that, as we've seen, bothers the critics of utilitarianism. If George defends only those special benefits that he himself enjoys, we have a right to question his sincerity, not to mention his logic.

It's commonly agreed that executive perquisites constitute an acceptable and ethical system of rewarding managers for their special skills. It's also commonly recognized that the system is abused, that "perk-pushing" is often the rule rather than the exception. Those who defend this system are generally forced to defend it, warts and all—as if the occasional infraction did not invalidate the design. By examining their arguments, though, we can see that the infractions are the design—and that only by constant ethical short-reining can perk-pushing be held in check.

Let's look at the three most common arguments in defense of the perk system, to see how this is so.

"Everybody does it." It's true that "perkism" is endemic, but if generality were an argument in favor of any practice, Indians would still be immolating widows and Americans enslaving blacks. The thoughtful manager who is offered a first-class plane ticket, a blank-check expense account, or the opportunity to balance his personal finances with a company calculator cannot simply pocket the benefit out of custom. George Gallup notes that "a sizable minority of business executives have reservations about using the perquisites that companies shower upon them." I believe those reservations are well founded.

The "standard practice" defense breaks down for the simplest of reasons: It is factually false. If it were true that "everybody" had access to the perks we are talking about, the cost of business would become prohibitive. Imagine the burden on your company if tomorrow *every* middle to senior manager suddenly started charging for lobster thermidor and nonexistent cabs. The result would be an accountant's nightmare. And that's not a fraction of the chaos that would ensue if the assembly line and the secretarial pool started putting *their* lunches on the company tab.

The sticking point for the general practice argument is the Kantian test of consistency. When business people speak of perk-pushing as common practice, they mean that certain extroardinary benefits are extended to a tiny fraction of employees—middle to upper management and the sales force—as a salary-enhancement package. Within that tiny group, an even smaller number of people choose to milk the system for all it's worth. And these are the people, by and large, who justify their extravagances with the general-practice defense.

So the first difficulty with the perquisite system is more than an ethical one; it is social. Perkism reinforces and indeed exacerbates class divisions. When President Carter proposed cutting back on business expense accounts in 1978, the outcry from the executive community was deafening. The working class did not share this outrage: A Harris poll found that 72 percent of the public endorsed the end of the three-martini lunch. The reason is not hard to find: The vast majority of the public pays for its own lunches.

The acid test for the general-practice argument is to take it on its own say-so, and to ask what would be the outcome if it were consistently, universally, realized; would its proponents defend it then? Alternatively, we could ask George to be the giver, not the receiver, of the benefit. Will he agree to have his secretary put her lunch on his budget? If he says no (and he will), the "everybody" plea falls down. And we are left with the Orwellian absurdity: All pigs are created equal, but some are more equal than others.

"They'll never miss it." The idea behind this contention is that corporations are so unimaginably wealthy that no amount of padding by an individual employee can possibly make a dent in their coffers. In the words of the worker referring to the use of the copying machine: "Big deal. It costs the company a penny a copy."

This utilitarian argument relies on the conviction that the company that pays for the unauthorized copying or the thermidor dinner isn't really hurt by the deception—that the slight degree of corporate pain is outweighed by the significant degree of pleasure afforded the employee. To anyone who has worked for a large organization, this is an attractive argument; it's surely the most commonly cited reason given for overcharging one's employer, whether the overcharger is an executive stretching his lunch budget or a secretary filching pencils. It betrays two basic flaws.

First, those who believe (or want to believe) that their firms can absorb the small losses associated with overcharging ignore the obvious fact that, in the aggregate, such perk-pushing can be very serious indeed. The cumulative effect of small swipes may be a whopping cost overrun, which in the long run will hurt the overcharging employee as well as the firm.

Second, even the smallest overcharge sets up an atmosphere of allowance in which the line between offenses becomes blurred. In isolated instances it may be possible to distinguish between the legal but ethically problematic perk (private use of a company car), the slight fudge of the system (eating at the best restaurant in town), and the outright scam (the cab not taken). But to most executives, in most situations, the lines are less distinct. And to draw them at all, people often resort to a simple dollars-and-cents calculus that is even less reliable as a measure of right and wrong than Bentham's hedonistic calculus.

Look, for example, at the money that might have been involved in George's little indiscretions. His use of the copy machine cost ABC maybe a dime. The calculator might have put the company out five or ten dollars. The cab overcharge was twelve dollars. The dinner with Brock, costing eighty dollars, was perhaps forty dollars beyond what ABC would have paid in any case. The long-distance call appeared as a fifteen-dollar charge on the hotel tab, the movie as another five.

Judged purely from the point of view of affordability, George's most serious infraction was the dinner, and the least serious one the copier use. Mathematically, moreover, the dinner was about three times as "immoral" as the cab, and having ABC subsidize his late-night voyeurism was less than half as bad. Clearly there are problems with this kind of ledger morality, even though it's commonly employed as a means of separating major offenses from modest ones. Referring to covert copying, one manager admitted, "It's a small expense and it's better to provide employees this benefit than experience lost time for them to go elsewhere to make copies." A pragmatically sound but ethically vapid justification.

There are two insupportable conclusions of the "They can afford it" argument. One is that you are not really doing anything wrong if you steal from someone with more money than you, even if the person you give the proceeds to is not the beggar at the gate, but yourself. The underlying justification for this belief was stated by Proudhon a century and a half ago. "Property is theft," he claimed, thus vindicating all attempts, no matter how self-serving, to right the social balance against an owner-dominated system. This anarchist position still enjoys support among lumpen Robin Hoods and their flacks; but it is difficult to imagine any but schizophrenic corporate managers finding it intellectually congenial.

The second, more modest conclusion is that although stealing big bucks may be wrong, stealing little ones is all right—at least if you don't get caught. The problem here is that the contention cannot be made universal. Indeed, no corporate manager would want it to be. The evidence for that is the zeal with which petty thievery in the stockroom and the secretarial pool is monitored, compared to the laxness that comes into play when the suspected thief wears a blue suit. Again, the inconsistency that arises from class bias is a serious argument against allowing filching of any sort. "Businesses don't furnish offices as a supply house for thieves," snarls one executive. Fair enough—but only if George's lifting of the calculator is judged by the same harsh standard as would apply if the thief were the supply room clerk.

In actual day-to-day business practice, of course, the higher you ascend the corporate ladder, the more you can get away with in terms of acceptable theft. I do not deny that this is the way of the boardroom world. But to those who would defend this situation on ethical, not just traditional, grounds, I recommend meditation on a possibly apocryphal but still trenchant story regarding George Bernard Shaw. Shaw is said to have asked a wealthy woman whether or not she would sleep with him for a million pounds. "I suppose so," she allowed. "How about one pound?" Shaw asked. Whereupon the woman expressed outrage. "What kind of a person do you think I am?" she demanded. "Madam," the playwright responded, "we have already determined that. Now we're just haggling over price."

"I've got it coming." The same problems that bedevil defenders of the "affordability" argument arise for those who feel that, to a greater or lesser extent, their companies owe them a living. The contention that "they owe it to me" rests on a peculiarly adversarial view of the worker-company relationship, and it is not surprising that this defense is popular among blue- and pink-collar employees who feel that their basic employment conditions are unfair. As a way of repaying a company that you feel is mistreating you, pencil pocketing can provide a psychological boost even when the material gain is negligible.

But the argument is by no means confined to the laboring class. The *Wall Street Journal* study quoted two traveling executives who used this defense for ordering the most expensive item on a company-billed dinner. The first said bluntly, "They owed it to me—I was out of town for 24 hours and they inconvenienced me." The second, a 68-year-old veteran of the road, explained, "You are out doing their business, so why not?" You could just as easily ask "Why?" The hidden message of this executive's question is "My company works me too hard, and has given me this small chance to get even; naturally I'm going to take it." The entire approach, combative rather than cooperative, denies the company the same respect that the executive feels the company itself has withheld.

The more direct, and respectful, method of translating the feeling of "I've got it coming" into practice would be to approach the company straightforwardly—to lay out your grievances and negotiate for a change in working conditions, payment, or benefits that would make this back-door revenge unnecessary. That of course requires a responsive and progressive-minded firm, and it is an arguable proposition that companies who are plagued with perk-pushing suffer this indignity because they have given their employees little sense of personal investment in the firm. If you want your firm to survive, you do not relish the idea of sticking it to them for a cab. Nor do you allow yourself to believe that the stockholders should provide you extra cushions because they're better off than you are.

But there is another way of looking at perk-pushing, one that is marginally more honorable than the ones I've just described. I'm saying that George's types of overcharges are wrong principally because they cheat stockholders. But what if they don't hurt stockholders? What if the particular perk being pushed actually enhances the business advantage of the firm? This is the point the older executive was making. If you are really "doing their business," and thereby increasing their profits, then perhaps stockholders should be paying. Let's look at this argument more closely.

I am not saying that there is no difference between the various abuses of the perk system. But I believe those differences should be assessed not on the basis of dollars lost but according to a simple qualifying test: "Does my use of this perk in this situation act in the company's best interest?" Or to rephrase it in terms of what I've called the manager's fundamental responsibility to stockholders, "Does this perk, in this situation, reflect wise management of my stockholders' money?"

The perk system, like the expense account system, was established by corporations as a way of bettering their market chances. The costs of George's hotel and dinner bills are reckoned to be acceptable because, by paying them, ABC is furthering its own interests. Such enlightened self-interest is the only reason that companies are willing to meet the real or imagined needs of their agents—and that is as it should be. It makes pragmatic sense for ABC to bankroll George's Bay City visit as long as he is doing their business—and only that long. When this irreducible quid pro quo of the perk system is forgotten or fudged, one stakeholder (George) is apt to be royally served at the expense of many others.

The only way to avoid this imbalance is to have expense accounts and perks understood as reimbursement for services rendered rather than as gravy that comes with the job. Many companies now feel obliged to spell this out in black and white. J.C. Penney's business ethics booklet warns that in accepting meals, "care must be exercised to ensure that they are necessary and that their value and frequency are not excessive under all the applicable circumstances." IBM, recognizing the dangers of imprecision, puts it this way: "Employees are entitled to reimbursement for reasonable expenses only if they are actually incurred. For example, to submit an expense account for meals not eaten, miles not driven, or airline tickets not used is dishonest reporting."

Even with such common-sense guidelines, though, many areas are still interpretable. Look again at George's sextet of offenses. It seems clear enough that his use of the office copier, his appropriation of the calculator, and his billing for the nonexistent cab served no reasonable company purpose. But what about the other infractions? Assuming that Preston Brock could be valuable to ABC's business, even an eighty-dollar dinner bill might be in order. The long-distance call, too, and even the midnight movie, could be defended as psychological necessities for George, enabling him to relax and thus be better prepared for the crucial ABC business in the morning. "You're out there doing their business, so why not?"

Obviously we are moving toward the absurd here—toward the "business as usual" realm where the hiring of call girls and cocaine dealers is justified by the oldest of arguments: It increases the hiring firm's chances of making sales. Consider three related problems:

What is company business? For anybody on an expense account, and especially for executives who work eighty-hour weeks, it's difficult to distinguish between activities undertaken on behalf of the business and those undertaken for oneself. George's midnight movie is a case in point. Was it a valid business expense, incurred to put him in the right frame of mind to sell on the following day, or a personal frivolity that George charged to ABC because he knew it would not be questioned?

One way out of this dilemma might be to adopt stiffer accounting and verification procedures, coupled with a more specific set of guidelines by which employees can gauge what is acceptable and what is not. This would involve further expense, of course, and it's understandable that many companies are loath to incur it. For many, the small expense of the occasional X-rated movie is more acceptable than the expense of extra accountants and guideline writers whose Sisyphean functions would include continual reassessment of restaurant menus. As a purely practical matter, most firms would rather suffer the peccadillos of a minority than Stalinize, at great cost, their supervisory apparatus.

Another way out would be cheaper, but would require a level of personal commitment to shareholders that, in the current climate of perkism, is bound to be rare, even in model companies. It would be for each manager, faced with the option of using a company perk, to apply the Golden Rule test and ask, "Would I use this benefit if I were the person paying? Would I preserve and protect *my* assets this way?"

Whose bottom line? Michael Rion, formerly of Cummins Engine and now president of Hartford Seminary, points out that while enlightened self-interest may be a good starting mechanism for evaluating decisions, it carries the hazard of reductionism. The manager faced with a choice involving the supposed self-interest of his firm might be tempted to ask *only* "What's best for the company here?" Without an external moral standard—for example, a Kantian or utilitarian standard—this could lead him or her to take the firm's interest as absolute. "That builds in a minimalist approach to ethics," says Rion, "that can clearly cause trouble on the margins."

For example, George might be convinced that treating Preston Brock to three hours of delirium in a downtown massage parlor would be good business for ABC; many field representatives, with the full support of their superiors, have come to similar conclusions. Putting Brock's massage bill on the ABC account would then easily be justified as honoring shareholders' needs. But what if the massage parlor is staffed by teenage runaways? What if they are overworked, underpaid, and expected to prostitute themselves as a condition of their employment? Is George justified in sustaining their enslavement so that ABC can get Brock's business?

The central problem, again, is that of balancing the needs of constituencies in conflict. It may not be obvious to George that the teenage hooker is one of ABC's constituents, but unless one is willing to adopt the extremist view that a corporation has no obligation to the society in which it does business, the conclusion is not far-fetched. And whether or not ABC accepts this reasoning, is not the hooker, by virtue of her status as an individual, worthy of the same respect as George or Brock or anyone else? In short, what is the ethical tradeoff between support of prostitution and maintaining the Brock account? As Rion explains, "There are certain situations where enlightened self-interest is a stumbling block to your thinking."

Perkism is inflationary. Even if the perk system can be justified morally and practically in most cases, the system itself may still generate more social harm than good. The villain here is corporate mimicry, and its handmaiden the ratchet effect. The outcome of perkism, taking the long view, is the principal economic ill of our time: inflation.

Expand the tableau at The Pines. Let's say that George has taken Brock to that particular restaurant not simply out of personal larceny but because he knows that various industry notables will be eating there, and he wants to advertise ABC's largesse. That's a disinterested enough motivation, but it doesn't stop there. All those notables, chances are, have come to the restaurant themselves out of the same mixture of motives. Thus an entire roomful of enterprising conference participants are found entertaining clients in an overpriced restaurant, and convincing themselves that they have to do this in order to stay competitive. The outcome is that not just ABC but several other corporations receive unreasonably high dinner bills.

This kind of one-upmanship charade goes on constantly in modern business. It is only the weak sisters in a competitive environment that do not feel obliged to keep up. It is not unknown, and not outlandish, for the Georges of the corporate battleground to say to themselves (and to their accountants if they are asked), "I *had* to take him there. Anything less would have put us at a disadvantage. That wouldn't have been fair to the company."

Thus, even if individual perks can be justified as enhancements of the firm's competitive advantage, and even if the system survives the inevitable abuses of the self-absorbed, perkism itself creates a problem that eventually can harm shareholders as much as anyone else. It hikes up the cost of doing business, so that everyone pays. A recognition of this fact lay behind Carter's ill-fated tax reforms. He sought to limit allowable business expenses not out of mean-spiritedness, and certainly not out of an anti-business bias, but because he understood a fundamental economic lesson: Under demand-pull inflation, spending drives prices upward. Overspending, such as that evident in perk-pushing, does the same thing, only faster.

In these days of wide public ownership, even in firms where managers themselves are major owners, one other factor influences managers' views of their obligations to the first stakeholder group. "There is an increasing tendency for managers," say Davis and Blomstrom, "to view their responsibilities as being primarily to the firm, rather than to owners." This is the indirect result of a shift in ownership from small groups to diverse, large groups; it's easier to attend to the needs of three or four big stockholders than it is to attend to, or even identify, the needs of 30,000 Mrs. Smiths. A reasonable way out of this difficulty is to claim that Mrs. Smith's needs will be met when the company prospers (not necessarily through maximization of profits). This twists the old proposition "What is good for the owners is good for the business" into its modern stewardship version: "What is good for the business is good for the owners too."

But if it were easy to determine what is good for the business the turnover in management circles would be a fraction of what it is. As we saw in the case of George's "acceptable" perk-pushing, it's common for managers to delude not only their firms but themselves in justifying questionable behavior on the grounds that it furthers company interests. I want to close this chapter by looking briefly at three areas of possible abuse that bring this issue into focus. All of them are mentioned in a recent *New York Times* survey of "me-first" management practices. Mark Green, the former Nader raider who is now writing a book on management waste and bureaucracy, traces them to "a bottom line stressing not profits and performance but rewards for managers...a prevailing business ethic [that] seems to be what's in it for me."

Pay and bonuses. There's no question that in the mind of the general public top executive pay constitutes a national scandal. A Harris poll conducted in the summer of 1984 for *Business Week* showed that 76 percent of those polled believed that corporate leaders were overpaid; only 14 percent felt that these managerial workers were worthy of their hire.

This poll was taken only a couple of months after the members of Detroit's inner circle voted themselves record bonuses for pulling the auto industry out of the competitive cellar. This extraordinary management blunder certainly contributed to the anti-business sentiment indicated. In view of the figures involved, that sentiment was hardly misplaced. When the wife of Ford chairman Philip Caldwell was asked whether or not he deserved his $7-million bonus, she shrugged, "How can I answer that without sounding like Marie Antoinette?" Obviously, she couldn't.

But public opinion is not the last word on ethics, and in spite of what the Bible says about avarice, greed is not in itself unethical. Using a "checked utilitarian" standard, we can say that the gobbling CEO becomes unethical when, in the act of gobbling, he takes food out of somebody else's mouth. To determine the rightness or wrongness of the bonuses, we need to know who was harmed.

The usual defense of executive greed is that no one was harmed: that six-figure bonuses are apt recompense for the preservation of shareholder assets and the continued viability of the firm. In a market economy, Caldwell explained on a national press show, top managerial talent must be bargained for like everything else. Numerous automobile executives had already been stolen by the Japanese, with the offer of even bigger deals. Wasn't the wisest use of stockholders' money to up the ante and keep Detroit's finest where they were?

The American public has generally accepted this reasoning. The Harris poll I just mentioned found that in spite of their disapproval of the giant takes, 71 percent of those polled felt that using profits in this way—to "keep able people" aboard—was justified. The public has ignored some minor glitches.

One: Since in many cases of massive executive compensation the executives involved sit on the boards granting the pay increases and bonuses, there's an obvious self-interest involved that may or may not be in the shareholders' or the company's best interests. It is a rare person who, given the opportunity of raising his own pay "for services rendered," will honestly assess those services to see if the hike is justified.

Two: If the bonuses were a reward for the company managers' skill in repulsing the Japanese invasion, then shouldn't those managers have been docked during the previous decade, when Honda and Toyota and Subaru were making them look like fools? How consistent, and therefore how ethical, can it be to expect extraordinary rewards for success and ordinary rewards for failure?

Three: What about the *other* stakeholders? The unionized workers at Ford, who had made major wage concessions to keep their jobs alive, obviously felt that they had been made to pay for their managers' record rewards—in other words, that they had been harmed. While it may be logically unprovable that voting down the bonuses could have helped those workers, it is perfectly obvious that voting them in generated psychological harm. That result would have been anticipated and avoided at Hewlett-Packard, where the 1970s recession led not to labor cuts but to a company-wide policy of time reduction; it would have been dealt with similarly at IBM, where a "no layoff" policy has been in effect for forty years.

Golden parachutes. The golden parachute phenomenon—a by-product of the recent takeover surge—has drawn fire from many quarters, although very few executives are willing to scrap it altogether. According to the *New York Times*, which in this instance seems to reflect public opinion, post-takeover payments to top managers "have often been arranged in the heat of takeover battles to guarantee corporate heads who may later fall out of their jobs a soft and cushy landing. Sometimes golden parachutes appear to be rewards for failure, which is not what the capitalist system is supposed to be about."

William Norris, founder, chairman, and chief executive officer of Control Data Corporation, says this view misses the mark. The golden parachute, he told me, was invented by CDC not as a cushion for the fallen but as a defense against the crash. The original point of such executive protection clauses was to make a potential hostile buyer think twice before making his play.

Control Data makes the incentive for thinking twice—or rather the disincentive for jumping the gun—extremely strong. John Tarrant, author of *Perks and Parachutes*, an illuminating guide to executive employment contracts, reproduces the CDC contract in his book. Clause 11 covers "Business Combinations," which would "necessarily result in material alteration or diminishment of Executive's position and responsibilities." To guard against such combinations, the contract allows an executive to terminate his contract on ten days' notice after the combination, yet to continue to receive throughout the life of the contract semimonthly payments of 200 percent his base salary!

Norris and many others in his position feel that such harsh disincentives are necessary to protect the integrity of their organizations. "Raiders are poisoning our environment," he told me. "If anybody takes over this company, he's going to get it without about sixty key executives." The parachute system, therefore, is supposed to be a kind of fail-safe machine, put in place to ensure the continuity of management that cares not just about the immediate stock price but the long-term viability of the firm.

Norris admits the system has been "perverted." Golden parachute clauses may work well in a company like Control Data where management is heavily invested, both emotionally and financially, in the organization's survival. In a company where the conjunction between management aims, stockholder needs, and long-term business needs is less clear, however, the system can be an invitation to bail out. Assuming that I buy the "me-first" approach to management, what incentive do I have for serving the shareholders wisely if the alternative is a million-dollar cushion?

The irony of the golden parachute system is that it works properly only when it is not used. Only when it remains a threat to raiders does it help to fulfill management's responsibility to stockholders. As with any deterrent system, implementation vitiates its value. When that happens, it's the owners who pay.

Greenmail. The situation is slightly different in the case of "greenmail," which is a kind of hush money paid to a hostile bidder to drop the takeover process. A notorious recent example was Walt Disney Productions' successful thwarting of financier Saul Steinberg's takeover bid by paying him an unconscionable $325 million for his 11 percent share in the company. "Ordinary shareholders," the *New York Times* explained, "were not included in the deal, and within a week of the buyback their stock had declined by 21 percent, to well below what Mr. Steinberg had been paid."

There's little defense in the business community for this practice, although executives at many firms have felt obliged to resort to it as a way of maintaining control. But is the maintenance of control worth the stock weakening that can be usually the spin-off of greenmailing? Do shareholders benefit more by continuity of management than they would by the takeover itself? Could Steinberg have run Disney better? And if so, wasn't the greenmail a waste of stockholders' assets?

The assumption on the part of those who pay greenmail is that the cost to the firm is slight compared to the chaos that would ensue after a successful hostile bid. That utilitarian argument—resting on the assumption that greenmail generates more pleasure than pain—may or may not be sound. The idea that continuity of management equals excellence of management is dubious at best. A convincing argument is made for the other side by New York raider Carl Icahn.

Icahn views greenmail as unethical not because it usually dilutes stock but because it bolsters incompetent management. Citing a "pernicious type of nepotism" (he means the old school tie) as the cause of floundering management, he recalls his unsuccessful attempt to buy a block of shares in a company as evidence that in some firms executives put their own jobs ahead of their stewardship responsibilities. Claiming that in this case he only wanted to "get involved" so that the company would better utilize its assets, Icahn says that the buddy system kept him out—and that the clincher to keeping him out was the offer of a $10-million profit "to go away and never come back." "That is greenmail," he concludes. "That is what they blame guys like us for." He does not say, incidentally, whether he took the bribe.

Icahn's unpopular opinion cannot be dismissed out of hand. In assessing management's fundamental charge to manage owners' money wisely, the offering of such payments must be examined on a case-by-case basis. It's conceivable that in spite of its nasty reputation, buying off a hostile bidder might be the most moral course of action. When the barbarians are at the city gates, it's not necessarily immoral to offer them money to leave. Nor is it necessarily immoral to welcome them in. In fact, if the city government is corrupt and unresponsive to its citizens, the truly ethical course might be to give the outsider a chance to do better.

All of the above problems, of course, appear in a somewhat different light when the executive in question feels himself or herself to be not simply a hired hand but part of a "team" or "family" organization. Fiddling with expense accounts and wolfing down lobster thermidor dinners and dreaming of cushioned landings are scenarios that are built into the psychological structure of only those enterprises that discourage identification of the individual's lot with the overall success of the firm. Such practices may be less common where workers feel themselves to be participants in, not parasites on, general corporate fortunes.

Mary Anne Easley, manager of public relations services at Hewlett-Packard, confirms this view. "I've worked in several large companies," she told me. "People here have a distinctive feeling about expense accounting." The feeling at HP, she said, is that employees are all "in this together," and that fiddling on one person's part hurts not just the company at large, but all the company's employees—the fiddler included.

There's a concrete financial reason for this. HP, like many progressive companies, has an extensive and equitably distributed profit-sharing plan that gives all workers the same incentive to treat company assets fairly. "Profit-sharing here," Easley explained, "is specifically a percentage of earnings. We all know that expenses figure heavily into earnings. So if you cheat on your expense account, you're really cheating yourself."

This type of conjunction between individual and corporate interests is a hallmark of those firms that I would call "employee stakeholder" companies. As we'll see in the following chapter, what these firms get out of their progressive attitudes is far more than a marginal cost savings on lobster dinners.

5 EMPLOYEE STAKEHOLDERS Running the Company "Family"

What is the HP way? I feel that in general terms it is the policies and actions that flow from the belief that men and women want to do a good job, a creative job, and that if they are provided with the proper environment they will do so....Clearly coupled with this is the HP tradition of treating each individual with consideration and respect, and recognizing personal achievements.

—William Hewlett
Cofounder, Hewlett-Packard Company

It is probably not love that makes the world go around, but rather those mutually supportive alliances through which partners recognize their dependence on each other for the achievement of shared and private goals....Treat employees like partners, and they act like partners.

—Fred T. Allen
Chairman, Pitney Bowes

It is fashionable today for corporate managers to speak of their employees as "family," suggesting that the sense of closeness and permanence that binds true family members binds their personnel too, and that the concern they feel for their people is akin to parental affection. Managers use the metaphor as liberally as eighteenth-century philosophers used "body politic," or as gridiron bureaucrats use "team." I have heard the family image invoked in companies that employ thousands of people, and with the same conviction displayed by the hardware store owner speaking of Carruthers and Son.

But there are families and there are families. When a usage becomes as popular as "family" is today, it is inevitably pressed into service in inappropriate situations. Since no one wants to acknowledge that he views his people not as family but as cogs in a wheel, it's important to understand what *kind* of family is meant when a manager uses the term.

The oldest use of the term is also the most invidious. In traditional smokestack industries, where the relationship between management and workers has always been adversarial, the boss may appear as a despotic patriarch rather than a loving father, and the family metaphor may evoke images of internecine combat rather than harmony. Just as the traditional paternalistic family tends toward dominance of the young, so a paternalistic company can revolve around the wishes of a leadership cadre, while the expressed needs of employees are dismissed as irrelevant or immature.

The fundamental problem of the "Father knows best" model is one of instability. In a democratic society, no matter how benevolent the paternalism, the eventual outcome is revolt. You cannot ask people to behave like adults as homeowners, citizens, consumers, parents—and expect them to become docile children when they walk through a factory door. In industries that have expected that—or, even worse, that have expected their people to behave like *rebellious* children, and treated them accordingly—the resulting resentment has caused low productivity, quality-control disasters, and a general bitterness toward Big Daddy (aka Big Brother) that threatens the entire economic system.

General Motors employee Martin Douglas, laid off in 1982 after eighteen years of service, acknowledges this bitterness:

> The apparent lack of understanding between labor and management stems from management's total failure to see its hourly workers as anything more than another labor-producing machine....The assembly line worker is the lowest man in the company hierarchy and seems to be only tolerated as a necessary evil. The contract between labor and management more closely resembles an armistice than a treaty for mutual benefit.

As Detroit's recent history indicates, such comments cannot be dismissed as the grumblings of one "bad kid." They articulate a basic ethical complaint, stemming from the perception that, as Kant would put it, people are being treated not as ends but as means.

A less traditional "family" structure is in evidence in those businesses that are owned and operated by workers themselves. In the dark 1970s, several failing businesses (the most famous was Weirton Steel in West Virginia) were bought out by employees who thought they could do a better job than Daddy. In most instances, employee involvement in the running of these reborn families is limited to stock ownership, with actual management being handled by a trust. In some firms, though, the employees' voices are being heard more directly; in over 200 workers' cooperatives around the country, ownership and day-to-day control are in the hands of the former "kids."

It's still too early to tell whether such efforts herald a wider collectivization of American business, or whether the new EO&O firms will follow their nineteenth-century predecessors into oblivion. It is clear, however, that when workers take over the store, a "family" structure evolves that is more pluralistic and more congenial to many workers than the old paternalistic model. A bookkeeper at a former A&P that was recently converted into an owner coop put the case with blunt cogency. "It's *my* store. We all feel that way about it. Owning the company gives us more incentive to make it a success."

Ownership as a work incentive. It seems an obvious point, but it's one that is frequently forgotten. The companies I'm surveying in this book don't forget it, and what I want to show in this chapter is how they give their people a sense of common ownership without becoming structurally as radical as the coops.

These firms use the family metaphor in a richer way than the way it is used at either the old-line paternalistic concerns or the new-fangled, "no head of the table" ones. In many of these companies, the line between "parent" and "child" tends to break down: The *functions* that line workers and managers perform may still differ sharply, but the *respect* afforded each individual family member is the same. Jobs may be variously performed and variously compensated in strict money terms, but everybody gets the same basic allowance for personal initiative and responsibility.

Nothing could be further, for example, from the old paternalistic style of management than the much-discussed "HP Way," the informal "family" philosophy that has put Hewlett-Packard onto so many lists of "best managed companies." HP president John Young explained to me, "The HP Way really begins with a belief in people. We offer opportunities for meaningful participation in a team effort, but only to people who can take responsibility for themselves. We aim for a naturally self-motivating environment, and we depend on people to do their jobs right." A dependence, it is very clear, that makes sense only in a community of adults. Instead of "Children should be seen but not heard," the operating principle at companies like Hewlett-Packard becomes "Everybody speaks, everybody listens—and everybody pulls his weight."

The link here to ethics should be clear. Kant's Categorical Imperative says that moral actions are universalizable, that they rest on respect for individuals, and that they are acceptable to those who receive them as well as those who do them. The grounding of the system is mutual respect. For that reason, the paternalistic family—in which parents "deserve" more respect than children because they are older and wiser—has significant limitations as a metaphor for progressive companies. The beginning of any moral treatment of employee stakeholders is the recognition that they are not children but responsible adults. Any obligations that a company may owe them derive ultimately from that recognition.

What are those obligations? Most people in business would agree that the fundamental obligation of an employer to its people is to pay them a fair living wage or salary for the services they perform. A corollary to this observation would be that it is unethical to underpay your workers—to give them starvation wages simply because it is possible to do so. There are problems, of course, in determining what is "fair" remuneration, but those problems do not undercut the principle: The first way an employer shows respect to his people is to pay them enough to live on.

It is also widely agreed that ensuring health and safety in the work place constitutes another obligation. Even if you pay your people far above the going rate, you cannct claim to be treating them ethically if you subject them to the constant threat of bodily harm as a condition of their employment. There are exceptions to this general principle—for example, the cases of high-steel workers or underwater welders—but they do not vitiate the rule, since such high-risk occupations are the domain of highly skilled volunteers who understand the risks involved, and who are paid especially well to take them. Today it is generally recognized that, for most employees, companies must provide places to work that will at least "do no harm." The judgments against chemical companies in recent years—most notably, Johns-Manville—grew out of a public perception that they had violated that ethical principle.

For the companies I am looking at in this book, the provision of adequate pay and a decent environment in which to earn it constitute only the first step in corporate obligations to employee stakeholders. These companies consider it ethically and practically essential to go beyond these basics, and to provide their people certain "extras" that will instill the ownership incentive the A&P worker mentioned above, and thus cement the stakeholder bond. To understand these extras, we need to backtrack briefly, to the early days of this century.

One linchpin of the Marxist argument against capitalism is that it inevitably immiserates workers. Marx believed that in their zeal for profit, owners would pay workers as little as possible and that they would get away with it because, in competition for a limited number of jobs, workers would bid each other down into starvation. In the absence of moral restraints (of which the bosses had none), a kind of auction-in-reverse among laborers would depress wages to an ultimately intolerable level. In Marx's scheme, this total impoverishment was one prerequisite for revolution.

The prerequisite didn't develop, for various reasons. First, the trade union movement in Europe and North America deflected workers' interests away from structural change of the system and toward an enhancement of possibilities within it. Early Marxists hated unions with good reason: They understood that, because of Samuel Gompers and his crowd, "wage slavery" was beginning to look attractive.

Second, reformist governments, fueled by public outrage at the excesses of Gilded Age capitalism, modified the laissez-faire system. The Supreme Court's decision in the notorious Lochner case (1905) enshrined the employer's right to do pretty much anything he wanted to workers—including paying them coolie wages and firing them at will—but throughout the next thirty years progressive legislation on minimum wages, child labor, and employee compensation gradually broke Lochner down.

Third, the capitalist system proved far more expansive, both structurally and geographically, than Marx had imagined it could be. In an imperialist, technologically sophisticated, and frequently war-driven economy, so many new employment opportunities were created that workers were afforded bigger and bigger slices of what seemed to be an infinitely expanding pie.

All of these reasons for the failure of Marx's prediction have been frequently observed. The final reason has not. That reason was the recognition by certain innovative business leaders that in the long-term interests of their firms, it was advisable to enhance rather than suppress worker satisfaction. In certain progressive companies at the turn of the century, management was working even harder than the unions to make people *like* their jobs.

Ida M. Tarbell is remembered chiefly for her influential muckraking history of the Standard Oil Company, which led in the years after its 1904 publication to federal action against the trust. In her *New Ideals in Business*, written ten years later, Tarbell took the other side, documenting how some business leaders were running their plants on what can only be described as a germinal "stakeholder" model. Speaking of a "silent revolution" in management, she described prodigious efforts throughout the country to transform American factories into models of safety, security, and worker satisfaction. New homes for workers, company gardens and clean lunchrooms, higher rates of pay, shortened workweeks, company-sponsored physical examinations—these were some of the developments that we take for granted today as part of a "fair pay" package, but that Tarbell saw as revolutionary in 1914.

Among the most revolutionary (and most successful) of the new "experiments in justice" that Tarbell described was the institution of profit-sharing and stock-purchase plans. The firms she profiled understood early on that if you wanted your employees to recognize their stake in the survival of your firm, you should give them ownership incentive.

Foremost in this regard was the Cincinnati company Procter & Gamble, whose stock-purchase plan had gone into effect in 1903. Tarbell devotes twelve pages to a description of this plan, and to a documentation of its enthusiastic reception among P&G's employees. "The chief problem of big business today," said then company president Cooper Procter, "is to shape its policies so that each worker, whether in office or factory, will feel he is a vital part of his company with a personal responsibility for its success and a chance to share in that success." As Tarbell's book recognized, one very effective way to meet this challenge was to give workers a financial stake in the business.

But Procter & Gamble was not alone. Consider these other examples of gaslight-era generosity:

- In 1909 the Armstrong Company, then just forty-nine years old, became the first company in the United States to offer free dental care for its employees. Four years later it instituted a pay differential for overtime, and in 1924 it established paid vacations.
- George Eastman, who ran Eastman Kodak until his death in 1932, was firmly committed to the stakeholder concept. A wage dividend program that he set up as a personal disbursement in 1898 became an official company policy in 1912. Seven years later Eastman parcelled out to his "family" one-third of his own stock holdings.
- The importance of profit-sharing has been institutionalized at Johnson Wax for three generations. In place since 1917, the twice-yearly payment scheme can boost a typical factory employee's earnings by 14 percent or more. CEO Samuel Johnson calls profit-sharing "part of the glue that holds our organization together."

This last comment is instructive. It suggests, quite appropriately, that the motivation behind all this involvement of the employee in the organization was not simple generosity but enlightened self-interest. Profit-sharing is put into place at Johnson Wax and Procter & Gamble because it enhances organizational stability. Armstrong treats its people well because it expects a long-term commitment, and is willing to drill a few teeth to get it. Johnson Wax's chairman, justly proud of the "family business" feeling that has long imbued his company, told me frankly, "We cultivate the family atmosphere because we feel that's the best way to gain the loyalty, motivation, and support of our people. It's a very practical approach."

Nowhere is this commitment to employee satisfaction as a way of ensuring stability better demonstrated than in those firms where job security is a principal focus of managerial attention. Dental plans and paid vacations are of only provisional value if at the first sign of economic trouble they go out the window with the workers. Many employee-stakeholder companies, recognizing this as a potential problem, make personal job security, as an element of organizational stability, part of the corporate design. They consider it a corporate moral obligation to keep their people on the payroll through troubled times, or at the very least to buffer the shock of necessary cutbacks by a variety of assistance plans.

One of the most surprising discoveries that American managers made about Japanese businesses in the 1970s was that they guarantee their people lifetime employment. Many Americans found it astonishing that a major industrial apparatus could afford to maintain a full employment policy in the face of free-market uncertainties. The Japanese, said the cynics, could make good on that promise only because they were crypto-socialist. All firms were under the hand not of Adam Smith, but of "Japan, Inc." It couldn't happen here—not in our decentralized, unplanned economy.

But those who linked Japanese lifetime tenure to central control ignored two basic facts. First was Japan, Inc.'s own internal buffers. In Japanese businesses, workers are expected to retire at the age of fifty-five, and women workers, officially considered temporaries, can be laid off at any time. Discounting the age and sex discriminations, the Japanese promise of lifetime work seems a little less astonishing.

Second, it not only could happen here; it does. And it's been happening for quite some time. In employee-stakeholder companies, lifetime tenure has long been considered the ideal. A few examples:

- *Hewlett-Packard.* At a 1975 management meeting, HP executives devised a list of concepts they felt illustrated the company's commitment to the individual. Among them was the importance of "security, permanence, development of people." This has never been an idle boast at HP. People who accept positions there know that, barring gross incompetency or larceny, they will never be asked to leave. The company has refused lucrative contracts that would require taking on additional personnel because they knew that once the contracts were delivered, they would have to release those people.
- *Delta Airlines.* The contentedness of Delta people is legendary, and in spite of the fact that some of it derives from the company's liberal benefits and perks (including free air travel for all employees), job security is also a major factor. In 1982, when the airline industry experienced one of the most disappointing years in its history, Delta kept all its people on, and raised their pay in the bargain.

- *Johnson Wax*. Chairman Samuel Johnson, like his father and grandfather before him, is proud of this decidedly family company's "culture of security." He sees the firm's longstanding no-layoff policy as only one element in a culture that is reluctant to let people go for *any* reason. "Employees are seldom fired," he says. "If somebody has to be fired, I consider it our mistake. Either we have put the person in the wrong job, we have promoted him to his level of incompetency, or we hired the wrong person in the beginning."
- *Procter & Gamble*. P&G vice-president Robert Goldstein, in a 1981 speech, cited the conviction of founders William Procter and James Gamble that it be "the policy of the Company to recognize that its interests and those of its employees are inseparable." To support this conviction, they instituted the profit-sharing plan that so impressed Ida Tarbell. And in 1923 the company set up a policy of guaranteeing its people regular employment for no less than forty-eight weeks a year.
- *IBM*. IBM's no-layoff policy is a direct outgrowth of Thomas Watson's belief in respect for the individual as the cornerstone of sound business behavior. Writing about his father, Thomas Jr. said, "He had known hard times, hard work, and unemployment himself, and he always had understanding for the problems of the working man. Moreover, he recognized that the greatest of these problems was job security." To alleviate that problem, IBM promised in 1914 never to lay anyone off for purely economic reasons. It has kept that promise for seventy years.

It hasn't always been easy. In late 1984 I asked Richard T. Liebhaber, then IBM's director for business practices and development, how the company managed to maintain its continuity of employment through hard times. "We work very hard at it," he said. "And we begin with an unusual premise—the idea that the individual comes first. A lot of companies begin somewhere else—with profit or productivity or growth—and try to work the individual in. We start with respect for the person and hang everything else on that concept. When you come at the business from that direction, decisions take on a very different tone, because the personal dimension is already built into your options."

He cited two examples. The first was the company's decision at the depth of the Depression to maintain its full payroll even though there was a severely diminished market for its machines. In a calculated risk that grew directly out of Watson's commitment to his people, employees were kept busy stockpiling parts, and in 1935 that difficult moral choice proved to be good business as well. When the Social Security Act was passed, IBM suddenly found itself with an enormous government contract—and plenty of inventory to supply it.

The second example was more current. When Liebhaber and I spoke, IBM was in the process of phasing out the last punchcard factory in the country, a small concern in Washington, D.C. that employed about 200 people. "We had known that plant had to go for years," he explained. "We also knew that you don't sell IBM people, so the people would have to stay. So the phasing-out process included plans for their retraining and relocation. Every one of those workers knows that when the plant closes down in the spring, he or she will already have a job waiting in one of our other facilities."

In today's uncertain environment, such contingency planning may be essential to the maintenance of an ethical system. Employee stakeholder companies don't just "let people go." They consider internal relocation, job-sharing, on-the-job retraining, and workweek reductions as ways of buffering the inevitable. With such flexible responses in place as part of the planning mix, employees understand that their needs are not irrelevant. And they are much more willing to sacrifice for the good of the firm.

A celebrated example of such flexibility occurred at Hewlett-Packard during the early 1970s recession. Orders had fallen off so badly that management was considering a 10 percent cut in the work force. Since laying off people was anathema, HP went a different route. It set up a working schedule of nine days out of ten for *everybody* in the company, from the CEO on down. The job-saving device stayed in place for six months, when orders picked up and the full ten-day schedule returned. William Hewlett explained how everybody profited from the experiment. "The net result of this program was that effectively all shared the burden of the recession, good people were not turned out on a very tough job market, and, I might observe, the company benefited by having in place a highly qualified work force when business improved."

Delta took a slightly different approach during a 1973 downturn, opting for job-juggling rather than time reduction. Instead of letting people go, the airline reassigned hundreds of people to other positions within the company. Their new jobs, Delta president David Garrett admitted to *Business Week*, were not as well paid, but at least reassignment sustained job security. "They still got paychecks," he said, "and they kept their seniority and all their medical benefits."

It's not only companies with an explicitly stated no-layoff policy that appreciate the value of shepherding their people through hard times, or of providing for their security as business changes. Control Data in Minneapolis has no such policy, yet with a massive in-house educational apparatus, an advanced health-care benefit structure, and a 24-hour employee counseling hotline, CDC obviously qualifies as a corporation that takes its commitment to "people needs" seriously. When that commitment was tested in a 1981 business crunch, the company set out a "rings of defense" strategy, including reassignments, a call for volunteers to take time off, and the assumption by CDC employees of jobs normally contracted out. Layoffs were kept down to 1.5 percent of the payroll.

The Aetna Life and Casualty Company is another firm where, although "no layoffs" is not a stated policy, job security is a major priority. Recently, a combination of automation and fierce competition has been pressuring the company to trim its payroll. So far, senior communications specialist Geraldine Morrissey told me, the company has been able to avoid that by focusing on in-house retraining and by maintaining a traditional commitment to providing "Aetna jobs for Aetna people." "We're undergoing a huge conversion process," she explained. "One charge of the newly created Office Automation staff is a humanistic one—it's to improve the job lot of our people by seeing that they get the training they need to take over the high-tech jobs when they're in place."

Beginning in 1984, that training was going on at the Aetna Institute for Corporate Education, housed in a sleekly attractive new complex across the street from Aetna's Hartford headquarters. When I spoke to John Filer, chairman of Aetna from 1972 to 1984, a few months before he retired, he referred with obvious pride to the structure; it represented to him that stability and continuity on which the insurance company's managers have long prided themselves. "I worry a bit," he admitted, "about our mid-level managers in their thirties. Unless they get themselves computer-literate very quickly, those people coming in the front door with their master's degrees and PCs are going to run right over them. That's why the number-one priority of the Institute is to improve the effectiveness of the education and training of our people."

The fact that Filer said this on the eve of his own retirement is, I think, illustrative. Top managers in employee-stakeholder companies are in the business not for what they alone can get out of it but for the long-term mutual benefit of employees, management, and the firm. Samuel Johnson said it well in a 1983 interview. "We don't manage our business for the next quarter or for the next year. We manage our business for the next generation of employees, the next generation of people in our community, and the next generation of consumers." That is security through space—and time.

A commitment to job security must underlie a company's attention to its people or there will be no people to attend to. It seems reasonable, therefore, for companies that identify their employees as stakeholders to cement the ongoing relationship with higher-than-normal pay scales, good benefit packages, in-house training, flexible cutback policies, and profit-sharing. All of these things make it easier for the workers affected to see that they really do have a stake in the firm.

But there are less tangible advantages in certain firms that are just as important to the people involved. Beyond the stability that is so desired, most of the companies I've looked at share one characteristic that relates just as directly to respect for the individual. This characteristic is more difficult to define than security, but it has to do with such "high-touch" concepts as networking, accessibility, openness, and the breaking down of hierarchy. All of these concepts are important to the Theory Z style of management that has received such attention in recent years, and all are implicit in the "productivity through people" approach touted by Peters and Waterman. The unifying concept here is one of *egalitarian discourse*. In companies that are truly committed to their employees as stakeholders, communication occurs among equals. To pick up the family metaphor, they are companies in which the dinner table is approximately circular. There's no real "head" of the table, because everybody is treated as an adult.

In many of the companies profiled here, the old distinction between blue- and white-collar work holds relatively little weight. Hewlett-Packard managers are known for their loose, peripatetic manner of "supervision," and for their use of first-name address with everyone from the rookie to the CEO. The same is true of Armstrong and Johnson Wax, where the familiarity is abetted by a smalltown atmosphere and where everybody eats in the same cafeteria. Aetna's Morrissey underscores the invidious "status basis" of the blue-collar/white-collar distinctions of smokestack America, and sees the lack of those distinctions as one of her company's strongest suits.

At some companies the vocabulary itself reflects egalitarianism. People Express, whose founder Donald Burr has been called "the boss who hates bosses," identifies all its employees as "managers." At J.C. Penney, since the days of James Cash Penney himself, workers have been known as "Associates." And at Pitney Bowes the conventional term "employee" shares time with the less conventional "jobholder," a term which parallels "stockholder" and which, as PB president Fred Allen explains, was chosen to stress "the similarity between the person who invests money in the business and the one who, as an employee, invests time and talent. Both are entitled to an accounting of the way their investments are used."

The commitment goes beyond vocabulary. In employee-stakeholder firms, it's embedded in the organizational structure. This ideal is manifested at the more progressive companies in a variety of ways.

First, many companies foster open communication through informal but regular exchanges between management and other employees. At Hewlett-Packard, which has made Management by Walking Around a catchphrase of business literature, the twice-a-day coffee break is viewed not as a respite from drudgery but as an opportunity to "encourage the exchange of useful ideas among various groups and operating levels." At John Deere, where line workers take an almost obsessive pride in their labor, quality control is a topic of regular discussion not just among QC supervisors, but among teams of management, foremen, and their crews. At both Delta and Johnson Wax, brainstorming sessions between blue-collar workers and senior management are scheduled every eighteen months. Pitney Bowes has developed two "devices through which management can talk effectively with employees on a two-way basis"—a monthly "council of personnel relations" and an annual "jobholders meeting" in which all members of the circular table come together for a "face-to-face review of the state of the business."

Second, employee-stockholder companies have carefully structured and widely advertised grievance procedures. Control Data uses a system called Peer Review, in which an unhappy employee's complaint is reviewed by a committee composed of a company counselor, two fellow workers, and one executive, all but the counselor chosen at random. Johnson Wax uses a hotline called "Just Ask," through which employees can address questions to management by means of a third party. The same concern for confidentiality, and the same checks against possible reprisal, are evident at IBM and Xerox. Both these firms use a combination of a no-holds-barred complaint system (at IBM it's called "Speak Up," at Xerox "Comment") and a formal Open Door policy under which an employee dissatisfied with the disposition of his grievance can ask for further managerial response, all the way to the top.

The IBM Open Door policy was set up by the elder Watson, who personally handled hundreds of complaints in his New York office. It is still a crucial part of IBM's employee-relations approach. As director Liebhaber explained, "Our business depends on creativity and initiative. We don't think our folks will continue to provide that unless we treat them fairly. So Open Door is serious business, and our managers know it. They know that if they don't take their people's problems seriously, they'll be taken higher up. And an accounting will be made."

Six pages of the Xerox personnel manual are devoted to employee communications. The manual specifies that "Comment" forms are to be posted on bulletin boards "readily available for use." And it emphasizes the immunity of an Open Door complainant: "Should an employee decide to seek resolution of a problem directly from a higher level of management, he or she may do so without fear of reprisal."

A third way in which progressive firms institutionalize open communication is through suggestion plans that offer the enthusiastic employee the same opportunity to reach management that the Open

Door policies offer the temporarily disenchanted. IBM is a leader here too. The company recognizes that the thousands of suggestions it receives from employees each year contribute substantially to profitability, and to acknowledge the contributions it gives not just recognition but cash awards. In 1983, the company estimates, employee suggestions saved it about $65 million; approximately $14 million of that amount was given back to the people who came up with the suggestions. Six employees received awards of $100,000 each.

The earliest, and still among the most generous, of employee suggestion plans is that of Eastman Kodak. Established in 1898, it now provides awards based on a percentage of cost savings achieved by each suggestion or, in cases where the idea leads to a new product, on a percentage of sales revenues. Kodak's average annual payback through this scheme is $1.65 million.

Probably the most generous, and certainly one of the most successful, of suggestion plans is that of Pitney Bowes. The Stamford, Connecticut company pays suggesters 50 percent of the money saved by a suggestion—more than double the average for U.S. industry. Since the company increased its internal promotion of the system in 1983—and upped the maximum award allowed to $50,000—the plan has taken off. Over $200,000 was saved in the first half of 1984 alone—quite an impressive figure for a company with only 6,000 employees.

Those who see corporations as mere expropriators of their people's talents tend to see such plans as disguises for managerial theft. Of course Kodak should pay its people for their cost-saving ideas, they say; so should every other company. The shame of working for corporate America is that when you perform your work badly you get summarily fired, and when you perform it exceptionally well, you get a pat on the head and a gold watch (or a piddling percentage of the sales take).

The argument is not dismissible, but I think it is misplaced when applied to companies like Kodak, that are far ahead on this issue, and that in any event are doing something they are not required to do. Under current patent law, those who work for major corporations have no legal claim whatsoever to the money their ideas make. If you design a widget that saves XYZ Industries 40 million dollars, XYZ owes you nothing. The law (and many corporate cultures) holds that what you do on XYZ time with XYZ resources is XYZ property.

Recently, for example, a large midwestern railroad was sued by one of its foremen on the grounds that it had, in effect, cheated him out of "royalties." The foreman, partly on company time and partly on his own time, had invented a car-coupling device that, it was duly determined, could eventually save the company many millions of dollars. The railroad's management gladly accepted the innovation, but declined to pay the foreman—and the state court ruled in their favor.

It is in this context, I think, that we have to evaluate such employee "royalty" plans as those in place at Kodak, Pitney Bowes, and IBM. The principle of a company "owning" the fruits of its workers' labor remains entrenched in law. It's because they see the moral limitations of the law that a few progressive firms go beyond it. Critics of the capitalist system may denounce the size of cash awards; but as long as such awards are voluntary (not to mention rare), it is hard to fault the companies involved for bad faith.

Minnesota Mining and Manufacturing, which is perhaps more famous than any other American company for fostering new ideas, takes a compromise approach to the subject. At 3M, ideas are considered joint property, rather than the property of either the company alone or of the individual who, under company auspices, comes up with them. The basic reasoning grows out of an environment filled with engineers, chemists, and other researchers. No idea springs full-blown from any individual's head; all are the products of team effort, and should be rewarded accordingly. Thus Art Fry, developer of 3M's "Post-It" note pads, receives no special royalty for his work—but his department is rewarded when bonus time comes around, and Fry himself gets a bonus as direct appreciation. In addition, 3M employees who suggest particularly successful ideas are eligible for the company's prestigious Carlton Award, winners of which are listed prominently in the St. Paul headquarters lobby.

The interesting thing is that in the companies we're talking about, such recognition seems to be enough. You do not get workers at employee-stakeholder firms buttonholing Mike Wallace to complain that they've been cheated. Apparently if you treat people with dignity and respect, if you give them bonuses in terms of recognition, accessibility, and formal thanks, financial rewards become relatively less important.

Does this progressive attitude toward employees work? What are the actual effects, long term, of treating the people who work for you not as means but as ends, not as children playing at being grown-up, but as actual adults, with responsibilities and needs and human value?

The effects are almost universally acknowledged to be excellent. In general, what happens at employee-stakeholder companies is that people come to understand and appreciate their stake, and work all the harder and more efficiently to secure it. Tarbell recognized this seventy years ago, when she quoted a granite-cutters association president reacting to the newly instituted eight-hour day: "They are working steadier, and Blue Monday is now unknown in our trade. They are more attentive, more in earnest."

That observation still holds true today. Specifically, firms that recognize employees as a prominent stakeholder group typically gain the following:

- Strong *continuity* and a very *low turnover* rate. At most of these companies, the managerial expectation that good treatment will lead to long tenure is consistently justified by the figures. Armstrong sells its new people on the "careers, not just jobs" concept, and the people stay. The same is true at Delta, J.C. Penney, Procter & Gamble, Hewlett-Packard, and John Deere. A team of Deere researchers recently found that most senior officers there had come to the company in their mid-twenties and stayed an average of 22 years. HP president John Young admits, "There's a little extra work that goes into providing our type of flexibility. But the cost is more than offset by the kind of people we're able to attract—and retain."
- *Few labor problems.* Of the twenty or so companies I'm looking at in this book only about a quarter are fully unionized. That's not necessarily because of union-busting. Progressive firms may be unfertile ground for unionization because when you can talk to your boss face to face, there's no advantage in hiring an outsider to do it for you. Since unions arose from the need for working people to protect themselves from abusive management, they are inevitably going to be less important to workers in firms that promote community, not conflict.

  Johnson Wax chairman Samuel Johnson recalled a conversation he had in the mid-1960s with a Wisconsin labor leader. "We don't have anything to offer your company," the unionist told him, "as long as you do two things: pay your people fairly, and listen to them. Once you stop doing either of those two things, we'll get you." Twenty years later Johnson Wax has still not been "gotten," and to its chairman the reason is obvious. "Companies need unions," he told me, "when the management is inadequate in communicating with employees. If you've opened up your communication and you have good first-line supervision by managers who listen to their people, there's no need for a union to provide the communication bridge."

- High degrees of *cooperativeness* and *flexibility*, even in times of economic distress. Witness the willingness of Hewlett-Packard employees to take a 10 percent time and pay cut for the overall good of the firm. Or the Delta people who, after the company had retained them even through the 1982 recession, bought the company a $30-million airplane—nicknamed the "Spirit of Delta"—as a gesture of appreciation. In an employee-stakeholder company, as Pitney Bowes's president Fred Allen explains, "An occasional reduction in force can be accepted because employees understand why it must be done. The reason: advance two-way communication, backed up by fair dealing." The lesson is clear. Cooperation and trust are reciprocal.

- Better *productivity* and *quality control*. People with a strong ownership incentive are less likely to lay down on the job than those who feel they are exploited. Furthermore, they are more likely to recapture that American phantom, pride in their work. Pride like that of the John Deere workers who, having inadvertently left a screwdriver inside an engine, apologized in writing to the buyer, explaining, "We do not want to make junk."

HP founder William Hewlett called attention to this final benefit (which may well be the most significant one of all) a few years ago, when he urged a business audience to look for "better solutions to the adversary relationships that have so long dominated the American labor scene." Linking quality, productivity, and employee satisfaction, he observed, "The United States is rapidly discovering that it must be competitive in world markets, and that both cost and quality are factors. Productivity is the name of the game, and gains in productivity will come only when better understanding and better relationships exist between management and the work force."

There is some evidence that Hewlett's warning is now being taken to heart, and that the face-to-face "circular table" approach employed by progressive management teams is gaining ground even in the old "Keep 'em in their place" industries. In the winter of 1983 *Business Week* documented the growth since 1980 of labor-management participation teams (LMPTs) in, of all places, the heavily unionized steel industry. Noting that "the old 'Do what I say, don't talk back' style of management had a lot to do with steel's decline," the magazine observed that the LMPTs, which give workers a voice in shop-floor operations, have already led to "better labor relations, improved quality and efficiency, and reduced absenteeism and grievance loads." A Cleveland shop foreman involved in one of the teams described their effect in terms that could easily have been lifted from a John Deere or HP memo: "When you give the hourly worker an input, his attitude changes and productivity goes up."

More recently, General Motors chairman Roger Smith, in an appearance on the Donahue show, applauded worker (even union worker) involvement in the development and manufacture of GM's new Saturn line. Speaking of "a whole new relationship with the worker," Smith acknowledged Detroit's reliance on its traditionally underrated family members ("We need them," he said frankly), and promised that future company decisions would consider the long-term interests of all concerned.

Of course there are some managers who, out of tradition, suspicion, or just plain pigheadedness, would prefer attitudes not to change. It is still too early to tell how widely and how quickly the "respect for people" model will be adopted in traditional industries. But one thing does seem fairly certain. If the progressive companies I'm profiling do *not* become the pattern for the future, that future is likely to be bleak. I don't mean just morally bleak. A John Deere company bulletin on "Basic Business Principles" clarifies why the old adversarial approach to the employee is economic as well as ethical suicide. The bulletin identifies *mutual advantage*—just what GM worker Douglas saw as missing—as the soundest basis for any business relationship.

> Any relationship—whether with an employee, dealer, supplier, stockholder, retail customer, or the general public—is a two-way affair. It requires understanding at both ends and appraisal of every question from the other's point of view. To be long-standing and valuable it must be beneficial to both parties.

You'll notice that this bulletin implicitly recognizes the multiple constituency model that I have borrowed from Cummins Engine, and that it echoes Fred Allen's focus on "mutually supportive alliances" as the key to reaching goals. Mutual advantage means not just looking at things from the other person's point of view (the Golden Rule principle), but also developing consistently profitable relationships. Again we see the conjunction of a business's ultimate self-interest with the interest of its constituencies, and again we are reminded that the Golden Rule works not in spite of but because of selfishness.

Mutual advantage and self-interest are particularly critical concepts at Miller Heiman, Inc., a California sales education firm whose partners, Robert Miller and Stephen Heiman, speak of mutual satisfaction as "the foundation of long-term success" in selling, and in any other aspect of business. The secret to maintaining healthy business relationships over time, they say, is in establishing "Win-Win" scenarios—scenarios in which all parties to a transaction feel that their self-interest has been served, and that they have therefore "Won."

Miller and Heiman are quick to denounce the adversarial "Do other men, for they would do you" approach to business as both ethically and practically unsound. They see Detroit's one-upmanship game with its unions, for example, as "a classic Lose-Lose scenario." I asked Bob Miller in August of 1984 what he thought of the notorious managerial bonuses; he echoed the Detroit columnist who called GM's 1982 accord with the UAW the "dumbest move of the year." "It's incredible," he said. "I can't believe the mind set there. It's like they were pathologically and categorically taking advantage of the situation, playing 'I Win-You Lose' with the unions. They'll get killed when contract renewal comes around, and that's just what they have coming. They're going to reap exactly what they've sowed."

When the UAW contract ran out at the end of 1984, of course Miller's prediction came true. The ensuing strike, which lasted almost two months, was only the latest in a series of labor-management debacles that prove one simple point: You cannot treat people disrespectfully and expect to get away with it forever.

However, this observation is not restricted solely to a company's treatment of employees. It applies to its treatment of all stakeholder groups. And as Miller and Heiman consistently point out in their sales training programs, it applies with special force to the relationship between a company with a product to sell and the people to whom that product is directed. The third stakeholder group, customers, provide the most telling test cases against which to measure the efficacy of the Win-Win, or mutual advantage, model. We turn to this third group now.

6 CUSTOMER STAKEHOLDERS Deconstructing "Caveat Emptor"

Win-Win salesmen and saleswomen don't overstock their customers. They don't pressure, threaten, or cajole. They don't ask for or offer mere "favors." They don't overpromise and underfulfill. They don't misrepresent the match between product and customer need. Instead, they work with their customers to provide satisfaction for everyone concerned....Far from behaving like their customers' sworn enemies, they act like partners instead.

—Robert Miller and Stephen Heiman
Coprincipals, Miller Heiman Inc.

Business never was and never will be anything more or less than people serving other people....From the beginning we have visualized customers as our neighbors, whom it is our neighborly privilege to assist toward buying what they need and want at the lowest fair prices....In other words, we interpret the golden rule as the mandate of service.

—James Cash Penney
Founder, J.C. Penney Company

The ethical baseline being used in this book is the Hippocratic injunction "Do no harm." That injunction, long recognized in our society as a common-sense rule of conduct, is being applied more and more in business, especially in cases where the potential harm is grievous and palpable, as for example in situations where life and limb are threatened. The current brouhaha over employer liability for faulty products and for hazardous workplace conditions (and the resulting massive judgments against such firms as A. H. Robins and Johns-Manville) highlight the public consensus that it is part of a corporation's basic duty to guarantee the safety both of those who make its products and of those who buy them.

Corporate attitudes on this issue are not uniform. Although most business leaders have foresworn "Caveat emptor," there is still considerable disagreement on pragmatic as well as philosophical grounds about the extent of a business's obligation to consumer safety. The harshest debate centers on employer liability for products that harm, or are thought to have harmed, many consumers. Perhaps the most notorious example is that of Robins's Dalkon Shield. The company is pleading a "multiple jeopardy" defense, saying it should not have to settle all the thousands of suits involved individually; yet the suits go on. *Business Week* writes that Robins and Manville "have come to represent the specter of mass suits that can threaten businesses in unprecedented proportions," and there is obviously wide sympathy for the manufacturers here. Wisconsin Senator Bob Kasten has even introduced a bill in Congress aimed at reducing the inefficiencies of a product liability system that he sees as so irrational that it is actually "starting to build disincentives for the manufacture of safe products."

An underlying theme of the current reaction against "pro-consumer" liability judgments is that a manufacturer should only be held liable for a defective or unsafe product if it "knew, or should have known, about its dangers." The tricky phrase is "should have," for even with prodigious quality control and testing procedures, mistakes do get through most corporate manufacturing lines. How much of the stockholders' investment is a manufacturer required to spend to ensure that he knows everything a court will later say he "should have" known? How does he know when he has spent enough? If negligence is seen as the result of potential rather than actual knowledge about your product, then are you not ethically required to bankrupt your company with testing rather than distribute a product you feel to be only 99 percent safe?

To avoid this absurd conclusion, businesses who care about their consumers aim for a prudent, middle-way approach: considering the 99-percent safety factor to be an acceptable risk, they take out hefty insurance policies and hope for the best. In a world in which "safe" automobiles and legal intoxicants kill far more people than defective merchandise, such modified caution is not morally inappropriate.

But all of this is preparatory. What happens when a product currently being marketed is discovered to be hazardous? What ethical obligation does a corporation owe its customers when it identifies a clear and present danger?

While most ethicists would find this a simple question to answer, this has not always been the case among business people. The notorious historical examples of corporate unwillingness to apply the Hippocratic injunction here include the various abuses of the robber-baron era—stock-watering, land-grabbing by railroads, sweatshops, vermin-infested food products—that were summed up in William Vanderbilt's anti-consumerist maxim "The public be damned." The most famous recent example is probably the Ford Motor Company's decision to continue distributing Pintos with reason to suspect that they were, in the chilling phrase of *Mother Jones's* Mark Dowie, "two million firetraps on wheels."

According to Dowie, Ford justified its inaction with a debased form of utilitarian reasoning that measured the costs of correcting the gas-tank defect against the benefits of people-not-burned-to-death. In an article in *Business and Society Review*, Dowie cites a leaked Ford internal memo indicating that, at $11 per car, the safety improvement would have cost the company $137 million; the estimated 180 burn injuries, calculated at $67,000 each, and the estimated 180 burn deaths, calculated at $200,000 each (these are National Highway Traffic Safety Administration figures, presumably related to expected insurance settlements) would cost only about $49 million. The arithmetic made the decision clear: Don't recall the Pintos.

This profit-line decision-making, aside from its ethical limitations, often backfires even in pragmatic terms. Although negligence was not proved in the Pinto case, the adverse press reaction alone must have made Ford think twice about the value of such cost-and-benefit judgments. In a separate case, the company decided not to recall for retooling models that were suspected of slipping out of "park" into "reverse," and running over their own drivers. Ford pled "driver error" in this instance—but the resulting liability judgments have already cost it an estimated $500 million.

It would be wrong, however, to take these examples as typical. Many companies are quick to respond to perceived or suspected hazards. Some examples:

The burning radios. In the early 1960s, the J.C. Penney Company received a small number of insurance claims on radios sold in its stores that had caught fire in customers' homes. Once its in-house testing revealed a potentially defective resistor, Penney's response was uncompromising. Although fewer than 1 percent of the tested units were defective, the company withdrew the entire line, informed the manufacturer, and placed national ads informing the public of the danger and offering immediate refunds. "This was before the Consumer Product Safety Commission even existed," Penney vice-chairman Robert Gill recollected. "I guess some people might have thought we were crazy, and said that liability insurance was specifically designed to take care of such problems. But we felt we just could not sell that kind of a product."

Penney, it should be noted, has been a standard bearer in this area for years. They were one of very few companies that, far from resisting the Product Safety Commission, actually helped to write its legislation. And recently they were cited by the business monitor Council on Economic Priorities as the retailing industry's leader in demonstrating a concern for customer welfare.

Johnson Wax and fluorocarbons. In the summer of 1975, the environmentalist cause celebre was depletion of the earth's ozone layer. After university scientists had suggested that this thin and fragile stratum of the upper atmosphere was being eroded by fluorocarbons released from aerosol cans, earth-watchers and the FDA alike mounted a media blitz to pressure manufacturers to withdraw the products containing fluorocarbons before the protective shell was gone and planetary life succumbed to universal skin cancer, or worse. Virtually every manufacturer of aerosol cans denounced the scientific findings as chimerical, and stood fast by their products. The exception was Johnson Wax.

"The science was difficult to prove," company chairman Samuel Johnson told me, "and in fact the fluorocarbon question is still technically unresolved. But the unfavorable publicity convinced us that summer that there was widespread genuine concern among our consumers about harm to the ozone layer. We made our decision based on that fact, and withdrew all our fluorocarbon products worldwide. This was years before the FDA ban. We picked up a lot of flak from other manufacturers, and we lost business in some areas, but I don't have any question we were right. When our customers are concerned, we're concerned. Our belief is that as long as you can make do without a potentially hazardous material, why not do without it?"

The Tylenol crisis. The classic, and classiest, example of a corporation putting its customers' safety before the bottom line was the Johnson & Johnson Tylenol recall decision of 1982. In October of that year, at a cost of approximately $100 million, J&J executives in New Brunswick, New Jersey decided to pull the most successful over-the-counter painkiller in history off the market because seven people in Chicago had died from ingesting cyanide-laced Tylenol capsules.

The aftermath of that decision is well known. In the months following the tragedy, the company mounted a massive media campaign to alleviate consumer fear and (not incidentally) to save its lucrative analgesic market. The campaign included the establishment of a consumer hotline at McNeil Consumer Products Company (the J&J subsidiary that makes Tylenol), extensive cooperation with the media, a widely advertised refund offer for capsules that frightened consumers had thrown away, an appearance on the Donahue show of J&J chairman James E. Burke, and the introduction of triple-sealed packaging that soon became a model for the drug industry.

What is less well known is the reasoning that lay behind the recall decision. Johnson & Johnson, a consumer-stakeholder company par excellence, issues every incoming employee a copy of the corporate "Credo" drafted by Robert Wood Johnson in the 1940s and reformulated slightly in the 1970s. The first line of the Credo reads: "We believe our first responsibility is to the doctors, nurses and patients, to mothers and all others who use our products and services." In thus putting the consumer stakeholder first, Johnson & Johnson had established the ground rules for decisions in the Tylenol crisis even before the crisis broke. "In that crisis," J&J corporate vice-president Lawrence G. Foster told me, "we reached for what we believed in, and that was the Credo philosophy. That philosophy said that protecting the consumer was a fundamental principle; given that principle, the recall decision was inevitable."

There was a practical aspect to this, too, which indicated the importance to J&J (as well as every other customer-stakeholder company) of maintaining credibility, not only with the consumer but with its own employees. Foster explains: "We had been telling our people for forty years that they were expected to live by the Credo. We were on trial more with them than with the nation. If we had compromised our principles during the Tylenol episode, the Credo would have looked like a sham. We really had no choice."

J&J chairman James Burke agrees. In the 1970s he instituted throughout the company a series of "Credo challenge meetings" to test the principles of the document among top managers. "It was hanging on the wall all over," he told me, "and we needed to see if it was a living document or just so many words. So we brought together managers from around the world and threw it open to them: Should we get rid of it, or rewrite it, or commit to it as it stood?"

The outcome of the meetings (which continue on a regular basis today) was that the Credo, with very slight revisions, was endorsed and thus reinstitutionalized throughout the business. Once that happened, the guidelines in the Tylenol case were clear. Burke explains: "We had spent a lot of time committing this corporation to a set of principles that clearly said the public comes first. If we had decided to violate that, every single employee in the world would have known what we were doing. So not only did we box ourselves in to a set of firm beliefs, but we were given in this horrible situation an opportunity to institutionalize them for a long time to come."

Only months after the Tylenol crisis, the Credo was tested again, when reports came in to New Brunswick that another J&J product, the prescription analgesic Zomax, seemed to be causing severe allergic reactions in some users. The number of cases was extremely small—so small that the FDA, to whom the company reported them, initially saw no need for a recall. A large number of doctors who were prescribing the drug agreed. But even though there was considerable support in the company for continuing to market Zomax, Burke and J&J president David R. Clare disagreed. Burke called Washington personally on the extraordinary mission of convincing the regulatory agency that the drug should be temporarily withdrawn—pending labelling changes.

The labelling changes were necessary, J&J top managers felt, because Zomax was being used "frivolously" by many patients. "It was so effective," Burke explained, "that people were taking it for backache, joint pains—many things for which it wasn't designed. So we had to contend with the wide misuse of a product that was already in about one and a half million medicine chests. If we had found a sensible, reasonable way to contact all those people and tell them the minimal but real hazards, we wouldn't have pulled the drug."

The Zomax case illustrates something more than J&J's zeal to protect the consumer from potential harm, even at great cost (the Zomax recall cost about $20 million). In both the Tylenol and Zomax cases, the company demonstrated a commitment to openness—with the press, with government, with the public. "After the withdrawal decision," says Lawrence Foster, "the most important decision in the Tylenol case was to give people all the information we had, to cooperate fully. Obviously that attitude operated in the Zomax case too, and in fact it operates throughout our culture. We don't say that we'll always tell you everything you want to know about our business, but we do follow one unequivocal rule: We've never yet told the press a lie."

This commitment to truthfulness, if not full disclosure, is a logical outgrowth of the fundamental commitment "not to harm." For there are many ways to harm a customer: Selling faulty or hazardous products is only the most extreme. Let's look now at some of the less extreme ones—specifically, at cases where a seller with a perfectly safe product "overpromises and underfulfills."

We've seen that corporate obligations to individuals or groups of individuals rest on the premise that each person is worthy of equal respect and deserves to be treated as an end rather than a means. In many business relationships, this could be stated in a more conventional manner: People have a right to be treated *fairly*. When the relationship is one between a company and its customers, fairness means not only not harming those who purchase products or services but ensuring that they have sufficient information about the purchase so that they do not make it under false premises. Without this information, a potential buyer is apt to be cheated or deceived. By selling someone something without telling that person exactly what he or she can expect from it, you are at the very least creating financial harm.

But specifically what information is necessary? Since the line between truth and falsehood is notoriously indistinct, it's important to have a realistic definition of "lying," and specific guidelines for determining when a company's promotion of its wares—whether in advertising or labelling—oversteps the indistinct line.

Two thousand years ago, Cicero posed a moral dilemma that speaks directly to this issue. In his essay "On Duties" he asked whether a grain merchant traveling to a famine-stricken town is obliged to inform the inhabitants that other grain merchants are behind him; and thus imperil the price he might get for his goods. Cicero claimed that he must, and in theory at least the Better Business Bureau agrees. Addressing "the ancient problem of truth" in one of its publications, it approvingly quotes the Roman sage: "All things should be laid bare so that the buyer may not in any way be ignorant of anything the seller knows."

This severe, "tell all" position has not been universally accepted. Thomas Aquinas disagreed with it, and so do many modern business people. I have mentioned Lawrence Foster's observation that, as zealous as J&J is in protecting the customer and maintaining good outside communication, the company has neither the intention nor the obligation to tell everything to anybody who asks. And this seems a reasonable approach. Suppose I own a small sporting goods store where I sell sweat socks for $2.59 a pair. Am I really ethically obliged to tell my potential customers that the K-Mart around the block sells the same socks for two dollars?

Perhaps a better way of getting at the question of truth and falsehood in customer relations is to ask not what should be said but to identify what must not be. Since the bulk of moral issues in the realm of advertising concern false or misleading claims, this makes logistical sense. If we know what types of claims a manufacturer or distributor is morally wrong in making, we should have a fair picture, in "negative" form, of the information a buyer ought to have to make an informed purchasing decision.

It is not necessary to say very much about blatantly false claims—those that are, in the simplest sense, lying. According to ethicist Richard De George, "Lying consists in making a statement which one believes is false to another person whom one has reason to think will believe the statement to be true." When an advertisement fulfills the two conditions implied here—that is, when an advertiser *intends* to deceive and expects to be *believed*—we're dealing with lying, pure and simple. Since the exaggerated or blatantly false claim is the oldest huckster's trick in the world, it's not surprising that the FTC, when it started reviewing advertising practices in the 1970s, began its regulation here. In a landmark 1978 Supreme Court judgment against Warner-Lambert, which supported an FTC ruling, the Court required the company to publish "corrective advertisements" to counter the long-standing allegation that its product Listerine "kills the germs" that lead to sore throats and colds. The tag line that set the record straight was a model of straightforward truth-telling: "Listerine will not help prevent colds or sore throats or lessen their severity." It remains to be seen whether other manufacturers will take the Warner-Lambert case as proof that honesty is the best course.

The issues are stickier when the claims made for a product are not patently false, or when one or both of De George's two conditions are not met. Here are four problem areas:

The selective ad. Since every product has an infinite number of characteristics, a company has great latitude in choosing which one to highlight. And since no one is obliged to tell everything, judicious companies focus on those characteristics that customers will find most appealing, and downplay any drawbacks. That's common sense. Toyota is expected to say, "You'll get 40 miles per gallon," not "The ride's not as smooth as a Buick." Buick is expected to highlight its luxury and prestige factors, not the mileage limitations of larger cars.

Selectivity only becomes a problem when, in focusing on the attractive aspects of his product, a manufacturer obscures information that is needed for the buyer to make a wise, and safe, purchase decision. Zomax is a case in point. J&J pulled that drug because it felt people were not being well enough informed to use it without endangering themselves. The same concern for public health and safety ought to be an operating principle in every company that manufactures food or beverages. The government recognizes this. That is why foods with high salt content must carry labels that warn away people with high blood pressure or heart problems.

The preemptive ad. The implication of a preemptive ad is that the claim being made for the advertised product is true of that product and no other. Suppose I am a textile maker, and I advertise a newly developed material as being "the revolutionary shrink-free fabric." If the fabric really is shrink-free, I am not strictly lying; but since numerous products already on the market are also shrink-free, I am distorting reality by suggesting that mine is the only product with this distinction. By failing to give the extra information that everybody else's fabric is also "revolutionary," I am creating the false impression of exclusivity.

Since consumers today are becoming increasingly sophisticated, advertisers who use preemptive ads often resort to the tactic of invoking secret ingredients or magic formulas to disguise their product's lack of exclusivity. So we hear about "MF 14" in a toothpaste or "Supersheen formula" floor wax—and are invited to believe (although we are not actually told so) that these ingredients make the product more effective.

The most famous example of this usage is probably the television commercial that claims that a certain analgesic contains "more of the pain reliever that doctors recommend most." That statement is strictly true, but the impression of exclusivity is misleading because the mystery ingredient is aspirin.

The statistical proof ad. The vague and unattributed use of statistics is another technique employed by advertisers to suggest what cannot be proved—or disproved. Whenever a customer hears that a given analgesic acts "3.9 times faster" than its competitor, he should ask for the test results, to see how this exotic figure was arrived at. The same goes for such unverifiable claims as the "13 percent more whitener" in various detergents, or the "eight ways" in which Wonder Bread is supposed to build strong bodies. Which eight ways? Why 13 and not 14 percent? To anyone with an elementary background in statistics, such claims are always suspect. But few customers have this background.

The suggestive ad. The statistical proof ad is really a special case of a much broader ad technique, designed to give customers the impression that the product being advertised is a passport not just to consumer satisfaction but to various extraneous benefits as well. Since suggestivity is at the heart of modern advertising, we need to go into this example in a little more detail.

It is a commonplace among advertising people, as well as among their critics, that sex sells more soap than soap does. "My men wear English Leather, or they wear nothing at all."Take it off, take it all off." "I'm Diana, fly me." Tag lines like these, used to hawk products as diverse as cologne, depilatory cream, and air travel, work only by linking suggestiveness and suggestibility.

That this sex-appeal appeal is effective is beyond doubt. One major corporation, Consolidated Foods, specializes in the prurient pitch: Its commercials for Hanes stockings, L'Eggs pantyhose, and Underalls body wear share a view of the American woman as an object designed for ogling. And Consolidated ranks No. 84 in the Forbes 500 listing.

But when I speak of the suggestive ad, I am speaking about a range of ads of which the sex-appeal variety is only the cutting edge. Focusing on the sexism of American commercials focuses the lens too sharply. The real suggestion of these ads, and of many ads that do not employ cheesecake as a marketing tool, is that if you buy the product you will fulfill hopes and avoid fears.

"In the factory," Revlon's Charles Revson once said, "we make cosmetics; in the store we sell hope." The flip side of that astute observation was described to me several years ago by the president of a West Coast electronics firm. "The foundation of most selling," he said, "is fear. If I can offer you something that will make you feel less stupid, less undesirable, less like a schmuck, I'm two steps out of three to the sale."

The truth of the dual proposition that hope and fear move products is evident on commercial television every day. Automobiles are sold on the hope premise: the suggestion that if you buy the newest dandymobile you will instantly become a composite of Indy 500 finalist, executive on the rise, and man about town. Household product ads rely principally on fear—specifically, the fear that something (floor wax build-up, sticky rice, ring around the collar) will intrude to shatter the Happy Home. Personal hygiene products are pushed with a combination of the two: the promise of Ultrabrite toothpaste, for example, is that you will get the job or the man (hope) by avoiding a fate worse than death, yellow teeth (fear).

But is there anything unethical about using hope and fear to push a product? What's wrong with a little exaggeration? Aren't consumers savvy enough to distinguish between fact and fantasy—and can't they make their buying decisions on the understanding that the promise of True Love is merely a device to catch their attention?

The answers to these questions depend on how smart you take the audience to be. The general approach to this issue, and the one that the FTC still uses, is that of the "reasonable man" test. If the "majority of reasonable people" would not be misled by a given ad (into believing, for example, that white teeth ensure wedded bliss), then it is not unethical. If, on the other hand, most reasonable people would take at face value a claim that is either false or misleading, then that ad is improper.

The problem with this approach, clearly, is that "reasonability" is difficult to measure, so that relying on it as a standard might allow advertisers to claim as ethical certain concepts that are misleading, or even patently false. The old Listerine ad, for example, was seen as factually true by millions of "reasonable" people, and yet it remained on the air for years.

Even greater difficulties arise when the target audience for an ad is too young to be considered "reasonable." Much of the turmoil over advertising today centers around ads pitched to children, an area of ethical muddiness precisely because the "reasonable man" principle falls down here. If you believe in Santa Claus and the tooth fairy, can you be expected to make a rational purchasing decision—or rather, to push your parents into making that decision—regarding the latest sugared cereal, action toy, or dress-up doll? The answer is obviously not, and some observers make a strong case for banning all television ads aimed at a preschool audience. De George makes the Kantian point well: "Such ads take advantage of children, and those who advertise in this way are morally culpable of manipulation and of treating children only as a means to their ends." Practically speaking, of course, pulling the ads would wreak havoc in the breakfast food industry and among its millions of employees—so that "kidvid" advertising may remain an ethical gray area that we all have to put up with.

Twenty years ago the social critic Jules Henry described advertising as a "philosophical system" designed to give credence to an unwarranted but revolutionary "pecuniary truth" that he felt was supplanting the "more traditional truth-logic" as an operating principle in commercial affairs. Convinced that advertising merely greased the gears of an implacable and insidious selling engine, he concluded that buying anything but absolute essentials was a proof of this system's irrationality. "If we were all logicians the economy could not survive, and herein lies a terrifying paradox, for in order to exist economically as we are we must try by might and main to remain stupid."

As extreme as this statement is, it does provide a rule of thumb by which observers of advertising might measure the ethical soundness of individual ads. Henry's ire against those who pander to the gullible is relevant only to situations in which guile, intentional deception, or reliance on hope and fear are the *principal* techniques for selling. Henry was loath to acknowledge something that will be obvious to anyone in business: that the majority of products are hawked not by simple recourse to these techniques but by an appeal to perceived customers' needs. And when you are selling to need, you don't need tricks to make your case.

This seems to be pretty generally the case in the companies that are profiled in this book. It stands to reason that a firm that takes customers as a stakeholder group will be slower to resort to the above practices than one that sees customers as marks, or merely as potential money in the bank. Procter & Gamble, the doyen of "close to the customer" companies, began market and consumer research back in the 1920s to determine what people wanted and needed; it is certainly no accident that its company history speaks of "P&G's partner, the consumer." With that enlightened attitude, you don't need sex to push your soap.

Steve Heiman has an interesting theory to explain why certain companies seem to favor underhanded tactics in the market, and specifically lying to the buyer. "When you're in a highly competitive market and you don't have a clearly differentiated product or service, backstabbing and lying may seem attractive. When you've got a solid, differentiated product line that meets actual customer needs, why lie? Even if you charge a lot more than the competition, you don't need to tell your customers anything but the truth. If you're that good, they'll know the premium price is worth it, because they're getting a value-added product."

That's a practical explanation of an observed ethical difference between those who will use any selling tactic that the FTC lets them get away with and those who have a vested interest in the truth. And it points to a further distinction between those who are out simply to sell and those who want Win-Win outcomes.

Many professional business people tend to think of supply and demand as the principal factor in pricing. Supply expands to meet a perceived increase in demand. When supply cannot keep up with demand, merchants have the opportunity to charge more for the items they do have to sell, knowing the market will absorb the price increment. That's Economics 101.

But there are obvious moral limitations to seeing perceived need as a chance to make bigger profits. Even when the need is not grievous—even when a customer will not be physically harmed by the lack of the desired product—to increase the cost of that product simply because a hungry market will absorb it is to treat the customer as a means, not an end. We have already seen why treating anyone in this manner can be considered unethical.

The problem is posed most sharply in cases like the one described by Cicero. The grain merchant facing a starving population that believes he is the sole supplier may or may not be obliged to point out his competitors' (possibly lower) price to them. But if he sells them the grain at an inflated price simply because he can get away with it, he is guilty in effect of cheating them; whether the situation is assessed in utilitarian or Kantian terms, he is taking unfair advantage of their distress.

Because the supply-and-demand seesaw can so easily be tilted against the consumer, medieval churchmen formulated the notion of the "just price," stipulating that profit to sellers and interest to lenders be kept within reason. Many observers of commercial activity have supported that notion, believing that taking "what the market will bear" is always, ethically speaking, a dangerous approach to pricing. Many attacks against capitalism at the turn of the century, for example, derived from this recognition. The utopian society proposed by Edward Bellamy in *Looking Backward*, a book that galvanized American social thought for two decades, eliminated the free market altogether, because Bellamy so detested the world of want into which "market forces" had driven the contemporary poor. Later, the reform movement under Presidents Roosevelt and Wilson singled out abuse of the pricing mechanism as one of the modern corporation's greatest sins. Behind the scrim of "pure competition," critics pointed out, the trusts continually conspired to keep prices artifically high—with the consumer as victim. The Justice Department's antitrust division today is dedicated to restoring competitive purity. However intrusively and fuzzily that division may do its job, it cannot be denied that its fundamental purpose is a noble one: to approximate that delicate balance between sellers' and buyers' right that a truly "free" market enjoys.

None of which is to say that under a just free market prices would always be low—only that they would be fairer, since they would be adjusted not only by supply and demand but by utilitarian considerations (potential pleasure vs. potential pain) as well. Unless some ethical framework is brought in as a corrective, the consumer is always in danger. It is not unethical to charge someone $14.95 for a bowl of soup unless (a) you have misinformed the buyer about the contents of the soup—saying, for example, that it contains a smidgen of ginseng root that will make him live to 120, and/or (b) you are the only soup kitchen in town. In the one case you would be lying. In the other, you would be taking advantage of short supply to profit unduly at the buyer's expense.

Obviously there's judgment involved here, which involves both practical and ethical intelligence. Ideally, the ethical business person judges each of his or her customers on a case-by-case basis. If the person wanting to buy your soup is dressed in top hat and tails, you may be justified in taking his $14.95 even if the kitchen around the block can give him an equivalent bowl of soup for twelve dollars. If he is obviously down and out, the supply-and-demand principles remain the same, but the ethical ones do not. From either a Kantian or a utilitarian viewpoint, it is clearly wrong to take anybody's last dime for a meal that he needs to survive—even if you are the only kitchen in town.

Miller and Heiman point out that to many companies the old adage "Any sale is a good sale" is still an operating principle. Companies that believe that are spared the trouble of investigating the effects of individual transactions, and frequently find themselves ethically foundering because they have overpromised or underfulfilled, or in some other way failed to satisfy the customer.

Customer satisfaction is a direct result of seeking to show the respect that, Kant says, all rational beings deserve. There's a pragmatic component here as well as a "philosophical" one. To a firm that is serious about meeting customer need, misrepresentation and overpricing are bad business. Bob Miller explains why. "If your philosophy is to sell anything to anybody anytime, you're inevitably going to end up selling customers who don't have a clearly defined need for your product. When that happens you Win but they Lose. You can get away with this once in a while, but eventually a customer that you trick into buying is going to find out. When he does, you can forget about repeat business, referrals, new leads—in other words, you can forget about everything that's keeping you in business."

The connection between meeting real needs and long-term business is especially obvious in today's high-tech markets, where products have become so sophisticated and so consumer-specific that "value added" marketing is the rule rather than the exception. Companies increasingly market their products and services to customers who are willing to pay a price differential for the assurance of knowing that they are getting top quality, reliable service, and custom-made design. That higher price is not ethically inappropriate; the added value correctly demands it.

The value-added approach to pricing is frequently linked to what Peters and Waterman call "quality obsession." It's as true of the companies I'm calling customer-stakeholder firms as it is of excellent companies in general that they dedicate themselves passionately to maintaining product integrity—and that they interpret that integrity to imply more than simple reliability. Consider, for example, the nation's chief farm equipment manufacturer, John Deere. A company story indicates that Deere quality obsession originated with the founder himself, and that it grew out of a practical as well as ethical consciousness. In 1850, according to the story, John Deere and his partner, Robert Tate, disagreed over improvements that Deere wanted to make in a plow that was already selling almost faster than orders could be filled.

> Mr. Tate felt that any plow selling in such numbers was quite good enough and that quantity production was now the main objective. He countered with some heat John Deere's suggestion of changing this or that in the design in order to achieve a slight improvement.
>
> "Damn the odds," Tate is reported to have burst out on one occasion. "They have got to take what we make!" "Oh, no," Mr. Deere replied quietly, "they haven't got to take what we make, and if someone else improves on our plow, we shall lose our trade."

Again, treating the customer decently—giving him what he really needs, with the highest quality possible and at a fair price—is seen as sound business *and* sound ethics.

The J.C. Penney Company also links value, fairness, and customer satisfaction. The first three items in its corporate testament, "The Penney Idea," pledge the business "to serve the public as nearly as we can to its complete satisfaction," "to expect for the service we render a fair remuneration, and not all the profit the traffic will bear," and "to do all in our power to pack the customer's dollar full of value, quality, and satisfaction." Penney vice-chairman Robert Gill wryly links the pragmatic and philosophical aspects of this pledge. "We must never lose sight of the fact," he told me, "that we are here to serve the customer. If we don't serve the customer well, another retailer will."

Or consider the story that Johnson Wax chairman Samuel Johnson tells on himself about an encounter with his father when the latter was company president and the former its first new-products manager. The initial new product to come out of the younger Sam's research was an insecticide that had the bad taste to contain no wax whatsoever. As Johnson tells the story:

> "Don't you realize," my father asked me, "that everything we make has wax in it?"
>
> I told him I supposed we could put some wax in it, but I doubted it would improve the product.
>
> "What's really better about this product?" he asked me. "How is it different from what's already out there?"
>
> I submitted that our insecticide was an easy-to-use aerosol, and that it had an attractive label, but had to agree with him pretty quickly that lots of other products had these features too. His final comment ended the discussion and sent me back to the research labs.
>
> "When you come up with something that's really better," he said, "then we can talk about getting out of the wax business and into insecticides."

This proved to be sound advice, for subsequent research developed an insecticide that *was* different: a water-based, pleasant-smelling product called Raid, which quickly captured the lion's share of the home insecticide market, and has kept it ever since.

In all these cases we see respect for the customer stakeholder being demonstrated by a commitment to sell not necessarily the least expensive product but the one that is best for the money. The same dedication to customer satisfaction applies in these companies when, in spite of the commitment to quality, something goes wrong with the product. In discussing his company's willingness to communicate during the horrors of the Tylenol episode, J&J's chairman James Burke said that the most successful consumer-product companies "have a long-standing love affair with their consumers. That's certainly one reason that Procter & Gamble is so successful. It's part of our success too." And part of that love affair means being able to talk when things are going badly.

To companies without this commitment to "talking it through," customer complaints can be seen as necessary evils—interruptions of "real" business. Quite the opposite attitude prevails at customer-stakeholder companies. "Adjustments" that need to be made after a sale is completed are viewed not as extraneous but as part of the long-term selling process. Selling, as Robert Miller and Stephen Heiman define it, is "a professional exercise in showing all the people to whom you sell that your product or service serves their individual self-interests." Since no one who is left sitting with a product he does not fully want, need, or understand will see his self-interest being served, this means following up on customer dissatisfaction is just as important a sales factor as selling the product in the first place. In the words of an IBM manager, "Getting the order is the *easiest* step; after-sales service is what counts."

We saw in the last chapter that at companies like Xerox and IBM, openness of communication was considered an essential aspect of employee relations, an essential element in an employee-stakeholder philosophy. Translated into the relationship between a company and its customers, this openness becomes a commitment to responsiveness and service. It is certainly no accident that IBM, widely admired as an "open door" firm for its own people, is also generally recognized as one of the premiere service companies of the world. Thomas Watson's second "basic belief," in fact, was the commitment to providing "the best customer service of any company in the world."

The same commitment to responsiveness is evident at Procter & Gamble, which set up the first 800 hot line in the nation in 1979 and fielded over 200,000 customer inquiries, (including both suggestions and complaints) in its first year of operation. It is evident at Caterpillar, whose promise to its customers that it will provide 48-hour guaranteed parts delivery anywhere in the world looks like "a mild form of lunacy ... until you look at Caterpillar's financial results." It is so important to the firms profiled in the Peters and Waterman study, in fact, that they identify *service* itself as the principal ingredient in customer relations: "One of our most significant conclusions about the excellent companies is that, whether their basic business is metal bending, high technology, or hamburgers, they have all defined themselves as service businesses."

Quoting ex-IBM executive Archie McGill (now at AT&T), Peters and Waterman hint strongly at the ethical basis of this definition. McGill endorses what he calls "customer focus" rather than a sharply delineated set of service standards because, he says, "overmeasurement of service (e.g., scores of variables) may actually detract from" true service. By focusing on figures rather than people, "one loses sight of the individual customer." Losing sight of the individual often means losing respect, and losing respect, as we've seen, is the first step toward ethical muddiness. The customer-stakeholder companies understand that service is built on respect; that is why they are perceived as good places to work—and to buy from.

A John Deere company letter, in itemizing the rights of customer stakeholders, summarizes many of the points made in this chapter. Former Deere chairman William A. Hewitt, now retired, wrote:

> Our customers are entitled to expect our products to be of high quality, to be reliable, to be safe if operated in a responsible manner, and to function in accordance with the claims we make for the product. Customers also have the right to expect us to pledge our full good faith in warranty of our products. They also are entitled to expect us to have repair parts readily available and to assure the

availability of competent service when repairs must be made.

The salient features of this statement are promises of quality, reliability, safety, proper representation, and service. All of them have in common a commitment to serving the customers' best interest as well as that of the firm.

The pragmatic benefits of such a commitment are just as obvious as the ethical ones. The negative lesson was suggested by John Deere's fear that if he compromised on quality he would "lose his trade." The positive lesson is evident in Thomas Watson's comment about his father's obsession with "respect" as an ingredient in long-term success: "He saw at once the value of the Golden Rule in business, for many people would buy his goods on the basis of what satisfied customers had to say about his products." An Eastman Kodak brochure makes the point even more concisely. Over a discussion of Kodak's obsessive product inspection procedures stands the maxim "Quality Means Repeat Customers."

But it is not quite so easy to satisfy customers today as it was in the original Deere's and Watson's and Eastman's day, and this fact points to an ironic and perhaps unexpected development in modern business. One might have assumed that increased competition would make business more cutthroat, less meticulous in terms of quality and service, but the opposite may actually be the case. In order to secure long-term market advantages, companies today more than ever are trying not just for dollars but for goodwill. Somtimes that means they are outbidding each other to be good. The companies I am calling customer-stakeholder companies may thus be the cutting edge of a trend.

In his stimulating assessment of the "next economy," Paul Hawken discusses that trend. As our economy shifts from a mass-intensive to an information-intensive one, Hawken says, companies that do well in the market will share a peculiarly "unmercenary" corporate culture. Whether these successful firms make data bases or machinery or fast food, their managers will operate on three basic assumptions:

- First, they will assume that people are "intelligent and are becoming more so. Companies that try to fool their customers or manipulate their employees will find themselves, sooner or later, competitively threatened by a company that does no such thing."
- Second, those who prosper "will treat their customers and clients as they would themselves." Hawken is speaking here of the importance of service and of enhancing "human contact and social conviviality." But his statement could hardly be a more clear-cut evocation of the Golden Rule.

- Finally, the successful firms in the informative economy "will no longer make a distinction between how they act in the world and how they want to see the world act." Again the Golden Rule, and again the implication that receiving a "high component of informativeness" —service, quality, responsiveness—is a direct result of giving it.

If Hawken is right, and the economy is undergoing a fundamental transformation from a mass base to an information base, then the importance that customer stakeholder companies have traditionally placed on meeting the real needs of their buyers is likely in the not too distant future to become an essential characteristic of all companies. Leaving your customers "surly but not rebellious" may have been a viable operating strategy in the days of caveat emptor, when consumers were more likely to shrug their shoulders in resignation if a company overpromised or underfulfilled. The combination of a tightening economy and a decade of consumer activism, however, have made those who buy products and services far smarter than they used to be. They know now when they are being taken advantage of—and they have options to correct it.

One social consequence of the information explosion, then, has been to alter the ground rules under which goods are distributed and consumed. The ethical implications, at least for businesses with a high social profile and an expectation of long-term business, can be startling. Today customers, no less than employees, recognize their right to demand fair treatment. In the near future, firms with little official commitment to fair dealing may be following the lead of customer-stakeholder firms, if not because they want to, then because they must.

7 COMMUNITY STAKEHOLDERS The Corporation as Good Citizen

Profit is the key word in moving an enterprise forward. But there is general recognition today that maximizing profit at the expense of social and human values is a losing game. The much more difficult game of balancing profit with social and human values is our present concern.

—Donald MacNaughton
Former chairman, Prudential Life Insurance

We believe that a well-integrated and comprehensive program of community involvement is not only good for the "bottom line," it is the bottom line.

—William A. Andres
Chairman, Dayton Hudson Corporation

Addressing the needs of shareholders, employees, and customers is widely accepted as a baseline moral obligation—and a baseline pragmatic imperative—of business today. Since these groups constitute a social triad without whose cooperation free enterprise cannot survive, even those who are nervous about the concept of moral "responsibility" in business acknowledge the needs of these three groups as valid corporate considerations. Practicality dictates nothing less.

The fundamental social question of business today is whether or not practicality, morality, or a combination of the two dictates *more.* Frequently that question is couched in a form that highlights "responsibility" as the sticking point: The debate about what business can, or should, do for groups beyond the basic triad generally revolves around the question, "What are the social responsibilities of business?" Corporate leaders today are as occupied with that question as their Reform Era counterparts were with questions about responsibilities to workers. In an age in which Big Business vies with Big Government as the dominant institutional force in public life, this is only natural. The increasing public pressure on business to "get involved" and the regulatory proliferation that seeks to define that involvement are only the most visible public sector responses to something that the private sector has known since at least World War II: that the principal question being asked of the twentieth-century corporation is "How far do your responsibilities extend to the society of which you are a part?"

For over twenty years Chicago economist Milton Friedman has led the chorus of those whose answer is "Not very far." The Friedman thesis, articulated in his 1962 book *Capitalism and Freedom*, is the now familiar one that the health of our economic system depends on capitalist leaders being able to perform their basic profit-seeking function with as little intrusion as possible from either government or special interest groups convinced that business must look beyond the bottom line. In a free economy, Friedman contends, business has "one and only one social responsibility—to use its resources and engage in activities designed to *increase its profits* so long as it stays within the rules of the game, which is to say, engages in open and free competition, without deception or fraud." When business leaders attempt to take on anything more than that, they are falling prey to a "fundamentally subversive doctrine," that is, the crypto-socialist doctrine that business is part of the State, and ought to behave accordingly.

Friedman's basic worry, of course, is not that business leaders will take on too *much* power but that once they begin to stick their necks into the social arena, they will be wrung by the feds. The initial problem of the "socially responsible" business person, Friedman correctly observes, is in defining responsibility itself. "Can self-selected private individuals decide what the social interest is?" Even if they can decide, will not their doing so transform them, ipso facto, from entrepreneurs into civil servants? And as civil servants, however disguised, will they not eventually be entrapped by their own overreach? Will the captain of industry not ultimately become a mere public flunky, "chosen by the public techniques of election and appointment?"

Thus the specter of government intrusion—of public control of private business—hangs over Friedman's entire portrayal of the "social responsibility" debate. Aware that Washington is ever ready to regulate fishing in public waters, Friedman counsels that the wise business leader take his tackle elsewhere. For even such modest muddyings of the laissez-faire waters as tax breaks for charitable contributions comprise "a step away from an individualistic society and toward the corporate state."

Harvard economist Theodore Levitt, four years before *Capitalism and Freedom* was published, voiced a related fear in a famous essay in the *Harvard Business Review*. Like Friedman, he felt that the business of business should be business—specifically, that "long-run profit maximization" should be "the one dominant objective in practice as well as in theory." Unlike Friedman, he felt that the principal danger of deflection from that objective was not state control but private abuse of power. If Friedman feared that businessmen would not be able to resist a public netting of their energies, Levitt thought they would be able to resist it only too well. The spectral end he envisioned was an "encircling business ministry" whose historical analogue was, to put it bluntly, fascism. Thus, from different directions, Friedman and Levitt arrive at the same conclusion: that looking beyond the bottom line means, ultimately, the loss of freedom.

This concern, while it is by no means a trivial one, is more likely to convince those who see any restriction on private liberty as an intolerable social outrage than those who see individual liberty—whether personal or corporate—as one of many elements in a complex social pattern that already includes numerous restrictions on liberty that are widely accepted as necessary for social health. Posing "loss of freedom" as a real social danger has always been the most attractive argument in the laissez-faire arsenal, and it is certainly no less attractive today than it was twenty years ago. But in analyzing the baneful effects of "social involvement" on our national life, surely it makes more sense to concentrate on the effects that have already taken place than to speculate on evils that may arise in some projected totalitarian future.

The fact is that corporations have been "socially involved" for several decades now, and the palpable effects on our society do not very closely parallel either of the professors' nightmare scenarios. The reason for this, I think, is clear. It is that we do not now live—nor have we lived for many years—in a truly "free" economy, but in one where business, government, and various interest groups are seen as uneasy but constant partners in the general social enterprise. Ours is a mixed economy and a mixed social system. The checks and balances model that was built into our constitution operates in the market as well, and well enough so that the abuse of power to which Friedman and Levitt fearfully point has not yet become a reality; nor is corporate intrusion into social welfare likely to make it so.

This is not to deny that there are risks involved when business takes on obligations beyond the bottom line. But I am less convinced than the Friedman camp that they are irreversible. Aetna's John Filer told me, when I asked him about corporate abuse of power, that while the danger certainly existed, it was generally ameliorated by the checks against power that were inherent in an open society itself. Yes, he admitted, big business had to be careful that it didn't simply "lead the parade" without looking back. "But I have great confidence in the capacity of the public to recognize and check that tendency. It's not as though we can do things today without any supervision." In a country with as strong a press and as large a regulatory apparatus as the United States, that's a wryly modest defense of social leadership.

I'll return to this issue in the following chapter, when I speak about corporate involvement in the widest possible social issues, such as public schooling and unemployment. Let me now take up Professor Friedman's second principal concern, the suspicion that in its zeal to perform "good works" for society, a corporation abuses its shareholders' trust and wastes their money. In *Capitalism and Freedom*, he condemned even modest charity—including contributions to educational institutions—as a squandering of corporate resources. One can imagine his view of such immodest social involvements as the funding of rape crisis centers and the rehabilitation of cities.

Friedman objects to the use of corporate funds for anything but the maximization of profit on fundamentally ethical grounds. The problem he identifies is that corporate managers, entrusted with money by their stockholders, choose to use that money in ways that do not bring those investors the best return on their investment. That, he suggests, is ethically unsound, because it involves an avoidance of every manager's primary responsibility—his duty to manage wisely.

The answer to this argument, I believe, lies in a redefinition of such terms as "manage" and "return on investment" and even "profit." Or to put it more precisely, it lies in recognizing that in our mixed economy and mixed polity those terms have already been redefined so that they bear only a passing relation to their meaning in a hypothetical "free" economy. More and more, wise management means attending to long-term profiles, including social profiles, rather than merely quarter-to-quarter profit margins. Since society "expects more of a corporation" today, and since long-term profitability is linked ultimately to public perceptions of a company, not just current sales figures, it is actually less responsible for a manager to go for the short-term take than to ensure, by socially responsible activity, that the firm will continue to enjoy public support.

"Buying public support" must be seen today not as a squandering of funds but as an essential part of doing business. Many of the managers I spoke to said that "putting something back" into the communities and society where they did business was not only a moral imperative but also the best way of fulfilling responsibilities to stockholders, because such social involvement acted as a pump-priming mechanism to ensure the kind of society in which business prospers.

Robert Roggeveen, manager of social investments for the Aetna

Foundation, speaks of the need to balance "self-interest and other interests" in administering corporate funds. He distinguishes between long-term and short-term profits in a way that speaks to Friedman's objection very well. I asked him how Aetna could justify giving money to various native American support groups. Since these groups were unlikely to become major purchasers of Aetna policies or stock, wasn't this throwing away stockholders' money?

"The return on investment of something like this," Roggeveen explained, "may be twenty years down the road. We feel it's important to invest in socially useful projects—and even in ones where the utility factor is not obvious—because we're part of the society we work in, and we're trying to make that society healthier for everybody concerned, including ourselves. We don't feel that's wasting our investors' money. On the contrary, it's a far better use of their funds than going for this quarter's profits while everything is crumbling around you.

"The same philosophy operates in Aetna's basic business of writing insurance. If our primary desire was to maintain a high stock price and high dividends, we'd concentrate on people making $60,000 a year, with houses in the affluent suburbs, and no health problems. We'd probably make more money that way. But we're not in the business of satisfying the needs of stock speculators. Our goal is to provide protection for as many groups as we can, and we're convinced that in the long run this is in the stockholders' best interest, because it helps create a more stable social environment."

Aetna's former chairman John Filer also takes a broad view of stockholder interests. "It is not written in stone," he told me, "that the only function of a corporation is the purely economic one of maximizing short-term return for stockholders. You have to manage a company for its long-term growth and success." Today that means getting involved in areas that a strict constructionist of corporate bylaws would see as the province of government. The logic of this involvement is that what Filer calls "the intelligent and voluntary use of our resources" for social needs helps to create an atmosphere—indeed, the only atmosphere—in which business itself can prosper.

The creation of such an atmosphere begins in those communities where a corporation actually does business. We begin, therefore, by seeing how Aetna and other firms manage what they perceive to be their responsibilities to local constituencies.

Corporations prove themselves to be good local citizens in a variety of ways. The three most common are to give money outright to community projects, to lend the talents and time of their people to those projects, and to work in financial and organizational partnerships with local government to generate improvements of value to all.

The first of these methods of demonstrating community involvement—straightforward dollar contributions—may seem the easiest to manage, but that is not always the case. Since many localities today tend to have more needs than resources to meet them, and since intelligent philanthropy means giving not indiscriminately but where it will do the most good, corporations with an established reputation for addressing the needs of community stakeholders are commonly beleaguered with more requests for funding than their resources can possibly meet, and are therefore having to decide, in every giving period, between equally attractive recipients.

The corporate dilemma thus created is chiefly a function of size. The small businessman who gives twenty dollars each to the neighborhood drug rehabilitation program, the local arts festival, and the United Way is seen as a good local citizen; the corporate officer who cannot release $200 to all these recipients, and a hundred more at the door, is seen as close-fisted and insensitive. William Brooks, secretary of the Prudential Foundation, complained to me, "The public looks at a company our size and sees huge pots of money; they don't realize that it's not ours to dispense at will." All companies, he pointed out, in order to satisfy the obligation to manage their owners' money wisely, must make judicious choices among many potential recipients of corporate largesse. This is as true of corporate giving programs as of the foundations funded by them.

To assess how managers make these difficult choices, and make them honorably, look at the experience of the Minneapolis business community. Two pillars of that community—the Dayton Hudson Corporation and the Pillsbury Company—have adopted local giving strategies that are both generous and effective.

As William Andres's comment at the head of this chapter indicates, Dayton Hudson has long been in the forefront of corporate community involvement. Since the 1940s, a singular element of that involvement has been the company's policy to contribute, largely to local causes, a minimum of 5 percent of its taxable income in charitable donations. That percentage is strictly budgeted, and although the policy is reviewed once a year at board meetings, it would be "a major change of policy," according to Dayton Hudson vice-president Peter Hutchinson, for it to be voted down now. "It's so well integrated into the way we do business," he told me, "that all of our managers 'own' the idea."

Hutchinson, who is chairman of the Dayton Hudson Foundation as well as a corporate officer, explains that in its search for the most appropriate areas toward which to focus its giving, the company aims for those where giving will set up a mutually profitable give-and-take between donor and recipient. "Our philosophy of service," he says, "is based on strategic self-interest: business prospers best in prosperous environments. Serving society is not optional to our business. It is the foundation upon which our business rests."

In the past, Hutchinson points out, most giving by corporations, even when it was generous, tended to be multidirectional and/or aimless. "There was a long period of irrelevancy. Then, about twenty years ago, giving programs started focusing better on real community needs—not just the president's pet project, but areas that really affected the community. That was what I'd call the period of relevance. Even in that period, however, giving was frequently ineffective. It addressed whatever problem area happened to be in the news in a given year, without any serious thought being given to how the problems related to business.

"We're moving now into a third, and I think clearly the most effective stage: that of *integrated* giving. The mistake often made in corporate giving is to try to be too broad and too disinterested. We say that giving should be *very* interested. It should be completely integrated into the business's major focus. The overall goals we have are goals that most effective giving programs have: to find linkages between our business and social concerns, and to use leverage with our funds so that you get the greatest punch for the dollar."

At Dayton Hudson recently this has meant concentrating the 5 percent on two overall areas: social action and the arts, each of which gets 40 percent of the total. Both of these areas connect structurally to Dayton Hudson's primary business, retailing. Social action is considered important because, as Hutchinson explained, you can't expect the poor and powerless to be very enthusiastic shoppers. "The solution is not to forget about those people, but to empower them so that we can help each other. This—not at all incidentally—also broadens our customer and employee base." The arts are considered important because "ours is a fashion business, oriented toward trends in color and design. So the arts are a natural linkage."

The same attention to "linkages" appears at Dayton Hudson's member companies. Since the Mervyn and Target store chains serve primarily young families, these companies' contributions focus on programs for children and parents. Recently Target, for example, bussed young schoolchildren to arts centers, and Mervyn's funded a bilingual day-care center in Oregon. The Dayton chain, alert to the plight of the female poor in the northern-tier states—and to the fact that 77 percent of its own customers are women—lent support to various programs helping rape victims, young mothers, and women with substandard work skills. And the B. Dalton bookstore chain committed $1 million to a nationwide adult literacy campaign.

The program contributions mentioned in Chapter 1 indicate the range of Dayton Hudson's 5 percent program. But whether the gift is large or small—whether it is $5000 for an Arizona halfway house or the million-dollar investment made in Minneapolis's Whittier neighborhood—a number of themes prevail.

First, the giving is local, in all but a minority of cases. Dayton Hudson is more committed than any other visible major corporate giver to the proposition that charity begins at home. "Home" here means not just Minneapolis but all those communities where the company has either an operating headquarters or a "presence." Only 2 percent of the contributions budget may be targeted for needs beyond these areas.

The reason for the local focus, Hutchinson explains, is purely practical. "That's where the action is, and it's where the long-term, stable government cooperation is. Besides, at a local level your giving is much more efficient, because practically everything you give goes into the targeted project. At the national level, a lot of it goes into overhead. If you really want to get services to folks, as we do, it makes sense to start at home."

Second, the giving is not purely philanthropic, but is keyed to strict accountability procedures. Since this is true of all charities, it should not be necessary to point it out, and I do so only to correct the impression, occasionally voiced in regard to Dayton Hudson, that the company enjoys "throwing its money away." The company publication, "Managing Change: Taking Direction from Our Communities," expresses it this way: "Priority will be given to programs that empower groups of socially disadvantaged adults or young people to attain or develop the tools needed for their own continuing self-sufficiency, rather than maintaining a dependency on government or charity for their survival." This "teach a man to fish" philosophy, along with the accounting process, ensures that Dayton Hudson stockholders' money is directed toward factual, not fanciful, social change.

Third, the giving is business-related. I have already mentioned Peter Hutchinson's view of "strategic self-interest" as a foundation of company involvement. Many grants, of course, are given in areas that do not connect obviously to retailing; but the priority areas remain programs that enable Dayton Hudson to "profit share" with its constituencies, socially and financially.

Dayton Hudson's 5 percent contributions policy began back in the 1940s, in response to the federal government's stipulation that up to 5 percent of pretax profits could be deducted from federal returns. At the time Dayton Hudson was thought both revolutionary and a bit mad. Since then, however, numerous other companies (particularly Minnesota companies) have followed suit, and one of the most satisfying aspects of the program now is the synergistic effect of multicorporate involvement. The Minnesota Keystone Award program, established in 1976 to recognize companies that contributed either the original 5 percent or, later, 2 percent, now has well over 100 members, and has long been a model for similar programs throughout the country.

Some of the members of this elite community service group are major corporations like Dayton Hudson; Price Waterhouse gives 5 percent, and both Honeywell and General Mills give 2 percent. Others are small concerns, like Anderson's China Shop and the Lieberman Music Company and Maxim's Beauty Salons. All of them share the conviction that good citizenship begins in the community; together they have helped make Minnesota a model for corporate involvement.

One of the most active members of the 2 percent giving "club" is another Twin Cities giant, Pillsbury. The food and food service corporation's focus is decidedly less local than that of Dayton Hudson—the company's educational and civic contributions are nationwide—but Pillsbury shares with the retailer a commitment to focused giving that is both strictly accountable and related to company interests.

Terry Saario, former vice-president, community relations, at the Pillsbury Company and now president of the Northwest Area Foundation, feels that simple, unfocused "nineteenth-century charity" is not only inappropriate for a corporation but "irresponsible" as well, because it deprives shareholders of dividends that they ought to be receiving. She describes a circular benefit that results when corporate giving is "targeted to a limited number of topics that are relevant to the nature of the business."

> The only way that corporations can really counter Milton Friedman's argument that they shouldn't be giving money away is for the giving to be tied directly to the corporation's image, so that our various publics recognize that we are being socially responsible, and respond by buying more of our products. I'm not at all uncomfortable with the cynic's view that this is "just PR." When corporations address social issues in their communities, they're quite deliberately enhancing their images. That's a perfectly legitimate use of profits. It enables them to sell more product, have happier employees and shareholders, have a better image in the financial markets—and continue to address community needs.

Pillsbury's focus areas recently have been on youth and hunger. The company's community relations report for 1984 explains the rationale behind these choices:

> The development of youth and hunger as foci for the Pillsbury Community Relations program is one that offers many synergies. As a premier food company, a pioneer in nutritional labeling and a leader in the development of food bank programs, Pillsbury has keen interests and knowledge relevant to the subject of hunger. As

> one of the nation's largest employers of youth, Pillsbury is also closely aware of the many needs and opportunities facing younger Americans.

The "food bank programs" referred to here are part of an ongoing hunger initiative under which the company contributes its own products to food-for-the-needy distribution centers. In late 1983, the company was given a special Keystone Award for using this program to provide over 750,000 meals to hungry people in three states. The company is a major youth employer through its Burger King subsidiary, and the subsidiary's own giving programs reflect the same attention to business-related areas as do the foundation's programs at large. Burger King's principal focus area in 1984 was the education of minority youth.

Every corporate manager I spoke to about community giving validated the belief, so visible at Dayton Hudson and Pillsbury, that effective giving had to be business-related. This doesn't mean that it has to be immediately reciprocal—that money given out has to be "repaid" directly—but only that in a long-term social investment strategy, the companies that have the greatest effect are likely to be those who work in areas, and with leverages, that they understand.

This common-sense proposition is evident in many corporate involvement programs, whether or not they demonstrate the intensely local interest of some of the Minneapolis firms:

- The Aetna Life and Casualty Foundation currently funds several neighborhood mediation programs that, programs officer Robert Roggeveen explains, grow directly out of the fact that Aetna, like all insurance companies, is "a virtual litigation factory." The company also funds legal research, encourages its own legal staff to do "pro bono" work in its community, and has developed alternative dispute resolution mechanisms for addressing conflicts in both the private and public sectors.
- Johnson & Johnson concentrates its giving in the health sciences and biological research. Chairman James Burke speaks of this focused giving as part of a "strategic plan." "Our money ought to be given, I believe, in a way that can be broadly defined as being in our own self-interest."
- At Eastman Kodak, involvement in local communities goes back to founder George Eastman, who coined the term "Community Chest." Today it encompasses aid for the United Way and numerous other civic programs, and the establishment of several "marketing education centers" in Kodak cities, where photography courses train local people to be wiser (and, not incidentally, more loyal) users of audiovisual equipment.

- Since Xerox, like all high-tech companies, has a profound impact on the changing labor picture, the Xerox Foundation now focuses heavily on such areas as employability, computer technology, and productivity. Foundation vice-president Robert Gudger articulates the rationale. "We feel there shouldn't be competition for meeting human needs, but that every need can and should be met by someone. Since we can't meet them all ourselves, we try to tackle those we know something about in a meaningful way."

Such examples of focused giving suggest not only the exigency of targeting limited resources judiciously; they suggest, by their popularity in many different businesses over a considerable period of time, that such a contributions approach benefits the giver as well as the receiver. Roggeveen calls effective corporate charity "a combination of self-interest and other interests." When those other interests grow out of, rather than away from, the primary business concern of the giving organization, you are most likely to get effects that transcend mere "philanthropy" and generate real transformations. One lesson of corporate charity, then, is the one we have also seen operating with regard to employee relations and customer relations: the Golden Rule can be good business.

A second way in which corporations meet their presumed obligations to local communities is to give not money but people. Firms who adopt this strategy often are able to generate both real social effects and tremendous public goodwill with a relatively small investment. In addition, having corporate employees involved at local levels reinforces that personal level of commitment on which community involvement really depends.

Many community-stakeholder firms encourage their employees to volunteer their efforts in local enrichment projects. Few do it as effectively or extensively as San Francisco's Levi Strauss Company. Both directly and through its foundation, the company nourishes employee activism on several levels. The first and broadest of these is the Community Grants program administered by the Strauss foundation.

The heart of the Community Grants program is a widely distributed network of Community Involvement Teams (CITs), composed of Levi Strauss employees formed within the company facilities to perform various service functions in local communities. In 1982, fifty-six communities in fifteen states profited from the work of these small teams. That work, which reflected the company's current target interests of aging, domestic violence, parent education, and employment, included such projects as these:

- In Charleston, South Carolina, Strauss workers developed plans and fund-raising events in support of a hospice for the terminally ill.
- In Boone County, Kentucky, a CIT landscaped and installed playground equipment in a new children's park.
- In Garland, Texas, CIT members, by volunteering their time and arranging for a Strauss foundation grant, enabled a health clinic to expand its delivery of services.

In all of these cases, and in scores of others like them, the initial CIT involvement served as the groundwork enabling the project to qualify for direct grants from the company. Community involvement at Levi Strauss is seen as a mix of money and time: In deciding where grant money should be allocated, priority is always given to areas where CITs are already active.

In addition to the Community Involvement Teams, the company also supports a three-part Social Benefits Program. It includes a straightforward matching-gifts function, under which the company equals an employee's donation to social service agencies; and in addition, two innovative functions that encourage direct worker participation in such agencies. Like the CIT program, these are a mix of time and money. Under the Local Employee Action Program (LEAP), Strauss employees and retirees may request grants of up to $500 for nonprofit groups to which they themselves donate time. And under the Board Service Program, somewhat heftier grants may be requested by employees who serve on such organizations' governing boards.

All of these programs, it should also be remembered, are part of a wide-spectrum foundation attack on deficiencies in both the national and local communities. The bulk of Levi Strauss's giving is directed to regional and national programs. But almost a third—which in 1982 amounted to $1.5 million—goes to Community Grants and Social Benefits. And nearly 14 percent of the total is targeted for higher education, which of course helps communities at all levels.

A similar multifaceted approach to community involvement is taken by Connecticut-based Xerox. The Xerox Foundation gives directly, and heavily, to community affairs projects including local capital campaigns and the United Way. Xerox employee participation, furthermore, is encouraged by two hands-on programs that illustrate very clearly the company's commitment to grass-roots involvement.

The Xerox Community Involvement Program (XCIP) invites comparison to the CIT program of Levi Strauss, since it too is an amalgam of local on-site organization and centralized corporate funding. Xerox employees in numerous communities (in 1983 it was nearly 10,000 employees in 200 communities) initiate social-service projects, donate their time and talents on an ad hoc or ongoing basis, and in certain instances are eligible for reimbursement of their expenses from the Xerox Foundation. To qualify for such funding, community and employee programs manager Marion Whipple told me, certain guidelines must be met. A company memo for employees considering XCIP projects asks them to be sure that any such project is "manageable, that the time frame is reasonable, and that there is potential for employee involvement." In addition, the project should have "clearly stated objectives" and should "meet a current need within the community." A final warning—"Do not make commitments you cannot keep"—shows the Xerox program to be not pie in the sky, but solid and results-oriented.

Most of the hundreds of projects undertaken by Xerox people each year address specific, short-term local needs. Some recent examples:

- In Jefferson City, Missouri, Xerox volunteers worked with the local Optimist Club and the police and fire departments to produce a one-day "traffic safety clinic"—complete with a miniature Safety City—for area children.
- In Albany, New York, Xerox technical reps set up an ongoing Saturday morning course in electricity and physics at a school for boys with social adjustment problems.
- In 1980, an Atlanta XCIP began rebuilding a ghetto church that had been destroyed by fire. Working weekends under the guidance of a local carpenter, they finished the project in 1983.
- Xerox volunteers in Middletown, Connecticut handled publicity and promotion for a fund-raising drive that brought in $50,000 for a shelter for the homeless.
- In Los Angeles, XCIP people from eight company locations trained handicapped students in computer literacy and other job skills.

These examples are representative. Most XCIP projects address not the structurally entrenched social problems that get most government and foundation attention, but the less glamorous, less fashionable dilemmas of marginal community groups. A consistent cluster of interests over the twelve years during which the program has operated has focused on the aged, the ill, and the handicapped.

A similar focus is evident in Xerox's other employee involvement program, the revolutionary Social Service Leave program instituted in 1971. Under this program, Xerox employees who wish to take time off from their jobs to "give something back" to their communities may do so, at *full pay*, for anywhere from a month to a year. Potential leave-takers specify what outside project they want to tackle, and for how long. Those who are chosen submit monthly progress reports during their leaves, but are not otherwise required to "justify" how they are spending the company's time. Furthermore, Social Service Leave is an employee-motivated and employee-supervised program. "This is the point that makes us unique," Whipple said. "The types of projects undertaken are generated by the employees themselves, and it's a group of employees, *not* managers, that decides who will be granted a Social Service Leave."

The range of projects (and of leave-takers who undertake them) is wide. "There's no set profile of a leave-taker. We've had vice-presidents and assembly line workers, secretaries and sales representatives. If the work you want to do is sound—if it can make a real difference to a community—we feel you should be given a chance to do it, no matter what your position." Officially, the president of Xerox can deny a request for leave if the applicant's service to the company seems absolutely fundamental and irreplaceable. But he's never done that yet.

Whipple acknowledges that there are real costs associated with the program. The ongoing salaries, for example. Since the company grants up to 264 months' worth of leave among the various applicants in any one year, the salary drain is substantial; Whipple estimated it at between $300,000 and $350,000 a year. There are occasional internal tensions too, she admitted, when a manager has to readjust his operation to account for the missing talent. But those problems are rare, and manageable. There's no question, she told me confidently, that Social Service Leave, like XCIP, is worth everything that Xerox puts into it.

The public relations element, I thought, must be an important consideration, but Whipple did not agree. "Of course we get some PR out of these programs," she said, "but that's not our primary intent. We recognize that we have a social responsibility as well as a business responsibility. We want the communities where we do business to know that we're not there simply to take something out, but to put something back. And we feel that our employees do that for us."

The employees benefit too—and so, quite directly, does the company, through the employee. Getting back a "better employee," Whipple stressed, is a major return to Xerox of Social Service Leave. There's no question, she said, that returning leave-takers are better rounded, more effective employees. "They've learned new interpersonal skills, they know what it's like in other organizations, they're better able to deal with people. That's a big gain for the company."

Xerox and Levi Strauss, of course, are only two of many corporations that encourage employee commitment to community stakeholders. We could mention the B. Dalton literacy program, which, though funded by Dayton Hudson money, was entirely staffed by B. Dalton volunteers. Or the IBM social service leave and faculty loan programs. Or the Dollars for Doers matching grants system for Aetna volunteers. Or J.C. Penney's "meals for the elderly" program in New York City.

The companies that run such programs share a growing recognition that local communities are vital to the health of any business. Most of them recognize as well that the investment of personnel can often bring as many benefits back to the organization as the investment of actual dollars.

By and large both corporate funding for community projects and employee voluntarism tend to focus on short-term, "doable" problems rather than the structural nightmares that beset our society at large and urban communities in particular. Part of the reason, in fact, that attention is often given to day-care centers and rape crisis centers and halfway houses for the dispossessed—all real, acute needs—is that progress seems possible in these areas, at least in incremental ways. A Special Olympics for sixty handicapped children has an immediate positive feedback; it gives those kids a good time, right now. That is both valuable and gratifying to corporate participants. It is seldom that an equivalent gratification is forthcoming when the problems are such pervasive and structural ones as America's current fatal triad: housing, education, and jobs.

Corporate attention to these problems has been slight in the past because corporate leaders, like the American public at large, have tended to see them as government issues rather than private ones. The fact that the federal government has often mismanaged all three of these fundamental dilemmas has not, up until very recently, generated widespread reassessment of the appropriate mix of public and private initiative in solving them. Almost two decades after Watts and Newark went up in flames, the United States still lacks a credible manpower policy, and the commitment to housing and education remains at the mercy of budgetary vacillation.

Whatever the ultimate outcome of President Reagan's budget of austerity for the poor, it is clear that the private sector (and especially corporations) will have to begin picking up more of the tab for social revitalization, unless they wish to follow our cities down the drain. This has been happening since the riots of the 1960s and is increasing in this decade, as select corporations understand that, far from being eliminable no-man's-lands, our great urban areas may be the only hope for a revitalized population. It's where the people live, after all.

But there are ethical as well as practical problems associated with a corporate assault on urban blight. To get an idea of those problems, and to understand how they relate to the general issue of community involvement, I want to look at three cases involving three different cities and three different corporations.

The Prudential in Newark. Throughout the late 1960s and early 1970s, the Prudential Insurance Company was in the forefront of corporate response to the problems of the inner city. Since the company's home base was Newark, New Jersey, site of some of the most violent racial riots of the 1960s, its managers were acutely aware that the Pru's own health and safety were linked to a viable city life.

In the wake of the riots, they understood, that meant first of all new housing, and to generate housing renewal the company, beginning in 1967, spearheaded a life insurance industry effort that made available to potential homeowners a vast bank of low-interest loans. By 1969 the industry investment was 2 billion dollars, to be used for residential loans and economic development investments in areas of severe dislocation.

It sounded great, but turned out to be little more than a noble gesture. The story of the post-riot years, in Newark as in so many other American cities, was the story of "white flight" to the suburbs, of a gradually shrinking tax base, and of increasing resignation and despair. Between 1967 and 1978, in spite of programs and investment efforts, Newark lost approximately 47,000 jobs.

Through it all, the Prudential stayed in Newark, and although as part of its decentralization strategy the company is now moving some of its urban base to the suburbs, company officials deny that it will ever "abandon Newark." Recent construction bears them out. As part of a "Renaissance Newark" package, Prudential invested heavily in real estate in downtown Newark, and has moved many of its remaining 3,000 employees into the new Gateway III office building a few blocks from its headquarters complex. In addition, the company maintains a schedule of "social investments," under which it invests funds, at lower-than-market rates, in projects with perceived social value across the country. The portfolio is now more than $300 million.

But a fundamental focus has changed. The real lesson of the low-income housing experience, public relations consultant Richard Mathisen told me, was that the company had to take a broader approach. "We said, 'Let's build low-income housing and watch the urban areas recover,' but it didn't work out that way. Now we take a more community-oriented approach, with emphasis on job creation and home ownership. One effort we support strongly is the Neighborhood Housing Service program, which is based on partnerships of community residents and representatives of local governments and financial institutions. The NHS programs offer comprehensive housing rehabilitation services to residents of locally selected neighborhoods. The key is to recognize that you don't have just a housing problem, you have a community problem. You have to find ways to address it on a variety of fronts."

Control Data in Minneapolis. Control Data chairman William Norris is one of the business community's most outspoken critics of the "handout" approach to community involvement. Philanthropy, he says, is not only nonprofitable but nonproductive. "People don't want philanthropy. They don't want a handout. They want assistance to become more productive." At Control Data that assistance is offered through investment and capitalization ventures that can be ongoing precisely because they bring a good return.

"Addressing society's major unmet needs as profitable business opportunities" is the reading line for one of Control Data's descriptive brochures, and a good shorthand description of both the firm's underlying philosophy and its business strategy. Among those needs, the brochure identifies health, education, productivity, energy, small enterprise, and both rural and urban development—a litany that, by any assessment, is a pretty fair appraisal of our problems. To Norris and his management team, the sophisticated products made by Control Data—computer mainframes, peripherals, and a huge range of tie-in services—can provide the bridge between a society where the above are trouble areas to one in which they are rich ground for entrepreneurship and economic advance. It's not by accident that CDC literature identifies as an early guiding principle the maxim "Need creates opportunity."

That principle was put into practice in an urban community as long ago as the late 1960s, when the company put a new production plant into a severely depressed area of north Minneapolis. Taking a decidedly holistic approach to this admittedly risky venture, management solicited the aid of local government, talked to community groups, and instituted a wide range of employee counselling and training services to ensure stability and thus their investment. Company lawyers bailed out workers who had ended up in jail over weekends. CDC provided transportation to work, assisted in setting up a day-care facility and, through its Commercial Credit subsidiary, enabled workers to take out low-interest automobile loans. "If you can't get businessmen to build in the slum," one executive commented, "you've got to get the slum out of the slum first. Then business will follow."

This investment in people and in hope paid off. The north Minneapolis plant eventually became profitable at a level competitive with Control Data's more conventional enterprises. And philanthropy had nothing to do with it.

Other such projects have not panned out so well, however, and Norris lays a lot of the blame at Washington's door. "People in the federal government," he told me, "don't have the sense of a partnership that you need to have to get things done." Lamenting the timidity, lethargy, and confusion that many business leaders see as endemic throughout the federal bureaucracy, he notes that the initiative for business-government partnerships has now passed to the states.

"The average person," Norris told me, "is unaware of the degree to which, for example, industrial policy—which is debated endlessly at the federal level without any consensus—is actually being implemented at the state level. There are about twenty states that have some form of enterprise zone legislation. They can't offer as attractive a package as the federal government, but they're still coming along very nicely. They get things done."

Whether the federal bureaucracy will eventually respond positively to the states' initiative in this area remains to be seen. One thing is certain, however. It's that, whether the focus is local, state, regional, or national, cooperation is the key to serving the community stakeholder well. Holism must be multifaceted not just in terms of the needs addressed but also in terms of the actors addressing those needs. This fundamental lesson of past community involvement is expressed forcefully in Control Data's own words: "Combining our own resources with those of other corporations, non-profit organizations and governments, is an effective way to leverage limited resources and to establish a comprehensive response to a major need."

J&J in New Brunswick. The observations made by Prudential's Mathisen and by Control Data's Norris about the importance of multifaceted response come together sharply in the efforts of Johnson & Johnson to help revitalize its once dying headquarters city, New Brunswick.

It is widely recognized now that the central New Jersey city's rebirth, after the long stagnancy of the late 1960s and early 1970s, began in earnest around 1978, when J&J announced plans to build a $75-million world headquarters there, thus consolidating an association between the town and the company that had existed since 1886. It is not widely recognized that the decision to breathe new life into New Brunswick had actually been made four years earlier, when then J&J chairman Richard Sellars hired an outside consulting firm to prepare a readout on the city's likely future. When the consultants envisaged New Brunswick as a model of public/private cooperation, Sellars asked noted architect I.M. Pei to prepare a land-use blueprint, and went to the city government with a unique co-venture plan. Within two years, the New Brunswick Development Corporation (DevCo) was formed, with Sellars as its chairman.

DevCo was the motive force behind the community concept New Brunswick Tomorrow, "a unique urban experiment in which business, government and community leaders founded a non-profit corporation with a board of directors representing each of those interests." With those interests working interactively, and with funding from local banks, Prudential in Newark, and J&J itself, the city began to move forward.

- The downtown area, once a vandalized and shabby eyesore, now boasts the new headquarters building and a new Hyatt Regency hotel, both paid for with J&J money. The combined tax revenues of the new buildings is about $2 million a year—as compared to $170,000 before.
- Several blocks away, in the middle of a brick-lined main street, what had been an abandoned department store is now Rutgers University's school of the arts. The dead store had been bought by J&J, and resold to the university at no profit.
- New Brunswick Tomorrow's operations include a human services task force that has set up an innovative home day-care system, a neighborhood task force that has set up a summer concert series, and a career preparation center that trains and places young people in local jobs.

Such projects are only a sampling, but they indicate well enough the multi-pronged NBT approach, and show what can be done fairly quickly when community stakeholders work together.

The problems have not all been solved, of course, as J&J officers are the first to admit. "One key problem that's still unsolved," says J&J chairman James Burke, "is the education system. Without an improved school system, you just won't get young families to build here and to provide that essential ongoing energy." To address that problem, J&J recently presented a three-day management training program for school administrators, focusing on such problem areas as performance appraisal, group problem solving, and stress management.

There are naturally some objections to Big Business being involved in urban rebirth at all, and those objections, although they are voiced by only a small minority of New Brunswick residents, do focus on the ethical issues inherent in such intense corporate involvement.

A preservationist contingent objects to J&J's grand design because it includes razing a small historical area and putting in housing and retail shops. The purely "pragmatic" utilitarian might find this a facetious obstruction, since presumably the presence of new shops and homes would bring more pleasure (at least economic pleasure) to local residents than the maintenance of a few ramshackle "sites." Yet the moral question implied here is not idle, since it involves the determination of who, rightly, should decide the character of traditional neighborhoods. A similar objection was raised in Hartford when Aetna funded improvements in a historic district. Does the financial ability to improve a given area give one the moral "right" to do so, especially when some community stakeholders are offended by the change? That is a question that any corporate manager engaged in urban revitalization must confront, and confront fairly. The real danger in urban revitalization, as in any massive social change, is that the opinions of minorities will be ignored.

This is much more baldly the case when the engine of progress displaces not historical buildings, but people. In both Hartford's Asylum Hill district and New Brunswick's "Golden Triangle" downtown, the majority of people displaced by the massive refurbishment were black or Hispanic, and poor. What ethical responsibilities do corporate managers (not to mention government officials) have to those people?

New Brunswick Tomorrow's work in the past year has included several initiatives designed to offset the "critical shortage" of housing; these included plans for senior citizen housing, for lease-purchase agreements, and for neighborhood improvement and development as part of the national Local Initiatives Support Corporation. Indirectly, of course, Johnson & Johnson contributes to all these efforts, through its ongoing support of New Brunswick Tomorrow.

But certain questions do remain. Do companies that initiate massive urban renewal efforts have an obligation to become directly involved in relocation, or is that the city government's problem? And what about gentrification, which the poor find predictably less attractive than the middle class who are its beneficiaries?

James Burke, while attempting to head off resentment through community involvement, admits that the vote in favor of corporate betterment of local communities is not, and never can be, unanimous. "We've tried to track our local constituencies here," says James Burke, "just as we tracked our consumers during the Tylenol crisis. We've tried to involve as many disparate groups in the planning process as possible. That hasn't always been easy. And it's been especially difficult because we're the only major business here that's been using its resources for change. Naturally somebody's going to get hurt in a project this size. You just have to do your best to minimize the dislocation and the pain."

Aetna's Filer, aware that the poor are frequently displaced during urban redevelopment programs, suggests that viable low-income housing may only become a reality as part of a wider refurbishment that includes, inevitably, gentrification. Before Aetna became involved in Asylum Hill, he said, it was "a potential disaster area." With a combination of a gentrification process (the creation of condominiums) and a major relocation effort, the company was able to "tip the balance, turning an unlivable section into one that survives." The revitalized section includes approximately 20 percent low-income housing units—which would not have been possible if the condos hadn't come first.

In a comment that echoed Richard Mathisen's observation that Newark had a "community problem, not just a housing problem," Filer summed up the Aetna attack on the decaying Asylum Hill. "We aimed for revitalizing the total fabric. The problem isn't really inadequate housing; it's inadequate income. If you fix the society so that people become income-producing, the housing will follow."

An interim shortage of low-income housing certainly seems like an acceptable price to pay for the general revitalization of a community, for the simple reason that such a revitalization brings more good to more people, eventually, than a maintenance of the status quo. The displacement of people, then, can be seen as a reasonable short-term cost that has to be incurred to fuel a process that eventually benefits everybody—even those who have been displaced.

All such analyses derive from an essentially utilitarian ethic, which measures the total good and total bad produced by a social decision, and judges the morality of the results on the basis of net loss or gain. To most utilitarians, the creation of some homeless people is an acceptable social pain when seen within the context of widening social pleasure. This type of argument has an honorable history, and it is hard to argue with the mathematics, but it leaves unanswered the question of what is to be done with, or for, the recipients of that "acceptable" pain.

I do not pretend that there are simple answers to this question. But to those corporate leaders who are faced, or who soon will be faced, with the type of exciting but difficult choices described here, I would advise that utility be tempered by a glance at the oldest and still most reliable of moral queries: What if it were being done to me?

In the context of urban revitalization, of course, that question must be asked not simply by corporate leaders but by those govvrnment and community leaders whose decisions, jointly, create progress. And this is all the more imperative when the progress being undertaken stretches beyond a single city and into the broad fabric of the nation. The questions being posed here, in other words, are fundamentally social questions. They focus a business's obligations not just to local constituencies but to the society at large.

8 SOCIETY AS STAKEHOLDER Reaching the Outer Circles

Business is a major social institution that should bear the same kinds of citizenship costs for society that an individual citizen bears. Business will benefit from a better society just as any citizen will benefit; therefore, business has a responsibility to recognize social problems and actively contribute its talents to help solve them.

—Keith Davis

Today more than ever, it is important that private enterprise be committed to strengthening the nation's economic and social system. Cutbacks in federal government spending for social programs will require more effort on the part of the private sector to fill some of the resulting voids. Our considerable economic and human resources can be used to help close some of these gaps.

—Robert A. Beck
Chairman, Prudential Life
Insurance Company

The new dimension that must be observed—a new "bottom line" for business, really—is social approval. Without it, economic victory would be Pyrrhic indeed.

—Thornton Bradshaw
Chairman, RCA

Corporations that take their local communities as stakeholders face problems of authority and decision-making and social control that, as we've seen, are not always amenable to easy solutions. When the corporation expands its influence and its accountability into the wider regional or national "community," those problems are frequently aggravated, not only because their scope increases, but also because the agencies addressing them multiply, and with them the potential for conflict. Since the American business community seldom enjoys the unqualified support of Washington lawmakers, conflict arises most often when the social issues are national. The irony is that it is on precisely the widest social issues that the business community's input is most sorely required.

In examining the difficulties that arise as companies reach toward the outer circles of commitment—that is, away from the inner circles of their owners, workers, and consumers and toward groups that have no direct connection with the business—we can begin by asking why a company might make this wider commitment in the first place. We've seen that Milton Friedman and his laissez-faire colleagues deny the ethical basis of this commitment entirely. What arguments exist on the other side?

The epigraphs to this chapter reflect three of the most commonly stated positions regarding the ethical obligations of business to society at large. In the first, business professor Keith Davis, hinting at a cost-benefit analysis, calls for business involvement as a basic citizenship cost—like taxes or jury duty—that companies owe society as payment for benefits received. Logically it is clear that freeloading (profiting from a collective benefit for which you have not paid any of the cost) is simply a form of theft, and thus morally unacceptable. The corporation, then, that profits from the benefits of a healthy society—and every corporation does, insofar as it enjoys access to open markets in such a society—without contributing to its maintenance is by definition a freeloader.

Critics of this anti-freeloader argument will say that business already pays its fair share toward social improvement through its tax contributions, and that to ask it in addition to address the problems that its tax money is supposed to be addressing, is to demand a double payment that individuals are not asked for.

This objection would have more weight if, under the current tax codes, businesses were not allowed such a wide range of depreciation, investment, and other deductions as a way of lessening their tax loads. The Internal Revenue Service and the various state governments tax corporations less heavily than they would tax individuals with equivalent incomes, and for a very good reason. The assumption behind all corporate tax breaks is that they will allow the benefited businesses to pass on their good fortune to the society at large, in the form of better products, more jobs, and general business expansion. It is precisely because this feedback mechanism has not always operated effectively—because many businesses have merely hoarded the goodies, rather than passing them on—that society is calling now for more "social responsibility." If supply-side theory had worked as well as its defenders predicted it would, we would not now be hearing such a clamor for corporations to pick up where federal social programs dropped off.

Which brings us to the second argument: Robert Beck's observation that the private sector today must make up for government cutbacks by applying its "considerable economic and human resources" to the social arena. This argument for corporate social involvement, which is enjoying a vogue today, is sometimes called the "capacity argument," implying that corporations should address social problems for the simple reason that they have the capacity to do so. The argument rests on the belief that moral behavior implies affirmative duties, not just avoidance of harm.

The distinction between negative and affirmative obligations was put especially well by John Simon, Charles Powers, and Jon Gunnemann in their 1972 book, *The Ethical Investor*. In that book they also devised a version of the capacity argument that they called the "Kew Gardens principle," named for the section in New York City where, in 1960, a young woman named Kitty Genovese was stabbed to death within sight and hearing of her neighbors. Michael Rion, Powers' former fellow manager for corporate responsibility at Cummins Engine, explains the principle this way:

> We tend to assume that in a case like that of Kitty Genovese, people should have helped. Who would disagree? But can we draw out characteristics from that case that would provide general guidelines for when help is morally required? The Kew Gardens principle says that when four conditions hold, and the more they hold, the more you have an obligation to go to the aid of another. The four conditions are need, proximity, capability, and last resort.

Applying this principle to the supposed obligation of businesses to address the needs of society, we can see that three out of the four conditions are easily met. There's little question today that, with or without Reaganomics, society has severe unmet needs, that businesses are close enough to those needs to address them, or that they have the capability—the "economic and human resources"—to do so. The sticking point is "last resort," and the whole supply-side vs. welfare-state debate today can be seen as an elaboration of the question of who—the private sector or government—is really the last resort for people in need.

Rion, while acknowledging that this is a sticky issue, counsels error on the side of overreaction rather than caution. "Since it's so easy to say 'Let somebody else do it,' it's better to let the benefit of the doubt get you involved than the other way around." That won't necessarily tell either an individual or a corporation how to react in a given situation, but it does provide "some categories to hang on to." The value of using those categories at a time when the federal safety net is shrinking should be obvious to even the staunchest supply-sider.

The third argument for corporate social involvement is essentially the "enlightened self-interest" argument. When Thornton Bradshaw identifies "social approval" as a new dimension in today's business, he is not simply referring to current heightened expectations, but harking back to one of the earliest recognized facts about the corporation: that it is a creature of society, and exists at society's pleasure. And since society's pleasure today clearly includes an increase in private-sector response to social problems, corporations that ignore the public mood on this issue risk incurring society's wrath.

Those who are accustomed to viewing the corporation as an unassailable behemoth with scant accountability to anybody but shareholders will see this risk as negligible. Business professionals will not agree. Davis and Blomstrom state their "Iron Law of Responsibility" as follows: "In the long run, those who do not use power in a manner which society considers responsible will tend to lose it." And Douglas Sherwin, in a provocative article on the ethical roots of the business system, acknowledges that the corporate free-enterprise strategy, which disallows most extra-economic involvement, is constantly being reviewed:

> Society always has this strategy on trial; it continually compares it with alternative strategies for securing economic good and monitors it for negative effects that business's economic behavior might have on other social goods it values. The signs are that society is nowhere near satisfied with business performance, governance, leadership, or values.

In the area of social involvement, that dissatisfaction is blatant. In the middle of President Reagan's first term, a Harris survey investigated people's views of private-sector response to social problems. By approximately a three-to-one margin Americans felt corporations were doing less than they should be doing in the areas of unemployment, education, and aid to the handicapped, elderly, and poor. The lesson is an old one. Corporations today may have to begin picking up more of the "social improvement" tab not to court public favor but to avoid its disfavor; a combination of the Kew Gardens principle and public outcry may force more of them to be good Samaritans.

Whether you favor the anti-freeloader argument, the capacity argument, or the appeal to enlightened self-interest, the question is how to direct proponents of corporate social involvement so that they generate the most *effective* use of economics and resources. Deciding where and how to direct these resources involves asking numerous anterior questions. Assuming your resources are not unlimited, how do you decide for one social project as against another? What areas of social disease ought the supposed curative of corporate attention attack first? Precisely what kinds of help—money, people, or a mixture—should corporations be giving to their most distant stakeholders?

All these questions were raised in the previous chapter, and I raise them here again to suggest that, rather than being distinct constituencies, the local and the national "communities" can be seen as elements of the same social continuum. The differences between corporate involvement with these two stakeholder groups are differences in scope and social management, not in the nature of the problems addressed. Indeed, as I mentioned in assessing the problems of the inner city, the problems of local (and especially urban) communities today *are* the major social problems of the nation at large.

Different corporations define different areas of interest with regard to these problems, but most progressive firms seem to agree that at the heart of our current social disequilibrium is chronic unemployment—and that this condition is intimately linked to a lack of appropriate education and skills training for America's "underclass."

Most of the business leaders I spoke to recognize this unsettling concatenation of joblessness and lack of preparation as a dangerous double-edged sword. Aetna's John Filer calls inner-city structural unemployment "this society's Achilles' heel." Control Data's William Norris champions computer-based education as a necessary tool for creating "a society that provides equitable access to education and training for all people," including those in low-income areas. And Robert Gudger, vice-president of the Xerox Foundation, which budgets nearly 40 percent of its funding toward education, pinpoints the link between "no jobs" and "no skills" very clearly. "The problem," he told me, "isn't unemployment. It's *unemployability*. Increasing people's ability to take on the new types of jobs being created has to be a basic component of any attack on unemployment."

Gudger's observation grows out of a recognition that the entire structure of work is now in transformation, a transformation which Paul Hawken has aptly described as the shift from a mass economy to an informative economy, and which has been less subtly (and less accurately) described as the shift from an industrial to a service base. The vaunted high-tech industries are only the cutting edge of the current labor revolution, for we are witnessing a shift from manual to cybernetic, from volume to quality, from routine to innovation, at all levels of the economy and in all industries. The dilemma of the chronically unemployed is that the number and types of jobs for which they are already prepared are rapidly becoming extinct.

But is this business's problem? Do corporations have an ethical obligation to shepherd the chronically unemployed—or anybody else, for that matter—through the brambles of the current transformation? I would say yes, for two reasons.

The first reason is based both on ethical utility and on the injunction against doing harm that we've identified as the basic "negative" ethical obligation. American business, as the chief architect of the developing informative economy, has necessarily put certain members of society at a disadvantage and others out of work, or at the least blocked their access to work by eliminating whole classes of jobs. Although nobody set out do to this—job elimination is an unfortunate by-product of the ongoing transformation—major corporations may still fairly be characterized as being responsible for the resulting pain. Should they not assume a countervailing responsibility to alleviate it?

The issue seems clearer if we consider the ethical responsibility of a single employer who, through no direct "fault" of his own, must lay off a single employee. Say I employ someone in a factory for twenty years, then automate that person's job, and am required to let him go. What, if anything, is my duty to that long-time contributor to my business?

We've seen that at companies like IBM, Hewlett-Packard, Delta, and other firms that take steady employment as an ethically desirable goal, it is considered imperative to stand by "family" members in hard times as well as good ones. At these companies, retraining, relocation, and sharing the burden of work reduction are taken not as extraordinary or beyond the call of duty but as part of the basic ethical obligation that the business has to its employee stakeholders.

If we extend this picture to the working society at large and see business as to some degree a generic employer of a population-wide work force, then does not business in general have an obligation to buffer the shock of unemployment and underemployment for those members of the work force whose (real or potential) jobs are being phased out by Progress?

There may be an objection that while a business may owe something to its own people, it owes nothing at all, except in a purely mystical sense, to those members of society whom it has never employed. However, this defense fails to account for one quite glaring inequity. What we call corporate America today was built with many tools, not the least of which was the sweat of manual labor. I phrase the inequity as a question: Is it just that the sons and daughters of former managers should profit from this combined effort, while the sons and daughters of former laborers (who far outnumber the others) should be rewarded with a bread line?

That is the first argument for corporations becoming involved in heightening the "employability" of potential workers. The other argument is more practical. It is that if corporate America does not attend to its "Achilles' heel," it will sooner or later find itself even more isolated and despised than it is now—and will find itself eventually in the middle of a social cataclysm in which it cannot do business at all.

Santayana's most famous observation—that those who ignore their history are condemned to repeat it—is relevant here. A hundred years ago, the United States was sharply and bitterly divided into what social reformers called "two nations": one of top hats and Delmonico dinners, another of child labor, tenement housing, and the fourteen-hour day. We are unlikely to reproduce that condition today, because the middle class has long intervened. But there are signs that the middle class is dying, and even if it survives, the nation is again being divided, this time into a nation of information-literate employables and another of the structurally forgotten. The outcome of the 1880s division was the most destructive class enmity this country has ever seen. If American companies today wish to avoid a repetition of that nightmare, they would do well to look to the underclass not as an inconvenient blot on the escutcheon of Progress, but as the most needy of society's stakeholders, whose economic evolution is in everyone's best interests—not least of all the corporation's.

To operate efficiently, businesses need skilled employees to create their goods and services, customers with enough money to purchase them, and a social environment that is stable enough to allow the transactions to go on. All three of these ingredients depend to some degree on an educational structure that is responsive to changing social conditions, and for this reason education—education for productivity, for purchasing power, for social harmony—is (or should be) of paramount interest to business leaders.

Many of the more progressive American firms have long recognized this fact. William Norris's Control Data is in the forefront in this area, for a solid business reason: CDC manufactures precisely the high-tech, sophisticated goods and services that can hasten the transformation from a mass to an informative economy. Norris's own pet project, the PLATO computerized education system, is specifically designed to educate for this new economy those who previously have been denied access. Another CDC program, Fair Break, utilizes PLATO technology to prepare the disadvantaged young to find employment; not coincidentally, it "benefits industry by enlarging the pool of skilled, dependable workers."

But the thrust toward enhancing employability is evident in many other companies as well, including many that have no direct tie-in with education. Many of them target a substantial portion of their funding to retraining and higher education, particularly for minority people.

Pillsbury, for example, gave 23 percent of its $4.2-million contribution budget in 1984 to education. The insurance giants Aetna and Prudential contributed about one-quarter and one-third, respectively, of their 1983 foundations funding to education; if you add in the money given to urban minority assistance, the figure rises to about 45 percent for both firms. Of the $10.5 million Kodak gave away in 1981, 47 percent went to education. Exxon and Atlantic Richfield, generally acknowledged to be the most socially alert of the giant oil companies, also contribute heavily to education. At ARCO, aid to education accounted for 32 percent of the 1983 foundation budget. Well over half of Exxon's 1983 contributions were to educational institutions, and the corporation also maintains a separate Education Foundation, which in the same year disbursed over $27 million on its own.

In donating so heavily to education, these firms acknowledge that enhancing educational chances for all people has become a fundamental element of progressive business enterprise. It is worth repeating that such enterprise remains firmly self-serving, no matter how richly it enhances the field for others. We are now in a crisis situation in this economy. But as Davis and Blomstrom point out in another context, the Chinese ideograph for "crisis" is an amalgam of the ideographs for "danger" and "opportunity." Business has a unique opportunity today to prove the Golden Rule in practice by contributing, either through direct philanthropy or through investment, in education-based employability. That opportunity—as the Golden Rule implies—can rebound to benefit the giver as well as the receiver. The ultimate social outcome—a more open, more mobile economy—can only help business itself. That, both on and beyond the bottom line, may be the most persuasive reason to reach toward the outer circle's needs.

Employability may be the most severe dilemma confronting our society today, but it is clearly not the only one. Nor are corporate responses to social issues on the broad national scale limited to the contributions and investment policies just described. One other area in which business can, and increasingly does, address society's stakeholder needs is that of minority advancement, and I want to look briefly at this area since it sharply focuses the opportunities (and the dilemmas) that face corporations when they take on broader social issues.

We do not need to review the lamentable history of race conflict in this country or to document the ubiquity of discrimination, both within corporations and outside. I take it as beyond reasonable argument that blacks and other minorities have been wronged in the past, and that in many cases they are still being harmed by both cumulative and current effects of racial prejudice. Since they are being unfairly harmed, their treatment is by definition unethical, and ought to be corrected. But how? What ethical choices must a corporation make in order to offset the effects of past discrimination and honor this society's stated goal of achieving equality of opportunity?

Progressive businesses, following the spirit as well as the letter of the 1964 Civil Rights Act, have tackled this problem head on on both external and internal fronts. Externally, they have encountered relatively little resistance, because the techniques they have taken to address the social issue of discrimination externally are merely extensions of conventional business practices. I mean the conscious attempt on the part of several corporations to purchase from minority suppliers and invest in minority businesses. Nobody complains when 3M is cited for record purchases from minority suppliers, when Aetna deposits millions of dollars at below-market rates in minority banks, or when Control Data establishes a Community Venture Fund licensed by the Small Business Administration as a Minority Enterprise Small Business Investment Company. Minority purchasing and MESBICs are widely considered legitimate uses of corporate power as a means of effecting a socially desirable outcome.

Internally, though, the use of such power is viewed with some misgivings, and not infrequently is considered ethically inappropriate, at least by those who feel themselves adversely affected by the "socially desirable outcome." Corporate attempts to do the "right" thing in this area are continually bedeviled by competing claims, and nowhere does the issue of conflicting stakeholder claims come to a greater head than in the area of affirmative action.

Virtually every large company today has an affirmative action program, and virtually all the firms discussed in this book administer that program aggressively, through a department or office at the vice-presidential or other high managerial level. Except for the occasional Neanderthal, nobody in business today questions the propriety of such departments or doubts that, as a general rule, corporations ought to be involved in enhancing job opportunities for groups that have hitherto been neglected. Problems do arise, however, in specific cases—and particularly at the shop-floor level.

Consider a typical scenario. Suppose you manage an engineering department in which a single opening occurs for a qualified electrical engineer. Your company is committed to affirmative action, and indeed a stated company policy is that managers such as you will be judged on their effectiveness in "increasing the proportionate representation of minorities." (The wording here is from a Polaroid company pamphlet, but it is typical of most progressive firms.) Like most managers, you take that to mean that you should aim for an unwritten percentage quota so that your company's racial mix approximates that of the society at large.

After reviewing several applications, you are left with the two engineers you consider best qualified, and must make a choice between them. One applicant is black and the other is white. The only real distinguishing characteristic between them is their color. Following the preferential hiring and promotion spirit that is implicit in affirmative action law, you veer toward the black engineer. But is this fair to the equally well-qualified white applicant? Isn't this a case of compounding rather than correcting a social evil—an example of what conservative writer Nathan Glazer calls "affirmative discrimination"?

As numerous court cases have indicated, these questions cannot be easily resolved, and certainly not definitively settled, in or out of court. The problem is one of balance. Managers and companies faced with similar choices are being asked to weigh the presumed long-range good of black advancement against the obvious and immediate harm done to individual white applicants who lose opportunities for the patently unjust reason that their skin is the wrong color. Is this fair? Or, to phrase the question in utilitarian terms, is the pleasure worth the pain?

Considering the nearly incalculable harm that has been done to American society by institutionalized negrophobia, it is difficult to deny that *any* improvement for blacks, whatever the cost to discriminated-against whites, is going to be a change for the better. The utilitarian hope in this area would be that over a period of time, as more and more minority groups are "preferred" over the historically dominant group, a social balance will be achieved, and that social harmony in general will be improved. Considering the potential vindictiveness of the human species, that is a debatable proposition, but it remains an honorable ideal. Corporate policies that move the society closer to that ideal must, at least in utilitarian terms, be judged as basically moral.

But there is no denying that, in non-utilitarian terms, affirmative action creates moral problems. The basic argument of the Kantian purist here—and of those self-serving individuals who hide behind a Kantian banner—is that, for the sake of consistency, discrimination against whites must be condemned as fervently as discrimination against blacks. It's the old "Two wrongs don't make a right" argument, and very difficult to assail. The only way it can be assailed, I think, is to acknowledge that in certain admittedly muddy areas, "two wrongs" may be the least disagreeable of available moral positions. Since *someone* has to suffer every time one appliiant is chosen over another, is it not morally preferable for the sufferer to come from a group that has traditionally been preferred than from one that has traditionally been abused? Might not this admittedly imperfect justice be better than no justice at all?

In opting for affirmative action and preferential hiring and promotion, though, we still need to observe a couple of qualifying guidelines to ensure that the system is not abused by well-meaning but fallible managers.

First, preference must not be extended so far that unqualified or poorly qualified minority candidates are chosen over qualified whites. This is as much a practical as an ethical consideration. A preference system that admitted to responsible jobs people who could not handle the work would, very rapidly, self-destruct. Such a system would ultimately frustrate everybody: the white worker denied employment or promotion in spite of his qualifications, the black worker promoted or hired too quickly to the level of his or her incompetence, and (not least of all) the shareholders whose assets would be mismanaged by ill-prepared personnel. No company has an obligation to make itself substantially less productive or less efficient as a way of achieving racial balance; that would be a clear violation of its principal charge, which is to manage the owners' money well.

Second, each choice must be made not in blind allegiance to the affirmative action principle—and far less in allegiance to a quota—but on the basis of its own merits and attendant confusions. This may seem too obvious to mention, but there is a danger that as affirmative action takes hold throughout corporate life, unimaginative managers will use it to simplify hard choices, under the erroneous impression that preference to minorities is an absolute rather than a contingent principle. Assuming all candidates for a job or a promotion are approximately equally well qualified, ethics cannot *dictate* in any given instance the hiring of one over another. It can merely suggest to people in positions of power that, other things being equal, a long-term hiring and promotion policy should include the goal of proportionate representation of minorities.

The most aggressive of affirmative action proponents might object to these qualifications on the grounds that since blacks have been systematically "put back" for so long, it is only simple justice for them to be pushed forward now—even when they are not equally qualified. I've already suggested why this argument seems to me untenable: Pushing the unqualified forward in this way would rapidly sap any business concern of its fundamental strength, its people's expertise. And without that, nobody would be better off.

But the objection points to a wider concern: the fact that in this area, as in all social areas, the problem is not uniform, but multiple—and so its solutions must be multiple too. Blacks have not been discriminated against historically because of the ill will of occasional employers, and they cannot be upgraded today by focusing on job opportunities alone. Again a holistic approach is called for. Affirmative action will become a vital reality only when it is seen as part of a package deal that includes improved education, retraining, and urban revitalization—the wide range of social issues we've been discussing in this and the previous chapter. And in all these areas, as many business leaders point out, the corporate community has a valuable role to play.

A final disheartening note. Even with the qualifications I've defined, affirmative action is going to be resented by a significant proportion of the American people, for the quite sensible reason that they perceive themselves as being harmed. Convincing these disaffected people—the many Bakkes of the world—that preferential treatment for blacks is in *their* long-term best interest is one of the greatest challenges facing our society today.

The managers in the progressive firms I spoke to seemed largely unsympathetic to my observation that advancement of minority employees might create resentment among those not advanced. I asked many of them whether or not, in their notably progressive companies, they had perceived internal problems with affirmative action. The response of William Brooks, secretary of the Prudential Foundation and himself a minority member, was representative. The Pru, he told me, struck him, when he first arrived there, as "a United Nations operation," because of the diversity of racial and ethnic groups. Yet nobody seemed to resent this plurality. "You get ahead here because you earn it, and for no other reason." And everybody understands that fact.

The implication—that there is no perceived contradiction at the Prudential between merit advancement and affirmative action—is one that I received from managers in virtually every organization I contacted. Unfortunately this perception of harmony is not shared by many members of the American work force. Anyone who has spent more than five minutes in a blue-collar bar knows that resentment against minorities for "taking white jobs" is widespread and intense. It may not surface—especially at places like the Pru—on the managerial levels, but at the wage-earner level may be no less severe today than it ever has been in our history.

Whether or not there is a clear "responsibility" to society in this area, the area of working class racial tension is one in which the example of responsible companies can do immeasurable good. It seems beyond question to me that the advancement in business of the single most severely deprived group in American society will, in the long run, prove beneficial to everybody in that society—even those white workers who initially feel the brunt of the advance. The more truly pluralistic, the more truly mobile, the more truly open for opportunity the wider society is, the better the chances for everyone to profit from industry and merit. The trick for business and government is in getting Archie Bunker to understand that, to see that his short-term loss is eventually his, and everybody else's, gain.

Currently, two conditions block the dissemination throughout the working class of the attitudes in place at the Pru's (and other firms') top echelons. First is the racialist bias that has plagued every chapter of our history, and that remains the single most formidable obstacle to the creation of true pluralism. Second is the shortage of jobs: that cyclical systemic nemesis that has always aggravated interracial turmoil and that, as the economy moves toward high-tech, becomes more and more an issue of race.

Again we reach an unavoidable conclusion: While the problems may be felt as piecemeal, the solutions must be holistic. Seeing housing as distinct from education, seeing discrimination as distinct from jobs, makes no sense in the real world. The hidden lesson of the MESBICs and of affirmative action is that only by a concerted effort on the part of both the private and the government sectors can *any* social problem be resolved.

The same observation could be made about any other presumably isolable social issue. I have focused here on employability and discrimination because they highlight with particular severity the ethical and practical difficulties involved in corporations meeting social needs. But there are obviously many other social problems that businesses can and do profitably address.

The rising cost and bewildering technologization of health care, for example, put severe pressure on the society, especially for the elderly and poor. The Robert Wood Johnson Foundation, largely funded by J&J, has been focusing for five years on cost-containment research and on providing care to the homeless and elderly. But many other businesses with no obvious business interest in more efficient health services are also involved in this area. Exxon devotes nearly one-fifth of its contributions budget to support of hospitals and health and welfare organizations. The Prudential Foundation, as a conscious response to federal cutbacks, has set up a special fund for local and regional health planning, and also funds health screenings for the elderly at hundreds of local health fairs.

Several of Control Data's subsidiary companies are involved in producing technology designed to simplify and contain costs in the hospital industry. In addition, in a move that is a bit surprising for a firm so committed to the profitable delivery of essential services, CDC also built a medical facility on the Rosebud Sioux reservation in South Dakota—a pilot project that the company hopes will help them "develop marketable programs to meet health care needs in other isolated rural areas and decaying inner cities."

Another broad area of mounting involvement by corporations is that of environmental "health care." One of the unfortunate by-products of rapid industrialization has been the gradual depletion of natural resources, including nonrenewable energy sources, and widespread pollution of air and water. In the wake of the ecological outrage of the 1970s, business attitudes toward these social problems have been changing quickly; impelled (sometimes unwillingly) by public and government pressure, business leaders are coming to recognize that unless the corporate sector attends quickly to its potentially negative impact on the ultimate stakeholder, the planet, responsibilities to all other groups will be of no avail.

To be sure, overall progress in this area has been slow, and has not been encouraged by the present administration. Nevertheless, progressive corporate leaders are acting on the understanding that such externalities as pollution and energy depletion are a legitimate societal concern, and one that business has a duty to address. John Deere, for example, maintains a corporate commitment to "building new facilities with the total environment in mind," and construction on its plant in Davenport, Iowa was begun only after intensive study of the effects the building would have on the surrounding area. The company in effect required its own environmental impact statement designed to head off damage before it could occur. Installation involved such protective measures as an area waterway check and a computerized space heating system that eliminated the need for sulfur dioxide controls.

The J.C. Penney Company has been involved for over a decade in energy conservation and recycling in its hundreds of operating facilities. Between 1973 and 1984, the company cut its energy consumption by over 50 percent, and in 1983 it reclaimed over 30,000 tons of waste paper and other recyclables; its assessment of corporate responsibility in this area acknowledges that this reclamation represented a savings "economically as well as environmentally."

Among the giant oil companies, the Atlantic Richfield Company (ARCO) has always stood out as particularly sensitive to environmental problems. The principal goal of its environmental protection policy is to "manage its operations with diligence and an awareness that its goal is to protect the environment by employing the best control mechanisms, procedures and processes which are proven technically sound and economically feasible." At ARCO that is not just eyewash. Kirk Hanson, a Stanford business professor whom the company asked to critique its own performance, pulls no punches in identifying problem areas: His mention of ARCO subsidiary Anaconda's labor problems, and of the company's slowness in integrating women into professional levels, are published in the company's own literature. But on balance, Hanson finds ARCO is managing its responsibilities well. Company officials, he points out, "are willing, amidst pressures to maximize profitability, to approve substantial expenditures for environmental control and community impact programs."

In the early 1980s those expenditures have been directed at such projects as the replanting of grasslands affected by mining, the construction of double-hulled tankers to minimize the risk of leakage or rupture, and the study of biologically sensitive areas on both the Atlantic and Pacific coasts as part of contingency planning in the case of an oil spill. Those who see the Seven Sisters as indistinguishable grasping leviathans might see this as mere window dressing, but few business observers agree. Milton Moskowitz observes that ARCO "often breaks ranks with the rest of the industry"—as for example, on the oil-depletion allowance and the windfall-profits tax issues. And one respected research organization, the New York-based Council on Economic Priorities, gives the company high marks on environmental management. In a 1976 CEP study, ARCO's refineries were determined to be the most attentive of all the oil companies to problems of emission control.

ARCO is willing to spend money on environmental control, and to do so without being forced by Washington, for the same reason that J&J is willing to fund health research, or any progressive company is willing to invest in minority programs that upgrade the skills of a potential new generation of workers. The reason is that it is as practical as it is "ethical" to do so. In an era of shrinking government, business becomes uniquely well suited to address those societal dilemmas that threaten the business environment itself. A business community in this decade that refuses to go beyond the bottom line will soon find itself part of a society where the bottom line itself is imperiled. Taking society as the final stakeholder, then, becomes a kind of insurance.

The real question for business today is systemic. It is much wider than the old-line, dollars-and-cents question that satisfied business leaders in the nineteenth century. The question the corporate community is now being asked to address is "What kind of a society do you want to live in, to do business in?" If the answer is "an open, progressive society, with ample opportunities for success and minimal social discord," then corporate leaders really have no choice but to pick up where government is leaving off.

What kind of a society do you want to live in? I discussed that question with Aetna manager Robert Roggeveen, and got some illuminating answers.

Many conservative business people, he acknowledged, resist the kinds of social involvement that Aetna supports. Why? The answer may have a lot to do with conflicting social ideals, with differences in the "kind of society" that the bottom-line camp seems to want, and the one that the more progressive business leaders are eager to encourage. "We believe," Roggeveen said, "that a more open, more mobile, ultimately more *democratic* society is a better one for all concerned. We're anxious to support social projects that nourish diversity and debate, as well as those that address people's physical needs, because we're convinced it's in the country's best interests for us to do so."

Sometimes such support for diversity can lead a company into peculiar situations. A short time ago, Roggeveen pointed out, the Aetna Life and Casualty Foundation gave a $12,000 grant to the legal defense and education fund of the National Organization of Womee so that it could study discrimination against women in public education. This same NOW fund is mounting a massive campaign against the insurance industry over risk classification of women—a campaign to which Aetna is strictly opposed, and which it is fighting with considerable money and resources. It may seem absurdly self-defeating for Aetna to be supporting its own bitter enemy, but Roggeveen sees the picture in a wider focus.

"It's like what Hegel called Greek tragedy," he told me. "A confrontation of two rights. Just because we disagree with NOW on risk classification doesn't mean that we question the importance of their work in trying to create a more equitable society, for men and women alike. We dispute their interpretation of 'equitable' in this case but continue to honor the principle of equity itself. So it's the old story of defending to the death somebody else's right to be wrong. Which is what democracy is all about."

Roggeveen is not saying (and I am not saying) that those opposed to corporate involvement in society are anti-democratic, or that corporations have an ethical obligation to fund their critics' attacks. I bring up the NOW example as a benchmark to indicate how, in a company that Roggeveen calls "principle-driven," caring for society as stakeholder can be seen as a higher priority than the immediate profit or prestige of the business. I mention it to illustrate too that when social health is taken as a guiding principle, short-term losses can be more easily justified, and even reconciled with the long-term good of the firm.

Roggeveen is not blithe about those losses. There are obvious costs involved, he says, in building a more democratic society. "If you believe in increasing democratization, it means you're going to have less power. We're saying that's all right." Just as John Deere says it's all right to spend more than the government demands on pollution control. And as Control Data says it's all right to build in high-risk northern Minneapolis. In every case where a business expends time or personnel or money in meeting a societal need, it runs the risk of overextension—and thus of wasting its owners' assets. More and more in socially conscious businesses, however, this risk is being taken as an acceptable business calculation.

There is nothing particularly noble or self-sacrificing about this development, for as society increasingly wants the private sector to address its unmet needs, the private sector has always needed a healthy, active society in which to perform its economic function. Reaching toward the outer circles, then—whether it means reforming the civil justice system or employing the handicapped, sheltering the homeless or cutting back on smokestack particulates—should be seen as part of a multifaceted private-sector enterprise of coordinating growth and stability within an increasingly diversified social structure.

In the long term that enterprise will surely not weaken the bottom line, but rather extend it and give it strength. Speaking of corporate giving as "a businesslike investment," Kodak chairman Walter Fallon makes the point well: "The financial contributions we make are investments in the future of society. They are designed to produce dividends for us all." And Aetna's Geraldine Morrissey, reflecting on her colleague Roggeveen's call for a mixture of self-interest and other interests, suggests this reasonable synthesis: "Being for yourself depends on others. What the spirit of public involvement does is to recognize that interdependence."

Part III

Problems and Prospects

9 A SIXTH STAKEHOLDER? Fairness in the Field

It is the intention of Pitney Bowes to compete vigorously for business, based on the strength of its offerings to customers, not on any real or perceived deficiencies on the part of its competitors. Legal, as well as ethical and moral considerations, dictate that competitive marketing activities be conducted fairly and honestly.

—"Business Practice Guidelines"
Pitney Bowes

In [a free] economy, there is one and only one social responsibility of business—to use its resources and engage in activities designed to increase its profits so long as it stays within the rules of the game, which is to say, engages in open and free competition, without deception or fraud.

—Milton Friedman

Intemperate critics of the Friedman thesis sometimes deride the minimalist approach to corporate responsibility as a sanction for subverting the game. If a business owes nothing to anybody but its stockholders, they say, then anything goes—or at least anything that can be written in black ink. Under the "profits first last and always" doctrine, avarice and guile go unchecked, and lead inevitably to marketplace bloodletting—a Hobbesian war of all against all that cries out for government control.

But this reading of Friedman is unfair. It ignores a small but significant proviso: the observation that the system only works when the "rules of the game" are preserved, that is, when competition is unpolluted by those basic moral errors, deception and fraud. Because of this proviso, it is perfectly possible to accept the Friedman thesis and yet be ethically opposed to such abuses as false advertising, unsafe working conditions, and the padding of expense accounts.

The proviso becomes even more useful as a check when we consider the practices that are most commonly cited as proof that business and ethics don't mix. When people espouse what De George calls the Myth of Amoral Business, they often find their "evidence" in cases of executive "wheeling and dealing." Since the scandal-rich 1970s, the wheeling and dealing has been most frequently seen as an untrammeled propensity to cheat, and specifically to secure unfair advantage by the use of expensive gifts, kickbacks, and bribes.

Thanks to the exposes of the last decade, nearly everyone in business is now convinced that under-the-table money is "wrong." This in itself is no small accomplishment, considering that for centuries before the scandals, grease and speed money in many businesses was thought of as simply a way of doing business. But it is not so clear *why* it is wrong. To phrase the question in terms of the "obligations to stakeholders" model that I've been using, who is the wronged stakeholder here?

I will go into the question of bribery a little later in the chapter. Now I want to put forward an unconventional proposition, one that both suggests why we find bribery offensive and raises other, more searching questions about the nature of capitalist enterprise.

The proposition is that, to the five stakeholder groups already discussed, we add a sixth constituency: *competing businesses.*

I'm aware that many business professionals would consider the competition the antithesis of a constituency and would be puzzled by the implication that a business "owes" something to its rivals. Yet only by taking the competition as a sixth stakeholder can we understand why bribery and various other offenses are repugnant to so many people. In this chapter I want to show three things: One, that competing firms do have moral claims on a business. Two, that these claims are widely, if not consciously, recognized. And three, that if they are *not* honored, free enterprise itself becomes threatened.

The reluctance of many business people to think of competitors as stakeholders can be demonstrated by reference to the accepted wisdom on a topic that has been much in the news in recent years: the problem of insider trading. What ethical difficulties are involved when a corporate employee privy to advance information about a stock issue, merger, or other company action uses that information for private gain? The SEC, of course, is strictly opposed to such profiteering, but that does not make it immoral. Is anyone really *harmed* by this common practice?

John A.C. Hetherington, assessing corporate social responsibility to stockholders a dozen years ago, articulated a negative response to this question. Writing in the *Journal of Contemporary Business*, he said:

> Trading by insiders on the basis of nonpublic information injures no one—what causes injury or loss to outsiders is not what the insiders knew or did; rather, it is what they themselves did not know....The purpose of imposing liability on insiders for trading on insider information is not to compensate outsiders for loss; rather, it is to discourage behavior which is considered unethical.

The question, of course, is *why* it is considered unethical, and that is a question that the artificial distinction between "what the insiders knew" and what the outsiders "did not know" fails to clarify. The view expressed here, that insider trading is merely benign finagling, does not fit the facts, for as Hetherington himself acknowledges, outsiders are injured by this practice. It is precisely because they are injured that the practice is morally suspect.

We can define the moral problem more clearly if we agree that for a business transaction to be considered ethical, all parties to the transaction must enter it freely and openly, and with enough relevant information to assess it judiciously. The requirement that no party to the transaction be a victim of (to use Friedman's terms) deception or fraud is as important when stocks are being traded as it is when goods are being purchased by consumers. The use of insider information tips the balance of awareness toward the privileged insider, thus putting at a clear disadvantage those who lack the information. De George's judgment on this case is an admirably direct one: "The use of inside information makes the transaction an unequal one, and hence an unfair one."

In the case of insider trading, the injured outsiders are other stockholders, and that is why the subject of inside tips is generally discussed in business texts under the rubric of "responsibility to stockholders." That makes sense if you think of those other stockholders as collective representatives of the company. If you think of them, however, as private individuals who are *competing among themselves* and with other stock market investors for pecuniary advantage, some interesting points arise.

Within a free enterprise system, trading in stocks, like trading in everything else, takes place within legal and moral parameters that are as much a part of the system as bid and ask calls or brokers' fees. To the Hamiltonian, those parameters must be strongly regulated, lest free enterprise turn into freebooting. To Dr. Friedman and others in the Jeffersonian tradition, the mere avoidance of deception and fraud seems both a necessary and sufficient rule of the competitive game. But to both sides of the regulation vs. laissez-faire controversy, a principal ideal remains to sustain that highest degree of "open and free competition" that is compatible with ethical fairness—however that may be construed. And here we come to the real reason that insider trading is suspect: It fouls the competitive atmosphere by in effect loading the dice—that is, by forcing certain parties competing for gain to play the game with a higher risk factor than others.

Risk is of course built into any business dealing, and I am not suggesting that it be eliminated, even if it could be. But the theory of "open and free competition" is sound only if all people competing for material gain at least start out with equal opportunity. Justice certainly does not require that all players of the stock market game end up with equal winnings. It does require that success be the result of industry, calculation, and equally distributed chance rather than privileged information.

Perhaps because of the stock-trading fiascos of recent seasons, most business professionals today seem to agree with this assessment. They seem to recognize too that the victim of this all-too-common practice is not only the unprivileged outsider but the spirit of competition itself. Without getting too mystical about that "spirit," it is reasonable to express apprehension about what Wall Street would look like if action on inside tips were permissible. Many executives in the position to profit from such liberalization are in fact doing just that.

A *Business Week*/Harris Executive Poll conducted in the spring of 1984, for example, found that an overwhelming majority of executives supported strong SEC restrictions on such deals. Two-thirds of those polled felt that the current restrictions should be maintained, and another 20 percent felt they should even be strengthened. When presented with the standard argument for reduced restrictions—that "investors would benefit because the market would reflect real values more quickly"—82 percent of the sample "emphatically disagreed." The same surprisingly high percentage condemned not just those currently illegal cases where a corporate executive profits personally from insider information, but also those currently legal cases where he or she passes that information on to someone else, and enjoys no direct advantage.

In many of the companies profiled in this book, insider trading is specifically identified as contrary to company policy. Levi Strauss, Pitney Bowes, IBM, and J.C. Penney are among the firms that spell out in their employee manuals a prohibition against buying or selling company securities on the basis of nonpublic information. To guard against possible misunderstanding of this legally sensitive issue, both Penney and IBM list typical insider scenarios to be avoided, and in both cases these include situations where the use of prohibited information concerns not just stock issues but future business developments in general.

The IBM new-employee manual "Business Conduct Guidelines," for example, prohibits stock gains based on information about IBM or about customer companies, but it also specifies, "If you have non-public information that IBM is about to build a new facility, you should not invest in land or business near the new site." In the J.C. Penney "Statement of Business Ethics," we find that an employee (Associate) makes an "improper use of Company information" by giving a neighbor company manuals that might help the neighbor in a new business. Obviously this injunction is based largely on Penney's desire to protect its own assets, but a tangential reason for the prohibition is that the manuals might give the neighbor an unfair market advantage over those "outsiders" without access to them.

You find a similar conjunction of reasons for prohibition in that complicated and frequently fuzzy area of ethical confrontation, "conflict of interest." Many large corporations today have detailed policy statements on this topic, and in many businesses the problem is drawing special, and mounting, concern. When I first wrote to corporations asking them for information about their ethical standards, I made no specific mention of conflict of interest, yet virtually everyone who responded with an ethical code included something on this sensitive area; the published codes of several companies suggest it is a dominant concern in today's ethically conscious boardrooms.

In the Procter & Gamble brochure "Your Personal Responsibility," for example, conflict of interest gets pride of place, appearing first among ten topics that P&G managers evidently feel are of ethical importance to their people. Seven pages of the Xerox personnel manual are devoted to the portmanteau subject "Business Ethics, Conflict of Interest and Illegal Conduct," while nearly half of the J.C. Penney ethics statement analyzes examples of possible conflict, including such arcane eventualities as "indirect interests and relationships" and "diversion of corporate opportunity."

There is a sound and obvious reason that corporate policy managers give so much attention to this subject. It is that conflict of interest, as usually defined, is an engagement of an employee in activities that deflect his or her attention from the best interests of the firm. The J.C. Penney policy statement on this point is as clear and comprehensive as any: "Each Associate of the Company shall avoid any activity, interest or relationship with non-Company persons or entities which would create, or might appear to others to create, a conflict with the interests of the Company." Specifically, this means that Penney discourages vested interests in competitors or suppliers, the owning of land on which a company facility might be located, and the holding of any public office involving decisions (regarding permits or zoning, for example) that might unduly favor the company, or even give the appearance of doing so.

Yet there is a curious inversion of language going on here, and it is one that is common to most of the company publications I've seen. The term "conflict of interest," as used in many of these publications and in common discourse, is really a linguistic misnomer, for it covers not just areas of real conflict but also areas where *lack* of conflict, not its presence, causes trouble. The employee of Company A who sits on the board of Company A's chief competitor is engaged in a clear-cut conflict of interest. But suppose a marketing manager for Company A sits on the board of Company B, which is Company A's chief supplier in the manager's department. When we condemn the manager for conflict of interest, we do not mean that his interests diverge, but that they do not diverge enough. A case like this one really involves a suspicious *convergence* of interest.

Ultimately, such a convergence often leads to conflict as well, because the employee who uses his company position wrongly here may be exposed to public scrutiny, and thus be judged to have harmed rather than helped his firm. The point to keep in mind is that in spite of the semantic confusion, the fundamental intent of corporate policies such as Penney's is to protect the company reputation by fusing each employee's interests with its own—and to provide detailed guidelines by which people can validate that fusion. The concern shown about the mere *appearance* of conflict—and it is a concern evident in many such publications—suggests that the ultimate villainy here is neither conflict nor collusion but the perpetration of any activity that could undermine confidence in the firm. In short, conflict of interest is immoral because it harms the primary stakeholders—the owners.

But that is only half the story. There is a second "constituent" that is harmed by conflict of interest, and, although it may not be their primary intention, the Penney and Xerox and P&G statements aim at protecting this constituent's interests as well. This other stakeholder is simply "the market" itself, composed of competing suppliers, customers—and rival firms. Avoiding conflict of interest translates on one important level as "playing fair with your rivals."

This may be surprising, but it is hardly inappropriate. As we saw in the opening chapter, business operation exists, and must exist, on a substratum of fundamental fair dealing. This substratum would be flimsy if it applied only to customers and employees and stockholders, and not to competing firms. Fairness in the field must apply to the competition as well, for the simple reason that if the competitive game is to survive at all, most firms must play by the rules. Corporate policy statements against insider trading and conflict of interest are ways of advancing that operating principle.

So are the elaborate and detailed instructions given to many firms' employees regarding the antitrust laws. At large companies like IBM and Xerox and Procter & Gamble, which may be expected to be constantly aware of the Sherman Act, these instructions derive from the basic recognition that in the area of antitrust as well as conflict of interest, Caesar's wife cannot even *look* like a whore. Procter & Gamble's basic policy is "for its employees to have no contacts with our competitors." "Be careful of your relationship with any competitor," warns the IBM guidelines manual; if a competitor so much as mentions pricing policy, costs, product plans, or marketing surveys, "you should object, stop the discussion immediately, tell the competitor firmly that under no circumstances can you discuss these matters and, if necessary, leave the meeting." Xerox gives the same advice—adding that, once you end the conversation, you should also "make a written record of your action and contact the law department as soon as possible."

The cynic might dismiss such statements as deriving not from a concern for open competition but from a paranoid fear of getting caught in the act of conspiring against it. While there does seem to be a paranoid tinge to much corporate policy on antitrust matters, that is understandable considering recent history—and in any event such self-interest, as I've pointed out earlier, is certainly not tantamount to immorality. In fact corporate pronouncements against collusion (imagined or real) with competitors seem to derive from the same conjunction of "self-interest and other interests" that Aetna's Robert Roggeveen identifies as a sound ethical motivator in business. In this area as in that of insider trading, we see policies that attempt to be fair first to the primary stakeholders, the owners, and then (and perhaps coincidentally) to all other firms in the market.

The same can be said of another Xerox policy: the innovative "No Comment" policy that the company enjoins its field representatives to adopt when questioned about competitors' products. This "iron-clad" policy is quite explicit: It bans "any comment whatsoever by Xerox personnel to customers, competitors, or any other outsider about competing copier or duplicator supplies." And it interprets "comment" with considerable latitude, to include not just overt statements but also tacit agreement to a customer's expressed reservations about competitors' supplies.

Xerox, a pioneer in this approach to avoiding possible trouble by avoiding comment, now has the company of other progressive firms. IBM counsels its people to avoid not only "false or misleading statements" (an obvious enough prohibition) but innuendo and unfair comparison as well. RCA prohibits "the dissemination of rumors or disparaging statements or other unfair action intended to damage competitors." And Pitney Bowes, which actually includes a heading "Responsibilities to Competitors" in its Business Practice Guidelines, explicitly denounces all disparagement, attempts to have potential customers cancel competitors' orders, and selling on the basis of company size rather than product quality.

The common thread in all these companies' policies is the understanding that knocking the competition, while it may most immediately harm the "knockee," carries an attendant, and more troublesome, risk of reflecting on the knocker as well. Before the No Comment policy went into effect, a Xerox publication admits, disparagement was an occasional problem—and one that always came home to roost. "When people wanted to take a fast shot at Xerox, it was all too easy to accuse our people of knocking competing copier and duplicator supplies—rightly or wrongly. Either way, Xerox was likely to wind up wearing the black hat." The IBM policy manual makes a similar point. To stress the deficiencies of the competition rather than the quality of your own product, it comments, "only invites disrespect from customers and complaints from competitors."

Sales consultant Robert Miller, whose company does business with several of the firms mentioned in this book, identifies a psychological component in such customer disrespect. "When you badmouth the competition," he says, "there seems to be an immediate decode in the customer's mind that works against you, not against the competition. The customer understands that you're really saying more about yourself than about the other guy. The immediate result is that you lose the one thing you can't afford to lose: credibility."

Stephen Heiman, Miller's partner and himself a former IBM sales executive, agrees. "When you knock the competition, it means you can only win out of somebody else's weakness. The implication is that you don't have any strengths of your own. Giving that message to a customer isn't just bad ethics; it's bad business. When I was at IBM, you got fired for doing that."

These comments reinforce the lesson that far from handicapping the ethical business person, an attention to fairness in the field may actually give him or her a long-term competitive edge. As every sprinter understands, there's far greater risk in cutting across another runner's lane than in pulling out all the stops in your own.

All of this comes into sharper focus when we consider the issue of kickbacks and bribes and the related issue of gifts given to enhance a company's market strength. I pointed out in Chapter 4 that offering associates such extras as dinner at an exclusive restaurant might be considered a reasonable use of the primary stakeholders' money, provided that the "gift" so offered actually enhanced the firm's advantage—or at least was intended to do so. But even when this condition is met, ethical problems remain when the amount being given is very large, or when it appears as a kickback or a bribe.

Judged by either a utilitarian or a Kantian standard, out-and-out bribery seems to most people to be a clearly immoral practice. A utilitarian defense of the practice is sometimes raised by people who feel that the retention of a lucrative contract by means of a bribe is worth the small impropriety if it brings pleasure to more people than it harms—if, for example, we weigh the happiness of all the workers whose jobs are saved by the contract against the minor inconveniences caused the participants, who must juggle company books to cover their tracks. But this "utilitarian" defense of the practice does not go far enough.

As Bentham insisted in his utilitarian calculus, and as De George points out in an excellent analysis of this type of case, it is not enough to measure the good and ill effects of those immediately affected by a bribe. An honest utilitarian also considers the broader societal effects, and weighs into his calculation the potential harm done to public confidence and integrity if bribery is accepted as moral. A judicious cost-benefit analysis of bribery illustrates that "once bribery is an accepted way of doing business, then people will no longer get the best for their money," but will have to settle for those goods and services that are paid for once over the table and once again under it.

De George uses essentially a utilitarian argument to show that such double payment cannot be condoned:

> If there is some doubt about whether the practice does more harm than good, we need only consider why bribery is not done openly....The obvious reason is that only a few people benefit from the practice at the expense of a great many other people and of society and business in general.

And this argument obviously is perfectly compatible with a Kantian analysis, which would condemn the practice for the simple reason that it is not universalizable—that is, that if it were widely practiced, business itself would fall apart.

But "business and society in general" comprise only one stakeholder group that is harmed by under-the-table payments. The immediate stakeholder harmed by such a practice is the group of competing firms who bid honestly and openly for contracts, and who are frustrated in their faith that everybody else is doing the same. Thus here, as in the cases of insider trading and conflict of interest, we see that business implicitly takes competitors, and the "spirit of competition" itself, as stakeholders worth defending—and condemns a practice vehemently because it subverts competitors' rights.

There is no question that business people in general do condemn the practice. And this is no recent reaction to the bribery scandals of the last decade. In both the 1961 and 1977 *Harvard Business Review* studies of reader opinions on business ethics, approximately a quarter of the respondents agreed that the principal area of offense was that of "gifts, gratuities, bribes, and call girls." In the sixteen years spanning those studies, the percentage of executives naming such practices as the top priority concern increased by only 3 percent, from 23 to 26 percent.

Virtually every company publication I have seen condemns bribery and gifts with the same enthusiasm shown in these two surveys. However, when we get down to the language of the prohibitions, problems arise that are inherent in the nature of this ethical problem.

The central difficulty is one of definition. Agreed that an out-and-out bribe is immoral because it subverts the rights of competitors and of society in general. But what constitutes a bribe? And how is it to be distinguished from casual, innocent gratuities that are exchanged between business associates every day, simply as a "way of doing business"?

A few quotations from company guidelines will indicate the stickiness of the problem.

- From the IBM booklet "Business Conduct Guidelines": "Gifts between employees of different companies range from widely distributed advertising novelties, which you may both give and receive, to bribes, which unquestionably you may not....In the case of gifts, services, and entertainment...there is a point of unacceptability. The difficulty lies in determining where that point is, unless, of course, laws make that clear."
- From the RCA policy guidelines on "Standards of Business Conduct": "No employee or representative of the Company shall make or offer to make any payment or gift...of such value that it might be construed as an attempt to influence such person in the performance of his or her duties."
- And from the Pitney Bowes "Business Practice Guidelines": "Company employees and representatives will provide no gifts, favors, or entertainment to customers except to the extent that they are in conformity with accepted business standards, with generally accepted ethical standards, and with any applicable laws."

Conformity with the law in these matters is a relatively simple matter, because the law is written out, and legal departments can be consulted in questionable instances. But, as has been pointed out frequently, the law is only a floor. The real difficulties arise in those cases where the law is being duly honored, but the transaction remains ethically arguable.

As the above representative guidelines make clear, there are two related problems here. One is in determining the *intent* of the persons involved in the transaction. The other is in determining what *amount* of gratuity transforms an acceptable gift into a kickback, payoff, or bribe.

It is easy to define in general terms what an immoral intent would be in this area. Since we have seen that business is, or should be, committed to honoring open and free competition, then activities that bend the rules ensuring such competition are de facto immoral. To offer a business associate some personal gain or advantage as an inducement to engage in a given transaction seems clearly a violation of the rules; if the transaction itself is understood to be a *precondition* of the personal gain, then we are clearly talking about bribery (if the gain precedes the transaction) or a kickback (if the reverse is true). It's not hard to see that when a person shifts the competitive edge toward his own company by offers extraneous to the deal, he is taking unfair advantage of the competition.

But there are a couple of problems here, not the least serious of which is that of terminology. What is meant by the words "understood" and "precondition" and "extraneous"? What kinds of "inducements" are to be seen as immoral, and what ones can be judged as acceptable? What about the case of a computer manufacturer who offers a major client extraordinary service terms on an initial contract? Is the manufacturer bribing the client to ensure the sale, or merely sweetening the deal? And what about the field representative who sends his best customers a bottle of scotch at the holidays? Is his action to be "understood" as an innocent gesture of friendship, or an unethical investment in future business?

One way of sifting through the problems here (or at least of diminishing their frequency) is to specify that employees receiving gifts from nonemployees not profit personally from them—and to insist on a similar "no personal profit" principle when employees give gifts to others. Penney takes this essentially hard-line approach in its analysis of gifts when it poses the example of a store manager who is offered complimentary tickets to the Caribbean by a local newspaper which annually gives this benefit to its largest advertisers. "A conflict of interest would exist," the company ethics statement decides, "if the store manager or other member of store management used the tickets personally." He could, however, use them as "prizes for a store contest or promotion." Again, the paramount interest, even in this high-minded firm, seems to be conflict of interest—the offense that disregards the right of both shareholders and the competition.

But the "no personal profit" approach, even if it could be enforced, would lead to labyrinthine uncertainties that, even if they were resolved, might disentangle the whole structure of business dealing—especially on the executive level. Imagine the shift in consciousness that would be necessary throughout corporate life to put in place an ethical system that saw every bottle of scotch as belonging unequivocally to the company whose employee had received it, rather than to the employee himself.

An idea of the flap that might ensue is illustrated by the current furor over "Frequent Flyer" coupons. The airlines that offer these "discount earned" premiums expect them to be used by the individual business flyers who have accumulated the required mileage—indeed, the coupons are officially nontransferable. Many companies that pay for the frequent flights in the first place do not agree, and it is hard to argue with their point. For an executive to earn a free personal flight to Acapulco because of his accumulated company mileage affronts both Penney's "no personal profit" rule and the principle, proposed in Chapter 4, that an ethical employee must use shareholder funds only to advance shareholder interests. Yet the airlines are standing firm, refusing to allow transferability because they feel, probably correctly, that this would reduce the incentive to fly.

The Frequent Flyer program really allows the unscrupulous executive to cheat his company twice: once when he takes unnecessary or unnecessarily long (that is, eccentrically routed) flights in order to accumulate mileage, and a second time when he receives for this accumulated mileage an individual reward for which not he, but his company, has paid.

Such chicanery may be extremely rare in a company like Penney, and indeed a review of the 1976 case in which three company officials were convicted on kickback charges suggests that it is rare, for the very good reason that when it occurs, it is dealt with harshly. Penney's own internal investigation brought the affair to light, and the company's expulsion of the offending executives was swift. But in companies with a flimsier "spiritual" base than Penney's, where small gifts and entertainment perks are de rigueur, it is hard to imagine a blanket rule against personal advantage taking hold.

Another way of addressing the problem of distinguishing between appropriate and inappropriate gifts is to tie culpability to excessive dollar amounts. This is a little more helpful, but not much. How much is excessive? Xerox, in its statement of buying policy, puts the issue this way:

> The small courtesies, the pleasantries, the kindnesses that occur between people who get on well and respect each other are all to the good. They help keep simple humanity in our business dealings. Then where do you draw the line? About here: A gift or service or consideration of any kind with a value over $10 must always be refused.

A good, clear guideline. But is it workable? Few firms would agree that it is, and I am not talking about the "bad guys" either. Many companies with as sound an ethical base as Xerox or J.C. Penney are still reluctant in today's business environment to monetize what is beyond the pale. Most progressive firms, when they consider the question of amount, resort to the inevitable weasel words: a gift, whether given or received, should not be "excessive" or "inordinate," but "nominal." Such terminology provides little help to the executive faced with accepting or refusing a twelve-dollar bottle of whiskey, but its very imprecision makes it closer to corporate reality than strict dollar prohibitions tend to be.

Moreover, the problem of determining the "proper" line between acceptable gifts and bribes can be complicated by the organizational positions of the people involved in the "transaction." Stephen Heiman, a former sales executive with IBM, a company that permits gifts of "nominal value" that are "customarily offered to others having a similar relationship with the customer," puts the problem this way:

> The issue gets very fuzzy because "appropriateness" depends a lot on expectations and the lifestyles of the people involved. It's probably all right to give a purchasing agent a bottle of scotch for Christmas—and obviously wrong to give him an entire case. But what if the recipient of the gift is the CEO of a billion-dollar company? With his earnings and expectations, the case might not be out of line. It might still be considered of sufficiently "nominal" value not to be taken as an inducement to unfair advantage. So how many bottles make a bribe?

Heiman's anecdote focuses very clearly the interlocking confusions of dollar amount and personality involved in any transfer of funds or services that are not strictly called for by contract. And it suggests with disturbing frankness the kind of ethical fluidity that exists in corporate organizations on this matter. Kant generally goes abegging here, as cases are decided on an individual basis according to the incomes, positions, and "lifestyles" of the people involved in the gift exchange.

Company publications frequently codify this very fluidity in their policy statements. In lacking those hard-and-fast rules that, as we've just seen, are largely impractical, even the most progressive firms resort to an appeal to "custom" or "common practice" or "accepted business practice," and leave the rest to good judgment. The trouble is that where good judgment is lacking, this procedure only adds smoke to the fog.

One technique for checking the fluidity is to require employees at all levels to report, in writing, any gratuities either given out or received. Strict accounting procedures in this difficult area would clearly cut down on the percentage of amenities transferred as a way of obligating the receiver rather than of expressing friendship or appreciation. Pitney Bowes and J.C. Penney, among others, do require such written notification. Obviously such a requirement serves both the shareholders, whose money is being used, and competing firms, who have a right not to lose competitive distance because someone else has greased the track.

But even this commendable practice is effective only in those cases where the accounting and legal departments, or the supervisory apparatus itself, is sufficiently attuned to the ethical problems of gift-giving to distinguish between amenities and bribes. That state of affairs is more easily defined than accomplished, and where such ethical scrutiny is not in place, the effect of relying on "accepted business practice" may simply be to pass the confusion upstairs.

The fundamental problem—that of intention—remains. Perhaps it is asking too much for corporate policies, even in progressive firms, to divine in individual cases whether someone who gives baseball tickets to a supplier is acting in good faith to create goodwill or stepping into the competitor's lane by offering the supplier an unfair "inducement" to do business. Perhaps all they can do is to put corporate employees on notice that "free and open competition" is still an ideal worth striving for, and that abuses against this principle will not be looked on lightly.

That in itself is an accomplishment. If the corporate statements I've quoted in this chapter do nothing more than sensitize employees to the fact that competitors deserve fair treatment, they will have served a major humanizing purpose. And that is in no way incompatible with a "hardball" approach to competition. An ethical stance toward the competition does not require that you let them win the game, only that you do not use tactics that you would deplore if they were used against you. On this point at least, Kant, Jesus, and Milton Friedman all agree.

10 CLASH OF VALUES Multinational Ethics

While company managements can—and in my opinion should—carry out ethical policies abroad, they must do so with due regard for local practice and sensitivities, in a flexible manner that takes account of local law and builds consent among their local partners, boards and employees rather than by exercise of a corporate sledgehammer.

—Stanley Cleveland,
Vice-president, international planning
Bendix Corporation

When I am at Rome I fast on Saturday. When I am at Milan I do not. Follow the custom of the church where you are.

—St. Ambrose's advice to
St. Augustine

Morality exists not in a philosopher's vacuum but in a social context. If sound decisions could be made using the tool of moral logic alone, ethical behavior would be a relatively simple affair. You could bring out your utilitarian calculator or consistency touchstone or golden rule, measure the choices, and act in clear good conscience, no matter what the social contingencies in the individual case. In a Kantian universe, such contingencies would be beside the point.

Not so in Kansas or Korea. In the real world, logically formal ethical judgments are constantly running into facts. Those facts, while they do not invalidate the ethical principles we have been discussing, do make their application difficult. In business, that is evident even in domestic markets. But it is more blatantly, and often more poignantly, evident when corporations do business abroad.

In the real world of human interaction, moral principle is only one of three fundamental social factors that must be taken into consideration when judging the rightness or wrongness of an action. The other two factors lack the cachet, philosophically speaking, of a Benthamite or Kantian analysis, but it is reckless, not to say impossible, to disregard them. They are on the one hand custom or tradition, and on the other hand law. These three sides of a conceptual triangle—morality, custom, and law—provide a metaphoric framework against which to assess real social decisions.

In an ideal society, the triangle would be equilateral, and the framework basically stable. Custom would enshrine those moral principles of justice and equity and fair play without which social concord is impossible. Law would codify custom. Nobody but the deranged would perceive a contradiction between personal moral inclination, traditional mores, and what the law allowed and disallowed.

In actual societies, however, the arrangement among the three sides is more delicate, and constantly shifting. Sometimes the law lags far behind ethical principle—as was the case in many "advanced" countries until the nineteenth century when slavery was still legal. Sometimes it is custom that lags behind—as was the case in the American South after 1954 when, in spite of *Brown v. Board of Education*, segregation was still widely condoned. Sometimes the three factors of judgment are conflated into an apparent but pernicious unity—as is the case today in many emerging nations, where torture and summary executions are justified by an appeal to a supposedly higher moral law espoused by the rulers.

The difficulty of reconciling law, morality, and custom can be a severe one even within a society that subscribes by and large to the same general principles. If it were not severe, those societies that are heirs of the Judeo-Christian tradition would not now be rent by factionalism over such issues as abortion, the insanity defense, and the death penalty. But the difficulty rises exponentially when the actors in a moral drama do not subscribe to the same general principles, when they must confront their ethical choices against the backdrop of clashing values.

Such a backdrop is frequently the setting for business transactions conducted abroad. Since these transactions comprise a significant amount of the total business conducted by companies based in the advanced nations—including most of the firms mentioned in this book—it is important to ask what kinds of special problems arise in a multinational context, and how they can be ethically resolved.

The public first became widely aware of problems in multinational ethics in the frothy wake of Watergate, when dozens of American corporations were discovered to have done under-the-table business with foreign officials so that their over-the-table business could prosper. For several years in the late 1970s, international bribery seemed as much a proof of the corruption of "the System" as did the CREEPing around of Mr. Nixon's "plumbers." In a typical emphasis of the time, in 1977 Brenner and Molander set up a *Harvard Business Review* study of business ethics by posing the most familiar of questions: "What would you do if the minister of a foreign nation where extraordinary payments to lubricate the decision-making machinery are common asked you for a $200,000 consulting fee?"

International bribery soon became such a cause célèbre that it eclipsed domestic skullduggery in the public eye, and became almost unilaterally responsible, in and out of the business schools, for a reassessment of corporate morality. The SEC, the *New York Times*, and the corporate community itself were in agreement that "questionable payments" to foreign officials posed a very serious problem indeed, and it is not stretching things too far to say that the current interest in business ethics grew directly out of the Lockheed and Northrup affairs. Two analysts of the Foreign Corrupt Practices Act, passed in 1977 to prevent such affairs, even conclude that the various ethical "codes, policy statements and manuals" that began to emanate from boardrooms at the time constituted a direct and immediate reaction to the bribery revelations.

Beyond the sound and the fury denouncing overseas payments as "immoral" and even "un-American," some tricky questions remained. Those questions, which are still being addressed today, concern the relationship between custom, morality, and law—a relationship, as I've said, that is continually being defined in all social and moral discourse.

As usual, the primary question is one of definition. As commonly defined in both domestic and international markets, a business bribe is something given to a person to induce him or her to influence business in the giver's favor. We saw in the previous chapter that bribery must be considered unethical because it gives undue advantage to the briber over competing firms; at the same time it distorts the rules of the free enterprise game, and so imperils competition itself. But our objection to the practice is predicated on the assumption that, in custom and in law, such inducements are generally seen as impermissible—as violations of the rules. What if that assumption is wrong? What if "open and free competition" and "fair play" as we understand them are less axiomatic than they are at home?

Although most business people seem to agree that the United States government acted rightly in banning overseas payments, a sizable minority disagrees. Their argument, which the FCPA may have muted but certainly has not silenced, speaks to the conflict between value systems that often occurs in international business and suggests that St.

Ambrose's advice is as applicable to foreign markets as it is to foreign congregations.

We condemn bribery in domestic business, they say, because it subverts the competitive process and affronts commonly agreed upon ethical strictures. But we cannot export those strictures to cultures where they would be alien. They play the game differently abroad. We must play by their rules, or lose business to those firms that do. We must abide by local customs and laws, even when doing so violates our own sense of right and wrong. To impose our standards abroad is not only arrogant; it is impractical. As high-minded as the endeavor might seem, it will eventually only lead to expulsion.

This argument sounds plausible enough, and adopting it may be innocuous when the conflict of values involves something as minor as fasting on Saturday or slipping ten dollars to a customs official to "facilitate" the processing of imports. As a practical matter, it may seem wiser to blink at such peccadillos than to bring down a puritan's "sledgehammer"—especially when the parties normally harmed by bribery, competing firms, are greasing just as many palms as you are. But there are logical and ethical difficulties in excusing questionable behavior solely on the grounds of custom and in allowing foreign practice to dictate how you will behave while abroad.

The fundamental difficulty is that, while foreign custom may be enlisted as an explanation for particular improprieties, it is quite unreliable as a *general* defense of multinational behavior. The tendency of the argument for letting custom rule is to allow the managers of the multinational concern to surrender their ethical judgment when they are abroad and to let the vox populi (or, in many cases, the vox dictatoris) tell them what is right and wrong in each context. Once managers make that fundamental tactical error, they open themselves and their companies up to an endless reign of moral blackmail. The "trivial" case of grease money, then, should be seen as the top of a very slippery slope. Once you let a single corrupt official, working under the aegis of "custom," rearrange your business ethics for you, you are wed to moral submissiveness as long as you do business in his country.

Ironically, some critics of the public outcry against venality abroad have used just this example of complicity leading to entrapment to exonerate American corporations for some of the blame in the bribery scandals. There's no question that they must share that blame with the "bribees," but some writers have gone so far as to suggest that when payment is demanded by a bribee rather than offered freely by a briber, the briber is in a "purer" moral condition than he would have been had there been no demand. Conclusion: Since Lockheed et al. were the victims of foreign government extortion, we shouldn't be too harsh on them for giving in.

Peter Drucker, in an arrestingly skeptical article on business ethics, presents the case clearly. In most discussion of payments abroad, he says, repugnance is directed at the wrong party; we should condemn less strongly the firm that pays a bribe than the person or government that demands it in the first place. "There was very little difference," he concludes, "between Lockheed's paying the Japanese and the pedestrian in New York's Central Park handing his wallet over to a mugger. Yet no one would consider the pedestrian to have acted unethically."

This argument misses a fundamental point: the fact that the consequences for noncompliance with the extortionist differ dramatically in the two cases. If the pedestrian refuses the unethical demand of the mugger, he stands to lose his life. Lockheed stood to lose the L-1011 contract. Granted that Lockheed had a moral obligation to pursue that contract aggressively to protect its workers' and stockholders' interests. But did it have the obligation to surrender exorbitant and unreported payments in order to protect those stakeholders? The SEC did not think so. Nor did the Japanese people, since the scandal resulting from the payments effectively toppled their government.

Which raises an interesting point about the plea to "custom" as a defense for international bribery. In the Lockheed case at least, American businessmen may have naively misinterpreted Japanese custom, assuming official venality to have been far more widespread and "acceptable" than it actually was; as Lockheed discovered after the uproar, the activities of the Tanaka government offended Japanese sensibilities as deeply as they would have offended American ones. Perhaps a similar misinterpretation of foreign custom was a factor in the other bribery and "questionable payment" cases of the mid-1970s. At least the case points to the unreliability of custom as a benchmark for business behavior. And it suggests that, to avoid being tripped up by its own cleverness, a multinational company would do well to take its ethical kit bag along when traveling to foreign climes.

But I do not want to put too much emphasis on the Lockheed case, because it is atypical. It has gotten the coverage it has largely because the numbers involved dwarf most others. Between 1967 and 1975, Lockheed was discovered to have given out approximately $25 million in questionable foreign payments; few of the other American firms implicated in such payments parted with more than one or two million. In addition, Lockheed had a genius for involving the most distinguished, and therefore vulnerable, of national leaders. What other multinational could match the Lockheed record of having implicated in improprieties the heads of state of four nations (Italy, Turkey, Japan, and the Netherlands)?

Most cases of international bribery take place on a much smaller scale, and though that does not really change the ethical principles involved, it does tend to lessen outrage and to make the examination of the pros and cons in individual cases a little less subject to spectacle. Speaking both practically and ethically, it's easier to justify the ten-dollar border bribe than the $10,000 greasing of a ministry. And it would be carrying moral rectitude to an extreme to suggest that the amount of a kickback or bribe had no bearing on the ethics involved.

This is tricky ground, to be sure. The same gray area that we saw operating in the cases of domestic bribes and expense accounts operates internationally with a vengeance. Especially in the area of "facilitating payments" (where a usually small amount of "speed" money is given to an official to perform a task he would have performed anyway, but more slowly) the ethical questions can be tricky. Many companies, says Clarence Walton, "do permit payment abroad when there is a recognized expediter, when the amount is insignificant, and when it is an accepted local practice." But what amount is insignificant? And how can a manager new to a foreign subsidiary tell which practices are "acceptable" and which are not?

The same difficult, and perhaps unanswerable, questions arise in cases where small gifts that would be considered beyond the pale in American culture are permitted, and even officially expected, in another. Walton explains that this situation is endemic among American firms doing business in Japan. In that country, he writes, it is "a time-honored tradition to offer small gifts when a person retires...or when an individual is promoted...or when an employee has played a significant role in completing a major event." AT IBM and GE, he points out, such gifts are considered "ethically appropriate within the Japanese culture." Yet the same type of giving would be denounced in the American press if it occurred here.

IBM and GE are not the only American firms that espouse and practice high moral standards at home and yet have trouble following them abroad. Because of the instability of the custom-law-morality triangle, progressive firms often have as much difficulty assessing what is "questionable" and what is not as anybody else. It would be against all the evidence, I think, to call Control Data or Xerox, Levi Strauss or IBM, Johnson & Johnson or Pitney Bowes, "unethical" enterprises. Yet in the 1970s all of these "good guy" firms were involved in some sort of questionable payments abroad.

Those who find business inherently corrupt will conclude from this fact that these firms are simply hypocritical. But there is a sounder, if more complicated, explanation: International business imposes special burdens of judgment on managers, because they are forced to balance not only the usual stakeholder claims but also the claims of sometimes conflicting business traditions—and to do so without the aid of a single, overlying moral code. Faced with that muddy situation, the best of us must be expected occasionally to founder.

Perhaps it is the lack of that overriding standard that is the real spoiler here. Two students of the Foreign Corrupt Practices Act, in assessing why it has failed to "clean up" multinational business, point to American domestic confusion rather than the much-touted discrepancy between our ("good") values and their ("corrupt") ones:

> There is no consensus within the United States as to what specifically constitutes ethical business behavior. Thus it was inevitable that when a law was written to export a moral standard to countries with different values and customs, the result would be even more intense confusion....The failure of the Foreign Corrupt Practices Act is grounded not only on its attempts to export an American ethic abroad, but also on the lack of a commonly agreed-upon ethic to export.

That is not to say that all "questionable payments" are alike, or that it is impossible to distinguish between honorific gifts, facilitating nudges, and bribes. It is only to suggest that in the world of international trade as in that of international politics, clarity begins at home. It may be that a diminution in exported palm-greasing may only come about after business professionals here have sorted out some of the confusion arising from such "accepted" business practices as the "thank you" tickets to the supplier or the three-martini lunch.

One possible benchmark is a negative one. The most common defense of grease and speed money is self-defense. I did it, the bribing corporate official says, to save my company's hide. In other words, no matter what you do, you cannot drop the red ball. While there is nothing wrong with such attention to company interests, the problem is in assuming that any loss of power, penetration, or effectiveness on the part of your firm is equivalent to dropping the red ball. The negative benchmark I would suggest here is for managers to take a modified approach to this attention to "company interests," and to be able to make precisely the same ethically pragmatic decisions abroad that they are constantly making at home: that they, in short, aim for reasonable growth within a complicated environment, rather than profit maximization and unlimited growth at all costs.

This may mean letting some business go. But that is not an insuperable problem. When the domestic manager who honors principles as well as profits is approached by an unscrupulous customer who demands a kickback as the price of a contract, he doesn't automatically throw up his hands and yell "Chapter 11." He lets that customer go and seeks another. The same thing can, and should, apply in international markets.

The bias toward economic growth, on both the macroeconomic and microeconomic scales, has had a quite pernicious influence on the way business is conducted. Who says that a business must grow at a minimum of X percent a year in gross sales if it is to remain viable over time? Who says that the loss of any individual contract is the death knell of any individual business—unless it is a business so badly managed that it has wed all its fortunes to one deal? Who says, finally, that all dollars are alike—that, as long as the chips roll in, it doesn't matter how the game has been played? The bias toward gaining "market share" at all costs may have done more (and may still be doing more) to undermine "open and free competition" than government regulation has ever done.

The solution is trust in the market. One of the first articles of faith for any capitalist is that the better product will capture the larger market—that the cream will rise to the top. Bribery, whether domestic or international, is an expression of bad faith with that principle. One of the great challenges, both moral and monetary, for the multinational firm today is to let the market work its magic unhindered by "influence," to see if, over the long run, the cream *does* rise to the top. It is to allow the market, and not "custom," to decide whether the combination of lesser products and greater grease will mean more or less, in the long run, than honest products honestly delivered.

Questionable payments are a factor in that segment of multinational business that precedes the signing of a contract. After the contract is signed, multinational firms continue to confront ethical difficulties, particularly in the marketing field. I want to turn briefly to that area, to see how the ethically minded manager selling abroad is confronted with slightly different choices than those that would confront him or her at home.

We have seen in Chapter 6 that a corporation has a basic obligation to sell its customers products and services that are honestly advertised and that will not harm them if properly used. In the United States this obligation is closely monitored by the federal and state governments. The ethical problems inherent in marketing products abroad—especially in the Third World—arise chiefly because there are weaker controls overseas.

The liberality of foreign governments when it comes to marketing possibilities does not necessarily lead to deceptive or dangerous practices. But the potential is there. Whatever your view of the federal regulatory apparatus, it must be admitted that the lack of such an apparatus in many Third World countries does create the opportunity for abuse by corporations less interested in distant stakeholders than in immediate profits. Some examples:

- Stung by the Surgeon General's increasingly strident warnings and anticipating a domestic market decline that never really developed, the Western tobacco giants began an aggressive marketing campaign in underdeveloped countries in the mid-1970s. Writer Albert Huebner explained in 1978 why they felt conditions for developing this new market were ideal. Governments on restricted budgets were likely to prefer the tax revenues from cigarette sales to the drain of money spent on anti-smoking campaigns. Farmers would easily be persuaded to convert their land from mere food to a hardy cash crop. "And because direct evidence of the health hazards of smoking is not yet visible in their countries," Third World inhabitants would be just as likely to lock in to "the subtle but powerful call of cigarette advertising" as did Americans in the 1960s and earlier. Thus the manufacturers of a clearly hazardous product were able to explore a vast untapped region without the noxious intrusion of the law or hostile opinion.
- Item in the *New York Times* for January 25, 1980: "The Federal Government has learned of plans by industry in the United States to dispose of poisonous wastes by shipping them overseas to developing countries...to solve the problem of disposal. Several of these countries are reportedly looking favorably at the proposal as a source of much-needed foreign exchange." So far this grotesque notion has not gone beyond the musing stage, but the thought is still instructive. And it focuses clearly the danger of a business circumventing real social problems by simply shifting its venue to an area whose people cannot afford to resist them.
- Beginning in 1968, the Swiss multinational chemical firm Ciba-Geigy distributed an insecticide called Galecron both in its host country and throughout the Third World. When the company's own internal research team and the World Health Organization agreed eight years later that its manufacture was too hazardous to continue, Ciba-Geigy pulled it off the market for two years while it tightened up safety precautions in its plants. Then, in 1978, Galecron was again available—but not in Switzerland. Told that Mexican field workers handling the compound were being exposed to exorbitantly high levels of the spray, a Ciba-Geigy spokesman blamed usage procedures and disclaimed company obligation. "We cannot be made responsible down to the last user and the last inhabitant," he said. Especially if they're not Swiss.

This last example raises two interesting, and related, questions about the marketing of various products in the Third World. First is the question of law.

"The Galecron story is not unique," a Swiss journalist wrote in 1983 for *In These Times.* "WHO estimates that every year about 500,000 people are poisoned by the 300 million kilos of pesticides that are dumped in the Third World." Chemical companies debate the figures, but nobody denies that substances that are illegal in host countries are being marketed widely in countries where the law is not so particular. For companies that operate within a democratic, mixed economy, this is at the very least a fudging of their faith in law. At worst it is profiteering from the ignorance of distant peoples whose own legal systems are failing them.

This assumes, of course, that the regulations that prohibit the marketing of Galecron in Switzerland, or of the dumping of toxic wastes in Kansas, are ethically appropriate to begin with. I am aware that many people in business do not believe them to be so. Logically enough, they see foreign marketing not as circumvention of the law but as the exercise of a legal and moral right that is being denied them at home by an unduly restrictive bureaucracy. This has become an especially popular defense of Third World penetration in our cancer-sensitive era, when the FDA is characterized by the makers of suspected carcinogens as a mere teller of tall tales that have the force of law.

The question of whether federal regulations are too severe or too lenient can only be decided on a case-by-case basis, and in many cases the judgment will not be in for many years down the road. Epidemiological studies in the early 2000s, for example, may begin to tell us whether the pushers of saccharin are right in seeing the FDA as a Nervous Nellie fan club or if the agency's extrapolation-from-rats testing method was scientifically sound in predicting human cancers. To me it seems obvious that, in the meantime, prudence dictates error on the side of the regulators—but then I am not a fan of processed foods or soft drinks, and can afford to be cavalier about additives.

But if the issue cannot be decided at this point, we can keep in mind one warning. Ethically speaking, the most hazardous course an American-based multinational can take in its marketing to the underdeveloped world is to take foreign law not as a floor but as a ceiling. To assume that whatever is legal is also moral is the coward's approach to decision-making. American history has shown repeatedly that if *all* an industry does is obey the law, it soon finds that law tightening up. It would be an economic as well as ethical tragedy to have that history repeated abroad.

The second point raised by the Galecron example is one that was also present in the most notorious multinational marketing venture of our time, the foray of Nestlé and other baby-formula manufacturers into countries whose people lacked the capacity to use their products safely. The question here is one of education. As we saw in Chapter 6, companies have an ethical obligation to give their customers adequate *information* about their products, so that they are able to use them wisely. In the Galecron case, Ciba-Geigy dutifully printed instructions on its canisters, but in many of its markets this was an empty gesture because (as Ciba-Geigy may or may not have known) most workers using the poison could not read. A similar confusion of the ethical responsibility to inform was evident at Nestlé until January 1984, when the firm, under seven years of pressure from consumer groups, finally agreed to marketing reforms.

Back at the beginning of the boycott against Nestlé, Massachusetts Senator Edward Kennedy defined the problem exactly: "Can a product which requires clean water, good sanitation, adequate family income, and a literate parent to follow printed instructions be properly and safely used in areas where water is contaminated, sewage runs in the streets, poverty is severe, and illiteracy is high?" You don't need to be much of a logician to see that the answer is no. Pushing infant formula on Third World mothers was like giving a book of matches to a child and saying "These can keep you warm."

Again the lesson is clear. Where law and custom do not adequately protect the consumer, it is not enough for a business to become a legal partner in destruction. Ethics requires more. It requires that, where people are clearly being harmed, you do better than the forces in control. Such a leadership role has been taken by American business in the past, and there is no reason it cannot be extended abroad.

Once again it's seeing the law not as ceiling but as floor. *Advertising Age*, hardly a bleeding-heart liberal publication, made just this judgment of Nestlé. "The lesson to be learned here," it said just after the boycott ended, "is that the absence of sophisticated regulatory mechanisms in the Third World should not be misconstrued as an open invitation to free-wheeling marketing behavior." That is a lesson that Nestlé learned well, if belatedly—and one that other multinationals should remember.

A third area in which multinationals experience special ethical problems is in the treatment of foreign nationals employed in their plants. This problem arises anywhere a Western firm hires non-Western workers, but it appears with particular severity in the workers' dystopia of South Africa.

The basic facts are indisputable and appalling. In the so-called republic ruled from Pretoria, a tiny minority of whites has since 1948 waged an economic and political cold war against a vastly larger population of indigenous blacks and "coloreds." The white population, on average, earns fourteen times as much as the black and lives on nearly 90 percent of the land. There are 100 times as many doctors per capita serving the white population as the black. The teacher/pupil ratio is one to sixty for blacks, one-third of that for whites. Under the official state system of apartheid, blacks are prohibited from engaging in the most rudimentary forms of social intercourse with their white neighbors. To add insult to injury, all nonwhite people are required to carry state-issued passbooks that, in enabling the police to "keep track of them," both symbolize and facilitate their oppression.

So repugnant is this obviously discriminatory system to many people, including numerous Western church groups, that they believe total and immediate withdrawal of Western industry from South Africa to be the only conscionable response. Their basic argument here is disarmingly simple: If you run your business on any principles of justice and equity, you cannot condone trading with tyrants.

A second proposed advantage of complete withdrawal is that it would shatter the apartheid regime. Left without the support of those Western industries that have helped create their economic hegemony, South African government officials would be forced to deal more equitably with the long-suppressed native population. The result might prove bloody, but it could hardly be less satisfying, ethically, than the current domination.

This elegantly straightforward proposal is attractive to increasing numbers of investors in the United States, who have been dunning their firms for a decade to pull out of a clearly bad business. But very few business leaders agree. For a variety of reasons, the managers of most firms now doing business in South Africa would prefer to maintain the commitment, in spite of the obvious social drawbacks.

Some of those reasons are clearly self-serving and cannot be interpreted to meet any honest test of ethical responsibility. The most obvious of these reasons is the one that you never hear admitted, that doing business in a country with vast natural resources, a huge supply of underpaid labor, and an ostensibly stable government can be a very profitable proposition. It seems easy to set morality aside, because it is hard to argue with the balance-sheet logic of no increase in overhead, no increase in taxes, no increase in government control—and a precipitous cutback in payroll costs.

A second self-serving argument is that the level of business involvement is so small that it really doesn't make much of a difference in South African society—so you might as well stay. This argument is groundless, considering the data on foreign investment. Although it's true that few individual U.S. firms have committed more than a fraction of their total operations to South Africa, the aggregate Western investment is substantial, and indispensable to the Pretoria regime. Writers from the right, left, and center agree that foreign capital built South Africa's economy and is keeping it in place today. To suggest that your firm may as well stay because it doesn't make a difference one way or the other is essentially the "cog in the wheel" defense that has always cemented lackeys to tyranny. It is as if Tamerlane's batman would whine, "Don't blame me for the slaughter; I only hold his sword."

A third argument for American presence is that the business of business is business, not politics. As long as the United States government does not object to our South African operations, one manager told me, we will continue to do business there. It is not our job, this argument goes, to dictate internal policies to other countries, but only to make a decent profit within the context of their laws.

I have already pointed out, in the discussion of international bribery, how dangerous it can be to adopt this kind of Good German attitude when doing business in countries with alien value systems. The person who follows an unjust law because he fears the penalties of refusal may perhaps be forgiven for being cowed. The person, or the multinational firm, that allows that law to benefit him while it harms others must be seen as a wolf in cow's clothing. And it does not help in the least to enlist Washington on your side in this effort, since for nearly two generations U.S. policy toward South Africa has been largely opportunistic and craven.

But there is one argument for staying that is not as self-serving, nor as transparent, as these. It is the utilitarian argument that American presence in South Africa does more good than ill, because the employment and general social practices of American firms are more progressive than those of their South African (or European or Japanese) counterparts.

You hear this argument in both negative and positive forms. The negative form is really a variation of the idea that being in South Africa is a dirty job, but somebody has to do it—and it may as well be us, because we do it more humanely than others would. Leave the field to the Germans and Japanese, the argument runs, and the progress made within American corporations would be wiped out overnight.

The positive form of this argument emphasizes that progress. IBM, which has been in South Africa since 1952, has made an obvious effort to carry its first principle of "respect for the individual" into a social context where such respect is actually against the law. By providing equal pay for equal work, technical training, and housing and educational assistance for black workers, the company has demonstrated a commitment, at least within its own sphere of influence, to a kind of social mobility that is anathema to South African custom. As circumscribed as it is, it is hard to deny that this has been progress.

IBM's former director of business practices and development, Richard Liebhaber, was visibly proud of this effort when I spoke to him late in 1984. "We were Sullivan signatories before there was a Sullivan Code," he said. "The Code itself is a direct result of U.S. corporate involvement. Our presence as role models has been part of the social maturation process. We feel that if ethical companies can set a new pattern, South Africa may evolve rather than fall into revolution." This view is widely held in the business community. Johnson Wax's Samuel Johnson points with pride to "the example of equitable opportunity set in our company, where the two races get along pretty well," and is convinced that this has had a positive effect overall. John Young cites the "contribution to the country" made by model firms like Johnson Wax, IBM, and his own Hewlett-Packard. And he agrees with Liebhaber's assessment of IBM's leadership role in this area. "They deserve a lot of credit," he told me, "for hiring the first black field engineers and standing right behind them in spite of resistance."

The ultimate goal behind such efforts, of course, is one that is far more congenial to progressive business people than it is to South Africa's leaders. Integration of American multinationals, it is promised, will eventually have a ripple effect throughout the society, and thus help to break down apartheid overall.

The consummation is devoutly to be wished, but has it yet borne fruit? To answer that question, we need to look at the progress that has been made in South Africa not just since American involvement began but specifically since 1977, when the code to which Liebhaber referred was adopted by several U.S.-based industries.

The aim of the Sullivan Code, drafted by Philadelphia minister and GM board member Leon Sullivan, was to capitalize on the momentum that U.S. companies had already created for social progress in South Africa by codifying a set of ethical principles to which all U.S. multinationals would be asked, in writing, to adhere. The six principles indicated clearly that the basic thrust of the code was to undermine the employment inequities that fueled Pretoria's caste system. Sullivan proposed that American firms pledge themselves to:

1. Nonsegregation of the races in all eating, comfort, and work facilities
2. Equal and fair employment practices for all employees
3. Equal pay for all employees doing equal or comparable work for the same period of time
4. Initiation of and development of training programs that will prepare, in substantial numbers, blacks and other nonwhites for supervisory, administrative, clerical, and technical jobs
5. Increasing the number of blacks and other nonwhites in management and supervisory positions
6. Improving the quality of employees' lives outside the work environment in such areas as housing, transportation, schooling, recreation, and health facilities

Since Sullivan wrote these propositions after consulting extensively with corporate leaders and representatives of the Pretoria government, there was general agreement, in 1977 and today, that they were realizable in principle. But implementation has been difficult, and there is now widespread disagreement on whether the Code has advanced or retarded social progress.

Arthur D. Little, Inc., the consulting firm, monitors the progress of American companies in addressing the tenets of the Code. The company has consistently given high marks for compliance to several of the progressive firms mentioned in this book, including Kodak, Exxon, and IBM. IBM management, at a 1981 stockholders meeting where disinvestment was demanded, cited the Little rating and called its people's activities in South Africa "exemplary." In the words of the *New York Times*'s correspondent Bernard Simon, "Even the most critical concede that Mr. Sullivan's credo has helped create a climate in which the blacks are making progress, albeit slow, in the workplace."

But there is a world of reservation in that "albeit," and not even the most ardent defender of U.S. corporate involvement in South Africa could honestly say that the Sullivan Code, or independent American efforts, have substantially altered the social structure, even within complying firms. In spite of training and fair employment practices, the menial jobs are still held largely by blacks, and the pay differential between the black and white populations is actually *increasing*. Most significantly, there are still virtually *no* black managers in American firms—a fact that derives partly from the lack of an established black educational base, but more blatantly from custom and law, under which no black may boss a white.

Even corporate defenders of the Sullivan Code admit that the fifth principle on the list—the obligation of firms to hire more black managers—has gone almost nowhere. And it is difficult to see how, without this principle being implemented, the caste system can ever be broken down. Ford now has a work-study program for black managerial candidates, and Kellogg has an innovative behavior-modification program for white workers to accustom them to black management. Johnson Wax, notes its chairman Samuel Johnson, plows back amounts ranging from 15 to 25 percent of its South African profits into advancement for blacks, and is training several black managers, including one "whom we feel could become our general manager there." Admirable as these advances are, though, they are straws on a sea of troubles, and they do little to address what Simon calls American business's ethical challenge in South Africa.

According to many observers, American business is not really interested in meeting that challenge, and has adopted the Sullivan Code as a cosmetic, and self-defensive, gesture. In a barbed and disturbing assessment of the "sluggish" progress made since 1977, Elizabeth Schmidt of the Institute for Policy Studies calls the Sullivan Code simple "camouflage" that has strengthened, not softened, repression:

> The Sullivan code has benefited the South African supporters of the apartheid system. It has allowed them to appear tolerant because they have not opposed the code's implementation. It has ensured the safety of American capital and technology, investments that strengthen and perpetuate the apartheid system.

These are serious charges, and they bring up a wider ethical question: Can even a provisional justice be created under an overarching cloud of repression? Asking whether or not Sullivan's principles are "folly in South Africa," *Business and Society* writer Lee Elbinger finds logical errors in all arguments for a sustained corporate presence. All such arguments, he claims, "use microeconomics to obscure macroeconomic truths." That is, they focus on small gains while ignoring the fact, as Jennifer Davis from the American Committee on Africa has put it, "that the whole structure of the society is carefully designed to prevent generalized equal opportunities for black and white."

Since that structure itself is heavily supported by American capital, taxes, and technology, it is not difficult to see why some critics of American involvement see the Sullivan Code as a way of simply polishing the shackles. Those who feel that on a utilitarian basis American presence is justified really have to meet this objection. As we saw in the discussion of Bentham's ideas in Chapter 2, a major difficulty in using the hedonistic calculus is that in weighing the good and evil effects of an action, people tend to weight immediate advantages more heavily than long-term, distant disadvantages—especially if those disadvantages happen to others. There's no question that the Sullivan Code has helped some black workers in American firms. But those workers comprise only a small fraction (less than 2 percent) of the total South African work force, and since the promised ripple effect is nowhere yet in evidence, American managers ought to be asking themselves one utilitarian question: Are the employment gains that my people are enjoying worth the support that my presence gives a system in which 98 percent of all black workers are still being harmed?

These questions are especially important for managers in high-tech firms. All the major American computer companies, including Control Data, Hewlett-Packard, and IBM, maintain presences in South Africa, and in the past all of them have sold computer capabilities directly to the apartheid government. Although they have now officially stopped doing so, it is naive to suppose that in a nation as centrally controlled as South Africa, this capability is not still being diverted to government usage. Do these companies, which stand firmly behind civil rights in this country, really want to extend the enormous power of their products to a government committed to their denial?

I do not suggest that complete and immediate withdrawal is the only conscionable action for American business to take. But at the very least ethical awareness requires that firms that do business *under* apartheid not do business *with* it. That means stricter controls on where products go, to ensure that the "innocent" computer you have delivered to an auto parts store in Johannesburg does not end up in a police station two blocks away. To critics of U.S. involvement, this is not nearly enough, since they see a corporate presence in itself as an inevitable prop for the regime. But if all companies in South Africa are equally condemned for lying down with vipers, a distinction can still be drawn between those that tolerate the vipers' presence as a necessary evil and those that actively feed them.

A few modest steps have been made in this direction. Several years ago Polaroid attempted to keep its products from the South African security police by having its distributor agree not to sell directly to the government; the company withdrew completely from the country when the distributor reneged on the agreement. More recently, Timothy Smith of the Interfaith Center on Corporate Responsibility notes, Control Data has refused business possibilities in South Africa after it "ascertained that its products would assist in repression rather than in humanization." And in 1983 the state of Connecticut dramatically revised its investment portfolio to drop not all firms involved in South Africa but those that were rated poorly by Little, that prohibited unions, or that sold "strategic products" to the South African police or military. Dozens of American municipalities and states have similar legislation pending.

One other approach that South African-based managers need to consider is taking a more active, vocal role in opposing the apartheid system. Up to now, virtually all American managers have been noticeably silent on this score, either out of a fear of expulsion or out of a misguided commitment to keeping politics and business separate. The truth is that in South Africa, as in any other country, politics and business are intimately linked. Silence about matters of government is as much a political "act" in the South African context as marching in an anti-apartheid demonstration. It is an act that lends support to the status quo, just as speaking out against the pass laws or the Bantu homelands policy is an act that challenges it. The argument that criticism of the regime is against the law is without moral weight; it will be readily remembered that before American firms adopted a leadership role in the area of employment, the principles embodied in the Sullivan Code were also against the law.

The key, as is often the case in the relationship of business and the state, is leadership. I think of Thomas Watson's comment on the dilatory nature of many business "leaders" regarding the social problems facing the nation in the early 1960s. He feared above all that their silence, their unwillingness to be part of the solution, would cause people to lose respect for their opinions. "And should the time come," he warned, "when our opinions mean nothing, we businessmen will have forfeited our claim to leadership in the United States." The point applies equally well today, to the situation in South Africa and to any other place where people of principle do business.

In a pointed critique of U.S. foreign policy in South Africa, the scholar Ruth Milkman identifies various "counterpressures" on the current supine American approach. Washington's tacit acceptance of apartheid "hurts its relations with the nations of independent black Africa," damages the chances of detente with the Soviet Union, and exacerbates racial tensions at home. Most important for the person concerned with the long-term leadership role of this country, it severely undermines "the U.S. government's credibility as an upholder of democratic values and human rights."

This last and most significant pressure operates in the private sector too, and it is one that no wise manager can afford to ignore. The most progressive American companies have built their reputations on credibility, and this credibility has always been linked to a respect for various stakeholders' rights. As these firms move ever farther abroad, the temptation will continually arise to leave principles and ethical codes at home, where they are appreciated, and to do business in less enlightened foreign markets with an eye solely on the bottom line.

Critics of corporatism in general and of multinational business in particular have no doubt that business's moral leadership will succumb, on every available occasion, to this dollars-and-cents temptation. They will eagerly seize upon evidence that the "good guys," no less than anyone else, simply blow with the prevailing legal winds. Multinational managers today have a historic opportunity, wherever custom and law collide with principle, to deny them that damning evidence.

11 DIVIDED LOYALTIES
Organization Men in Turmoil

The institutional context for the exercise of managerial judgment is a critical feature of ethical management....Firm and visible top management commitment, and especially a history of such commitment, is essential to keeping ethical dimensions of management on the agenda of operating managers.

—Michael Rion
Former corporate responsibility director,
Cummins Engine

The formula is simple: American corporate leadership is clearly in a state of crisis. Communication is...the pathway out of this crisis, and top management is the focal point for the effort.

—Richard Ruch and Ronald Goodman

In July of 1970, Frank Camps was a senior design engineer for the Ford Motor Company, with over fifteen years of experience in testing vehicle safety standards. That summer, in response to competition from Volkswagen and the new Japanese imports, Ford was preparing to market its own compact, the Pinto. Camps was responsible for overseeing the model's test crashes and reporting the results to the government. When those results proved disappointing, he became involved in a cover-up that brought him into bitter conflict with his employer, pushed his personal values to the limit, and eventually cost him his job.

The Pinto's initial problem was that its windshield was too weak. Camps and his colleagues solved that problem by creating another one. Using what he called "a clever engineering ploy," they diverted the kinetic energy generated by a crash away from the windshield and, via the drive shaft, toward the gas tank. Ford was happy with the solution and, Camps admits, "The corporate reasoning was sound. Windshield retention was a federally mandated area of certification. Fuel system integrity, at that time, was not."

The tragic results of this solution have by now become well known. They began to be evident to Camps as early as 1972, when the first of the Pinto gas tank explosions were reported in the national press. Aware of his inadvertent complicity in these tragedies, he experienced a crisis of conscience and started a private campaign within the Ford organization to remedy the design defect so that further tragedies could be averted.

The company's response was first to ignore his warnings, then to instruct him to withhold information from the government, and finally to reassign him to a more junior position where he would not have to worry about federal safety standards. Camps continued to pursue the matter for almost five years, finding himself rebuffed in turn by his direct superiors, the company's Corporate Safety Office, and its Office of General Counsel. Finally, in 1978, he resigned, initiating litigation against Ford charging them with job discrimination and asking the court to absolve him of responsibility for injuries he had attempted to prevent in vain. He thus joined a small but growing fraternity of corporate "whistle blowers" who, faced with a conflict between company policy and personal conviction, choose disloyalty over dishonor.

But why should he have been forced to choose at all? Why did so many of his superiors at Ford, in his words, "confuse my dissent with disloyalty"? Why did no one see that in attempting to correct a defect, Camps was actually trying to further the corporate advantage, not undermine it? As in so many other cases of companies that stonewall rather than respond to employee misgivings, what we have is a distorted concept of "loyalty" that pervades many large organizations and that, unchecked, can lead to the ethical nightmares of groupthink. Under the proper conditions, loyalty to a single leader or organization impairs ethical judgment so severely that the outcome is a Watergate or even Dachau.

In the business world, the outcome is seldom that world-shattering, but the moral implications are the same. The corporate employee who knows about but winks at his company's misdeeds is in the same shaky moral position as the participant in a government cover-up or the miscreant soldier who is "just following orders." And he usually ends up in that position for the same reason that they do—out of respect for a "loyalty" that is supposed to transcend personal misgivings.

The pressure put on employees not to subvert that respect can be both subtle and intense. Often the threat of economic reprisal is only one of its features. In many cases, psychological sanctions against dividing the company "family," against talking to the "enemy" outside, are also important. The difficulty that Frank Camps had in deciding to blow the whistle (remember that it took him six years) is experienced every day by employees who are not only afraid of losing their jobs but reluctant to break the unwritten code that binds them, like good soldiers, to the organization. *Harvard Business Review* editor David Ewing calls "the prejudice against ratting" probably "the highest hurdle in making constitutionalism effective in organizations." It is also a major hurdle to judgment.

A generation ago, William Whyte called attention to the pressure on employees to conform in his classic study *The Organization Man*. Addressing the dilemmas of lower and middle management, Whyte claimed that the modern corporation had become a "citadel of belongingness," and he lamented the fact that in his zeal to "fit in" with the style and designs of his firm, the young manager had become "imprisoned in brotherhood." Afraid to appear peculiar, he had become a company pawn, a mere functionary who, in the name of unity, was in danger of jettisoning independent thinking, personal idiosyncrasies, and moral choice.

Whyte was writing in the notoriously conformist 1950s, when according to liberal caricature everybody in corporate life wore a gray flannel suit, lived in a ticky-tacky house, and spoke to his superiors only to say "Yes, boss" and "I'll get right on it, J.B." The picture is overdrawn, but it is not entirely off the mark. Middle managers in the 1950s did experience real pressure to conform to company guidelines, and you did not read about corporate whistle-blowing in the Eisenhower years because that pressure was largely effective. Before about 1960, the superior's word was law, and widely accepted as such.

Are things very different today? Not according to middle management. The gray flannel suits and crew cuts may have given way to designer jackets and styled hair, but in the field of moral decision-making, the game of "follow the leader" is still very much a factor in organizational life. As numerous studies have shown, junior and middle managers still feel constant pressure to compromise their personal values when they conflict with the values of the marketplace and the firm.

Business Week, in a 1977 article summarizing the results of three studies, pointed out that in the post-Watergate era most business managers admit to feeling pressure "to compromise personal ethics to achieve corporate goals." When the managers surveyed in those studies were asked whether or not subordinates "automatically go along with superiors to show loyalty," over two-thirds of the respondents replied that this was common practice. An even more depressing finding was that a majority of the managers surveyed felt that this compliance with superiors' wishes even extended, for most managers, to the marketing of off-standard and possibly dangerous items. Obviously Frank Camps was not alone in perceiving conflicts between his personal values, his job security, and his company's corporate designs.

The difficulty of maintaining loyalty to superiors in the face of value conflict has become a major sticking point for young executives. Steven Brenner and Earl Molander, reporting in 1977 on changing business values for the *Harvard Business Review*, found that troubled relations with superiors had become "the primary category of ethical conflict" for young managers. After interviewing over 1,200 executives at all levels, they found that "respondents frequently complained of superiors' pressure to support incorrect viewpoints, sign false documents, overlook superiors' wrongdoing, and do business with superiors' friends."

But this finding did not apply equally to all the executives surveyed. Significantly, "follow the leader" was perceived as a less compromising game by the leaders than by the followers. The lower the respondents were on the corporate ladder, the more pressure they felt from the top to behave badly in order to keep their jobs.

University of Georgia professor Archie Carroll, who has surveyed hundreds of corporate managers on the issue of company loyalty, finds this pattern of response "particularly troubling." In one survey, 64 percent of his respondents admitted there was pressure on managers to compromise personal values. But when he broke those respondents down into categories of top, middle, and lower management, the pattern was very different: Only 50 percent of top management agreed with the observation, as opposed to 65 percent of middle management and 85 percent of the lower tier.

Carroll concluded, reasonably enough, that there is a severe "gap in understanding" between higher and lower management levels about ethical problems—and that this gap has a special relevance to lower management's moral qualms. The implication is that top managers don't know when they are twisting their subordinates' arms. "This breakdown of understanding, or lack of sensitivity by top management as to how far subordinates will go to please them, can be conducive to lower level subordinates behaving unethically out of a fear of reprisal, misguided sense of loyalty, or distorted concept of the job."

The problem here is not so much personal as institutional. It's not simply that Mr. Big bullies young Jones into silence, or that Jones insulates Mr. Big from the dirty laundry out of timidity. We have to see both of them as parts of a business system that encourages the abrogation of personal responsibility and seeks, whether consciously or not, to chop down as many individual trees of conscience as possible for the sake of the corporate wood.

It is therefore misguided to "blame" either senior or lower

management entirely. All managers today are at risk of being overwhelmed by the corporate structure, where responsibility is commonly diffused, where the conflict between ethical goods and economic goods is often fuzzy, and where, because of the pace and pressure of decision-making, it is easy for managers at every level to be honestly ignorant of their own questionable practices right up to the moment that they see them denounced on the six o'clock news.

Because of the nature of corporate decision-making, therefore, the gray flannel is often worn inside rather than out. As the firm grows and the complexity of decisions grows with it, the focus of responsibility (and of blame) becomes increasingly difficult to identify, and the corporation comes to resemble what Edmund Wilson called American capitalism in general—"a vast system for passing the buck." It may be pointless in this situation to try to ferret out who is ultimately "at fault" for the passing of a bribe, the selling of a dangerous product, or the shredding of compromising files. Everybody, and nobody, is the culprit, because corporate life has entered the phase of what C. Wright Mills called a condition of "organized irresponsibility."

In describing the "managerial demiurge" of the 1950s, Mills noted the ease with which personal responsibility could be avoided in many areas of modern industrial life. "We do not mean merely," he wrote, "that there are managers of bureaucracies and of communication agencies who scheme...but...that the social control of the system is such that irresponsibility is organized into it." He was speaking largely of government structures, but as anyone who works in a modern corporation can attest, organized irresponsibility is just as common a condition in business as it is in business's sometime nemesis. Size creates fuzziness, and fuzziness lends itself to buck-passing, no matter how ethically sound Jones, or Mr. Big, or the managers between them in the hierarchy might be. And this is not necessarily bad for business. As Harold Johnson recently observed, it may even make the firm run more smoothly. "Decisions may be facilitated—and top officers protected by—an ignorance of some of the messy details of tough business. Perhaps you won't be pilloried in the press, sued in the courts, or fined by regulatory agencies if you plead ignorance about deplorable corporate practices. Somebody else is responsible."

When that somebody else is a junior executive, the hazards of organized irresponsibility become clear. Junior managers are understandably reluctant to accept responsibility for dubious practices when their superiors have given tacit approval for those practices and yet do not own up to the approval in public. One of the sobering discoveries of the current ethical crisis is that, when the buck is passed, it often ends up on the desk not of the person in charge but of somebody who was "just doing his job" and yet got stuck with the tab. In the view of many junior managers, the disheartening finale of Watergate is being played out again and again in the boardrooms: Mr. Big, who is supposedly supervising corporate decisions, is pardoned by the public and the press while young Jones loses his reputation for carrying out what he thought to be a company policy.

It's important to remember that we're not talking only about the Frank Camps kind of case, where an employee gets a direct or hinted order to violate the law. Few ethical dilemmas in business involve this kind of clear-cut transgression. In most cases, the order is not "Lie to the feds or you're fired" but some variation on "It doesn't have to be good, it has to be Tuesday"—the implication being that if you have to bend the rules to make it by Tuesday, your superiors will look the other way.

W. L. LaCroix points to the understated but understood pressure to conform to superiors' wrongdoing as a major cause of resentment among today's executives. He describes three kinds of directives to younger managers that can lead to moral confusion. The first directive, "Act questionably," is relatively easy to deal with, since it has the virtue of clarity if not honor. More difficult are the directives "Do the right thing but also produce" and (worst of all) "Produce or else." It is the potential conflict between having to produce and wanting to maintain your integrity that puts the worst pressure on men and women in the middle. "This pressure shifts the responsibility for results to the middle manager, and yet those who apply the business pressure within an organization do not clarify the limits of the pressure," La Croix concludes. As a result, Jones is forced indirectly "to act at times unethically to achieve the organization's economic objectives and to sacrifice...objectives one should ethically support." And this all happens inferentially, without direct commands. It's as if, in the game of "follow the leader," Mr. Big leads Jones into a darkened room and then hides behind the door as the newcomer stumbles into furniture.

It is hardly surprising that in this atmosphere of inference, buck-passing, and scapegoating, younger executives have begun to demand more specific ethical guidelines. The clamor for "examples from the top" has become a major refrain in the business literature. In the Brenner/Molander study, respondents identified the behavior of superiors as the chief factor influencing their own ethical decisions within their companies, and they widely agreed with the idea that "corporate steps taken to improve ethical behavior clearly must come from the top and be part of the reward and punishment system." In the words of Pitney Bowes CEO Fred Allen, commenting on a survey of his own management, "Managers want the leadership to show them what to do. They want to believe their particular job can be done with a high degree of ethics. It is up to corporate management to confirm this belief."

But what happens when they don't? What happens when, in a situation where stakeholders' claims are in conflict, junior managers are asked to carry the ethical weight while the CEO is sipping mai tais in Aruba? Increasingly, what happens is that they make Frank Camps's unwelcome choice and come out against their firms.

When they do so, of course, they are immediately branded as deserters. At a time when business is despised by much of the public, the good company soldiers are understandably upset when one of their ranks goes over to the "enemy," presenting to government or the press inside information they need to make things even tougher than they are. It's never easy to break corporate ranks, because the concept of company loyalty still commands considerable respect. That is why the whistle-blowing phenomenon is both morally and legally complicated: It involves fundamental contradictions between definitions of loyalty itself. And these definitions, right now, are in the process of changing.

"Loyalty," a French medieval term, referred originally to the feudal obligations that a vassal owed his lord, and vice versa. These obligations—for example, the vassal's duty to give military service, and the lord's duty to protect—were strictly defined by feudal law. "Loyal," in fact, means "legal."

The underlying medieval meaning of "loyal" as roughly equivalent to legal is still applicable today. In common parlance, the word loyalty is used more freely, of course: Usage often suggests that it means simply "obedience to superiors." But that usage is unwarranted, for in the notion of loyalty there is a crucial distinction between blind obedience and obedience to a duly constituted authority exercising its legal rights. Law, and the social mores that law is supposed to embody, are still indispensable elements of any workable definition of loyalty.

Medieval people recognized this perhaps a little better than we do. If Richard were to ask Tancred not to kill Saracens but to pillage the local church, Tancred would have every right to refuse. The illegal request would not have to be honored according to his feudal obligations, and indeed by making the request, Richard would be breaking those obligations and undoing the whole concept of loyalty.

But even though corporate life is far more complicated and far less well defined than medieval vassalage, the basic principle remains that a superior in a corporate context can demand loyalty from his or her subordinate only so long as that loyalty is consistent with the law. No employer can ask or expect you to do anything, no matter how good it is for business, that is in conflict with the law. This principle, which has long been an element of good business practice, is enshrined in the legal principle of *agency*, by which employees are bound to obey their principals (employers) only within the limits of the law.

This principle has been tested many times in the courts, and it is now well established in law not only that agency does not extend to illegalities but also that an employee may not be fired for refusing to so interpret it. Ruling on whistle-blowing cases in the 1970s, several state supreme courts awarded damages to employees who had been fired for refusing to break the law. In addition, the courts extended legal protection to employees who were in danger of termination because of refusing to violate consumer credit codes, engaging in union activity, serving on a jury, filing worker compensation claims, opposing sexual discrimination, or refusing to falsify records. Because of these decisions, "company loyalty" is no longer the reliable excuse it once was for employers to fire troublesome workers.

But if legal protection for whistle-blowers extended only to those unwilling to break the law, it would not have shaken up the idea of company loyalty nearly as much as it has done. The real threat to the equation of "loyalty" with "obedience to superiors" has come from other court decisions—decisions that have dramatically altered the traditional worker-boss relationship. The earliest of these decisions came in an Illinois court in 1968, with the case of *Pickering* v. *Board of Education*.

In this case an Illinois schoolteacher named Pickering was fired for writing a letter to the local newspaper criticizing the allocation of school funds. The school board acted as many employers had been acting up to that point in interpreting the teacher's action as disloyalty. The U.S. Supreme Court disagreed. It ruled eventually that the board had overstepped its bounds and that Pickering could not be fired for exercising his First Amendment right to free speech.

This decision, even though it covered only public-employee disloyalty, became a precedent for whistle-blowers in private industry as well. As a result the climate for those whose values are in conflict with their firms' business goals has become a little less hazardous than it was in the 1950s. In the spring of 1981, Michigan enacted the first Whistle Blowers Protection Act, and since its passage, other states have followed suit. As Alan Westin points out in his valuable case compendium *Whistle-Blowing*, the courts in the last ten years have significantly altered the old relationship under which an employee could be fired at will. Several courts have now said that "if the employee could prove that a dismissal had been prompted by motives or reasons that would contravene 'public policy,' there would be grounds for judicial intervention."

That is a far cry from saying the courts will step in only if Mr. Big orders Jones to commit a crime and he refuses. If judicial intervention is possible in cases where the conflict is only ethical and not legal, then the problem of divided loyalties becomes much more complicated than it was in the Frank Camps case. And if "public policy" is to be a factor in future whistle-blowing cases, then employees and managers alike have a right to ask who makes that policy and in what cases loyalty to public policy overrides loyalty to the firm.

By invoking the public interest as a factor in weighing company loyalty, the courts are both harking back to the medieval notion of obedience to God superseding obedience to mere mortals, and looking forward to the multiple stakeholder concept that I have been using in this book. Increasingly today that concept is forcing managers to modify the old-fashioned "follow the leader" model as a guideline for blameless judgment. At today's moral crossroads, managers consistently must weigh the claims of various constituencies against the bottom line and against the expectations of superiors. This enterprise forces many of them to recognize that, in certain cases, going *outside* the organization may be the only honorable option.

Legalizing that option does create its own problems. One that many managers have pointed to is the lack of assurance that whistle-blowers, now or in the future, will be on the side of the angels. The whistle-blower's assessment of the facts could be wrong. He could simply hold a different view of the public welfare than his employer. And as a defender of whistle-blowing admits, not all whistle-blowers are as clean as their whistles. "There is always the danger that incompetent or inadequately performing employees will take up the whistle to avoid facing justified personnel sanctions." Even more pointedly, Peter Drucker draws the logical connection between whistle-blowing and "informing," and suggests that, except where the company misdeeds "so grossly violate propriety and laws that the subordinate...cannot remain silent," whistle-blowing always creates more difficulty than it alleviates. The problem remains, oo course, to determine where that line of gross violation is reached. All of which means that, partly because of and partly in spite of the recent spate of whistle-blowing, the questions that ethically torn managers will have to ask themselves in the coming years will not yield easy answers.

Even when whistle-blowing is clearly indicated by the situation, the fallout from adopting this choice is often so intense that it makes compromise, in retrospect, seem attractive. The reasons for this are as much personal as economic. I want to tie up this chapter by looking at the personal side of the issse, and then showing how, in firms that are committed to what William Hewlett has called "the human side of management," structures and procedures long in place often obviate the need for "going outside."

The truly effective sanctions against telling the world that your employer sells substandard goods or pads his expense account are not the economic ones of possible termination but social and psychological ones: loss of friendships, peer pressure, and the realization that as you go to the press, thousands of other employees are continuing to do precisely what you refused to do, and sleeping quite soundly besides. Ratting on your friends—even to save your fellow citizens from faulty tires or tainted milk—is still seen by many people as the social equivalent of banning yourself to Siberia. Many doubt whether coming clean is worth the trouble.

Say you are a rising young Jones and have been with your company for ten years. You have built up not only a reputation for reliability and hard work but a network of friends and colleagues who are quite as important to you as your salary. You discover that one of those colleagues—your golfing buddy, Bob—has been manipulating sales figures on the quarterly stockholders' reports. What's your first reaction? Is it "If I go to the press with this, I'll lose my job"? Or is it "What a mess for Bob. I wish I could avoid turning him in"?

Unless you're a complete cynic or a complete sentimentalist, of course, you will have both reactions, and a great many more besides. And you will seek desperately for a way to solve your moral dilemma without sacrificing everything you have worked for—including Bob's friendship—over the years. Here lies the real tragedy of divided loyalties in the corporation: not that companies sometimes foster value conflicts and make hard moral choices necessary, but that in making those choices, the person of conscience frequently has to hurt those he admires. When there are lives or public health at stake, he may find it relatively easy to act honorably. When the dilemma involves something as minor as sales figures, that choice may not come so easily.

The Supreme Court in the Pickering case refused to consider employee loyalty a determining factor because the "disloyal" teacher had, in writing to the press, ruptured no discernible bonds of harmony between himself and his superiors. But the Court foresaw that, in other cases, such bonds might indeed be ruptured, and it warned that rulings might be different in cases where "the relationship between superior and subordinate is of such a personal and intimate nature that certain forms of public criticism of the superior by the subordinate would seriously undermine the effectiveness of the working relationship between them."

Of course, once you've blown the whistle, that relationship is already undermined. Even if an employee escapes dismissal after calling attention to an employer's misconduct, it's obvious that his action will still create internal friction, and this friction could easily hamper both his personal contacts and his ability to do his job properly. Having blown the whistle with legal impunity, many conscience-torn employees are still confronted with the unpleasant question "Do I really want to work here now?"

The difficulty of answering that question, and the fear of having to confront it, put many people in what they see as a no-win situation. They see themselves as having only two ways of dealing with an ethical conflict. If they choose to turn in a wrongdoer to a higher authority, they hold onto their jobs only at the price of great personal strife. If they choose to ignore the conflict, they retain their jobs at the price of what Albert Carr has pungently called "toxins of suppressed guilt." Thus cooperation with evil and resistance to evil bring about the same result: a severely damaged work environment.

There is a third choice, however, and at the more "people oriented" companies, that choice has been offered for many years. It is to have in place a universally understood communications mechanism that can head off employee grievance before it ever gets to the stage of whistle-blowing. "In America today," write Goodman and Ruch, "our corporations, our society, and our government need a new quality of leadership and the honesty, directness, and truthfulness in communication that are its prime ingredients." The conjunction expressed here between the standard virtues of honesty and truthfulness and the functional virtue of communication is far from accidental. Whistle-blowing, like any other instance of employee dissatisfaction, does not arise in most ethically managed companies precisely because clear standards are in place throughout the firm, and this fact is continually communicated to people at all levels. Companies where ethics support, rather than subvert, the bottom line demonstrate a commitment to "organized responsibility" that directly corrects the organized irresponsibility that irked C. Wright Mills in the 1950s.

I would identify three interrelated aspects of this "organized responsibility": commitment, communication, and response.

Commitment. By commitment I mean commitment at the top: a deeply felt and consciously articulated belief among senior management that the operating principles of the company include ethical as well as financial ones. Division of loyalties among middle managers is not created in the top executive suites but it is certainly nourished there, by leaders who either do not understand the moral hunger of their juniors, or are willing to ignore that hunger in their devotion to the bottom line. In the words of the *Wall Street Journal*, "Many corporate employees have behaved improperly in the misguided belief that the front office wanted them to. If standards are not formulated systematically at the top, they will be formulated haphazardly and impulsively in the field." One pressing challenge of the 1980s is for top management to demonstrate that this "misguided belief" is in fact misguided, and that the American corporation has as solid a commitment to good behavior as it obviously has to success.

It would be difficult to overestimate the importance in meeting that challenge of the chief executive himself. Ruch and Goodman speak of "the critical role of the CEO" in providing leadership, both in areas of public policy and in those areas of worker management that frequently intersect with it. Many writers have pointed to the necessity of the CEO (or COO, or president) to "set a tone" of ethical direction, and observed that if this tone is lacking, there is little that middle management can do to instill confidence in supposed corporate values.

Numerous historical examples indicate the importance of the company head in this area. Many of the firms profiled in this book, for example, did not evolve accidentally into basically moral concerns but got that way early on, through the example and insistent direction of a highly principled founder. James Cash Penney, the Missouri preacher's son, called his first retail store The Golden Rule, and in his business dealings took that name as far more than a gimmick. William Procter and James Gamble, according to their biographer, brought to their dealings with others "a kind of Biblical rectitude." J&J founder Robert Wood Johnson was championing corporate social involvement at a time when most business leaders thought ethics was best confined to Sunday sermons. IBM's reputation for integrity is a direct result of Thomas Watson's belief in the importance of respect for the individual.

But the lesson is still true today. It is no accident that ARCO became the oil industry's ethical standard bearer under the joint leadership of Robert Anderson and Thornton Bradshaw, or that Aetna's social involvement grew under a man who, as head of the Filer Commission, had recommended an increase in corporate philanthropy. Johnson & Johnson's determination to stand by its customers in the Tylenol crisis rested firmly on chairman James Burke's and president David Clare's belief in the company Credo. And there is no question that Cummins Engine's commitment to enhanced opportunities for blacks in the 1960s emanated directly from chairman Irwin Miller's office.

Communication. Commitment at the top would be useless if it were not regularly, and clearly, communicated downward. Communication of ethical principles is both the most complicated and the most challenging of tasks in "organizing responsibility." It involves institutionalizing what always threatens to become window dressing, or the conviction of an isolated few. To get the ethical principles out of the CEO's office and disseminated among the troops, progressive companies rely on various strategies.

One of the most popular strategies is to publish, for general employee consumption, an official set of principles or ethical code. While having such a code is certainly no prerequisite to (and no guarantee of) moral behavior, specifying in writing what you expect of your employees does seem to limit the chances of moral fudging. At the very least it sets up certain ground rules against which decisions can be judged; the absence of these ground rules, as we've seen, is a primary cause for anxiety in companies that "play it by ear."

There is no single best format for setting up these guidelines. As the examples in the Appendix illustrate, the principles of ethical business practice may be expressed in a brief statement of goals ("The Penney Idea"), a more elaborate description of corporate responsibilities (the J&J "Credo"), or in management policy statements and discussions of philosophy, such as that given by William Hewlett in the booklet "The HP Way." Even periodic "chairman's letters" like those that preface annual reports can serve as vehicles for reinforcing ethical guidelines. The point is that to be effective, they must be *reinforced*, not just stated and forgotten.

Reinforcement is crucial because, as we've seen, organized irresponsibility seems a natural development in large human structures. Michael Rion, formerly of Cummins Engine, feels that the absence of this reinforcement is a fundamental reason for ethical slippage. "It's not that people are focusing exclusively on profits," he says. "It's that they put a disproportionate emphasis on short-term organizational goals and are allowed to forget that there's more to the business than that. They've got to be reminded regularly, or the basic principles get lost."

They might be reminded in a relatively structured format like the "ethics workshops" that Rion helped to set up at Cummins in the 1970s, or the "affirmation ceremonies" at which J.C. Penney middle managers formally pledge themselves to the "HCSC" principles of Honor, Confidence, Service, and Cooperation. The Cummins workshops permitted managers to clarify and make visible the ethics necessary for their work. Investiture ceremonies like Penney's do the same thing, and can also have a psychological impact that can carry an employee through a lifetime of commitment. Penney vice-chairman Robert Gill, who joined the company in the 1950s and received his HCSC pin from James Cash Penney himself, thirty years later recalls his affirmation ceremony as "a very moving experience."

Some firms institutionalize their principles by making them a part of the general decor. The J&J Credo, for example, hangs on the wall, visible to all, in hundreds of company facilities around the world. Penney Associates are given wallet-sized cards displaying the seven precepts of the Penney Idea—a continually visible reminder of what the firm is about. At most companies, the reminders appear in the less constantly visible formats of entry-level brochures; but in the best of these—such as Xerox's brilliantly executed brochure, "An Understanding"—the personalized plea to "do good" still comes through very clearly.

But framed creeds and wallet cards and slick entry folders can easily degenerate into gimmicks if they are not themselves frequently reassessed, and this points to another significant feature of the communication process in progressive firms: It is always ready for review. In Chapter 5 I mentioned the open communication traditions of companies like Hewlett-Packard and Johnson Wax, Delta Airlines and John Deere, Xerox and Control Data and IBM, and suggested that one reason for the extraordinary success of these companies with their own employees is that those employees are constantly aware that if a grievance arises, there is a tested and universally respected *internal* mechanism for handling it. Control Data's Peer Review, Johnson Wax's "Just Ask" line, Xerox's "Comment" program and IBM's "Speak Up" system—these are good examples of inner channels through which a worker upset by an ethical or other problem can seek advice and redress without fear of stonewalling or reprisal.

Hewlett-Packard's senior management found out in 1979 how critical periodic review is in fostering open communication. When the company implemented its Open Line survey, seeking to measure employee perceptions of the company, it found (amid general enthusiasm) some fear of openness itself: The Open Line experiment, some said, was sometimes "frustrated by feelings of threat." However small the percentage of people who felt threatened, this was still disturbing to a company that for forty years had deemphasized hierarchical authority and stressed internal discussion.

The company's response was typical. Instead of backing off from the Open Line process, HP reinstitutionalized it. With encouragement from Palo Alto, some HP organizations "restated a crystal-clear HP policy that says any attempts by managers to block the use of Open Door will not be tolerated." And company president John Young, in several messages in the HP house organ "Measure," reiterated two fundamental company principles: "the accessibility of managers to their people and the need to establish a work climate of openness and trust." This jibes well with something Young told me in the fall of 1984: "In every company training session we run, no matter what the subject is, we have something on managing people. We provide constant reinforcement for that principle."

A similar rededication process occurred in 1976 at J&J, when, at James Burke's insistence, managers from all over the world were gathered together to "challenge" the Credo that had been laid down in the 1940s by General Johnson. "We were especially concerned," Burke told Edwin Newman, "about the effect of the Credo on our new, young hires. Would they see the document as pretentious or self-serving? The challenge meetings were set up to see whether, as J&J management got younger, the General's words should be retained, revised, or—if they didn't mean anything—gotten rid of altogether."

The outcome of that review process—which continues on a regular basis today—was to revive and make universally visible throughout the organization what might have become mere verbiage. The effect of the revivification was made clear in the Tylenol crisis of 1982, when the precepts of the Credo were communicated in word and deed not just to new young hires, but to an entire society. The final lesson here is the same as the lesson of HP's Open Line experiment: that putting practices and principles to the test on a regular, ongoing basis is a sound method of ensuring that they do not degenerate into platitudes but remain integral elements of a developing corporate strategy over time.

Response. The final element of a corporate culture that "organizes responsibility" at all levels is a continually reinforced tradition of response to both positive and negative interpretations of the company "code."

On the positive side, this means, in the apt words of business ethicist Thomas Donaldson, "implementing reward procedures which utilize moral considerations." Noting that employees, management included, are generally rewarded for "increased productivity, reliability, longevity, and ability to cooperate," Donaldson asks whether the criteria for individual excellence ought not to be extended. "Should not raises, promotions, bonuses, and vacations also be tied to responsible behavior?"

At many of the companies discussed here, rewards for adherence to principle are as clearly a factor in managerial advancement as bonuses for record quarters. This is seldom a quantifiable factor. That is, promotions do not come as a clear-cut result of so many good works or so many instances of respect for employee rights. But attention to people—by which I mean all a company's stakeholders—is still considered a necessary variable in judging employee performance at many progressive firms. At Hewlett-Packard, for example, after the Open Line initial experiment, all supervisors were officially reminded that effectiveness in establishing an open work climate would always "be taken into consideration in the evaluation of managers." In the past at J.C. Penney, invitation into the management profit-sharing plan was contingent upon establishing a one-year or two-year history of ethical reliability, and ethical reliability is a concept that continues to apply at Penney's. At Dayton Hudson, managers know they are judged primarily on their ability to anticipate and track trends—and that very clearly means social as well as fashion trends. "We look at social issues along a bell-shaped curve," says Dayton Hudson Foundation chairman Peter Hutchinson. "Trend management means above all being able to see what's coming in on the left side of the curve and what is going out on the right side. That's the single most important thing we do in running this program. Our managers all understand that they're constantly being assessed on their ability to do it well."

On the negative side, response may mean coming down hard on employees who fail to live up to the code. At Penney, Xerox, and numerous other progressive companies, new employees are asked to sign an ethical "compliance" statement that resembles not so much a loyalty oath as a reiteration of fundamental principles. When in the mid-1970s Penney learned that three of its employees had violated the company's principles by accepting either substantial payments or services in a New York City building scheme, the company's response was tough and decisive. The culprits promptly became ex-employees. In addition, an internal investigation was mounted to ensure that the problem was not more widespread. "We wish these things would not happen," Penney vice-chairman Robert Gill told me, "but people are human, and so they do. We just have to deal with these cases according to the principles we believe in."

PBS commentator Robert MacNeil elicited much the same response from Johnson & Johnson when he queried chairman Burke and then-president David Clare about company response to violations of the Credo. Has anybody ever been fired over the Credo? MacNeil asked. Yes, the two responded. And yet, as both of them made clear, it was never a case of draconian justice but of incompatibility with a design that could not, on basic principles, be altered. "When a J&J manager runs afoul of the Credo," explained Clare, "we assume first that he or she needs more education and more exposure to its precepts. If that doesn't work, we try counseling. Only after that too has failed do we consider severing the relationship." Burke concurred that incompatibility rather than "disobedience" generally was responsible for dismissals over the Credo. "We don't tell people 'You're being fired because you ignored this document.' But people have been fired because they weren't able to function comfortably and profitably with its principles."

Such a moderate, conciliatory response is to be expected from a company that places such value on individual development and performance. But the softness of the response should not disguise the basic fact that at J&J as in many other progressive firms, when a conflict arises between one employee's performance and "the code," it is the code that must be maintained. In the quaint but powerful words of IBM's Thomas Watson: "Any organization...must have a sound set of beliefs on which it premises all its policies and actions....If an organization is to meet the challenges of a changing world, it must be prepared to change everything about itself except those beliefs."

Commitment, communication, response—this triad of structural features comprise a "game plan" for corporate management that is, I believe, not only ethically but practically sound. One solid piece of evidence of its soundness is that the firms I have profiled here have not been plagued by the whistle-blowing that has attacked many competitors. The reason is simple. In a company culture in which communication about problems is encouraged rather than stifled, whistle-blowing is beside the point.

The consumerist and environmentalist movements of the 1970s established in the American mind a sense of business's responsibilities that is far more moralistic and far less forgiving of commercial foibles than it ever was before. Whistle-blowing itself is but the desperate cutting edge of that sense. Perhaps corporate America's greatest challenge today—greater than the challenge of foreign competition or failing productivity—is to convince people both within and outside the corporate walls that it has expanded its historical mission and is seriously engaged in questioning not only how to make a living but also how to make a life. Those firms that find this challenge irrelevant will (increasingly in the years to come) find themselves beset by unwitting fifth columns, forced into corporate "disloyalty" by the shocking disjunction between their own values and those of the people they work for.

The firms that are most likely to prosper, on the other hand, will be those that recognize and accept the challenge. They will be led by sound business people who know that the mission has expanded, and who know too that part of business's new mandate is to forge an intimate connection between profit and fairness to all those who make it possible. These firms will understand, as one executive put it, that people "don't want one set of ethics during the day and another at five o'clock in the afternoon." And they will understand the necessity of creating corporate cultures where that juncture between personal and organizational ethics is possible.

If you believe, as Kenneth Walters has said, that "much whistle blowing occurs only because the organization is unresponsive to early warnings from its employees," then eliminating it and other revolutions from within may not be a terribly complicated task. It may require only a dedication, at all institutional levels, to the basic ethical beliefs that your own people bring to you. Once that dedication is in place, people may be loyal to the firm out of personal conviction, not fear. And the anguished decisions that the Frank Camps of the corporate world have had to make may gradually become things of the past.

12 CAN THE GOOD GUYS FINISH FIRST?

The governing rule in industry should be that something is good only if it pays. Otherwise it is alien and impermissible. This is the rule of capitalism.

—Theodore Levitt

Our early emphasis on human relations was not motivated by altruism but by the simple belief that if we respected our people and helped them to respect themselves the company would make the most profit.

—Thomas J. Watson, Jr.
Former chairman, IBM

Nearly seventy years ago, in her study of the progressive labor practices of the time, Ida Tarbell wrote, "No permanent good can come in industry from anything which is actuated by patronage or charity." Few business people, then or now, would disagree with that assessment. We've seen that among contemporary business leaders who actively engage social problems, there is broad disagreement about the extent of disinterested giving that corporations should undertake. But it is important to remember that no responsible corporate manager completely rejects return on investment, however that may be measured, as a factor in making allocation decisions. Terry Saario, former secretary of the ostensibly "philanthropic" Pillsbury Foundation, makes the point clearly. "Corporations are not charitable organizations," she told me, "and they shouldn't be expected to be. In fact, I believe strongly that simply giving money away, without measuring the effects, would be an example not of corporate responsibility but of blatant irresponsibility. We must have accountability to satisfy our duty to our stockholders."

Peter Hutchinson of the Dayton Hudson Foundation agrees. I told him of his fellow Minnesotan William Norris's comment that philanthropy was "nonprofitable and nonproductive." His response was to deny the supposed distinction between the "hard" and "soft" schools of corporate involvement. "I don't think we're that far apart. The angle and the rhetoric are different, but nobody just throws money at problems and forgets about it. We think of our giving as an investment of a kind—an investment in a healthier community from which we expect a long-term return. Control Data expects the same things. We're really partners in a broad social effort." And (he might have added) that partnership has a physical manifestation. Dayton Hudson is a major supporter of the Minnesota Seed Capital Fund, a profitable pump-priming organization for new business, of which William Norris is president.

The distinction between the "hard" and "soft" approaches to corporate involvement, then, is more semantic than real. The tactics for meeting social needs are distinct, but the long-term strategy is the same. It is to make the investment of corporate funds and resources part of a multisector attack on problems that beset us all, and thereby to help create a society in which business continues to profit. Peter Hutchinson is just as committed to that bottom line as William Norris. The real distinction to be drawn is not that between the "investment" and "philanthropic" approaches to corporate involvement, but between those who feel that meeting the needs of multiple stakeholder groups threatens those of the primary shareholder group and those who believe that it strengthens them. Virtually all of the corporate leaders I spoke to in the course of researching this book are convinced of the latter proposition. Virtually all of them agree that extending the arm of business into the community—beginning with the workplace "community" and reaching toward the society at large—is a financially sound, not just ethically gratifying, endeavor.

They do readily acknowledge that returns to shareholders in a community-conscious business may not always be as swift as they might be in a number-crunching firm. William Norris admits that investors in Control Data sometimes have to have the corporate strategy explained to them. But this in no way diminishes his faith. "Our programs are much longer term than is usual in most corporations. That doesn't make them bad. I'm absolutely convinced that in the long run, because of our programs, we will have a more stable, more enduring, and more profitable business."

Nor is the return on shareholder investment in a public-spirited firm always as tangible or immediately satisfying as a semiannual dividend check. I think often of Robert Roggeveen's assessment of the money the

Aetna Foundation has targeted toward native American communities. While admitting that the return on such investments might not be visible for a generation, there was no question in his mind that the risk was worth the potential rewards. Those "rewards," when they came in, would be measured in terms like demonstrations avoided and able-bodied people kept off welfare. Even the hardest-nosed book-balancer would have difficulty in denying that such a "return" would benefit business as much as anyone else.

But such a return would not be bankable, at least not immediately, and shareholders tend to be less concerned with the shape of society in the next century than they are with the size of their dividend checks in this one. It's perfectly reasonable for investors, when they consider backing a "good guy" corporation, to ask of that corporation the same questions they would ask of any other corporation: How will my money be managed? What will I get for my support? Society, too, has a right to expect of a public-spirited company that, in seeking to address multiple responsibilities, it not slight its primary economic function. To revert to the analogy suggested by the J&J manager at the 1976 Credo challenge meeting, a company must always remember that in juggling the several white balls and one red one, the one thing it cannot do is drop the red.

As I've been suggesting throughout this book, I see no inevitable conflict between any corporation's observance of ethics and its awareness of the bottom line. Whether the stakeholders under consideration are employees or customers, shareholders or communities, there is plenty of evidence that doing good is not incompatible with doing well. Moreover, it can be persuasively argued that, other things being equal, ethical conduct even enhances corporate health. In this concluding chapter, I want to suggest three areas in which this may be true.

The first area is productivity—a productivity that comes from (and only from) a work force that sees itself as a partner rather than an antagonist to management. As we saw in Chapter 5, companies that practice a "people centered" management style are frequently "paid back" by their employees with strong job loyalty, cooperation, flexibility in hard times, and heightened productivity and quality control. "It's so obvious," says Johnson Wax chairman Samuel Johnson, "that it's surprising more companies haven't seen it sooner. The attitudes of employees are crucial to productivity and creativity. One reason we've done well is that we will not cut corners in that area."

Companies that extend this commitment to people into the community through employee outreach programs can reap even greater internal gains: Remember manager Marion Whipple's observation that the primary benefit to Xerox of its Social Service Leave program was a better, more productive employee.

In a 1982 evaluation of Control Data's social programs, William Norris named "the favorable reaction by employees" as the first, and certainly not the least, of benefits to the company:

> Our programs provide the opportunity for employees to participate directly and visibly in serving society as part of their work responsibilities. As a result, they have a sense of pride and gain a special kind of enjoyment.... Prospective employees, especially those just entering the work force, also view our strategy very favorably, as demonstrated by a college recruiting success rate much higher than other companies.

Hewlett-Packard president John Young made the same comment to me about his company's college recruitment success, and it is a success that is mirrored in other progressive firms. Clearly, if you develop a reputation for doing good, internally and externally, good people will beat a path to your door. Once those people are part of a team effort that stresses employee satisfaction, gains in productivity almost always follow.

A second area is public relations—an area that it is easy both to underestimate and to give undue importance. Critics of corporatism tend to do the latter, assuming that business involvement in social problems, not to mention simple fair treatment of customers and employees, derives exclusively from a desire for good press coverage. The natural tendency of business, they say, is to treat people like expendable parts; if the occasional business does otherwise, it's only because it looks good by doing so.

Considering the relative space that the popular press has given in recent years to corporate scandals and corporate social responsibility, it is hard to see this argument as much more than knee-jerk commercophobia. An oil company's inadvertent fouling of a shoreline is trumpeted on the front page of the *New York Times*—as of course it should be. Yet the same company's sponsorship of minority education, because it is not a "newsworthy" item, gets an inch and a half on page 20. One can hardly blame a corporate PR department for attempting to redress the balance by announcing public service projects as loudly as possible. But it would be false to conclude that the exclusive purpose, or the major effect, of such projects is to generate public goodwill.

As Aetna's John Filer points out, corporate social involvement is an "expensive and inefficient" way to generate good public relations. In speaking of his company's social investments, he says that "anybody who thinks of this as public relations just hasn't been around. PR is a substantive function in itself," and should not be confused with corporate social involvement. "You get a PR plus from it, but if that's the reason you're doing it, you're wasting an awful lot of money, because you can get that plus much cheaper with advertising."

Which is not to say that the PR plus is negligible. Marion Whipple, Xerox's community and employee programs manager, agrees that the public relations gain is an attractive though incidental aspect of the company's programs. "Getting PR is not our intent," she says, "although it comes anyway. When our communities see Xerox people out on their own time, on weekends, helping in various ways, of course the company benefits. We do get positive feedback."

She mentioned the example of a "Corporate Follies" that Xerox, Pitney Bowes, and several other Stamford companies in cooperation with a local volunteer agency had mounted in the spring of 1984 to entertain senior citizens. The show, which featured performers from ten local firms, drew applause not only from a delighted audience but from an appreciative community as well. As numerous letters to the editor of local papers testified, the show generated widespread favorable publicity for the companies involved. And this was a one-time community-enrichment event in one Connecticut city. It is hard not to be convinced that, over time, those firms that take their "people commitments" seriously do realize a PR advantage over those who are simply counting numbers.

Such an advantage is not to be minimized, especially at a time when public attitudes toward business fluctuate between the merely tolerant and the actively hostile. Although the intense distrust of business that characterized the 1970s has softened somewhat, numerous polls indicate that the American public's suspicion of institutions, including corporate institutions, is still firmly entrenched.

It's clear that people feel business is not doing enough to address major social difficulties, and that there is a small but growing contingent who feel that the social welfare ball, recently passed off by President Reagan, should be carried now by the private sector. If business fails to meet this challenge—and if it fails at the very least to treat its own internal constituencies well—we may expect a resurgence of that anticommercial sentiment that historically has always led to a call for more government control.

This points to a third advantage of a public-spirited approach to business: It can keep both government and nongovernment regulators off the private sector's back. Or, to phrase the advantage negatively: Businesses that fail to respond to public expectations may sooner or later lose their customary power.

IBM's Thomas Watson, Jr. recognized this danger early on. In the 1963 lecture series that was published as *A Business and Its Beliefs*, he chided conservative business leaders who were resisting the then infant domestic welfare programs either as being too expensive or as involving too much government intervention. He understood that one likely effect of this resistance would be an increase in public distrust.

> If the American people ever come to believe that we businessmen can always be counted on to shout "No!" they will not only regard us as being against them—they will cease to have respect for our opinions. And should the time come when our opinions mean nothing, we businessmen will have forfeited our claim to leadership in the United States.

Watson was speaking here of business leaders' antipathy to social security, regulation of the stock exchange, and federal aid to education—all of which, in today's climate, seem fairly modest intrusions of the public into the private sector. But the point is as relevant today as it was in 1963. The hidden message of Watson's observation was that if business continued to oppose social developments that the people obviously wanted, those developments would go through anyway—but at business's expense, rather than with its input.

That message is hardly hidden today. If the federal regulatory apparatus has grown into a hydra-headed monster, the corporate sector must certainly take some of the blame for feeding it too well. If there had been no reckless stock speculation in the 1920s, would there now be an SEC? If Detroit had not botched its public safety charge, could Ralph Nader have gotten off the ground? Would we need an Environmental Protection Agency today if the industrial giants had themselves acted to reduce sulfur and hydrocarbon emissions?

The sad fact is that, until very recently, most American business has been slow to respond to the perceptions of its various constituencies that it was harming, not helping, the nation. One outcome of that slowness has been increased government regulation. Harvard sociologist Daniel Bell made the observation pointedly during Bentley College's first conference on business ethics. Automobile manufacturers, he pointed out, were "virtually unregulated" in the early 1960s; by the late 1970s, they were trammeled by dozens of agencies because they had failed to react to "evident signs on the horizon." At the same conference, General Mills vice-president Mercedes Bates made a similar comment in reference to the consumer movement—itself the seedbed of countless agencies:

> The consumer movement exists today because of the failure of business to satisfy consumer needs. The movement did not spring full blown into being for no good reason....Business is paying for its own inadequacies, and there has been a long, long history of them.

It is not outlandish to suppose that had that history been different—had Ida Tarbell's "new ideals in business" been the rule rather than the exception in this century—the business community might now be closer to that paradise of laissez-faire that so many dream about but which few have done anything to make real.

The same comment can be made about the effect of corporate responsibility on another attempt at control, that which is couched now in the debate over corporate "governance" or corporate "democracy." Ten or fifteen years ago the idea of broadening the representation on corporate boards struck most business people as a mere leftist fantasy, one with as much popular appeal as "worker council control" or (in some areas) the closed shop. Today the appeal is much broader. Thomas Donaldson identifies "attempts to alter corporate behavior by altering corporate structure" as among the "most promising" proposals made by critics of corporate ethics. Bentley College's fifth annual conference on business ethics, held in the fall of 1983, was devoted entirely to this once "radical" idea: The title of the conference was "Corporate Governance: Institutionalizing Ethical Responsibility."

A description of corporate democracy by four prominent critics of corporate power implies a significant overlap between this proposal for "controlling" the corporation and activities that are already going on in the more progressive-minded firms. The four, calling modern corporations "private governments," say they are run by undemocratic elites. To correct this social inequity, they propose that corporate judgments be made by "a combination of executives selected by a representative board, a board genuinely elected by beneficial shareholders, and other 'stakeholders' of the corporation such as workers and communities where companies are located."

Obviously the concept, if not the reality, of such a governing body is already in place at many of the corporations profiled in this book. Just as obviously, there is a tactical advantage to including the needs of multiple stakeholders in your company decisions before the loyal opposition gets ahold of the concept and uses it to dislodge your management. If you're a corporate critic who has just discovered the newly sharpened ax of democratization, the places you will look to sink it will not be those firms that have already anticipated democracy and have incorporated it into their company practices, but those firms that have implacably resisted the broadening of the corporate base. Resistant firms will always be the initial targets of reform.

H.G. Wells put the case with precision: "It is not creative minds that produce revolutions, but the obstinate conservation of established authority. It is the blank refusal to accept the idea of an orderly evolution toward new things that gives a revolutionary quality to every constructive proposal." That observation, which appears as a coda to the above-mentioned article on corporate democracy, is as germane to the current evolution toward greater corporate involvement as it was to the potential revolution in labor that Wells was writing about 100 years ago. The lesson of both eras is the same. The organizations that survive will be those that are able to adapt to changing circumstances—including those circumstances in the minds of the American people that are calling for industrial reform.

Whatever your feelings about its utility or appropriateness, outside regulation of the corporation is a fact of modern life—and is going to continue to be so. A principal challenge for business in this and the following decade is to become the initiator, rather than simply the reactor, in a process of widening responsibility. If, as has often been the case, business ignores its moral and social imperatives, closing ranks against the external "attack," the adversarial bloodletting that has long characterized labor-management relations in many companies could easily spill over into the wider relationship between the corporation and society at large. Business professor Norman Bowie suggests that the ultimate result could be systemic and devastating:

> When corporations begin to take moral shortcuts, either the government steps in and further constrains business or a Hobbesian state of nature develops in which each business ends up trying to cut the throat of its competitors. Either result undermines the conditions of capitalism....To the extent that corporations undermine the ethical foundation that made capitalism possible, they engage in behavior that will bring about their own destruction.

But this result is not inevitable. If more businesses follow the lead of the firms profiled here, they will very likely find that attending to more than mere profit-and-loss statements is an excellent technique for keeping vulpine cries from the door. This will not solve business's problems, to be sure. But it might help to generate an atmosphere in which they can be more effectively addressed.

Better employee relations, enhanced public goodwill, and the deflection of external controls—these gains comprise a convincing triad of arguments in favor of looking beyond the bottom line. But what *about* the bottom line? Whatever its productivity figures, public image, and autonomy from external control, a corporation still rises or falls on the basis of annual reports. What of the given stock market wisdom that you can't both do good and do well?

Considering how much print has been lavished on the causes of profitability and on the role of ethical behavior in the marketplace, it's surprising how little has been expended to investigate the connection between the two. Journals like *Business and Society Review*, *Business Horizons*, and the various business school reviews carry occasional notices that social responsibility is not a losing game, but this news seldom reaches the popular press. For the most part the general public is left with the unchallenged assumed wisdom because it has not seen the data that disprove it.

But that data, even though it is still fairly sketchy, is extremely encouraging to anyone who wants to believe that doing good and doing well are compatible. Since the early 1970s, several independent studies have demonstrated that the given wisdom is a fiction. I'll mention four as representative.

An early foray into this field appeared in 1972 in *Business and Society Review*. In an article entitled "Choosing Socially Responsible Stocks," contributing editor Milton Moskowitz made what he called "the beginning of an attempt to assess corporate responsibility" by reviewing the work of fourteen socially responsive companies and then asking managers of several investment and mutual funds to comment on "the concept of a socially responsive investment portfolio." These were his fourteen companies:

Chase Manhattan	New York Times
Dayton Hudson	Rouse Company
First Pennsylvania	Standard Oil (Indiana)
Jewel Companies	Syntex
Johnson Products	Weyerhaeuser
Levi Strauss	Whirlpool
Mutual Real Estate Investment Trust	Xerox

The reasons each of these companies was chosen varied widely, and Moskowitz was careful to acknowledge that inclusion on this preliminary list did not suggest across-the-board impeccability. Not only were the standards for measuring social "performance" still unconstructed, but companies varied internally depending on what was being measured. For example, "While a company may be strong in one area, such as pollution control, it may be laggard in another, such as minority hiring." The conceptual and judgmental problems suggested here obviously have not disappeared over time.

The money managers' comments on socially responsible portfolios tended to support the suspicion that profit and principle were compatible. Royce Flippin, head of First Spectrum Fund, a mutual fund that in 1973 already had several of Moskowitz's choices in its portfolio, suggested that "socially responsible companies...are very likely good investment vehicles in that their behavior reflects those qualities of management vision and statesmanship that also produce profits." Harold W. Janeway, research director of White, Weld, and Company, agreed. "The more socially responsible companies," he wrote, "tend to be more profitable, but it is not at all certain which comes first. One can also argue that the more profitable companies can afford to be more responsible."

Comments like that, of course, are often hurled at visibly benevolent corporations as proof that their charity is somehow suspect because it comes after the fact. This chicken-and-egg question may interest psychologists, but it has little bearing on the central issue of whether or not money and morality can go together. According to these two managers, they clearly can—regardless of which comes first.

Janeway made one other observation that is germane to that central issue. He cautioned potential investors against placing all their bets on mere goodness, and advised that "from a performance standpoint it might make more sense to concentrate on avoiding the 'socially irresponsible' companies than to try to profit from a portfolio of the most responsible companies." His rationale for avoiding the "bad guys" was that insensitivity to social problems might indicate other management blind spots—failings that could lead to real dollars-and-cents losses. "Earnings per share," rather than long-term profitability, he pointed out, "are likely to continue to be the name of the game."

That fairly obvious conclusion was endorsed five years later in a study undertaken by Ohio State business professors Frederick D. Sturdivant and James L. Ginter. In a *California Management Review* article, they assessed the management attitudes and economic performance of sixty-seven companies that BSR's Moskowitz had recently "rated" on the basis of social responsiveness. Moskowitz had divided the firms into three categories—Best, Worst, and Honorable Mention—and Sturdivant and Ginter compared the earnings-per-share growth over a ten-year period (1964-74) of the three groups.

Since I am interested here in models to be emulated rather than shunned, I will not list the twenty companies that Moskowitz identified as "Worst." Instead, here are the eighteen firms that Moskowitz, Sturdivant, and Ginter chose in 1977 as "Best":

Aetna	McGraw-Hill
CNA Financial	Owens-Illinois
Cummins Engine	Quaker Oats
Dow Chemical	Rouse Company
First Pennsylvania	Standard Oil (Indiana)
Jewel Companies	Syntex
Johnson Products	Weyerhaeuser
Levi Strauss	Whirlpool
Lowe's Companies	Xerox

And here are the twenty-nine companies to which Moskowitz gave an "Honorable Mention":

American Metal Climax	AT&T

Atlantic Richfield
Bank America
Campbell Soup
Chase Manhattan
Citicorp
Citizens & Southern National Bank
Consolidated Edison
Dayton Hudson
Eastern Gas & Fuel
General Electric
Giant Food
Hallmark Cards
Hoffmann-La Roche
IBM
Kimberly Clark
Koppers
Marcor
Masco
Mobil Oil
Mutual Real Estate Investment Trust
Peoples Gas
Phillips-VanHeusen
Polaroid
Ralston Purina
RCA
Sperry & Hutchinson
Wells Fargo

To avoid the obvious methodological errors of comparing apples and oranges, Sturdivant and Ginter broke the sixty-seven companies into four "relatively homogeneous categories: petrochemical, industrial, retailing, and nondurable consumer goods." They then aggregated across the four categories the relative-share growth of the Best, Worst, and Honorable Mention groups, and came up with an encouraging conclusion. Although the difference between the Best and Honorable Mention categories was negligible, there was a statistically significant difference in economic performance between both these groups and the Worst group; the data showed across the board that the more socially responsible groups also did better on the bottom line.

Sturdivant and Ginter's explanation as to why this was so was provocative and compelling. Since corporate social response and traditional economic performance are linked closely to management attitudes, the Ohio State professors made a case for seeing those attitudes as the key to a firm's "responsiveness" on all fronts. "A company management group which reflects rather narrow and rigid views of social change and rising expectations might also be expected to respond less creatively and effectively in the traditional but also dynamic arenas in which business functions." Therefore, they implied, not only does a social consciousness not impede economic performance, it may actually be an indication of a mental agility that enhances it.

A third study of the connection between good works and profits was undertaken in 1983 at the behest of J&J's chairman James Burke. "I have long harbored the belief," Burke told the Ad Council late that year, "that the most successful corporations in this country, the ones that have delivered outstanding results over a long period of time, were driven by a simple moral imperative: to serve the public in the broadest possible sense better than their competition." To test that belief, a J&J staff worked with the Business Roundtable's Task Force on Corporate Responsibility and the Ethics Resource Center in Washington, D.C. to compile a list of "public service" companies whose long-term earnings could be assessed against those of corporate America in general.

"We looked for companies," Burke told me, "that fulfilled two criteria. One, they had to have somewhere in their literature a long-standing document that defined, as our Credo does, a responsibility beyond the bottom line. Two, we had to be convinced that the current corporate culture reinforced and lived by that document. With those criteria in mind, we came up with an original list of twenty-six companies that we would examine with regard to sales and profitability." They were:

Aetna*
Allied Chemical*
American Can*
AT&T
Coca-Cola
Dayton Hudson*
General Foods
Gerber Products
Hewlett-Packard*
IBM
J.C. Penney
John Deere
Johnson & Johnson
Johnson Wax*
Kodak
Levi Strauss*
McDonald's*
McGraw-Hill*
3M
Pitney Bowes
Pittsburgh National Corporation*
Procter & Gamble
Prudential*
R.J. Reynolds
Sun Company
Xerox

Because of a lack of "comparable data," the eleven companies with asterisks above were later dropped from the list, leaving the J&J researchers with a final list of fifteen. Studying the economic performance, in terms of profits and returns to stockholders, of these companies over the thirty-year period 1952-82, they reached some provocative conclusions.

Profits for the fifteen-company composite were considerably above the national average, showing an 11 percent compound growth rate over the thirty-year period. That compares favorably, to say the least, to a 3.1 percent growth of the GNP in the same period. And although the composite figure was somewhat skewed by Xerox's phenomenal 25.2 percent increase, even the slowest growing member of the group—John Deere, with a 6.7 percent increase—still outperformed the GNP by over two to one. The bottom line? In 1982 the GNP was two and a half times greater than it had been in 1952; the net income of the public-service companies was twenty-three times greater!

As for the shareholders—those primary stakeholders whom the bottom-line fanatics are always afraid of leaving in the lurch—they would have had no reason to complain if they had invested exclusively in these "good guy" firms. Burke makes the point with a pithy comparison. "If you had invested $30,000 in a composite of the Dow Jones thirty years ago, it would be worth $134,000 today. If you had put that $30,000 into these firms—$2,000 into each of the fifteen—it would now be worth over $1 million."

Similarly impressive conclusions were reached by a fourth study, conducted by the Center for Economic Revitalization, a Vermont-based investment research group that reports on socially conscious companies in the bimonthly newsletter *Good Money*. Five years ago the Good Money staff compiled a Center Corporate Responsiveness Average (CCRA) to measure the economic performance of "good" firms, as the Dow Jones Average measures "typical" industrial performance. Companies on the CCRA index had to meet both economic criteria (they had to be publicly traded major industrials with a good stock market history) and social criteria. To meet the social criteria, companies had to:

1. Produce nondestructive goods and services, contributing to the overall quality of life, and/or
2. Have responsible employee/labor relations, and/or
3. Engage in community service work, and/or
4. Support philanthropic or public service programs, and/or
5. Demonstrate an ethical concern for and response to major social problems and issues.

Although the Good Money staff designed averages for socially responsible industrials, utilities, and transportation companies, it is their industrial index that is most fully developed, and most relevant to the firms profiled in this book. This index tracked the following thirty companies:

Aetna
American Greetings
Ametek
Atlantic Richfield
Browning-Ferris
Coleman
A.T. Cross
Cummins Engine
Digital Equipment
Disney Productions
Esquire
Federal Express
Fort Howard Paper
General Motors
Hershey Foods
Johnson & Johnson

Kroger	Norton Company
Levi Strauss	Norton Simon
Matsushita Electric	Polaroid
Maytag	Smucker
MCI Communications	Snap-On Tools
Melville Corporation	Wang Labs
New York Times	Worthington Industries

When the stock performance of these firms was compared to that of the Dow Jones firms for the period between late 1981 and the summer of 1984, the result was a difference of eight percentage points. The Dow rose 27 percent, the CCRA firms 35 percent.

This was statistically a modest difference. Convinced, however, that "socially responsive investing really pays off over the long run, and that short-term fluctuations can be misleading," the Center extended its analysis back to 1974, a year when, as Good Money put it, "we didn't exist but was the year of the last great market low." Over this longer span (1974-84), the difference between the CCRA and Dow averages was startling. The Dow had gone up 55 percent, the *Good Money* index 240 percent. Hardly a compelling argument for corporations to stick to nuts and bolts and stay away from social concerns.

What do these studies suggest? Looking at them in the aggregate, two conclusions stand out. First, although they were conducted over a twelve-year span and by people with obviously different motivations and research methods, the studies singled out many of the same "socially responsible" corporations again and again. This I believe is not simply a case of researchers feeding off each others' data (although that may be a factor) but of the facts looking approximately the same, over time, to different eyes.

When I began this study, I had no idea which corporations were well regarded by business ethics experts. Yet a consensus began to emerge very quickly. In assessments of progressive business practices I constantly came across the names Cummins and Xerox and Levi Strauss, Aetna and Johnson & Johnson and IBM. These names appeared not just in professional and academic studies like the ones I have just cited, but in the popular press as well. They are well represented, for example, on *Money* magazine's 1976 survey of "Ten Terrific Companies to Work For" and on *Fortune's* 1983 and 1984 "most admired corporations" listings. These firms do not reappear in the literature because of isolated PR gestures but because of consistent records of attending to people's needs.

Second, in spite of their differing interpretations of social responsibility and their different sampling methods, the researchers all reach essentially the same conclusion. That conclusion, which flies in the face of the given wisdom, is that social responsibility and a sound bottom line are not incompatible propositions. On the contrary, there is very good evidence that those who behave ethically toward their various constituencies are also those who make the most money.

But there are two seemingly plausible corollaries to this conclusion that are merely attractive non sequiturs. The first is that the connection between morality and profit is not just coincident but causal, and that by extension the more good works you perform, the more profitable you will be. As the negligible difference in profitability between the Best and Honorable Mention companies in the Sturdivant/Ginter study suggests, such a proposition is probably wishful thinking. Because social projects are a drain on company resources, there may be an upper limit (different for each firm, of course) beyond which reaching out becomes economically unfeasible. That's common sense. If it were not, Dayton Hudson might now be giving 10 or 15 or 25 percent of its pretax income to charity, and getting richer all the time by doing so.

Nor is it clear from the evidence that once you have taken on a socially responsible role, you will have done everything necessary to secure a steady market advantage. The goodwill of various constituencies is a fundamental component of success in many of the companies I've profiled, but it's obviously not the only one, and it may not be the determining one. The business of business is still business, after all. The basic economic functions of the corporation—manufacturing, R&D, marketing, finances, service, and so on—can obviously be performed effectively within an ethical context. But it is nonsense to suppose that the context itself will get them done.

The second corollary to avoid is the obverse of the first one. It is that since good works and success are compatible, the lack of good works must lead to failure. This essentially religious conviction—that God will bankrupt the wicked—also is not borne out by the evidence. We all know business people who regularly knife their employees in the back, lie to their customers, foul the air and water, and in general thumb their noses at society—and laugh about it all the way to the bank.

There are people in corporate life—people of experience and acumen—who believe that this type of behavior eventually leads to destruction. Richard Liebhaber, proud of the fact that at IBM "the company is the people," sees the impersonal management style of some old-line businesses as "confusing the factors of production." There are numerous managers, he explains, "who have forgotten that it is not capital but the folks who use the capital who count." The long-term competitive chances of those people, he is convinced, are very poor. When I asked him if "good guys" could finish first, he answered immediately, "They're the only ones who will finish at all."

Gulf Oil vice-president Jayne Baker Spain shares the view that dirty pool in business is self-destructive. Reacting to the press beating that her company took in the mid-1970s as a result of illegal contributions, she confessed to a Bentley College audience, "We now realize ... that by not doing our business well—by not doing it in full accord with the law and ethical standards—we can get hurt and hurt badly."

Maybe. But the bottom-line evidence is still sketchy. Certainly Gulf lost public esteem because of the contributions, but esteem is not money. In an engaging study of adverse publicity and corporate offenses, Brent Fisse and John Braithwaite found no evidence that corporations suffer significant financial setbacks because of ethical blunders. After reviewing numerous celebrated scandals—including the Pinto case, the Exxon and Lockheed bribery cases, and the problems of Allied Chemical with kepone—they concluded that public exposure in such cases generally leads only to modest and temporary sales losses. As for the stock market, they say, "It is impossible to be certain that negative publicity had an adverse effect on the stock prices of any of the companies studied." So on this point the jury is still out.

But it may not be out for long. Clearly one effect of the current information explosion has been that customers, employees, and the citizenry at large are far more keenly attuned to what large organizations can do, what they are doing, and the frequent discrepancy between the two. This puts both Big Government and Big Business on notice, and business probably more than government because, for all its power and resourcefulness, it is the more vulnerable to attack. I have mentioned the challenge now facing the private sector in the intricately overlapping areas of ethical conduct, social involvement, and government control. That challenge can be turned into opportunity only by companies that understand how little support simple, bottom-line ethics now has—and will continue to have—with most people. More and more, the future lies with those firms that take the admittedly important needs of shareholders as one among many factors to consider in formulating long-term management objectives.

I believe that two key phrases will bracket all future discussions of business ethics. They are the phrases "goodwill" and "long term."

Earning the goodwill of constituencies is neither platitudinous nor visionary. This endeavor, in fact, has long been a pragmatic foundation of the most successful, and most enduring, organizations. H.F. Johnson said it well in a 1927 profit-sharing speech to Johnson Wax employees: "The goodwill of the people is the only enduring thing in any business. It is the sole substance. The rest is shadow." He was speaking to, and about, company employees, but the dictum applies to everyone—all those who, in a mixed and democratic economy, have a stake in the survival of business. J&J chairman James Burke reflected this view recently, when he told an audience of business executives that the success of any business enterprise, and the success of "this democratic capitalistic system that means so much to all of us," depended above all on the leverage to be gained from "our most important asset: the goodwill of the public."

Goodwill is half the battle. The other half is managing that asset not for this year's returns only but for the life of the corporation—and indeed for the life of society. This means accepting short-term losses and being able to ignore the Wall Street gurus who claim that a dipped earnings growth this quarter will soon spell economic disaster. It means having the courage to take on marginally profitable investments because of their long-term social utility, in the belief that a better society down the line means more profits for us all. It means, in short, having faith in the system. Not just the corporate, competitive system, but the "democratic capitalistic system" of which it is a working part.

Two managers' observations speak especially well to this faith. One is the comment of Dayton Hudson vice-president Peter Hutchinson on the need for company managers to track social as well as fashion trends if they expected to survive in the Dayton Hudson system. Hutchinson made it clear that the DH commitment to social progress was as much an economic as a "philanthropic" endeavor: that the management tracking of fashion and "social needs" trends were two parts of the same large picture. In that picture, corporate giving—even at 5 percent—made sense because it breathed life into the society without which no corporation could prosper.

The other observation came from Robert Roggeveen, the Aetna manager who championed Aetna's support of NOW in spite of NOW's opposition to the insurance industry, because "a more democratic society is a better one."

Few people would disclaim that observation in the abstract. Yet it must be admitted that for most of American history, the visible majority of corporate managers have moved staunchly in the other direction. It was precisely this retrograde trend that Thomas Watson castigated in 1963 as a "stubborn doctrinaire approach" to social progress. Is it any wonder that, in spite of numerous progressive exceptions, the American people in general still regard corporations as grasping giants, insensitive to anything but bottom-line concerns?

If the corporation is to continue to play a central role in the evolution of democratic capitalism, it will itself have to evolve. Its managers must recognize the fact that public expectations, of business and of every large organization, have dramatically changed since the laissez-faire gospel was laid down centuries ago. In Thomas Donaldson's pointed phrase, today's society *expects* more of a corporation. This does not necessarily dictate any specific social involvements on the part of given corporations; it does indicate the need for the private sector in general to engage its "people" problems, whether internal or external, in a much more active fashion than it has done in the past.

To some in the corporate hierarchy, this will come as bad news. I am not sure it is, although engaging social issues will obviously, in the short run, cost business more than traditional book-balancing would.

But even if such short-term constriction is necessary, the good news is not far away. The good news is that, as we move inexorably toward a society in which more rather than fewer people make decisions, in which allegiances are increasingly multiple, in which the image of the corporation as Big Brother is gradually being replaced by the image of the corporation as a working partner in an irreversibly mixed economy, business organizations can do very well by understanding and responding to this transformation.

Unquestionably the corporation will continue to exert a vital and major impact on American and international life. But it is now only one player in an elaborate social mix that also includes the small business enterprise, the federal and state regulatory apparatuses, consumer and other pressure groups, employees, local governments, foreign peoples—an entire range of stakeholders that hardly had to be considered a hundred or even fifty years ago.

Some corporate leaders respond to this development by railing against regulation, denying the inevitable, and focusing ever more sharply on the bottom line. Others see the writing on the wall and try, like many of the leaders quoted here, to coordinate "social profits" with the traditional corporate mission of making an economic profit by supplying needed goods and services.

As the evidence in this chapter suggests, over the long run such attempts at coordination are likely to prove not just ethically but financially sound. I have little doubt that, in time, Richard Liebhaber's prediction will come true: that corporate villains will fall by the wayside, leaving the finish line to those businesses that play the game hard, but fairly. As democracy and competition both increase, earning the public's goodwill will become less and less an ancillary preoccupation, and move ever more forcefully to the forefront of managers' attention.

Managers who respond to this challenge will prove in the long run most successful not because they slight Theodore Levitt's "rule of capitalism," but because, given changing conditions, they honor it best of all. They will most consistently demonstrate what the companies profiled in this book have been demonstrating for years: that public service is good not only because it's "the right thing to do," but also because it pays.

APPENDIX
Corporate Ethical Statements

The chief response of many corporations to the business scandals of the 1970s was to issue official "codes of conduct," yell "Mea non culpa" at the press, and go about business as usual. As a result, corporate ethical statements have had about as much credibility with the general public as Mr. Nixon's exculpatory cry "I am not a crook." Many observers of the business scene, asked to categorize such statements in a word, waver only between "hypocrisy" and "fiction."

Such cynicism is understandable. But as I have tried to show in this book, it is not equally applicable to all firms. There are corporations that actually try to live by the principles set forth in their codes; if they do not always succeed, that is a failing of human and organizational nature rather than of faith or nerve.

Statements from four of these companies follow. Taken together, they suggest the diversity of today's corporate ethics, and serve to challenge the assumption that company codes are just sound and puree, signifying nothing.

Naturally, many firms with less well-defined codes—and many with no written codes at all—are just as earnest about acting fairly and honorably as the four firms I have selected here. I do not mean to imply that these four are the "most" or "only" moral corporations in the world—only that, in their statements as well as their actions, they come as close as anyone does to what "business ethics" is about.

HEWLETT-PACKARD
What Is the HP Way?

This statement, written by William Hewlett to introduce the company publication "The HP Way," is a classic definition of the "people centered" management style in which HP excels.

Any group of people who have worked together for some time, any organization of long standing, indeed, any state or national body over a period of time develops a philosophy, a series of traditions, a set of mores. These, in total, are unique and they fully define the organization, setting it aside for better or worse from similar organizations. At HP all of this goes under the general heading of "the HP way." I want to emphasize that the "HP way" cannot be demonstrated to be unique, and that although based on sound principles, it is not necessarily transplantable to other organizations. But what can be said about it is that it has worked successfully in the past at HP and there is every reason to believe that being a dynamic "way," it will work in the future. If this is true, and if it differs from more conventional practices, then it is important that whatever this "way" is that it be conveyed to, and understood by new HP people.

What *is* the HP way? I feel that in general terms it is the policies and actions that flow from the belief that men and women want to do a good job, a creative job, and that if they are provided the proper environment they will do so. But that's only part of it. Closely coupled with this is the HP tradition of treating each individual with consideration and respect, and recognizing personal achievements. This sounds almost trite, but Dave [HP cofounder David Packard] and I honestly believe in this philosophy and have tried to operate the company along these lines since it first started.

What are some examples of this application of a confidence in and concern for people? One was a very early decision that has had a profound effect on the company. That decision was that we did not want to be a "hire and fire" operation—a company that would seek large contracts, employ a great many people for the duration of the contract, and at its completion let these people go. Now, there is nothing that is fundamentally wrong with this method of operation—much work can only be performed using this technique—it's just that Dave and I did not want to operate in this mode. This one early decision greatly limited our freedom of choice and was one of the factors that led us into the business in which we are now engaged.

There are a number of corollaries to this policy. One is that employees should be in a position to benefit directly from the success of the organization. This led to the early introduction of a profit-sharing plan, and eventually to the employee stock purchase plan. A second corollary was that if an employee was worried about pressing problems at home, he could not be expected to concentrate fully on his job. This, and the fact that in the early days Dave and I were very closely associated with people throughout the company and thus had a chance to see firsthand the devastating effect of domestic tragedy, led, amongst other things, to the very early introduction of medical insurance for catastrophic illness.

As the company grew and it became evident that we had to develop new levels of management, we applied our own concept of management-by-objective. When stripped down to its barest fundamentals, management-by-objective says that a manager, a supervisor, a foreman given the proper support and guidance (that is, the objectives), is probably better able to make decisions about the problems he is directly concerned with than some executive way up the line—no matter how smart or able that executive may be. This system places great responsibility on the individual concerned, but it also makes his work more interesting and more challenging. It makes him feel that he is really part of the company, and that he can have a direct effect on its performance.

Another illustration of the HP way occurred in 1970. During that time, orders were coming in at a rate less than our production capability. We were faced with the prospect of a 10 percent layoff—something we had never done. Rather than a layoff, we tried a different tack. We went to a schedule of working nine days out of every two weeks—a 10 percent cut in work schedule with a corresponding 10 percent cut in pay for all employees involved in this schedule. At the end of a six-month period, orders and employment were once again in balance and the company returned to a full work week. The net result of this program was that effectively all shared the burden of the recession, good people were not turned out on a very tough job market, and, I might observe, the company benefitted by having in place a highly qualified work force when business improved.

The dignity and worth of the individual is a very important part of the HP way. With this in mind, many years ago we did away with time clocks, and more recently we introduced the flexible work hours program. Flexible or gliding, time was originated within the company at our plant in Germany. Later it was tried for six months or so at the Waltham Division in Massachusetts, and then made available throughout much of the company. Again, this is meant to be an expression of trust and confidence in HP people as well as providing them with an opportunity to adjust their work schedules to their personal lives.

Many new HP people as well as visitors often note and comment to us about another HP way—that is, our informality and our being on a first name basis. Both Dave and I believe we all operate more effectively and comfortably in a truly informal and personal name atmosphere. Hopefully, with increasing growth we can retain this "family" way of operating with the minimum of controls and the maximum of a friendly "help each other" attitude.

I could cite other examples, but the probbem is that none by themselves really catches the essence of what the HP way is all about. You can't describe it in numbers and statistics. In the last analysis it is a spirit, a point of view. It is a feeling that everyone is a part of a team, and that team is HP. As I said at the beginning, it is an idea that is based on the individual. It exists because people have seen that it works, and they believe in it and support it. I believe that this feeling makes HP what it is, and that it is worth perpetuating.

J.C. PENNEY COMPANY
The Penney Idea

The company publication "Business Ethics at J.C. Penney" calls The Penney Idea—first formulated by James Cash Penney and his partners in 1913—"the cornerstone upon which the success of our Company is based." It is composed of seven objectives:

> To serve the public as nearly as we can to its complete satisfaction.
> To expect for the service we render a fair remuneration, and not all the profit the traffic will bear.
> To do all in our power to pack the customer's dollar full of value, quality, and satisfaction.
> To continue to train ourselves and our associates so that the service we give will be more and more intelligently performed.
> To improve constantly the human factor in our business.
> To reward the men and women in our organization through participation in what the business produces.
> To test our every policy, method and act in this wise: "Does it square with what is right and just?"

JOHNSON & JOHNSON
Our Credo

Johnson & Johnson's corporate Credo, written originally by Robert Wood Johnson in the 1940s and revised slightly in the mid-1970s, proved its value as a living document during the Tylenol crisis. It reflects the multiple "stakeholder" model that informs much contemporary corporate thinking.

> We believe our first responsibility is to the doctors, nurses and patients, to mothers and all others who use our products and services. In meeting their needs everything we do must be of high quality. We must constantly strive to reduce our costs in order to maintain reasonable prices. Customers' orders must be serviced promptly and accurately. Our suppliers and distributors must have an opportunity to make a fair profit.
>
> We are responsible to our employees, the men and women who work with us throughout the world. Everyone must be considered as an individual. We must respect their dignity and recognize their merit. They must have a sense of security in their jobs. Compensation must be fair and adequate, and working conditions clean, orderly and safe. Employees must feel free to make suggestions and complaints. There must be equal opportunity for employment, development and advancement for those qualified.
>
> We must provide competent management, and their actions must be just and ethical.
>
> We are responsible to the communities in which we live and work and to the world community as well.
>
> We must be good citizens—support good works and charities and bear our fair share of taxes. We must encourage civic improvements and better health and education.
>
> We must maintain in good order the property we are privileged to use, protecting the environment and natural resources.
>
> Our final responsibility is to our stockholders. Business must

make a sound profit. We must experiment with new ideas. Research must be carried on, innovative programs developed and mistakes paid for. New equipment must be purchased, new facilities provided and new products launched. Reserves must be created to provide for adverse times.

When we operate according to these principles, the stockholders should realize a fair return.

AETNA LIFE & CASUALTY
Philosophy and Direction

This statement by Stephen B. Middlebrook, vice-president and general counsel at Aetna, appeared in the 1982 company report "Taking Part." Another corporate recognition of the multiple constituency model, it is an articulate defense of private-sector involvement in social issues.

Is a corporation's concern for the collective needs of society in conflict with its profit-producing role? Debates over the role of the modern corporation in its society have captured much attention in recent years—in both public and private settings. By now, most respectable thought has moved beyond the narrow notion that "the business of business is business." But there are some who still maintain that a corporation's profit motive severely constrains the extent to which it can respond to social and public needs.

Our view at Aetna Life & Casualty is that there is no inherent inconsistency between these two objectives. Indeed, tending to the broader needs of society is essential to fulfilling our economic role.

As a member of many communities, we have a vital interest in whether they are good places to live, to recruit qualified employees, to market our products, and to invest our financial resources. We are similarly concerned about the educational preparation of those entering the labor force, the buying power of those to whom we sell our products, the safety and accessibility of our offices, and the productivity of all segments of society.

Not long ago people and organizations could take the health of these communities for granted. Steady economic growth allowed most people to improve their standard of living; government and a few private agencies were equipped to aid those in need of assistance; and the network of community and charitable institutions, commonly called the third sector, was strong and well-supported by private and government funds.

That time has passed. We are now faced with a long-term prospect of slow economic growth, taxpayer resistance to costly entitlement programs, and a general perception of government excess in social engineering. Corporations and other members of the private sector are being asked to become more active in ensuring the health of the nation's communities. The President's Task Force on Private Sector Initiatives, on which Aetna's Chairman played an active role, documents why this must be done and gives numerous examples of how it can happen.

Quite clearly, our business decisions do have an impact on the communities that surround us, just as decisions made by those communities have an impact on our business objectives and success.

Examples include our approach to educating and training employees as affected by the public education system; the health, safety and longevity of our employees and customers as influenced by their working and living conditions; and the resolution of insurance claims and other disputes as dictated by our civil justice system. At an even more elementary level, our products and services must be perceived in today's competitive marketplace as comprehensible, affordable and relevant to modern financial needs. In all of these respects—and in many others—our business practices must respond to our public environment or we will have no business to practice.

Corporate public involvement is our expression of these evolving concepts. Fundamentally, we are concerned with "the impact of corporate performance on people." It is an operating principle that recognizes the relevance of our business to our numerous constituencies.

It embraces such topics as *privacy*—the right of Aetna customers, sales agents and employees to know what data we have filed on them and what we share with others; *affirmative action*—the responsibility of this corporation to develop programs that can reflect in its employee population the diverse communities in which we do business; and *suitability*—the development and marketing of products and services that meet the real needs of a financial services marketplace.

Corporate public involvement also embraces such complicated and sensitive areas as responsible use of investment funds, consideration of community impact factors in selecting office locations, the methods by which we gather and select data for rating purposes, and the extent to which we encourage employee voluntarism.

At Aetna, we are persuaded that this increased attention to corporate public involvement is appropriate. Together with labor groups and the private not-for-profit organizations, we can and should provide the leadership necessary to assess community needs, attach priorities to them, and seek intelligent implementation plans to meet those needs effectively. Of course, the public sector—which more and more will come to mean state and local government—will and should continue to assure that our perceptions of community needs are in line with the reality of public expectations. For us, a critical issue is how the private and public sectors can best combine their strengths and skills to upgrade the quality of life in America.

Our goals are lofty ones, but we do not delude ourselves as to our limitations. It would not be appropriate, nor does the public expect us, to respond by turning the full focus of the corporation and our employees to solving the nation's social problems. Corporations cannot be "do-gooders," but they can and must interject a concern for social issues in their consideration of what their multiple constituencies—employees, agents, shareholders, customers, and the public generally—demand of them.

NOTES

Chapter 1

3 The Dickens quotation is from *Martin Chuzzlewit*; James Cash Penney's is from his book *Fifty Years with the Golden Rule: A Spiritual Autobiography* (Harper & Row, 1950), p. 52; oxymoron: *Wall Street Journal*, May 5, 1983, p. 1.

4 polls: The July 1983 Gallup results appear in Gallup Report No. 214; the October Gallup poll was reported by Roger Ricklefs in a four-part *Wall Street Journal* series, Oct. 31-Nov. 3, 1983; the Harris survey results appeared in a Nov. 17, 1983 Harris press release on confidence in institutions.

4 "Most businessmen": Emily Stipes, *The Businessman in American Literature* (University of Georgia Press, 1982), p. 150.

5 *Agricola*: cited in Howard Mumford Jones, *O Strange New World: American Culture, the Formative Years* (Viking, 1967), p. 206.

6 Fortune report: Irwin Ross, "How Lawless Are Big Companies?" in Fortune, Dec. 1, 1980.

7 "If it were true": Richard T. De George, *Business Ethics* (Macmillan, 1982), p. 4.

8 Gallup survey: See Ricklefs.

9 "Corporations today": Thomas Donaldson, "Ethically, Society Expects More from a Corporation." A "conversation with Thomas Donaldson" in *U.S. News & World Report*, Sept. 6, 1982, p. 30.

9 "Business is not simply...": MacNaughton is quoted in Carlton E. Spitzer, *Raising the Bottom Line: Business Leadership in a Changing Society* (Longman, 1982), p. 19.

10 Levi Strauss: The 1979 cash awards are mentioned in Milton Moskowitz, Michael Katz and Robert Levering, *Everybody's Business: An Almanac* (Harper & Row, 1980), p. 156; the previous year's distress payments are noted in the "Company Performance Roundup" section of *Business and Society Review*, Spring 1979, p. 75. The 1984 benefits are mentioned in *Business Week*'s Nov. 5, 1984 cover story, "Who's Excellent Now?"

11 "the case example": Richard S. Ruch and Ronald Goodman, *Image at the Top: Crisis and Renaissance in Corporate Leadership* (Free Press, 1983), p. 40.

11 "a company willing": *The Washington Post* is cited in J&J's publication "The Tylenol Comeback," put out by the Corporate Public Relations department.

11 "landmark in urban planning": Harvey Shapiro in the *New York Times*, June 17, 1979, Section III, p. 1.

13 Its spokesmen explain: Dayton Hudson program officer Terry Barreiro is quoted as saying, "We'll not increase our percentage until many other corporations get much closer to 5 percent. For us to increase our share to 10 percent would put us at a competitive disadvantage." See Michael Fedo, "A Most Generous Company," in the *New York Times*, Feb. 28, 1982, Section III, p. 4.

14 "partners dealing with the same problem": Quoted in Ruch and Goodman, *Image at the Top*, p. 39.

Chapter 2

15 Aristotle's comment is in Book I of *Nicomachean Ethics*; Shaw's is in "Maxims for Revolutionists," part of the preface to *Man and Superman*.

16 Plato's allegory of the cave appears as Chapter 25 in Francis Cornford's translation of *The Republic* (Oxford University Press, 1963), pp. 227-35.

16 "genuine moral dilemmas": Report of the Committee for Education in Business Ethics, sponsored by the National Endowment for the Humanities and supported by Fel-Pro, Inc. (1980), p. 7.

18 De George's analysis of ethical relativism, from which the quoted material is taken, appears on pages 30-34 of his *Business Ethics* (Macmillan, 1982).

20 "value in question": Bentham's qualifiers on his calculus are explained in De George, p. 42.

20 "policies, laws, and actions": Ibid., p. 45.

21 "cheating our own conscience": Max Lerner, ed., *The Essential Works of John Stuart Mill* (Bantam, 1961), p. 211.

21 Joseph Butler: The bishop's bon mot is mentioned in D.H. Monro's illuminating article on utilitarianism in the *Dictionary of the History of Ideas*, Vol. 4 (Scribner's, 1973), p. 444.

23 "To universalize cheating": Norman Bowie, *Business Ethics* (Prentice-Hall, 1982), p. 42.

24 "an extensive reworking": Bowie, p. 40.

25 Watson's statement of first principles appears in *A Business and its Beliefs*

(McGraw-Hill, 1963). The Johnson Wax promise is part of the company credo "This We Believe." Seibert's observation is from his introductory letter to the company pamphlet "Business Ethics at J.C. Penney."

Chapter 3

27 Schacht and Powers comment in "Business Responsibility and the Public Policy Process," in Thornton Bradshaw and David Vogel, eds., *Corporations and their Critics* (McGraw-Hill, 1981), p. 28.

27 Hutchinson's observation is in *Foundation News Magazine*, Sept.-Oct. 1984.

27 Donaldson: see note to page 9, Chapter 1.

27 Howard R. Bowen is cited in Keith Davis and Robert Blomstrom, *Business and Society: Environment and Responsibility*, 3rd ed. (McGraw-Hill, 1975), p. 10.

28 "turn to other challenges": Ibid., p. 5.

28 "viable in the system": Ibid., p. 80.

28 "the long-term viability": The Business Roundtable, "Statement on Corporate Responsibility," (New York, Oct. 1981), p. 1.

28 MacNaughton: see note to page 9, Chapter 1.

31 "close to the customer": This concept is articulated in Chapter 6 of Thomas Peters and Robert Waterman, *In Search of Excellence* (Warner Books, 1984).

32 Harold Johnson's essay "Ethics and the Executive" appears in *Business Horizons*, May-June 1981.

32 The J&J manager's metaphor of the juggler's balls was suggested at the company's "Credo challenge" meeting; my thanks to J&J for letting me view a videotape of that meeting.

33 C.C. Peterson's comments were made in a speech on "Ethics in Business" in Ottumwa, Iowa on Mar. 2, 1982. I thank the John Deere public relations department for sending me a transcript.

35 "The Decalogue, after all": Clarence Francis, in a 1948 speech for the Harvard Business School alumni conference, printed in Harwood F. Merrill, ed., *The Responsibilities of Business Leadership* (Harvard University Press, 1949), p. 8.

36 "Most of the debate": *The Ethical Investor* was published by Yale University Press in 1972; the quotation is from page 36.

36 Michael Rion's observation is in his article "Training for Ethical Management at Cummins Engine," in *Doing Ethics in Business*, ed. Donald G. Jones (Cambridge, Mass.: Oelgeschlager, Gunn & Hain, 1982), p. 32.

36 For the quotations from Schacht and Powers, see note for page 27, this chapter.

36 "informative economy": The term comes from Paul Hawken, *The Next Economy* (Ballantine Books, 1983). See especially Chapter 5.

Chapter 4

41 The Davis/Blomstrom quotation comes from their book *Business and Society: Environment and Responsibility*, 3rd ed. (McGraw-Hill, 1975), p. 259. Bradshaw's observation is in his article "The Changing Status of Business," Chapter 11 of Donald G. Jones, ed., *Business, Religion, and Ethics: Inquiry and Encounter* (Oelgeschlager, Gunn & Hain, 1982), p. 142. GM chairman Murphy's famous remark is quoted in Milton Moskowitz et al., *Everybody's Business* (Harper & Row, 1980), p. 271.

42 "It is one thing":Richard Eells and Clarence Walton made the comment in their book *Conceptual Foundations of Business* (Richard D. Irwin, 1961), and are quoted in Davis/Blomstrom, p. 259.

42 shareholder legal rights: Davis/Blomstrom, p. 247.

43 The survey results appear in Steven N. Brenner and Earl A. Molander, "Is the Ethics of Business Changing?" in *Harvard Business Review*, Jan.-Feb. 1977.

43 George Craig: a fictional composite.

44 *Wall Street Journal* survey: See the Ricklefs survey cited in Chapter 1. George Gallup is quoted in the second part of the Ricklefs *Wall Street Journal* series, Nov. 1, 1983.

46 President Carter's tax proposals: the Harris survey results were released to the press on Mar. 23, 1978, and published by the Chicago Tribune-N.Y. News Syndicate.

47 "Businesses don't furnish offices": quoted in the Ricklefs *Wall Street Journal* survey, Nov.1, 1983.

48 *Wall Street Journal* study: quoted in Ricklefs's first article, Oct. 31, 1983.

49 The J.C. Penney Company guidelines appear in the company "Statement of Business Ethics"; the IBM version is in the 1983 booklet "Business Conduct Guidelines."

52 "an increasing tendency for managers": Davis/Blomstrom, p. 242.

52 "what's in it for me": Green is quoted in Ann Crittenden, "The Age of Me-First Management," *New York Times*, Section III, Aug. 19, 1984.

52 Harris Poll results: *Business Week*, June 25, 1984, in an unsigned article "Top Executive Pay Peeves the Public."

53 "Marie Antoinette": Betsey Caldwell is quoted in the Ann Crittenden article, p. 12.

54 "a soft and cushy landing": Crittenden, p. 1.
John Tarrant's book *Perks and Parachutes* was published by the Linden Press (Simon & Schuster) in 1985.

55 Saul Steinberg's takeover bid is described in Crittenden, p. 12.

55 Carl Icahn is quoted ibid., p. 12.

Chapter 5

57 Hewlett's comment is in "The HP Way," the company report on its business philosophy. Allen's is in his article "Business Communication" in *Leaders* magazine, Jan.-Mar. 1979.

58 "The apparent lack": Martin Douglas, "Reflections from the Assembly Line," *Business and Society Review* (Spring 1982-83), pp. 44-47.
Employee owned and operated businesses are described in John Egerton, "Workers Take Over the Store," *New York Times Magazine*, Sept. 11, 1983.

59 "It's my store": Egerton, p. 164.

62 Procter & Gamble's stock purchase plan: Ida M. Tarbell, *New Ideals in Business* (Macmillan, 1917), pp. 238-49. Cooper Procter's statement appeared in a post-World War I speech, cited in the company history, Oscar Schisgall's *Eyes on Tomorrow; The Evolution of Procter & Gamble* (J.G. Ferguson, 1981), p. 62.
The Armstrong, Kodak, and Johnson Wax examples are taken from Robert Levering, Milton Moskowitz, and Michael Katz, *The 100 Best Companies to Work for in America* (Addison-Wesley, 1984).

62 "part of the glue": From an interview with Samuel Johnson in *Cornell Executive* (Cornell University Graduate School of Management, Summer/Fall, 1983).

63 The Japanese lifetime employment promise is discussed in William G. Ouchi, *Theory Z: How American Business Can Meet the Japanese Challenge* (Avon, 1982), pp. 15-22.

64 The Hewlett-Packard principles are in "The HP Way"; the stories are told in Levering et al., *100 Best Companies.*
"If somebody has to be fired": Samuel Johnson interview in *Cornell Executive.*

64 The Robert Goldstein speech I received as a reprint from the Procter & Gamble publicity department; the 48-weeks-out-of-a-year promise is cited in Levering et al., *100 Best Companies.*
"He had known hard times": Thomas J. Watson, Jr., *A Business and Its Beliefs: The Ideas that Helped Build IBM* (McGraw-Hill, 1963), p. 14.

65 "The net result": Hewlett in "The HP Way."

65 "They still got paychecks": Garrett is quoted in Levering et al., *100 Best Companies.*
66 "rings of defense": ibid.

66 "We don't manage our business": *Cornell Executive* interview.
"high-touch": See John Naisbitt, *Megatrends* (Warner Books, 1984), especially Chapter 2.

67 Peters and Waterman: See *In Search of Excellence*, pp. 218-23 and 235-78.

67 Fred Allen: See note for page 57, this chapter.

69 IBM cash awards: The figures come from the company's 1983 annual report, p. 23.

69 The Kodak figures are from Levering et al., *100 Best Companies*.
The Pitney Bowes figures are from the company newsletter *PB News* for Aug.-Sept. 1984.

70 Art Fry: The "Post-It" discovery is described in Levering et al., *100 Best Companies*.

70 "They are working steadier": Quoted in Tarbell, *New Ideals*, p. 168.

71 Anecdotes from Levering et al., *100 Best Companies*.

71 "Spirit of Delta": The Delta employees' gift is described in Michael VerMaulen, "When Employees Give Something Extra," *Parade* Nov. 6, 1983.
"An occasional reduction in force": Fred Allen in *Leaders* magazine, Jan.-Mar. 1979.

72 "The United States is rapidly discovering": William Hewlett's executive lecture, "The Human Side of Management," was delivered at the University of Notre Dame on Mar. 25, 1982.

72 LMPTs: see "Steel Listens to Workers and Likes What It Hears," *Business Week*, Dec. 19, 1983.
Roger Smith spoke on the Donahue show, Feb. 26, 1985.

72 The Deere bulletin is No. 5, dated Dec. 1, 1975.

Chapter 6

75 The Miller/Heiman Win-Win philosophy is outlined in their book *Strategic Selling* (William Morrow, 1985); the quotation is from the Introduction, p. 12.
Penney's statement appears in his book *Fifty Years with the Golden Rule: A Spiritual Autobiography* (Harper & Row, 1950), p. 232.

76 "specter of mass suits": On the Robins suits and the Kasten bill, see the unsigned article "Unsafe Products: the Great Debate over Blame and Punishment," *Business Week*, Apr. 30, 1984, pp. 96-104.

77 Dowie's article "Two Million Firetraps on Wheels" is in Business and *Society Review*, Fall 1977.

77 "an estimated $500 million": The figure, which is debated by Ford, is from the Center for Auto Safety, a consumer group cited in "Unsafe Products."

78 The Tylenol case has been extensively covered in the press. My information and quotations come from Richard Ruch and Ronald Goodman, *Image at the Top* (Free Press, 1983), pp. 34-40; the J&J publication "The Tylenol Comeback"; and my personal interviews with Lawrence Foster and James Burke.

81 Cicero: The grain merchant's dilemma is recounted in Thomas Donaldson, *Corporations and Morality* (Prentice-Hall, 1982).
The Better Business Bureau publication is "History and Traditions," written by B. Charles Wansley and published by the Council of Better Business Bureaus (rev. ed., 1982).

81 "Lying consists": Richard T. De George, *Business Ethics* (Macmillan, 1982), p. 188.

82 Listerine: The case is discussed in William Sklar, "Ads Are Finally Getting Bleeped at the FTC," *Business and Society Review*, Spring 1978.

83 "we sell hope": Charles Revson is quoted in Theodore Levitt, "The Morality (?) of Advertising," *Harvard Business Review*, July-Aug. 1970.

84 "Such ads take advantage": De George, *Business Ethics*, p. 194.

85 "If we were all logicians": Jules Henry, *Culture Against Man* (Random House, 1963).

88 "quality obsession": See Peters and Waterman, *In Search of Excellence* (Warner Books, 1982), pp. 171-82.
"Mr. Tate felt": The story is related in a Deere company bulletin on "Product Quality and Reliability," dated Dec. 1, 1975.

88 "The Penney Idea": Reproduced in the Penney broadsheet "Business Ethics at J.C. Penney."

89 "When you come up with something": The elder Johnson is quoted in an interview with Samuel Johnson, *Cornell Executive* (Cornell Graduate School of Management, Summer/Fall 1983).

89 "a professional exercise": Miller and Heiman, *Strategic Selling*, p. 156.

90 "Getting the order": quoted in Peters and Waterman, *In Search of Excellence*, p. 161.

90 "the best customer service": See Thomas Watson, A Business and Its Beliefs (McGraw-Hill, 1963), pp. 29-41.
"a mild form of lunacy": Peters and Waterman, *In Search of Excellence*, p. 171.
"One of our most significant": ibid., 168.

90 Archie McGill is quoted ibid.
"Our customers are entitled": Hewitt's letter, "To John Deere Employees," is an internal document sent to me by the company.

91 "value of the Golden Rule": Watson, *A Business*, p. 30.
The Kodak brochure is "More than Photography: A Visit to Eastman Kodak Company."

91 "three basic assumptions": See Paul Hawken, *The Next Economy* (Ballantine Books, 1983), pp. 176-78.

Chapter 7

93 MacNaughton is quoted in Carlton Spitzer, *Raising the Bottom Line* (Longman, 1982), p. 18.
Andres's statement is in the Dayton Hudson social action report "Managing Change: Taking Direction from Our Communities" (1982), p. 1.

94 *Capitalism and Freedom* was published in 1962 by the University of Chicago Press; the quotations in this chapter are taken from pp. 133-36.

94 Theodore Levitt's essay is "The Dangers of Social Responsibility," in *Harvard Business Review*, Sept.-Oct. 1958, pp. 41-50.

98 "Our philosophy of service": Hutchinson is quoted in Dayton Hudson's "Managing Change." All other statements by him in this chapter are from our interview.

99 The giving programs of Dayton Hudson's member companies are described in "Managing Change."

100 Information on Minnesota's Keystone Award programs is available from the Business Action Resource Council of the Minneapolis Chamber of Commerce.

101 "development of youth and hunger": Quoted from Pillsbury's 1984 Community Relations annual report, p. 3.

103 The Strauss CITs are described in the company foundation's 1982 report, "A Commitment to People."

104 Social Benefits Program: ibid.

108 "abandon Newark": John Rosenberg examines Prudential's current Newark presence in "Prudential Lessens Newark Base," *New York Times*, Aug. 17, 1980.

109 "get the slum out of the slum": The unnamed Control Data executive is cited in Michael Fedo, "How Control Data Turns a Profit on Its Good Works," *New York Times*, Jan. 7, 1979.

110 "Combining our own resources": From the CDC report "Addressing Society's Major Unmet Needs as Profitable Business Opportunities," p. 3.
J&J in New Brunswick: My information on New Brunswick's revival comes from my interview with J&J chairman James Burke and vice-president Lawrence Foster, from New Brunswick Tomorrow's 1983 annual report, and from an excellent survey of the city" progress, "Gems of New Jersey: New Brunswick," by Gordon Bishop in the *Newark Sunday Star-Ledger*, Mar. 11, 1984.

Chapter 8

115 The Keith Davis epigraph is from his article "Five Propositions for Social Responsibility," *Business Horizons*, June 1975. Robert Beck's comments are in Prudential's 1981 pamphlet "A Social Report."
Thornton Bradshaw is quoted in the Atlantic Richfield Company's social progress report, "Participation III."

117 "capacity argument": The term is used by Howard Sohn in a report on the highlights of Bentley College's second (1978) national conference on business ethics, published by the college's Center for Business Ethics.
"Kew Gardens principle": See John Simon, Charles Powers, and Jon Gunnemann, *The Ethical Investor* (Yale University Press, 1972), pp. 22-25.

118 "Iron Law of Responsibility": See Davis and Blomstrom, *Business and Society: Environment and Responsibility* (McGraw-Hill, 1975), p. 50.
"Society always has this strategy": Douglas Sherwin, "The Ethical Roots of the Business System," *Harvard Business Review*, Nov.-Dec. 1983, p. 192.

118 The Harris survey cited was released to the Chicago Tribune-New York News Syndicate on Dec. 10, 1981.

119 "underclass": The term was popularized by Ken Auletta; see his book *The Underclass* (Random House, 1982).

119 Paul Hawken's analysis of the current transformation appears in his book *The Next Economy* (Ballantine, 1983).

121 PLATO and Fair Break are described in Control Data's publication "Addressing Society's Unmet Needs as Profitable Business Opportunities."

122 Throughout this chapter, data on foundation interests come from the companies' respective foundation reports; data on Exxon and ARCO come, respectively, from the publications "Dimension 83" and "Participation III."

122 "Chinese ideograph": Davis and Blomstrom, *Business and Society*, p. 426.

124 "proportionate representation": The pamphlet cited is "Polaroid and the Community," which I received through the kindness of public relations specialist Peter Schwartz. Nathan Glazer's book *Affirmative Discrimination* was published by Basic Books in 1975.

127 "develop marketable programs": Control Data, "Unmet Needs," p. 38.

128 "building new facilities": See the John Deere Company pamphlet "A Concern for the Total Environment."
The J.C. Penney Company statistics come from the company's 1983 annual report.
"manage its operations with diligence": Atlantic Richfield Company, "Participation III."

128 "are willing, amidst pressure": Kirk O. Hanson, Atlantic Richfield Company, ibid.

129 "often breaks ranks": Moskowitz, Katz and Levering, *Everybody's Business* (Harper & Row, 1980), p. 491.

131 "dividends for us all": Walter Fallon's comment appears in the company brochure "Sharing: The Kodak Commitment."

Chapter 9

General note: Unless otherwise indicated, the company publications cited in this chapter are as follows: IBM: "Business Conduct Guidelines" (1983); J.C. Penney: "Statement of Business Ethics"; Pitney Bowes: "Business Practice Guidelines" (Feb. 14, 1983); Procter & Gamble: "Your Personal Responsibility" (1983); RCA: policy bulletin #10229 (Sept. 19, 1983); Xerox: Personnel Manual (July 1, 1983) and the new-employee brochure "An Understanding," including policy statements on conflict of interest, antitrust, and the ethics of buying and selling. All these publications were provided to me through the kindness of the respective public relations departments.

135 Milton Friedman's famous observation appears in *Capitalism and Freedom* (Chicago, 1962), p. 133.

136 Myth of Amoral Business: De George, *Business Ethics* (Macmillan, 1982), pp. 3-5.

137 "Trading by insiders": John A.C. Hetherington, "Corporate Social Responsibility, Stockholders, and the Law," *Journal of Contemporary Business*, Winter 1973, p. 51.

137 "The use of inside information": De George, *Business Ethics*, p. 212.

138 The Harris poll on insider trading appears in *Business Week*, May 28, 1984, p. 16.

143 "once bribery is an accepted": De George, *Business Ethics*, p. 52.

143 "If there is some doubt": ibid., pp. 52-53.

143 Results of the 1961 and 1977 surveys are reported in Steven Brenner and Earl Molander, "Is the Ethics of Business Changing?" in *Harvard Business Review*, Jan.-Feb. 1977.

146 "Such chicanery": The Penney kickback case was reported frequently in the *New York Times* in 1976.

Chapter 10

149 Stanley Cleveland's remarks were made at the second annual Bentley College conference on business ethics (1978), and recorded in its Center for Business Ethics highlights report, p. 25.
St. Ambrose's advice is reproduced in all standard collections of quotations.

151 "What would you do if": Brenner and Molander, "Is the Ethics of Business Changing?" in *Harvard Business Review*, Jan.-Feb. 1977, p. 57.
Two analysts: See George C. Greanias and Duane Windsor, *The Foreign Corrupt Practices Act: Anatomy of a Statute* (Lexington Books, 1982), p. 109.

153 "There was very little difference": Peter Drucker, *The Changing World of the Executive* (Truman Talley/Times Books, 1982), p. 237.

153 $25 million: The overseas payments figures have been widely reported in the press. My source here is Greanias and Windsor, *Foreign Corrupt Practices Act*, pp. 20-21.

154 "do permit payment abroad": Clarence Walton, ed., *The Ethics of Corporate Conduct* (Prentice-Hall, 1977), p. 182. Subsequent Walton quotations are from the same source.

155 "There is no consensus": Greanias and Windsor, *Foreign Corrupt Practices Act*, p. 124.

157 "And because direct evidence": Albert Huebner, "Tobacco's Lucrative Third World Invasion," *Business and Society Review* 35 (Fall 1980).
Item in tte New York Times; cited in Charles Levenstein and Stanley Eller, "Are Hazardous Industries Fleeing Abroad?" in *Business and Society Review* 34 (Summer 1980).
Galecron: See Ernest Beck, "Swiss Dump on Third World," *In These Times*, Feb. 2-8, 1983, p. 7.

157 "Galecron story": Ibid.

159 "Can a product which requires": Kennedy is quoted in Fred Clarkson, "The Taming of Nestle," *Multinational Monitor*, Apr. 1984, p.14.

159 *Advertising Age* quotation: ibid.

162 The Sullivan Code principles have been widely printed. See, for example, Lee Elbinger, "Are Sullivan's Principles Folly in South Africa?" *Business and Society Review* 30 (Summer 1979).

163 consistently given high marks: See Bernard Simon, "At a Crossroad in South Africa," *New York Times*, Nov. 6, 1983.
"Even the most critical concede": ibid.
"exemplary": See *New York Times*, Apr. 27, 1981.
increasing: The widening pay differential has been reported often. See Elbinger, "Folly"; and Elizabeth Schmidt, *Decoding Corporate Camouflage: U.S. Business Support for Apartheid* (Institute for Policy Studies, 1980), pp. 28-29.

164 "The Sullivan code has benefited": ibid., p. 46.

164 "use microeconomics": Elbinger, "Folly," p. 40.
"the whole structure": Davis is quoted ibid.
98 percent: Employment figures from the American Committee on Africa

165 "ascertained that its products": Timothy Smith, "The Ethical Responsibilities of Multinational Companies," in Thornton Bradshaw and David Vogel, eds., *Corporations and Their Critics* (McGraw-Hill, 1981), p. 81.
The Connecticut divestment is cited in Tamar Lewin, "Reverend Sullivan Steps Up His Anti-Apartheid Fight," *New York Times*, Nov. 6, 1983.

166 "And should the time come": Thomas Watson, *A Business and Its Beliefs* (McGraw-Hill, 1963), p. 96.
"hurts its relations": Ruth Milkman, "Apartheid, Economic Growth, and U.S. Foreign Policy in South Africa," in Martin J. Murray, ed., *South African Capitalism and Black Political Opposition* (Schenkman Publishing, 1982), p. 443.

Chapter 11

167 Michael Rion's comment is in his article "Training for Ethical Management at Cummins Engine," in Donald Jones, ed., *Doing Ethics in Business* (Cambridge, Mass.: Oelgeschlager, Gunn, & Hain, 1982) p. 32. The comment by Ruch and Goodman is from their book *Image at the Top* (Free Press, 1983), p. 22. Frank Camps tells his story "Warning an Auto Company about an Unsafe Design" in Alan Westin, ed., *Whistle-Blowing: Loyalty and Dissent in the Corporation* (McGraw-Hill, 1981). The version of the Pinto case given here is Camps's.

169 "prejudice against ratting": David W. Ewing, *Freedom Inside the Organization: Bringing Civil Liberties to the Workplace* (E.P. Dutton, 1977), p. 82.
"citadel of belongingness": William H. Whyte, Jr., *The Organization Man* (Simon & Schuster, 1956).

169 The unsigned 1977 *Business Week* article is "The Pressure to Compromise Personal Ethics," Jan. 31, 1977. Brenner and Molander's study is "Is the Ethics of Business Changing?" *Harvard Business Review* Jan.-Feb. 1977.

170 Archie Carroll: See his study "Managerial Ethics and the Organizational Hierarchy," in *Proceedings of the Second National Conference on Business Ethics* (University Press of America, 1978).

171 "managerial demiurge": See C. Wright Mills, *White Collar: The American Middle Classes* (Oxford, 1951).

171 "Decisions may be facilitated": Harold L. Johnson, "Ethics and the Executive," *Business Horizons*, May-June 1981.

172 W.L. LaCroix: See his *Principles for Ethics in Business* (University Press of America, 1978).
"corporate steps taken": Brenner and Molander, "Is the Ethics of Business Changing?"
"Managers want the leadership": Fred Allen is quoted in *Business Week*, "Pressure to Compromise."

174 "whistle-blowing cases in the 1970s": The cases are reviewed in "Armor for Whistle Blowers," *Business Week*. July 6, 1981.

Pickering: The case is outlined in Kenneth D. Walters, "Your Employees' Right to Blow the Whistle," *Harvard Business Review*, July-Aug. 1975.

174 "if the employee could prove": Westin, *Whistle-Blowing*.

175 "There is always the danger": Ibid.

175 "so grossly violate": Peter Drucker, "The Matter of Business Ethics," in *The Changing World of the Executive* (Truman Talley/Times Books, 1982), pp. 252-53.

176 But the Court foresaw: The warning about "a personal and intimate nature" is quoted in Walters, "Your Employees' Right."

177 "toxins of suppressed guilt": Albert Carr, "Can an Executive Afford a Conscience?" *Harvard Business Review*, July-Aug. 1970.
"In America today": Ruch and Goodman, *Image at the Top*, p. 21.

177 "Many corporate employees": *The Wall Street Journal* of Feb. 24, 1977 is quoted in Carroll, "Managerial Ethics."
"critical role of the CEO": Ruch and Goodman, *Image*, pp. 13-20.

178 "Biblical rectitude": Oscar Schisgall, *Eyes on Tomorrow: The Evolution of Procter & Gamble* (Doubleday, 1981), p. 5.

180 "frustrated by feelings of threat": My information about HP's communications experiment comes from the company report "Open Line."

180 "We were especially concerned": Edwin Newman interviewed James Burke in February 1978. Johnson & Johnson provided me with a videotape of that interview.

181 "implementing reward procedures": Thomas Donaldson, *Corporations and Morality* (Prentice-Hall, 1982), p. 206.

182 "more education and more exposure": Robert MacNeil interviewed Clare and Burke in April 1980. Johnson & Johnson provided me with a videotape.
"a sound set of beliefs": Thomas Watson, *A Business and Its Beliefs* (McGraw-Hill, 1963), p. 5.

183 "much whistle blowing occurs": Walters, "Your Employees' Right," p. 161.

Chapter 12

185 Watson's comment is in his book, *A Business and Its Beliefs* (McGraw-Hill, 1963), pp. 18-19. Levitt's is in "The Dangers of Social Responsibility," Harvard Business Review, Sept.-Oct. 1958, p. 48.
"No permanent good": Ida Tarbell, *New Ideals in Business* (Macmillan, 1917), p. 357.

190 "If the American people": Watson, A Business and Its Beliefs, p. 96.

190 "evident signs on the horizon": Daniel Bell's comments appear on page 6 of Bentley College's report on its first annual conference on business ethics (1977). "The consumer movement exists": Mercedes Bates, ibid., p. 13.

191 "attempts to alter corporate behavior": Thomas Donaldson, *Corporations and Morality* (Prentice-Hall, 1982), p. 206.
"a combination of executives": The four critics are Mark Green of Congress Watch, Alice Teffer Marlin of the Council on Economic Priorities, Victor Kamber of the AFL-CIO, and Jules Bernstein of Laborers' International Union. Their article "The Case for a Corporate Democracy Act" appears in *Business and Society Review* 36 (Summer 1980).

191 "It is not creative minds": Wells's statement, from his 1921 book *The Salvaging of Civilization*, is quoted in Mark Green et al., ibid., p. 58.

192 "their own destruction": Norman Bowie, *Business Ethics* (Prentice-Hall, 1982), p. 154.

193 An early foray: Milton Moskowitz's article and the comments by Royce Flippin and Harold Janeway appeared in *Business and Society Review* 1 (Spring 1972).

194 The Sturdivant/Ginter study "Corporate Social Responsiveness: Management Attitudes and Economic Performance" appeared in *California Management Review*, Spring 1977.

195 "I have long harbored": James Burke spoke to the Ad Council on Nov. 16, 1983. I am grateful to him for making available to me a copy of his speech, and the results of the J&J study of public service firms.

197 "If you had invested $30,000": Ad Council speech.
CCRA index: I am grateful to Ritchie Lowry and the Good Money staff for sending me data on the CCRA index.

200 "We now realize": Jayne Baker Spain is quoted on page 25 of the Bentley College report cited in the note to page xx, this chapter.

200 "It is impossible to be certain": Brent Fisse and John Braithwaite, *The Impact of Publicity on Corporate Offenders* (SUNY Press, 1983), p. 231.

200 "The goodwill of the people": H.F. Johnson is quoted in the Johnson Wax booklet "This We Believe."
"this democratic capitalistic system": Burke speech to the Ad Council.

201 "stubborn doctrinaire approach": Thomas Watson, *A Business and Its Beliefs*, p. 97.

INDEX